MAX AND THE HIDDEN VISITOR

D.P. BOWKETT

Dippy Bee

First published in 2023 by Dippy Bee Publishing

This book is a work of fiction, and, except in the case of historical fact, any resemblance to actual persons or aliens, living or dead, events or locations is entirely coincidental.

Cover illustration by Alex at PerkyVisuals Book Covers
Interior Formatting by Kelley at Sleepy Fox Studio

A very special *thank you* to my beta readers who encouraged me to get this far.

eBook ISBN: 978-1-7395583-1-4
Print ISBN: 978-1-7395583-0-7

BISAC codes YAF019000, YAF056000, YAF001000

Prologue

After more than two thousand years on your planet, I've lived in many different countries, and the one thing that never ceases to amaze me is humankind's ability to be consistently inconsistent with its rules and regulations.

During the period of my life covered by this biography, I am living in England, and it may help if I explain some of the way things are currently done here.

First of all, the school system is grouped as follows:

- Primary education – 5-11 year-olds (primary or junior school).

- Secondary education – 11-16 years old (secondary or senior school). GCSE exams are taken around May/June at age 15/16.

- Further education – 17-18 years old (college). A-level exams or similar are taken around May/June around age 18.

- Higher education – 19-21 years old (university).

Secondly, you are not allowed to learn to drive a car on public roads until you are 17 years old, and until you have passed a driving test with an official examiner, you must have a qualified driver with you as a front-seat passenger at all times. As a learner driver, you are not allowed to drive on motorways.

There are so many more peculiarities I could mention like it is illegal to handle a salmon in suspicious circumstances or to have a sleeping donkey in your bathtub after 7 p.m. in England. Mind you, bathtub-sleeping donkeys are also illegal in Arizona. However, I think I'll let you get on and experience the craziness of my life.

1
THE ACCIDENT

Catherine Thomas was late yet again. She had arranged to meet her uncle, Max Thomas, at the Willow for dinner at 7:00 p.m. But it was already 7:20 p.m., and everything seemed to conspire against her.

As a busy doctor in central London, any dinner invitation always came with a caveat of give or take an hour. Unfortunately, the Trust Property Planning Meeting at Imperial College in St Mary's Hospital had overrun by twenty minutes, not the best end to an eleven-hour day.

At least she could catch the Elizabeth underground line at Paddington, which would give her just under ten minutes to relax, followed by a five-minute walk to West Street. She pulled out her phone and messaged Max to say she was running around thirty-five to forty minutes late before descending towards the Elizabeth line platform.

She sat on the train, impressed with how clean and modern it looked in its purple livery compared to the dirty and dated trains on some of the other London Underground lines. Her mind turned to thoughts about her family's involvement with

Max. It felt like he had been around forever, a little like that favourite but mysterious uncle who pops up from time to time with some magical tales and a present or two but who would disappear almost as quickly.

Uncle Max was different; that difference had brought him and her family together a long time ago. She also knew that what he did was, at times, dangerous but also highly secretive. As a child, she often asked him, 'What do you do, Uncle Max?' He would reply, 'Saving the world, my dear, just saving the world.'

Uncle Max wasn't her real uncle, nor was Thomas his surname; his real surname was Janus. But the one thing she knew with absolute certainty was that whilst biologically Max was human, he was anything but human. He certainly looked human; in fact, he was almost identical in looks to her father, and they could easily pass as twins. They were a little under five feet eleven inches; both had a full head of still naturally curly hair and a mischievous smile that could charm and disarm in equal measure. They also had a playful sense of humour. Putting the two of them in charge of any event would surely result in an unforgettable occasion, although only sometimes for the right reasons.

But there were differences. Since Catherine's father retired as a neurological consultant three years ago, aged sixty, he had started to enjoy the good life, maybe a little too much. As a result, he was noticeably heavier than Max, or as he put it, a touch portly, and he had grown a beard. However, Max had a few more battle-earned scars on his face, was generally clean-shaven, and two fingers on his left hand were bent due to an accident which damaged his ring and little finger.

Why they were so similar was only revealed to her three years ago when she turned thirty and was in the final few years of her training in general surgery.

It turns out that mysterious but loveable Uncle Max was a Shadower, an ancient race from a distant world that has been on Earth for thousands of years trying to protect humanity from other Shadowers with less honourable intentions for Earth and its inhabitants.

Catherine knew her family had a long history with medicine going back several centuries, but she also discovered that her family had kept Max alive for all those years. Shadowers can be killed, but they can survive or cheat death if given a chance. If they can touch or be touched by another living thing within seconds of the human body dying, they can pass their energy soul into that other person or animal. If they cannot do it, their energy soul vaporises, leaving just the dead body behind.

The exact process was going to be explained to her tonight by Max. Her father was also due to join them but had to cancel this morning due to some unexpected problem at the hospital where he used to work. All she knew was that once the energy soul was in the other body, it spent some time building some form of DNA structure based on its host. After six months, the energy soul could separate from the host. Using the DNA structure, it had made an identical copy of the host, which protected the energy soul from Earth's weaker gravity compared to their home planet.

The underground train speaker fired up, breaking her thoughts, 'We are sorry to announce that this train will terminate at Bond Street due to a derailment. Please change at Bond Street for the Central line to complete your journey to Tottenham Court Road. We apologise for any inconvenience.'

Catherine considered her options, either what is sure to be the cramped foul air of the Central line or an extra 15-minute walk through the equally congested streets of Soho. The Central line won, so she quickly messaged Max again and joined a crush of tourists, evening commuters and locals squeezing onto the tube. While walking the long corridors between platforms, Catherine started to feel uneasy. Her father and Uncle Max had drummed it into her to be aware of her surroundings. She also seemed to have a sixth sense if someone was watching or following her, the Uncle Max gift her father called it.

She looked around as she walked, but with so many people from all walks of life and all parts of the planet always in London, she couldn't see anyone or anything out of place. However, the hairs on the back of her neck prickled.

She squeezed into the carriage and then considered waiting for the next train. She stepped back to the platform to see how long it was for the next train, but it would be another five minutes, so she decided to put up with this one and stepped back on. Her suspicions were confirmed in that fleeting moment of getting on, then off and back on again.

She knew she didn't imagine it. As she stepped off the train, a man at the far end of the carriage wearing a black hoodie and jeans had done the same thing, and when she decided to go for this cramped journey and stepped back on, he did the same.

Max sighed and leaned back in his chair at the Willow. Catherine's first message had said she would be thirty-five to forty minutes late, and the latest one added another ten minutes to that delay. He knew Catherine was the antithesis of her father, Michael, when it came to timekeeping. Michael was a stickler for time and order, 'Always be in the right place at the right time, ready to do the job properly' was his mantra. Catherine had followed her mother Agathe's more laid-back Caribbean style, always working hard but with a view that if it gets done, why worry if it is done now or later?

Max sided with her father on this point. He hated being late, but his affection for Catherine and his gratitude for how her family had cared for him for centuries gave them a free pass on tardiness. But something niggled with him about Catherine's messages, particularly how she said in her last message that she was being followed.

Why would anyone be interested in Catherine, and why would they be following her?

As a Shadower, he was always on guard, constantly aware that other Shadowers like him could lurk among the humans. Since arriving on Earth back in the Roman era as part of a team of Shadower Enforcers, Max was tasked with chasing down dangerous Shadowers known as Deceptors who had been tracked to the planet. It was a task that he took seriously. He had been doing it for centuries and developed a keen sense for detecting other Shadowers, especially Deceptors.

Of course, not all Shadowers on Earth had criminal intent. Some were like him, working away in the background protecting the planet from the criminal element from their home planet. Others had just settled into a human lifestyle, settling down with partners and living an everyday planet Earth life. But there was a dark side to the Deceptors. They knew their abilities gave them an incredible advantage over humankind. So they regularly popped up, trying to exploit that and take everything they could.

Some Deceptors had even reached the point of controlling whole countries, using their skills and powers to manipulate humans to ensure they enjoyed enormous wealth and privilege. These were the hardest to bring down as they were usually heavily guarded. But in many ways, the small-time crooks were the bane of his life. Deceptors who just skimmed along the surface of petty and mainstream crime, taking enough to keep them in comfort whilst destroying so many other lives around them. They rarely flagged up on any of the Shadower enforcement team's radars.

Max looked straight into one of the many mirrored columns adorning the Willow. He liked dining there as it afforded him two significant benefits. The first was meeting and mixing with the exclusive clientele who frequented the establishment. This enabled him to befriend and call upon them to open doors to people and places that may otherwise have been locked shut.

The second advantage was the bountiful reflective surfaces. Mirrors reflected other mirrors and glass, which bounced light and reflections around the room. It enabled Max to see large swathes of the restaurant with minimal effort. But, more importantly, he could see people's reflections which could be a matter of life or death for a Shadower.

The only sure way to spot a Shadower, whether good or evil, was to see their reflection. Another Shadower could see a distinct glowing aura around the Shadower's image. This aura was invisible to most other beings, including humans.

Some humans claim to be able to see these auras assigning particular meanings to the various colours. However, Max had other ideas, believing it was due to a genetic mutation in the person's ancestry. Max knew that when a Shadower used a human as a host, there was often the risk of leaving some trace of Shadower's genetic code behind. Depending on what that code was, it could give the human some advanced 'gifts', which could be passed down from generation to generation, or equally, they could fade away from the family genetic line.

It was almost unheard of for humans to develop significant Shadower abilities. But, over the two millennia he had spent on this planet, he knew of a handful of cases where this had happened, resulting in a powerful human. However, spotting auras was undoubtedly one of the more uncomplicated talents left in humans more often than other skills.

Max looked at his watch and then at his reflection in the mirrored column and smiled. When Michael had acted as host 34 years ago, perhaps some of Michael's genetic code had transferred onto Max's energy soul instead of the other way around, with attitude to time-keeping being one, and also a fondness for a good malt whisky.

Max returned to scanning the busy restaurant for signs of danger and was content with the knowledge that everything seemed in order.

The tube stopped at Tottenham Court Road station, and Catherine hurried out. As she did, she looked for the hooded man, but he seemed to have either vanished or at least blended into the mass of people rushing for the escalators. Catherine ran through the busy tunnels and walked quickly up the left-hand side of the escalator, cursing the people on the way who didn't seem to understand the underground etiquette of keeping right for standing so people in a hurry could pass on the left. As she got near the top, she moved quickly to the right and used the long drop down the escalator to look for the man in the hoodie, and there he was halfway up but now also stood to the right with his head down.

Catherine moved quickly. In a far-from-typical move by her, she rudely pushed her way to the barriers, tapped her card, and darted out onto Tottenham Court Road, ignoring the disgruntled heckles from those she barged past. A quick left and she was moving as quickly as possible south toward Cambridge Circus.

Glancing back, she still couldn't see anyone, but her nerves were dancing like crazy. Had she imagined the hoodie man was following her? Maybe he was making the same judgement call about squeezing onto a packed carriage or waiting for the next one. But then, he quickly averted her gaze every time she glanced down to that end of the carriage.

She decided to cross the road even though it was not where she was going and spotted him doing the same thing. Catherine's heart began to race, and she knew she had to do something. 'OK, Catherine, think it's all about self-protection and staying safe.' Max always told her there was safety in numbers, and the more boisterous the crowds were, the easier it was to hide. Well, you don't get much more raucous than

Old Compton Street on a Friday night, she thought and turned right. The crowds were undoubtedly enjoying the warm air with rainbow banners everywhere.

She kept moving quickly and took a left into Moor Street, opening several different routes for her to take. She kept moving, and as she reached Cambridge Circus, she decided the direct way, straight across and down West Street, was the better option over Charing Cross Road and Litchfield Street. It also meant that as she reached West Street, she could stop and look back for the hooded man.

Catching her breath as she entered West Street, she paused by the fast-food chicken shop and peered back towards Moor Street to the right of the Palace Theatre. Many people were bustling about, but there was no sign of the hoodie man. Instead, a couple of young lads came running out of Moor Street and turned to their right, heading up Shaftesbury Avenue; a young couple also appeared that way, looking agitated before heading into the theatre; maybe they were late for the show. After a minute or two, Catherine convinced herself that she had lost him or it was just a coincidence. The only people who had headed her way were a woman in a white blouse, a couple of older gentlemen holding hands and a few more young lads who looked like they were about to have a serious debate with several pints of beer.

Catherine turned and headed down to the Willow, feeling a little easier but still tense. The journey to the Willow had been long, stressful, and tiring, but Catherine finally arrived safely, and she was relieved to see Uncle Max waiting for her at his usual table.

Max spotted Catherine walking into the restaurant and waved. He never tired of seeing her warm and radiant complexion. She was undeniably the daughter of her father and mother, with high cheekbones, full lips, and almond-shaped eyes. She was a mix of the best features of both her parents. Her hair was brown almost to the point of being black, and she always kept it short, in her words, 'to ensure it took as little effort as possible in the morning.' As she moved across the restaurant towards him, her athletic and toned body with long and lean limbs carried her with grace and confidence, he could see she was now a woman who knew how to handle herself. Her style was a mix of professional and trendy, reflecting her busy lifestyle and fashion sensibilities.

They hugged and exchanged the usual welcoming pleasantries as Catherine ordered a glass of wine to calm her nerves.

As they perused the menu and placed their order, Catherine shared the details of her long day at the hospital, including the incident on the tube. Max listened intently, agreeing that being aware of your surroundings and trusting your instincts was essential. Finally, the dinner arrived, and Max asked after Catherine's father.

'How are Thomas and Agathe?' he said, 'I've not seen them for a couple of weeks as I've been away.'

'Oh, they're fine. Papa was so sorry he couldn't make it, but they asked him if he could call in at his old hospital. I'm not sure what the problem is, but I think some VIP had specifically demanded that Papa see to him. As for Mama, she's doing her usual of feeding everyone. I think she said she was supporting a homeless shelter this evening.'

'Some VIPs do get a little above themselves, thinking they can demand the earth because of who they are. Did Thomas say how long he would be and who the VIP was?'

'No, I didn't get to speak to Papa in person to ask. He just messaged me to say he was sorry he couldn't make it and explained why. It's unusual for him to message and not call, though. He's a bit of a Luddite with things like that.'

'Have you tried to call—' but Max's attention was suddenly distracted. Did he see an aura in one of the mirrors? Max's eyes widened as he scanned the room, his eyes darting from reflective surface to reflective surface.

'Max, are you OK? What's the matter?' Catherine asked, concerned about her uncle's sudden change in behaviour.

'Something's not right. I think there may be another Shadower in here. At least, I hope it's just a Shadower and not a Deceptor. I'm sure I saw an aura. I know you can't see auras but is anyone looking suspicious or watching us?'

'Max, look at that waitress over there. She seems to be wandering around but not serving. I swear she passed me when I was looking for the guy with the hoodie,' Catherine said, trying to indicate in the direction of one of the waitresses without making it too obvious.

Max turned his head toward the waitress and then flicked back, scouring mirrors and windows to spot her in a mirror. In one of the mirrors, he saw what he was looking for, the purple haze of an aura, but it was a reflection of a reflection, and he couldn't see more than just the edge of it. He tried moving his head to see the body it was emanating from, but he moved the wrong way, and it disappeared.

Max tapped his pocket and felt the familiar bulge of what appeared to be an old fountain pen, but it was actually his immobiliser. The device is thin and narrow, and the press of a button sends a pulse wave which immobilises a Shadower's energy soul in the human body for up to an hour, preventing their escape from the body. But the immobiliser's aim was far from perfect, and its range is only a metre or two. Whilst this hardly sounded, hi-tech Max was proud of how he had improved on the one he had when he arrived on Earth. Version one needed to be held against the Shadower when the button was pressed, so getting it to send a pulse had been a significant leap forward. But, unfortunately, he hadn't been able to increase the range for fear of hitting innocent civilians because whilst the pulse only immobilised a Shadower, it could seriously injure a human.

Max had also realised he needed to ensure the device stopped working if it didn't detect his energy soul within a few metres of range and disguised it as an everyday object which would help prevent it from falling into the wrong hands. So with each new mutation, he would build a new one into a device that fitted with his new persona, and this time an old Dunhill pen seemed perfect.

Max pulled out his immobiliser and said to Catherine, 'I'm going to wash my hands.' He whispered, 'Keep an eye on the waitress and see if she watches me or starts moving towards me. I'm going to try to spot her reflection.'

Max started walking towards the toilets, bringing him closer to the waitress. He avoided looking directly at her but kept looking around the room as if enjoying the décor and checking out the mirrors while trying to remain inconspicuous. Then Max saw the unmistakable purple aura surrounding the waitress in a mirror. He could not use the immobiliser on her in such a crowded place, so he decided to continue to the toilets. However, the waitress was now also walking in his direction. He had noticed she kept looking towards his table and Catherine.

Max and the waitress were on a collision course, but then the waitress must have sensed something because she suddenly looked up and locked eyes with Max. Panic set in as the waitress started to run, causing chaos in the restaurant as people scrambled out of the way. Max followed closely behind, dodging tables and chairs as he chased the Deceptor into the street.

He knew he had to act fast before the Deceptor could harm anyone, but he had to find out why she seemed so interested in Catherine.

The pursuit took them across Cambridge Circus and through the colourful streets of Soho. The queues and crowds for the clubs and bars give Max little opportunity to chase as fast as he could. Finally, the waitress turned into Dean Street and looked back to see if she was still being pursued. While running, she tapped her watch to make a call to someone.

They were soon fighting through the busy crowds of Chinatown and heading towards Leicester Square. Max's mind was racing as he tried to devise a plan to capture the waitress. He had to keep his focus and not let her get away. He knew he was far from running at full speed but was surprised how easily he could keep pace with her, given her much younger and fitter body.

He needed to find a way to get her to head somewhere quieter, but she seemed to know where she was going. He'd noticed her tap her watch, so had she arranged for backup, was he heading into a trap or had she sorted an escape plan for herself? All he could be sure of was that they were heading towards Piccadilly Circus. Until this point, it seemed like she was trying to stay in crowds, but if she got to Piccadilly Circus, she would also have the underground and many other ways to hide and escape.

Just as he spotted the impressive facade of the Criterion Theatre, he collided with a delivery person who sent him sprawling across the pavement.

He scrambled to his feet, offered profuse apologies to the delivery person, and scanned for the waitress as blood started trickling down his face.

He realised it was futile. The waitress could be anywhere by now. The blood blurred his sight, and his leg hurt from the fall. He limped across to the entry to the underground outside the theatre and glanced down, hoping that maybe she was hiding where she could see him run past and then make her escape, but he couldn't see her.

He saw a group of teenagers sitting at the base of the statue of Eros and hobbled over to them. 'Excuse me, guys, did you see a blonde-haired woman in a white blouse and black trousers running past?'

'Nah, buddy,' one of them mumbled as he munched on a burger.

Max stumbled up the steps at the statue's base, hoping the elevated position would help him spot her. As he looked around, there seemed to be one large red double-decker bus after another, but all were moving remarkably quickly for this time of the evening. Max presumed it unlikely that she would have double-backed the way they had run, so he looked up Shaftesbury Avenue, but his line of sight was obscured by all the buses. He then scanned across to his left as the buses and cars passed until he looked down Piccadilly.

His phone rang, and he saw it was Catherine. 'Yes, my dear, how are things there?'

'A little crazy but getting back to normal. I've been asking the staff, and no one knows who she is. They all assumed she was just some agency worker, as they get them when it's busy. Are you still following her?'

'No, I think I've lost her. We got as far as Piccadilly Circus, but I tripped, and by the time I got up, she had....'

Max spotted the waitress standing in the first arch of the building on the corner of Shaftesbury Avenue and Glasshouse Street. He knew several entrances to the tube station were dotted around, so when he tripped, she could have quickly gone into the one by the theatre and emerged from another on that side of the road. So why was she standing there staring at him instead of escaping? Admittedly she was standing well back, blending a little into the shadows, but her white blouse and face were illuminated by her phone.

'I can see her,' Max said quickly, 'got to go.'

He tried to hit the call end button but missed it as he stuffed the phone back into his jacket. His eyes were fixed on her, and he knew she wouldn't escape this time. He leapt off the statue base, keeping her in his gaze, but his injured leg started to crumble, and he lurched forward as he landed.

A squeal of tyres followed as Max was hit by a black limousine, leaving him sprawled on the road and close to death in the street.

'Max, what's happened?' Catherine screeched down the phone. She'd heard the tyre squeal and then a sudden loud impact. People were screaming, and car horns seemed to be going off. There were muffled voices of several people, but she couldn't make anything out.

Catherine babbled to a waiter about the bill, but he just told her to go. Max had been a patron of the Willow for many years, and they all knew Max, Catherine and her father well. Now was not the time to worry about his bill.

She knew he was around Piccadilly Circus from her call, so she ran towards and then down Shaftesbury Avenue. The traffic was already backing up, and she had a terrible foreboding. She put the phone on speaker and kept running.

Max's mind raced as he lay on the ground, the sounds of car horns and shouting people slowly fading away. He had been close to capturing the Deceptor, who had been masquerading as a waitress.

Max realised this might be the end as he lay there, feeling his energy draining. He had been alive for centuries, chasing down dangerous alien criminals on Earth, but now it seemed his time was finally up. He closed his eyes and braced himself for the end, or with luck, enough time to get into another host.

The last thing he remembered was that familiar feeling of his energy soul tearing out of his body.

'Hello, is anyone there?' a voice crackled from the phone in Catherine's hand.

Catherine shot the phone to her ear, turning off the speaker. 'Yes, who is this, and why are you on my uncle's phone?'

'Oh, I'm really sorry, but I think your uncle has been in an accident, and his phone must have fallen out of his pocket when the car hit him,' the female voice explained.

'Where are you? I'm just running down Shaftesbury Avenue past the, uh yeah, the Apollo, but everything seems gridlocked.'

'You are almost here. The accident was right in the middle of Piccadilly Circus. I heard the bang and turned to see him lying on the floor by a big black car. Some boys ran over to him, but a woman came along and told everyone to stand back, saying she was a doctor and nobody should touch him,' the voice continued. 'When you get here, I'm by the Eros statue facing the accident, but please prepare yourself, my dear.'

Catherine tore into the crowd with a string of, 'Excuse me,' 'Let me through,' 'I think it's my uncle,' and 'Please, can I get past.'

Then she saw the car and circling to the left; there was the unmistakable figure of Max lying in the road, his body broken and shattered from the collision.

Catherine screamed. 'Max' as she pushed through to reach his body. 'Please, it's my uncle. What happened?'

A familiar voice came from behind her. 'Hello dear, I think we were just speaking on the phone. Here is your uncle's phone.'

'What? Oh, thank you,' Catherine said, her eyes filling with tears. 'What happened, and has anyone called an ambulance?'

An American man in the crowd near Catherine confirmed one had been called, 'There was a female doctor here until a few minutes ago, but I don't know where she went. She kept us all back as she checked his pulse, but then she stood up and said he had died, so she needed to call the police to report it, and that was the last time I saw her.'

'What did she look like?' Catherine demanded.

'Around your height and similar age, but she was white with blonde hair. She was wearing a white blouse and black pants,' the American man said.

Catherine looked at the old lady who had handed her the phone. She had one of those kind grandmotherly faces and a voice that seemed to make everything seem not quite so bad, 'Please, Mrs um.'

'Beatrice, my dear, call me Beatrice,' the old lady replied

'Please, Beatrice, you mentioned some lads helping my uncle. Where are they?'

'Oh, they left after the doctor intervened, my dear. I guess they thought she was in charge now.'

Just then, sirens interrupted everything as an ambulance, and two police cars came the wrong way up the bus lane into Piccadilly Circus.

2
THE AWAKENING

'Bobby, Bobby wake up,' the little girl shouted.

Max was confused. Where was he, and why was a young girl bouncing up and down on him or at least on his bed?

His head hurt, his body ached, and he could only remember parts of what had happened in the accident. Had his life been saved? Was he now in hospital, and would this girl please stop shouting and bouncing up and down as it is very annoying?

He opened his eyes and saw a girl aged about four or five years old was the budding trampolinist. He glanced around the room and saw all the hallmarks of a teenage boy's bedroom, complete with posters of pop singers, some old cuddly toys and a—

'Get out of my room,' a voice shouted.

'It's time to get up, Bobby. Mummy sent me to wake you,' said the girl.

'It's Sunday morning Lily. Go away,' said the voice belonging to someone called Bobby.

OK, so Max now knew the girl's name was Lily, and there was also someone called Bobby in the room.

'Of course, I know it's Lily. Why wouldn't I? Why am I thinking like this and in a weird old man voice?' the voice called Bobby asked.

'Mummy said dinner will be half an hour, so you have to get up,' said Lily. 'And who are you talking to?'

'Nobody, just go so I can get dressed,' the voice known as Bobby snapped back.

Max felt his body start to move, accompanied by several groans and felt his hand rubbing his head.

Unable to grasp precisely what had happened, he asked, 'Excuse me, but can you tell me where I am?'

Bobby screamed, 'Who the heck said that?'

'I did,' replied Max.

'But who are you, and where are you?' Bobby asked.

Max figured that somehow, he was now inside this Bobby person and that they would have to work together to figure out what to do next.

'What the actual hell do you mean you are inside me?' Bobby demanded.

Max sighed and rubbed his temples, realising that he had much work to do to help this boy understand what was happening. Although, to be honest, he was still putting the pieces together himself.

'*I need you to stay very calm whilst I explain this to you, but first of all, I need to ask you a question,*' Max said as calmly as he could, thinking the words rather than saying them.

'Why?' challenged Bobby.

'*Because it will help me understand what has happened and make it easier to explain to you. Also, you don't need to speak out loud; think what you want to say, and I can hear it, just like I am doing now. Were you in Piccadilly Circus recently and saw a man hit by a car? Also, when was this, and what day is it today?*'

'*Yeah, it happened on Friday. Some old guy asked us about seeing a woman, and then he ran out in front of a big black whip. The guy never stood a chance.*'

'*A whip?*'

'*Yeah, a whip, you know, a big limo, I think it was a Merc, but it certainly damaged the guy more than he damaged it. Oh, and it's Sunday today.*'

'*What happened next?*' Max asked, realising he would be learning a whole new language of teen English.

'*Well, me and the guys ran over to check on him. A few others did too. I did first aid at college, so I was checking for a pulse when this woman came over and told us to stand back as she was a doctor.*'

'*Ah, that explains it,*' Max said as the jigsaw pieces started slotting into place. '*Was the woman blonde and wearing black trousers with a white blouse?*'

'*Yeah, she was. Were you there as well?*'

'*You could say that. In fact, not only was I there, but I was the old guy as you kindly described me.*'

'WHAT!' shouted Bobby.

'*Shh. We don't want anyone else in the house coming in now.*'

'Bobby, are you up yet?' a female voice shouted up the stairs.

'Yes, Mum, just getting dressed,' Bobby shouted back.

'*Look, there is no easy way to say this, so please, no more shouting and listen,*' Max said reassuringly. '*My name is Max. I'm over two thousand years old, and I'm—*'

'Bull,' retorted Bobby out loud before thinking, '*Nobody can live that long.*'

'*No human can, Bobby, but that is what I was about to explain. I'm not human. I'm from a planet many light-years away.*' Max sighed as he mentioned his home world. '*Human astronomers have not spotted the planet, so it has no human name, but we call it Zephyrion.*'

'*So if you are alien, why are you here, and how come you looked human?*'

'*A long time ago, our planet started to change. The change happened gradually, but we were so advanced that we thought we could engineer our way out of it. Then, the atmosphere started getting denser to the point where our bodies struggled to function. But scientists had a breakthrough and worked out how to separate our energy souls from our bodies. Not only did this mean we could exist as an energy force without the intense pressure of gravity pulling against our physical being, but it also eradicated all illnesses and, to a large extent, death. We could only die if our energy souls were destroyed.*

'But this only delayed the problem, and as other creatures started dying around us in increasingly greater numbers, we could see that it meant our planet was doomed, but by the time we realised what was happening, it was too late.' Max hadn't thought about his home planet for a long time, and explaining it like this never got any easier.

'But how did you end up on Earth?'

'When people started converting to energy souls, it made travel easy. We could transport people using energy transporters. It's like sending an electrical signal down a power line or using a laser. However, you need the right equipment at the start to break down and code each energy soul to decode you at the other end restoring you. This created many opportunities for space travel but also for criminals. My job was as an Enforcer, or you might say I was a policeman or spy. I infiltrated the criminal gangs and brought them down. I was very good at it, even if I say so myself.'

'Hello,' said Bobby, *'can you speed it up? My dinner is waiting!'*

'Fine, well as the planet's climate started to collapse, we realised we needed to find alternative planets, which resulted in Operation Exodus. The plan was to send people to various habitable planets and rebuild our civilisation. Despite our planning, we knew we risked picking planets that may already have intelligent life, which could have created a significant cultural destabilisation, so each exodus included a group of Enforcers to ensure stability if that happened. We were also tasked with preventing criminal gangs from taking over the new settlements.'

'*Well, I guess you dropped lucky with Earth then, as there is little intelligent life here.*'

'*Yes, well, Earth was never supposed to be used. We knew it had primitive but civilised life forms, so it was deselected early in the process. However, whilst working as an Enforcer, I discovered gangs were using an Exodus machine to send Shadowers to Earth.*' Max said.

'*What are Shadowers?*'

'*It is the name we use for ourselves, or at least it is the closest human word to what we use. The criminal Shadowers we call Deceptors for the same reason.*'

'*So these Deceptors were coming here, and you chased after them to bring them back to your planet?*'

'*Sort of, yes. A small group of us Enforcers were selected to come to Earth along with a scientist, an engineer and a technician who would build an Exodus machine for the return journey, but we had a problem.*'

'*What was it?*'

'*Because Earth had been deselected very early in the process, we hadn't any data on the atmospheric density. This meant that with the much lighter Earth's atmosphere compared to ours, the first few sent over vaporised,*' Max explained. '*Earth wasn't dense enough to hold our energy souls together.*'

'*How did you survive then?*'

'*As a senior Enforcer, I had done some interplanetary expeditions and had gone through light atmosphere survival training, but with time running out, most of the group had only been given a brief level of training, and we didn't appreciate how quickly they would need to react. Within seconds of landing, I jumped into a nearby human and tried to bring a few other humans to the arrival point.*

'*Other Shadowers arrived, and I managed to save a few other Enforcers and the technician, but the scientist and the senior engineer both perished. The technician knew the principles of the Exodus machine but didn't have the skills to build the technology from scratch, which made this a one-way trip.'* Max sighed. He had recounted this tale many times over the years, but it never got any easier.

'*So where are the others, and what happened to the technician?*'

'*Us Enforcers agreed to separate to cover different parts of the planet, and the technician's location remains a secret. Nobody knows what the technician now looks like, but a couple of us know the code words and the correct response should we need to reveal ourselves to him. The technician said he thought he might be able to build a new Exodus machine, but it would take a lot of testing, time, and money. However, we underestimated how lacking in technology humans were at that time. Only now is it getting to a basic enough level where he can start testing his theories with workable models. In the meantime, we keep jumping from one human to another because the bodies we inhabit age the same as other humans.'* Max stopped, feeling he had probably already said too much.

'*Woah, back up a bit, cowboy. What do you mean you keep jumping from one human to another? Does this mean you are staying inside me forever?*' Bobby said worryingly.

'*No, not forever. I ensured the other Shadowers learned how to use human DNA to create their shells. It takes us about six months to do it, and then we can separate using the shell to hold our energy souls. So effectively, it's a bit like building a clone. Once the process starts, you must separate once the shell is ready, or both the Shadower and the host will die.'*

'SIX MONTHS?' Bobby spat the words out. 'Are you telling me you will be in my head for six flipping months?'

'*Yes, but stop talking. Just think, and I'm not just in your head; I occupy all of you. Think of it like a flatshare.'*

'*Hey cowboy, my body ain't some sort of Airbnb, you know. And what do you mean you occupy all of it?*'

'*I need to create a full copy of your body for it to function properly under my control.'*

'*Yeah, but ALL of it? Even my erm, well, you know, like everything?*'

'*Yes, Bobby, everything, but don't worry, I've been a human male before, so there is nothing to worry about.*' Max tried to reassure Bobby.

'*That may be, but you haven't been this human male before. It's cringe.*'

'*Cringe? Ah, yes, it makes you feel awkward about the situation.*'

'*Why did that feel like you were hunting for the word in my brain?*'

'*Because that is basically what I was doing. From what you told me, I've been inside you for maybe a day and a half. The first few times, I'd be conscious straight away, but each jump into a new body seems to take a little longer to wake up and get used to the new host. So I'm still just getting to grips with how you work internally. Don't worry. Another day or so, and it'll be as if we are one. Well, that is until I can separate.*'

'*This is mega-scale cringe, and hearing some creepy-voiced old man inside me seeing everything and knowing all my thoughts doesn't help.*'

'*Oh, that's easily fixed,*' said Max switching to a young female voice.

'*Woah, like, what the hell was that?*'

'*Well, I thought you might find a female voice easier to cope with. I've been just about every type of human, even a couple of dogs, but that's another story, so I can use any voice you prefer internally.*'

'*Well, stick to the old guy. It's bad enough knowing I got a geezer inside me without thinking there's a woman inside me, seeing everything and knowing what I'm thinking.*'

The bedroom door flew open, and Lily stood there, hands on her hips, looking pleased with herself. Then, shouting down the stairs, she said, 'I was right, Mummy. He's still in bed.' Lily turned back towards the bedroom and added, 'Bobby,

Mummy wants you downstairs now; dinner is ready, and leave that glowing thing behind you.'

'OK, I'm coming now,' said Bobby flinging back his duvet in a grand gesture to prove he was getting up. He reached for a pair of jeans and a white T-shirt and dropped them on his bed.

Lily seemed pleased with the reaction she had been responsible for and ran back down the stairs informing half the neighbourhood that Bobby was getting up.

'*Are you not changing your socks and underwear?*' Max queried.

'*They were clean yesterday morning, thank you.*'

'Good grief, I'm living in a slob.'

'Rent free, I'd like to point out,' Bobby retorted.

Ignoring the last comment, Max changed the subject, saying, '*By the way, your sister is very loud.*'

'*You're telling me? I have to live with her.*'

'*So do I, it seems, for the time being,*'

'*What do you think she meant by that glowing thing?*' Bobby asked.

'*Do you have a mirror?*'

'*Yeah, in the bathroom.*'

Walking into the bathroom, Max picked up the smell of dampness and mould.

'*Dad always said this was going to be the first room he sorted out after Granny Mosley died, but he never got around to it,*' Bobby tried to explain.

'*No need to explain. I've seen far worse. Now, before you look in the mirror, I nee—*'

Shutting the bathroom door to reveal the full-length mirror on the back of it, Bobby's mind screamed, '*What the heck.*'

'*Yes, that is what I was about to explain. Anything inhabited by a Shadower has an aura. But before you panic, only other Shadowers and a few former hosts can generally see them.*'

'*Well, I can flipping see it, and so could Lily.*'

'Of course, you can see it as I am inside you, but your sister is a bit of an enigma. I have heard of young children having more advanced skills, which diminish as they age, but this is the first time I have encountered it myself.'

Max took the opportunity of standing in front of the mirror to look down at the body he was now inhabiting. It looked reasonable, not athletic, but with an average build. Nevertheless, he was pleased as being an Enforcer meant staying fit. The one advantage of being inside a younger body was that at least training would be easier.

'Woah there, cowboy, why are you eyeing up my body?'

'Relax. I was just seeing what I had to work with because I need to get you fit, which means plenty of exercise.'

'Well, stop it, it's a serious cringefest,' replied Bobby, returning to his bedroom and quickly pulling on his jeans and t-shirt. *'Besides, I know of very little that can be improved with excessive exercise. Talking of which, I'm going down for dinner now to exercise my jaw and stomach, so whatever you do, stay quiet, OK?'*

'Yes, OK. Oh, and it's lunch at this time of day. Dinner is in the evening.'

'Whatevs,' Bobby shot back before half jogging down the stairs.

At the bottom of the stairs, Bobby turned left and went through the living room, scowling at Lily as she poked her tongue out at him as he passed into the kitchen.

'Hi, Mum, what's for dinner?' Bobby inquired.

'Lunch,' Max reminded him.

Bobby ignored Max and walked over to where his Mum was plating up.

'Morning champ, or should I say afternoon? It's sausage and mash, as things are tight this month,' his mother replied.

'That's OK. I like sausages, but can I have more gravy, please?' Bobby said before grabbing his plate and wandering into the living room to eat it off his lap.

'Hah, stinky, you never even had a shower,' Lily said. Bobby sat on the sofa near where Lily sat on the floor, eating her dinner off her plate perched on the coffee table.

Bobby ignored her and stared at the television, playing yet another children's cartoon that his sister had seen for what seemed like the gazillionth time.

'*Where is your Dad, Bobby?*

'*He died in a car crash just over five years ago, just before she was born,*' Bobby looked in Lily's direction.

'*I'm sorry to hear that. Is it just you three now, then?*

'*Yeah, just me, Lily and our Mum. Oh, by the way, her name is Pat or Patricia if you want to wind her up.*'

As he finished thinking, Pat entered the room and sat at the other end of the sofa. Max tried to study her without it being obvious. She looked to be in her late thirties with long brown hair, a slim build, and a tired but weary smile.

'*Hah, she'd love you,*' Bobby pipped up, '*She's 42 this year.*'

'Lily, turn the telly over. I want to watch the news,' Pat said.

'Aww, Mummy, I've not seen this one,' Lily squealed.

'You mean you've not seen it in the last half hour,' Bobby chipped in.

'Shut it, scummy,' Lily said, glaring at her brother.

'Lily, I said don't use words like that and change the channel now, young lady,' Pat replied.

Lily grumbled but flicked the remote button. A few adverts flickered across the screen before the local news started.

'In the news tonight, the Greater London police are appealing for witnesses to come forward to Friday night's awful accident in Piccadilly Circus. They are particularly keen to speak to a group of teenagers who were first to reach the elderly gentleman after he was hit by the car,' the newsreader announced.

The screen flashed images of the accident, showing the limousine, flashing lights from police cars and ambulances and police officers trying to hold back the crowds.

'Didn't you say you saw that accident, Bobby?' Pat asked.

'Uh yeah, me and me mates were there.'

'*Shhh, deny it was you who came to me,*' Max said urgently. '*The appeal is probably a Deceptor plan to find you all.*'

Bobby stuttered, then continued, 'But we didn't get involved. Some other lads ran to him before a woman arrived, saying she was a doctor. So we just left them all to it.'

'Is the woman the police are talking to by the black car the doctor?'

'Uh, no, she was driving the car that hit him.'

Bobby was staring at the screen; well, actually, it was Max doing the staring; Bobby seemed to have lost the ability to move his body.

'*What's going on? I can't move,*' Bobby thought.

'*Shh,*' Max responded, '*Sorry, I need to see this. I think it's her. Quick, can you rewind and zoom in there?*'

'*Zoom in? Are you kidding? This telly is so old it's not even got internet access, but if it's connected to the smart box, we can rewind.*'

'Mum, can you rewind it a bit? I think I recognise someone,' Bobby said.

Pat rewound the images until Bobby said play. The camera panned across from the Eros statue, over the crowds and stopped at the car as the reporter replayed what they believed to be the dead man's movements before the accident.

'*Can you see the blonde-haired woman with the white top in the background?*' Max asked.

'Yeah, that's the doctor over there,' Bobby said.

'Which one?' Pat asked.

'Oh, sorry, I was thinking out loud. But yeah, you see that woman on the far side of the car in a white top with blonde hair? She was the one who told us to step back, erm, the crowd, I mean, and she shooed off the guys helping him.'

'Strange she's not still assisting if she was the first doctor on the scene,' Pat mused.

'*Yes, my thoughts exactly, except she's no doctor. She was the Deceptor I was chasing,*' Max said. '*That's why she wanted you all to stand back so she could stop me transmuting.*'

'*Transwhatting?*'

'*Transmutation is the term for transforming from one being into another. In this case, me moving out of Maxwell Thomas's body and entering yours.*'

'*Please stop saying things like being in me or entering me. It's cringe,*' Bobby pleaded.

'*OK, if it helps, but she wanted to stop me transmuting from Maxwell into you or anyone else.*'

'*But couldn't you just transthingy into her or, like when you first came to Earth, just quickly move into the crowd?*'

'*A Shadower cannot occupy anything that already contains another Shadower so she could freely touch me. She probably wanted to use her immobiliser to stop me from leaving Maxwell's body, which would have meant I died.*'

'*Her what?*'

'*It locks a Shadower into a body and immobilises them and the body. If you use it on a body that's dying, the Shadower is trapped and if the body dies, so does the Shadower most of the time. Occasionally the death of the body seems to release the Shadower, but they've only got about five seconds at the most to find a new host. Which reminds me, we must build a new one as soon as possible.*'

'*Where is the nearest Immobilisers'R'Us then?*'

'*We just need a DIY store or some electrical retailer to get what's needed, or ideally, we could go to see my friend Catherine. Just in case she was given my belongings.*'

'It's your turn washing up, champ,' Pat said.

'Aww, Mum, I'm meeting the guys in town, besides it's Lily's turn.'

'She's five, Bobby, come on. I'll let you off this time, but you're on double shifts tomorrow.' She smirked at Bobby, and he just felt her love.

'OK, Mum and thanks. I might be late back as I've got a few things to do.'

'OK, son, but don't be too late as you've got a driving lesson tomorrow.'

Bobby wandered into the kitchen, scraped the remains of his dinner into the bin and left his plate on the side. Then, passing through the living room, he said, 'I'm off now. I'll be back around ten.'

'OK, champ, have a nice time,' Pat replied.

'Laters loser,' Lily chimed in.

Bobby ignored Lily and headed for the front door.

3 Hinton Court was a traditional mid-20th Century council house in the North London borough of Haywood. Not grand but functional. Upstairs comprised of 3 bedrooms with a family bathroom whilst downstairs was a lounge, kitchen, toilet and utility room. It was a bit tired and needed some modernising, but it was a loving family home.

'*Yep, that's home,*' Bobby said, '*It used to be Granny Mosley's house, but the council let Mum and Dad inherit it when she died as we were living here caring for her. Dad had so many plans to buy it, add an extension with a garage, and expand upstairs into four bedrooms until, well, you know.*'

'*Sorry I wasn't criticising it; it seems like a lovely place. Oh wow, it's a bit old, but it's a Focus ST, let's go.*'

'*What are you on about? That's Mum's car. Besides, I've not passed my test yet.*'

'*You mean?*'

'*Yeah, we're walking to the tube station. But I've got a driving lesson tomorrow, and my test is in a few weeks.*'

It was less than 10 minutes to the tube station, and Bobby saw Adam at the end of the road.

Adam Lee was the sporty member of Bobby's group of friends. He was always up for a game of football, a round of golf or any sport, but he was ultra-competitive, albeit in a good-natured way. He was average height but fit in every way you could imagine. In Bobby's eyes, if you drew the perfect dark-haired, browned-eyed teenager, it would be Adam, and his wicked sense of humour made him even more perfect.

'Hey, Adam, how are you?' Bobby asked.

'Oh, hi, Bobby. I'm good, thanks. Dazza and Avery said they'd meet us in Bond Street, but I've not heard from Danny.'

'Danny is grounded for hacking some college exams. But Abi is going to meet us by Oxford Circus.'

'*Wow, you like Adam,*' said Max.

'*Yeah, he's a cool guy.*'

'*No, I mean you find him attractive. Have you told him how you feel?*'

Bobby blushed.

'You OK, buddy?' Adam asked as they approached the tube station.

'Yeah, I'm good, just worried about Mum, but all fine,' Bobby replied, thinking for Max's benefit, '*Shut up, I'm not gay; he's just my best friend.*'

'*Your body says he's more than just a best friend.*'

'Just do one,' Bobby said out loud.

'You what, buddy?' Adam asked.

'Oh, sorry, Adam, I was just thinking out loud, durrr.'

Bobby and Adam boarded the tube, which was almost empty as their station was at the end of the line. Bobby glanced at Adam, thinking about what Max had said.

'*Tell him how you feel,*' Max said.

'*I can't. He'd hate me, my family would disown me, and besides, I like someone else more.*'

'*Hmm. I can't see all of your thoughts yet, but I can see you're confused about your emotions.*'

'*Wow, the depth of your wisdom is truly awe-inspiring. You're in my brain, yet the best you can come up with is I'm emotionally confused. Let me grab a pen to jot down that moment of brilliance.*'

'Did you see the game last night?' Adam asked. 'Watford got stuffed again. Those Mancs were so lucky. We deserved a penalty.'

'Uh yeah, although we were awful,' Bobby replied.

Bobby watched as the stations flicked past whilst Adam chattered about Saturday's football matches. Wembley Park, Finchley Road and then the tannoy announced, 'The next stop is Bond Street. Please change here for the Central Line.'

They followed the crowd along the platform and up the escalator. Then, hitting the fresh air, Adam said, 'The guys said they'd wait by the Disney shop.'

Crossing Oxford Street, Bobby spotted Avery.

'*Ah, you're one of us,*' Max said.

'*What do you mean?*' Bobby replied.

'*Just that you see everyone as we do, all as equal regardless of gender or race. Although not strictly like us. Shadowers have transcended beyond gender or race. Now we are pure energy souls.*'

'Get out of my head, will you? She's just a friend.'

But Max could see that Bobby saw Avery as so much more. In Bobby's mind, he could see that Bobby thought of her as bright and artistic, always creating something, whether it was paintings, sculptures, or even doodles in her notebook. Her personality was vibrant, and her creative mind made her stand out from the rest of the group. To Bobby, she was truly unique and fun to be around. Her curly black hair, vivid imagination and contagious energy made her so perfect in Bobby's eyes.

'Hey, Bobby darling,' Avery said, hugging him before turning to Adam. 'Hi Adam, what's up,' she added, kissing Adam on the cheek.

'*See, she fancies Adam,*' Bobby thought defiantly.

But Max was already unravelling Bobby's mind. He was starting to understand the confusion, fear, clarity, and simplicity of Bobby's emotions, making him smile. Bobby seemed to see the good in everyone.

'*Except Lily,*' Bobby thought jokingly in response to Max's musing.

'Hey, Dazza, how's things?' Bobby asked.

'Good, thanks. How's Doctor Bob? Killed any old geezers recently?' Dazza replied.

Darius 'Dazza' Turner was a bit of a joker. His role in life was all about making people laugh as far as he was concerned, with a contagious energy that was always lifting the mood of those around him. However, it was a mask to hide his insecurities. At six foot four inches, he was the group's tallest but also the heaviest. Dazza was self-conscious about his weight even though, at 95 kilograms, he was healthy despite his food addiction.

'I'm good, thanks, big man,' said Bobby, 'No, not killed anyone recently. In fact, that old geezer may not be dead, I reckon.'

'*What are you doing?*' said Max, '*You can't tell them about me for their safety.*'

The big man phrase always hurt Dazza, but he knew his friends never meant it maliciously.

'Hey, Dazza, how's you?' Adam asked, hugging his mate tightly.

'Yeah, all OK,' said Dazza feeling awkward at such a public display of closeness from Adam, but they had been friends longer than the rest of the gang since their mothers had been school friends.

'Abi said she'd meet us by Oxford Circus,' Bobby said as they headed in that direction.

'*Are you listening to me? I mean it. You can't tell them about me.*'

'*So what do I tell them?*'

'*Nothing if you can help it. The less your friends know, the less at risk they'll be.*'

'*What do you mean risk?*'

'*Well, that Deceptor saw an opportunity and wanted me dead. I didn't recognise her and certainly wasn't aware of any Deceptors actively pursuing me, well, no more than usual. So if I am a target, anyone I'm involved with could also be at risk.*'

'*But you were chasing her, which hardly sounds like the action of someone after you.*'

'*True, but at times it almost felt like she slowed down to ensure I didn't lose her.*' Max said, confusion running through his thoughts. '*I need to speak to Catherine and try to distance myself from your family.*'

'*Are you saying Mum and Lily are in danger?*'

'*Not in immediate danger, as the Deceptors don't appear to know who you are. That's why they put that appeal on the news for you and your friends to come forward. Talking of which, do you have a phone as we need to speak to my friend.*'

'Hey, all, I just need to make a call. I'll catch up with you,' Bobby said to his friends.

'OK, Bob,' Dazza replied as they started to leave Bobby behind.

'*Why does Dazza call you Bob, emphasising the second b, when everyone else calls you Bobby?*'

'*Oh, don't. It was an old comedy show where a character was, I think, a woman disguised as a man and used the name Bob in that way, and it's sort of stuck. It annoyed me for ages, but I think of it as Dazza's way now. Who am I calling?*'

Max looked down at Bobby's battered old smartphone with a crack across part of the screen. He typed a number into it, hit the dial button and held it to his ear, '*Don't try and speak. I'll do the talking.*'

'*Yes, boss, after all, it's only my body and voice.*'

A familiar voice wafted from the phone, 'Catherine Thomas here.'

Max felt relief at this glimmer of normality, 'Hello, Catherine, it's Max.'

'*Woah there, cowboy, like, what the actual hell was that?*' Bobby asked.

'*It seems that trying to sound like me isn't working with your voice box.*'

'Max, is that you? You sound so different,' Catherine said, 'Where are you, and are you OK?'

'I'm fine,' Max continued, 'Are you at home today? I need to see you.'

'I'm at Mama's. Papa has messaged again, saying he'll be away for a few days, and after what happened to you, I just wanted to be with someone. I'm popping out to get some groceries, and I've got a few chores to do while I'm out, but I'll be back around five-ish.'

'OK, I'll get there before six then. I'll explain when I see you, but just be careful, Catherine.'

'I always am, Max. You taught me well. See you later.'

The line went dead, and Max stared at it.

'*You care about her, don't you?*' Bobby said.

'*Of course I do. I've known Catherine and her family for generations.*'

'*Ha! Now it's my turn to see your thoughts, cowboy, and I can see it's more than that. Oh no, sorry, no, I didn't realise. I'm so sorry, Max. Does she know?*'

'*Nobody knows or can even be certain without tests, but yes, there is a chance she could be part of me. But only her parents and I know there is that possibility.*'

'*But how? Can Shadowers have babies with humans, then?*'

'*Once we separate from our hosts in our transmuted shells, we are often infertile, although occasionally the shells are such perfect copies, they produce the appropriate gametes to reproduce the human DNA. But during transmutation? I'm not sure, as I always avoid intimacy. We were trained as Enforcers to never engage in reproduction whilst transmuting as we were warned it could be dangerous. Not that they ever said what the consequences would be.*'

'*What the hell are gametes? Ah, they're the respective male and female organisms like eggs and—*'

'*Yes, that's right. I can see you're adapting to me quickly and reading my thoughts. I'd go as far as to say you seem to be adapting exceptionally quickly. As for how, let's just say Michael and Agathe, Catherine's parents, had a moment whilst I was transmuting inside Michael. Only the three of us are aware of it, plus now you are, of course.*'

'*I'm a quick learner, cowboy, and don't worry, your secret is safe with me. We need to get a shift on now. I can't even see the others.*'

Bobby jogged down Oxford Street, avoiding the throng of tourists and afternoon shoppers. When he got to Oxford Circus, he realised he'd made a rookie error in agreeing to meet Abi there. The place was swarming with people, and the friends hadn't said which underground exit or shop to meet at. He panicked, cursing Max for separating him from his friends and dragging him into this mess. He scoured the mass of people, desperate to find anyone.

'*Look, I'm sorry for dragging you into this,*' Max said, '*I promise as soon as I can, I'll let you go back to your normal life.*'

'*It's OK,*' Bobby replied, still anxiously looking across the crowds.

'*I know you're being kind and lying. I'm grateful for that, but neither of us can lie to each other as we know what the other is thinking and—there look, that's Dazza over on Regent Street, isn't it? You can see him above the rest of the people.*'

They crossed the road and shouted out to the rest of his friends.

'Hey Bobby, where have you been?' Abi asked.

'Sorry, Abi, I needed to call someone. Great to see you. When did you get back? Oh, before I forget, I need to shoot off at five to meet someone in Kensington.' Bobby said.

'I landed yesterday morning, but everyone told me about what happened Friday night. It sounds awful.'

Abigail 'Abi' Jenkins was the social butterfly of the group. She was always the one organising get-togethers and making new friends. She was outgoing and confident, bringing plenty of energy to the group. Bobby often wondered if her ginger hair and lanky build had given her a choice of being outgoing or bullied. Either way, he was pleased she chose the former.

'Well, if you've got to be in Kensington, why don't we all go to the V&A for an ice cream?' Abi suggested.

They set off down Regents Street, heading for Piccadilly Circus station, aiming to catch the Piccadilly line down to South Kensington. As they went, Abi regaled them with what she did on holiday, including sharing all the posts on her numerous social media accounts.

Max grumbled, *'What is it with everyone nowadays sharing everything about where they are and what they are doing?'*

'Get with it, cowboy. Everyone is doing it. Besides, if you get successful, you can make a lot of money.'

'I value my privacy over money, thank you. Oh, and why do you keep calling me cowboy? It is rather annoying.'

'Dunno, I guess it's cos your voice reminds me a little of that old toy cowboy in that kid's cartoon film.'

Bobby's internal conversation was interrupted by Avery.

'Who do you know in Kensington anyway?' Avery asked. 'It's a bit swanky for you, isn't it?'

'Oh, just an old family friend, and it's actually Earls Court,' Bobby quickly replied. 'Mum asked me to pop in to collect something.'

'Talking of swanky, has Avery told you her news?' Adam asked.

'No, what's going on, Avery?' Bobby asked.

'Oh, it's nothing too special, but Dad said work is going very well, so Mum, Dad and I can go on a luxury holiday this year. He's going to book a swanky villa and take us to Rome,' Avery replied, 'I've heard it's so special.'

'Avery, Romam petis? Euge! Urbs pulchra est, plena amoris et romanticismi. Tibi ibi placere certe debet. Stadionem Domitiani visitare debes, certe spectaculum magnificum spectabis,' Bobby said in Latin.

They all turned and looked at him. Dazza's jaw dropped as if he wanted to make a joke, but no words came out.

Switching smoothly into Italian, Bobby apologised, saying, 'Mi scusi, quello che volevo dire è Avery, vai a Roma? Che bello! È una città bellissima, piena di amore e romanticismo. Ti piacerà sicuramente. Devi assolutamente andare allo Stadio di Domiziano, vedrai uno spettacolo magnifico.'

'WHAT THE...' the others all said in unison.

Bobby blushed.

'Nice one, cowboy. How're you getting us out of this one?' He challenged Max.

Max said, 'Sorry, I slipped into Latin, then Italian. I love Rome so much. I meant to say how wonderful! Rome is such a beautiful city, full of love and romance; I know you will enjoy it. And as you love history, you must go to the Stadium of Domitian; it's a magnificent spectacle under the Piazza Navona.'

'See,' thought Max, *'Just keep it simple, and they'll be fine.'*

'You think?' Bobby replied, *'Let's—'*

Adam interrupted Bobby's thoughts, 'What do you mean you slipped into Latin, then Italian? You can only just about manage English, and even that's a push.'

'Well, erm,' Bobby faltered.

Abi said, 'And how do you know what to see in Rome?'

'Yeah, Bob, how do you know? You get a nosebleed if you set foot outside the M25. I bet you've never even done that,' Dazza responded, laughing at the mere thought of his friend being a seasoned traveller.

'That's not true,' Bobby replied, trying to defend his honour. 'I've been to Vicarage Road to watch the Hornets play many times.'

'Well, I suppose someone has to support them,' Dazza added.

'*Watford's football ground is inside the M25,*' Max thought.

'But, you've proved my point. The case for the prosecution rests,' Dazza said, laughing.

'Oh, whatevs,' Bobby responded.

'Bobby, I think you've got some explaining to do,' Avery said rather forcefully.

3
In it Together

'*We've got to tell them now, thanks to you. Besides, if we don't, what if one of them responds to the police appeal? You said yourself it was a Deceptor trap to find us.*'

Max thought briefly, then relented, '*OK but let's keep it simple and not reveal too much. The less they know, the better.*'

Max took a deep breath and sighed; he had always been meticulous about only letting his very close friends know his identity and, of course, anyone who hosted his energy soul.

Bobby looked at his friends' faces and said, 'Guys, listen, I need to tell you something, but it's confidential. You've got to promise not to say anything to anyone else, right?'

'Wow, get you, the man of mystery and intrigue,' Dazza chipped in.

Avery shot Dazza a look that made it clear he should keep quiet before saying, 'Of course we will, Bobby. What is it?'

They had made it down to the station platform, and Bobby said, 'I can't tell you here; it's too busy, but if we can find a quiet area at the V&A, I'll tell you what I can.'

The 10-minute journey to South Kensington passed with little more than small talk in the packed carriage. Abi chatted to Avery and Dazza about her holiday whilst Adam and Bobby stood by the single door at the front of the carriage.

'What's going on then?' Adam asked. 'Is everything all right at home? I know the last five years have been tough since your old man died.'

'Yeah, it's all cool there. Mum seems to be moving on with things, and cos he died before Lily was born, she never even mentions him, but I still miss him,' Bobby looked away, trying not to cry in front of his friend.

'Hey, it's OK to be sad, buddy,' Adam added, putting his arm around him and giving him a friendly hug. 'If you ever need to let it out, I'm here. We all are.' He nodded towards the other three friends.

'Thanks, Adam,' Bobby replied, turning to face him. He studied his friend's face for a second or two. There was no denying Adam was good-looking, and his love of sports meant he had an athletic build that you couldn't help but admire. But, above all, Bobby saw Adam as a true friend who would do anything for those he cared for.

'*You'd have been better off going into Adam,*' Bobby thought. '*He's everything I'm not.*'

'*Don't put yourself down, Bobby. I'm still getting to know you and your friends, but the one conclusion I'm already coming to is that you all have different strengths and weaknesses, but your combined friendship makes you all special. As for you, I think I've ended up in a pretty decent guy. And remember, I am quickly learning everything about you.*'

'Hey, lovebirds, it's our stop,' Dazza shouted in Adam and Bobby's direction.

'What, oh yeah,' Bobby said. 'Sorry, Adam, was I staring?'

'Nah, all good. I think you were just lost in thoughts about your Dad,' Adam smiled. Then leaning forward as if he was about to kiss Bobby, he glanced towards Dazza and shouted, 'Besides babes, he's only jealous.'

They all started laughing and shoving each other as they got off the train and headed back up the escalators into the warm, pleasant fresh air of South Kensington. They turned right, heading towards the Victoria and Albert Museum, passing the Sunday afternoon café crowds on Exhibition Road before reaching the museum and running straight into the central courtyard.

'Dazza, Abi, grab those seats to the left of the café entrance. I'll get us some ice cream. 99s for everyone?' Avery said. 'Bobby, you and Adam can be my labourers.'

'No flake for me,' Abi shouted as she headed towards the empty seats with Dazza.

Avery, Bobby and Adam headed towards the snack shack.

'What's this all about, Bobby?' Avery asked. 'Since we met up, I've noticed you're constantly looking around, but it's more like you're looking past people rather than at them.'

'I know it's been a tough few days,' Adam added. 'Did that old guy dying bring your Dad's death back to mind? Especially with cars involved with both deaths.'

'*What is it with you lot? I was only just over 60. You all make it sound like I was ancient,*' Max grumbled.

Bobby laughed, causing his friends to stare in disbelief at this sudden change in their friend's behaviour.

'*Well, technically, as you admitted, you're over 2,000 years old; you are ancient, cowboy,*' Bobby chuckled.

'Sorry guys, you won't believe what I'm going to tell you, but yeah, saying the old geezer affected me is fair,' Bobby said out loud.

After handing out the ice creams and sitting down, they turned towards Bobby.

'OK, Bob, what's happening then?' Dazza asked.

'Abi, you said they told you about that guy we saw killed at Piccadilly Circus?' Bobby asked.

'Yeah, Avery and Dazza were telling me more about it when we were on the tube.' Abi said, adding, 'Avery's Mum saw the police appeal on the TV too.'

'Mum wanted to call the number to say we were there, but I asked her to wait until I'd seen all of you this afternoon,' Avery said.

'You can't let her call,' Max said urgently. 'That goes for all of you. Under no circumstances respond to that appeal. If anyone asks, say that you were there but didn't see anything because of the crowds.'

Silence fell as the friends looked at each other and then back to Bobby.

'What?' Bobby asked.

'Why did you change your voice like that?' Abi queried.

'Ah, yeah, umm, that's part of what I need to tell you,' Bobby replied.

Over the next 30 minutes, Bobby tried to explain what had happened at the accident scene and how things had progressed over the last two days.

'So that pensioner is now inside you?' Dazza asked.

'Oi, I am here, you know, and can see and hear everything,' Max responded. 'As Bobby explained, I may be over two thousand years old, but age doesn't mean a thing to my people. We have evolved beyond time, so in a way, I'm young and old at the same time.'

'Sorry, Bobby, but this is freaky. Seeing your lips move, but a slightly different voice coming out is weirding me out,' Adam shuddered.

'It's like someone took the old Bobby, dropped your voice lower and gave you electrocution lessons,' Dazza added.

'I think you mean elocution lessons,' said Abi rolling her eyes.

'Yeah, them too,' Dazza replied, blushing a little.

Abi interrupted, 'If Max's people can rebuild DNA....'

'We don't rebuild DNA. Instead, we adapt and replicate it,' Max corrected her.

'OK, but if you can adapt and replicate DNA to create this shell thing, why don't you just rebuild the DNA to make the existing body you are in young again and repair any injuries?' Abi continued.

'Not technically correct, but in principle, it is entirely possible, but until now, doing it has been hazardous,' Max replied.

'Why hazardous?' Bobby asked before adding, 'Ah, I see.'

'OK, dudes, look, the twin voice thing is freaky, but the twin voices having a conversation with each other is a whole new level of what the heck,' Dazza said, keeping his eyes fixed on Bobby.

'Never mind that,' Abi interrupted Dazza, 'what do you mean by "Ah, I see" Bobby?'

'Sorry, Abi, it's just that whilst I am being hosted in Bobby's body, we can see everything the other is thinking, and over a short period, we learn to read each other's memories too,' Max explained. 'Bobby asked why it was hazardous to rebuild the DNA out loud but then saw the answer in my mind, well, in our mind actually at the moment.'

'Oi, cowboy, it's my mind you're just squatting,' Babby replied.

'So why is it dangerous?' Abi asked.

'Could you end up giving us two heads or give us bigger muscles or something?' Dazza asked before adding, 'Actually, if you can make things bigger—'

'Not now, Dazza,' Adam interrupted, 'Sorry, Bobby, Max, you were explaining about rebuilding our DNA to reverse ageing.'

'It's not exactly rebuilding it,' Max continued. 'Your DNA structure is fine. You only age due to how your epigenetics change over time. Think of it like raw meat.'

'Eww, I'm vegetarian,' Abi squirmed.

'OK, think of it like a piece of fresh fruit then,' Max tried to continue.

'Eww, I'm anti-fruitist,' Dazza said, laughing at himself.

The others stared at him while Max continued, 'Think of it like something fresh, be it vegetables, raw meat or whatever. If you leave it out, it will start to rot or decompose, and the more it rots, the faster the rot happens.'

'That makes sense,' Avery said.

'Controlling your and other animals' bodies is a brain,' Max replied.

'Except in Dazza's case,' piped up Abi, which resulted in her getting a friendly punch in the arm from Dazza and laughter from the rest of them.

'Anyway, your body includes proteins and chemicals that tell your genes what, how and where to do things. It's a bit like a computer with microchips that turn circuits on and off. The changes to control the genes, turning them on or off, are called epigenomes. They are the chemical marks on your DNA,' Max continued. 'Over time, your epigenomes get corrupted. They are flipped in the wrong direction or corrupted in other ways. The more corruption you get, the worse your body responds, and it ages before finally stopping. Like that meat decaying at ever-increasing speed or your computer getting a virus which allows more viruses to get in. Whether it's in the brain or other organs or cells.'

'But if that is how it works, and you know how to stop it, then why not just do it?' Avery queried.

'That is down to mankind, I'm afraid,' Max replied. 'You have existed for thousands of years accepting death and ageing as inevitable. When we came to Earth, it didn't take too many accusations of witchcraft and demonic possession to realise we needed to blend into your circle of life and reversing ageing or repairing near-fatal injuries was not a good approach.'

'So that's why you let bodies age and then jump into a new one when it starts to die?' Avery said.

'Quite correct. All we had to do was find a new host to allow us to transmute over the six months. Then, after leaving the host, we assume a new alternative identity.'

'Is it that easy just to create a new identity?' Avery asked.

'It used to be very simple until recently because records were inaccurate and poorly kept. You could say you were any name you wanted and pick a location a reasonable distance from your host, and that was it.'

'What's changed?' Avery queried.

'Control is the best way of describing it. The last 100 years or so have seen tighter and tighter controls to track everything about people. From birth to death, with modern passports starting in the 1920s, national identity numbers, driving licences, ID cards and more recently, biometric data, everything about everyone is being tracked and monitored. Nowadays, we need to find a person who died when they were younger, adopt their identity and hope their death hasn't been linked to it, or else remove the death records from any systems. But, you need a computer hacker who can keep ahead of technology.'

'Danny!' they all replied.

'Who's Danny?' Max queried, then he saw him in Bobby's mind, 'Ah, yes, I see. He seems like a brilliant guy.'

'Too smart sometimes,' Dazza replied with a chuckle.

'This all sounds good if you can get a host to accept you, but what if they don't want you inside them?' Abi asked.

'I've only experienced that rarely. Usually, I have identified potential new hosts and, over time, built up a friendship and trust, so at the right moment, it is not a problem.' Max replied.

'But not always?' Adam asked, getting intrigued by what he was hearing.

'No, not always. Sometimes, like on this occasion, our old bodies meet their end unexpectedly. We have to move into whatever person or animal is most convenient. It nearly always freaks them out to start with, but most of the time, they realise I mean no harm, and actually, it can benefit us both.'

'Can't see you'll benefit much from Bob,' Dazza joked.

'You'd be surprised, Dazza. When you spend six months inside someone, you learn a lot about them and the things they know. The benefits can continue even when we exit. There can be residue elements left behind in the host, and we take things about them into our new shells,' Max continued.

'What sort of things?' Adam challenged.

'It varies by person. Remember I mentioned we could spot other Shadowers by their auras in reflective surfaces? Well, sometimes the host retains that ability after we split. Likewise, you humans still do not use your bodies and minds to their maximum ability. I'm not saying we do either, but we have learnt how to improve how human bodies work significantly. For example, the way you run is based on the contractile limits of your muscle fibres which dictate how quickly you can apply force to the surface you are running on. If you apply those elements correctly, you can reach around 35 to 40 miles per hour. Sometimes, the host retains some of that ability and becomes a much faster athlete. It is very random.'

'Wow, you'd be breaking world records like that,' Adam added, 'I'm sure the current 100-metre record is only around 25 to 26 miles per hour.'

'27.5 miles per hour, actually,' Avery chipped in, adding, 'So you're saying after you leave a body, the host might be able to do things a Shadower can do?'

'Certainly, they can retain some abilities,' added Max, 'Sometimes those benefits or at least the prospect of some of those benefits help us to persuade the host to relax and accept us.'

'And if they don't?' Adam asked.

'Well, in the most severe case, a Shadower can take control of the host and leave them as an effective passenger, along for the ride without any control,' Max explained.

'Yeah, he did that to me when we watched the news earlier,' Bobby butted in, 'It freaks you out. It's like watching TV, but you are in it and can't control anything.'

'Do all Shadowers have the same abilities and skills?' Adam asked, 'You know, like the ability to make humans run faster.'

'Most have the basic abilities, but like with humans, some seem to have special skills which others don't have,' Max replied.

'What's your special skill, Max?' Abi queried.

'Not dying,' Max responded flatly.

'What next, then?' Avery asked, 'Where do we go from here?'

'Well, you guys just need to keep a low profile. Except for Abi, the rest of you can't deny you were in Piccadilly Circus if anyone confronts you. Don't do anything to offer up that information, so please do not discuss this with anybody. Where possible, stick to the line that you were there but didn't see much as the crowds rushed to the injured man.'

'But what about you and Bobby?' Adam challenged.

'I need to keep a low profile too, but first, I need to speak to the person I was having dinner with before this all happened. She is an old family friend and someone I can trust. Next, I must find out what happened after the accident and if she saw anything. I think that Deceptor wanted me to follow her.'

'But what about the accident?' Adam added.

'I think that was just unfortunate. Because I had tripped, I had blood in my eyes, and my leg was injured, so when I leapt forward, my leg gave way, and I just didn't see the car. But I'm presuming that whatever her reasons were for getting me to follow her, once she saw I was badly injured, she decided to take the chance to kill me instead?'

'Wow,' replied Dazza, 'Have Deceptors tried to kill you before?'

'It goes with the territory of being an Enforcer. There is always someone who would like to see me dead.'

'Have they ever succeeded?' Dazza added.

The others looked at Dazza before Adam said, 'Dazza, what do you think?'

'Oh yeah, good point,' Dazza replied. Then, trying to deflect his embarrassment, he added, 'But won't seeing someone from your former self put you and Bob at risk?'

'Potentially, yes, but I can't take the risk that the Deceptors may already know about Bobby and me. I need to get ahead of them. You've already seen their influence on the media and the police. I am sure they will pull other strings to get hold of any CCTV footage of the Piccadilly area to track everybody there and where they went when they left. Talking of which, I need to go.'

Avery blocked his path. 'Hang on a minute Max or whatever your real name is. By association, you have potentially put our friend, us, and our families at risk. You just admitted that it is just a matter of time before they get hold of the CCTV, identify and track us down.'

'Possibly, but I can't risk getting all of you involved even deeper,' Max pleaded.

'Look, dude; it's a bit late for that. Bob is our friend. If he needs help because of you, then you are going nowhere without us,' Dazza stood firm beside Avery.

Adam and Abi joined the line blocking Max's path.

Abi chimed in, adding, 'Look, I know we are no alien superheroes or anything, just very ordinary people but in some ways, that's our advantage. We can go places without anyone getting suspicious.'

'Nobody is putting my buddy at risk without me putting up a fight. So wherever you are taking him, we are coming too.' Adam added, puffing out his chest to emphasise that he was ready for a fight.

Max sighed, 'Fine, but I need to make this very clear if I say something, you need to do it, and when we get to my friend's house, let me do the talking. This is going to be hard enough as it is.'

They hardly spoke as they headed back towards South Kensington station to catch the tube to Earls Court. Max felt like the friends were forming a protective circle around him and Bobby, with Adam just in front, Dazza behind and Abi and Avery on either side.

'*They are my friends,*' Bobby thought, '*It's what good friends do.*'

'*I understand,*' Max replied. '*I've always tried to keep people at a distance as it's safer for them and, in many ways, safer for me. Catherine and her family are probably the only exceptions. I've known the family for almost two hundred years as they have helped protect me down their generations.*'

As they emerged from Earls Court Station, Bobby turned left, heading down the road.

'Hey, there's a burger joint there. Can we grab some nosh? I'm starving.' Dazza added, 'It is nearly 6, and I'm missing my tea.'

'It's only 5 minutes further, and I'm sure Agathe will rustle up something if I ask,' Max replied, trying to hurry them along.

'Is Agathe the friend we're going to see?' Avery asked.

'Sort of, but it's her daughter Catherine I need to speak to,' Max replied, not noticing the look on Avery's face.

As they arrived at 12 Glenthorne Crescent, a grand four-storey late Victorian townhouse, Dazza whistled, 'Wow, Max, your pal is loaded.'

Max rang the bell and stood back.

The door opened, revealing a thin, dark-skinned woman in her early sixties with greying hair and a laconic smile.

'Hello,' Agathe said, 'Can I help you?'

Stepping forward, Max said, 'Hello, Agathe, it's me, Max.'

'Max, my darling,' said Agathe as she flung her arms around him in a bear hug and almost lifted him off the floor. 'Catherine warned me you had gone through another change, but my word, she never said how young you were now.'

Bobby glowed redder than a beetroot at this strange woman's affection.

'*Sorry, Bobby. I really should have warned you that Agathe is an off-the-scale hugger!*' Max thought.

'Agathe, the other person here is Bobby,' Max said, pointing at himself, 'And these are his friends. Can we come in? I'm here to see Catherine.'

'Of course. Please come in. Max, I'm sure you know the way to the Drawing Room. Catherine should be home soon, and you can use Michael's study to talk privately.'

Max walked into the house with Abi pushing her way to the front to be next.

'Good evening, Mrs ....'

'Agathe, my dear, just call me Agathe. Nobody calls me Mrs Thomas unless they are after money,' Agathe replied with a wink.

'Good evening Agathe. I'm Abigail or Abi,' Abi said confidently.

'Well, I'm charmed to meet you, Abi,' Agathe responded, 'Just follow Max. Knowing him, I bet none of you have eaten. Would you like something to drink and eat?'

A chorus of yes pleases followed as the rest of the friends trooped through the door and introduced themselves to Agathe before following the others up the stairs.

By the time Dazza entered the first-floor Drawing Room, Max was already sitting in a large armchair near the fire but positioned neatly in front of a pillar between two of the three large windows. Adam had taken the other armchair in front of the second window pillar with the other friends sitting on various armchairs and sofas in the room, mainly positioned around a large marble coffee table in the centre of the front half of the room.

Towards the back of the room was a large solid bookcase masking the stairwell from that side of the room, with four more armchairs in a circle around a more discreet wooden coffee table. Finally, a relatively well-stocked drinks cabinet was at the back of the room.

Dazza looked around in amazement. 'This place is incredible. This room must be around ten metres by seven metres at least. Even that room downstairs is bigger than our front room!'

Before Max could reply to Dazza, he heard the front door open and close, someone running up the stairs, and a familiar voice shouting, 'Max.'

In a flash, Catherine shot across the room towards him.

'How did you know which one was me?' Max asked.

'Too easy, Max. Who else would pick the chair hidden from the buildings opposite, with a clear view of the stairs and the furthest from it to give them time to switch to fight or flight?' Catherine said with a huge smile on her face.

'Come on then, aren't you going to introduce me?' Catherine continued.

'Well, the young man I'm currently sharing a body with—' Max started to say.

'I'm Bobby,' Bobby interrupted. 'Your friend Max latched onto me when I went to check his pulse after the whip hit him.' Then, adding for Max's benefit, '*Will you stop talking about my body and sharing it, jeez.*'

'The whip?' Catherine asked with a puzzled look on her face.

'Yes, apparently, that is the latest buzzword to describe a limousine,' Max sighed.

'*You're so out of touch, cowboy,*' Bobby chuckled.

'I'm pleased to meet you, Bobby, and I'm glad you've been able to help my friend. Who is everyone else?' Catherine said, indicating the others.

'These friends were with me when Max got hit,' Bobby said. 'Well, apart from Abi, who was on holiday,' he added, nodding in Abi's direction.

Bobby proceeded to introduce his friends; just as he finished, Agathe arrived carrying a large tray which she placed in the middle of the marble coffee table. 'Here you go, grab some drinks and biscuits whilst I pop down to bring the other trays up.'

Adam jumped up, 'I'll give you a hand if you want, Mrs, err, Agathe.'

'That would be very kind of you,' Agathe replied as she and Adam headed downstairs.

As Dazza dived into the biscuits, Max looked at Catherine and said, 'Shall we go into your Dad's study? Your Mum said it would be OK to use it.'

Max and Catherine headed back towards the stairs and down a corridor between the back of the bookcase and the stairwell.

'I wouldn't be too long if I were you,' Abi shouted after them. 'Dazza seems to love Agathe's cooking.'

A harrumph of 'Don't know what you mean' tumbled from Dazza's mouth, along with several large crumbs of food.

Almost an hour passed as Max and Catherine exchanged their recollections of what had happened on Friday evening.

They emerged from the study and walked back towards the Drawing Room. The coffee table was almost a wasteland of empty plates, and the chairs were unoccupied as they entered the room. Then, turning towards the back of the room, they saw Bobby's friends crowded around the bookcase, pointing at various pictures.

'Is this your home then?' Avery asked, looking confused.

'Yeah, why are there so many pictures of the old you? It looks like you were married to Agathe. Is Catherine your daughter?' Abi added.

Catherine burst out laughing, 'Oh, don't. I loved Uncle Max so much, but I don't think I could have coped with him being my Dad,' She added.

Bobby felt Max emotionally sag inside him. '*Come on, cowboy; you do have a pretty mad lifestyle. I've only just boarded for the ride, and I'm already finding it crazy. How is she to know there is a possibility you could be her father? Even you admitted nobody knows the truth.*'

Bobby felt sad for his new friend for the first time and was compelled to speak up, 'Look, everyone, in the same way, Max is now transmuting inside me; a long time ago, he did the same with Catherine's Dad, Michael. When he splits from the host, they look like twins, so that is why those pictures look like the guy we saw run over.'

'Oh no, you mean in six months there will be two Bobby Morris's running around? Stop the World. I need to get off,' Avery joked.

'Ha, flipping, ha,' Bobby replied. 'I'll remember that, Avery,' he added, giving her a scowl followed by a huge grin.

'Hey, I don't want to be a buzzkill, but we should be heading for home. It's getting late, and we're on the wrong side of town, so it will take a while to get back.' Adam said.

'Yeah, Adam, you're right,' Max replied. Then, turning to Catherine, he added, 'I'm sorry, Catherine, but we need to go. Please thank your Mum for the food, and can we catch up later this week? There is still so much to do, and I need to find that Deceptor before she finds any of us.'

'Yes, of course, Max and once again, so nice to meet you, Bobby.' Catherine replied, leaning in to kiss him on both cheeks and sliding something into Bobby's pocket, adding, 'I forgot to give you this when I gave you your phone.'

Catherine exchanged pleasantries with Bobby's friends, and they turned and headed downstairs. Agathe emerged from the kitchen with a glass of white wine.

'It's been an emotional evening,' she said to Catherine before turning and wishing the friends well, inviting them to return soon.

They all chattered about the day's events as they returned to Earls Court underground station.

'Oh no, it's Monday tomorrow. That means revision exams,' Avery wailed.

'Yeah, me too,' replied Dazza.

'You'll both smash it,' Adam replied. 'What about you two?' he added, turning to Abi and Bobby.

'I've got a free tomorrow, so I'll just be chilling and maybe do some socials,' Abi replied, 'What about you, Bobby?'

'I've got a driving lesson just before lunch. It's my test in a few weeks, so I need the practice,' Bobby replied.

'Oh no, send out emergency alerts. Bobby Morris will be driving down the streets of London tomorrow morning. Everyone hide!' Dazza responded as the rest burst into laughter.

With that, they boarded the train heading for home. On the train, Bobby pulled out the object Catherine had slipped into his pocket earlier.

'Oh, that looks well-loved. Was it Max's pen?' Avery asked.

Bobby hesitated momentarily and then said, 'Yeah, it is.'

As they reached Green Park, the friends exchanged goodbyes with Avery as Adam, Bobby, Abi, and Dazza swapped for the Jubilee line towards Haywood, leaving Avery to continue towards Lychbar.

They repeated the goodbye routine when Abi disembarked at the penultimate stop.

Bobby, Adam and Dazza finally arrived at their stop. Dazza said he had to pop to the shops and pick up something for his Mum whilst Adam and Bobby walked towards their homes.

Adam turned to Bobby and said, 'Bobby, if you ever want to say anything to me, I promise I won't be shocked. It is the 21st century, after all.'

'*Do you need a big red sign saying speak now?*' Max asked.

'*No, I just have enough confusion in my life as it is for now. I'm not sure I'm ready for even more,*' Bobby replied.

Bobby blushed but replied, 'Cheers, Adam. I think the last couple of days have been so crazy that I'm all over the place emotionally. I'll be fine. Well, this is my street. I hope you have a great game tomorrow, and I might pop around before tea to see how you got on.'

'Yeah, sure, Bobby. See you tomorrow,' Adam replied. 'Oh, I'll be going for a run between two and three, but I'll be home after that.'

'Can I join you on that run? Max said I need to get fitter,' Max said, doing his best Bobby impression.

'Yeah, of course. Just come around anytime before two. It's just a friendly game tomorrow, so I'll be home around noon,' Adam said before heading toward his house.

'*Why did you do that?*' Bobby asked.

'*Because you need to get fitter, and Adam will make a good exercise buddy.*'

'*Well, that had better be the only reason.*'

Opening the front door to 3 Hinton Close, Bobby could hear the television through the open living room door.

'Hi Mum, it's only me,' Bobby shouted.

'Oh, hi, champ. Hope you had a good afternoon?'

'Yeah, it was cool hanging with everyone. But I'm so tired I'm going straight to bed; night, Mum. Love you.'

'OK, night, champ, love you more.'

Bobby smiled at this usual battle of the loves and went upstairs. Tomorrow was going to be a long day.

4
Drive Time

'Morning, sleepy head. You've got a big day today with your mock driving test, so you'd better get up,' Pat chirped as she put a mug of tea on the boxes by his bed.

'Hiya Mum, yeah, OK,' Bobby replied, adding, 'Thanks for the drink.'

'I'm going now. The car won't start, so I need to walk Lily to school before catching the bus to work,' Pat said as she walked towards the stairs. 'Love you, champ and good luck today.'

'Thanks, Mum. Love you more.'

A few seconds later and the front door slammed shut.

'*What is it about mothers that they think a cup of tea and getting up early makes everything better?*' Bobby thought.

'*I don't know about the tea thing; I'm afraid that's British logic which I've always found rather illogical, but I've also learned you cannot dare to question the sacred cuppa. But your mum is right about the need to get up. We have things to do.*'

Max flung back the sheet, sat up, and took a long sip of tea.

'*Eurgh, what is that? It tastes like a dessert rather than a drink,*' Max scowled.

'*What's wrong with it? I only have three sugars in my tea.*'

'*We need to refine your palate, young man.*'

'*You need to remember you're in my body, old man, so it's my rules,*' Bobby responded, reaching for his grey jogger bottoms.

'*Now hang on, putting up with sickly sweet tea is one thing, but you need a shower. You stink. You also need to change your socks and underwear.*'

'*This is like having a parent monitoring my every move. Fine, OK, I'll have a shower.*'

Bobby glugged some more of his tea, in his mind a punishment for Max's ordering ways, then pulled off his socks and headed towards the bathroom. He shut the door and reached over the bath to turn on the shower before stepping into it.

'*Aren't you forgetting something?*' Max asked. '*You've still got your underwear on.*'

'*I know. I can't strip with you here, can I?*'

'*Why not?. I have been a male quite a few times, you know. Besides, you'll have to change out of your wet underwear anyway.*'

'*Fine, whatevs,*' Bobby snapped before throwing his boxers across the room and grabbing the shower gel.

Twenty minutes later, Bobby wandered into the living room and let out a blood-curdling scream.

'*What on Earth is that pain?*' Max asked.

'*That, cowboy, is the worst pain a human can ever feel,*' Bobby replied, extracting the plastic building block from his foot.

Limping into the kitchen, Bobby opened the fridge and pulled out the milk carton before turning and grabbing a glass off the draining board. He opened a cupboard door and groaned, '*Why did they invent ready-salted crisps? I mean, who eats plain crisps? They're always the ones left until last.*'

'*Don't tell me you plan on having crisps for breakfast?*'

'*OK, I won't tell you then,*' Bobby replied, reaching into the cupboard and pulling out a packet.

'*You can't eat crisps for breakfast.*'

'*Well, I can't flipping drink them, can I?*'

'*That's it. I'm taking charge,*' Max replied, making Bobby's hand fling the crisps back into the cupboard.

'*You can't do this; it's not right,*' Bobby moaned.

'*You're quite correct. Doing this is not right, so I'll stop. Sorry, I meant I'll stop once I've prepared us a proper breakfast, so you sit back and enjoy the ride.*'

Max opened the cupboards and the fridge, took a quick look in the freezer and then pulled out several ingredients. A few minutes of chopping that wouldn't look out of place in a professional kitchen was followed by whisking and frying before Max said, '*Ed ecco una frittata.*'

'*It's an omelette,*' Bobby said, '*Mum makes them quite often, but they're so boring.*'

'*It's a lot more than an omelette, thank you. Just try it.*'

Bobby reluctantly tried some, then took another forkful, and before long, he'd cleared the plate, '*Wow, that was incredible.*'

'*Thank you, I've had to change the recipe over time, but Caesar used to say it was one of his favourite meals,*' Max said, feeling proud.

'*No way. I watched all those ancient Batman shows with my Dad, and The Joker was my favourite. I can't believe you just cooked me one of Cesar Romero's favourite meals.*'

Max sighed, '*No, not Cesar Romero. I mean Julius Caesar. You know, that guy who used to be big in Rome back in the day.*'

'*Nope, never heard of him,*' Bobby replied, wiping the plate clean with a slice of bread.

'*This is going to be a tougher challenge than I thought. Let's get this washed up before your driving instructor arrives.*'

'*Mum always does it when she gets back from work.*'

'*And that's why we're going to do it. We made the mess, so we clean it up.*'

'*You made the mess actually, so you clean....*' Bobby stopped mid-sentence, realising what this meant just as Max retook control, washing up not just their breakfast pots but all the cleaning up in the kitchen.

Just as they finished washing up, there was a knock at the door. Bobby walked through the living room, picking up his favourite black and yellow Izumi jacket off the back of the sofa.

'*That was your Dad's, wasn't it,*' Max asked.

'*Yeah, it was. It's my lucky jacket now,*' Bobby replied as he opened the front door to see his driving instructor Mr Prosser standing there.

'Morning, Bobby. Are you ready to show me what you can do?' Mr Prosser said with a broad grin as Bobby handed him the money for the lesson.

Ian Prosser always took pride in his appearance. He was 65 years old, of slim build, and just 5 foot 8 inches tall. One of his favourite jokes concerned not spending much at the hairdresser, even though he'd been almost bald for twenty years. He had the persona of something so unremarkable you'd struggle to name anything that unremarkable, but Ian had a secret beneath that dull science teacher persona. Before retiring fifteen years ago, he'd spent twenty years as an advanced driving instructor with Greater London police until his wife persuaded him to retire and do something a little slower. Becoming a driving instructor seemed like the obvious choice, although he'd witnessed more accidents as a civilian driving instructor than he ever did in the police force.

'Great, let's start with the eyesight check. Read the number plate of that orange car down there,' Mr Prosser said cheerily.

Bobby squinted a little, then said, 'KVJ 533P.'

'Well done, now the tell-me question. Where can you find this car's correct tyre pressure information, and how should you check them?' Mr Prosser said.

'*Is he for real?*' Max asked sarcastically.

'*Shush, I need to concentrate,*' Bobby replied, adding for his instructor's benefit, 'In the car handbook for the pressures, and then using a reliable pressure monitor when the tyres are cold, oh and not forgetting the spare tyre.'

'Great, that's very good, Bobby. Let's go. In you hop,' Mr Prosser said, waving towards the driver's side of the car.

'*I swear, if he calls you a good boy, I may have to hit him,*' Max responded.

'*Will you pipe down,*' Bobby pleaded, holding back a chuckle.

Bobby got in the car and did all the preliminary checks. In his mind, he was going through the checklist he'd memorised, including seat position, seat belt, steering wheel, mirrors etc., before finally starting the car, indicating and pulling off.

The test got off to a mundane start. First, Mr Prosser directed Bobby into a car park, where he made him forward park into a parking bay. Then as soon as Bobby pulled away, he got him to reverse park into another bay.

'*I thought you were having a driving lesson?*' Max grumbled, '*They should call this a parking lesson.*'

Mr Prosser then directed Bobby around the streets and roads in the area, which took him down the busy High Street, across roundabouts and then turned left into a side street. He told Bobby to pull over and said, 'We will now practice the emergency stop. I'll get you to proceed down this road, and when I lean forward and tap the dashboard, I want you to stop safely and quickly. Do you understand?'

'*I'll tap him in a minute,*' Max moaned.

Bobby ignored Max and said, 'Yes, Mr Prosser.'

Bobby then pulled the car back into the road and proceeded down the quiet street, glancing towards Mr Prosser at every opportunity.

He saw Mr Prosser glance in the door and rearview mirrors on his side, leaning forward slightly to get a better view, and then.

'*Get ready, Bobby, any second, NOW,*' Max shouted, bringing the car to a quick stop.

Unfortunately, Bobby's reactions boosted by Max had meant Mr Prosser was still leaning forward as the car came to a halt, and he head-butted the windscreen.

Mr Prosser sat back in his seat, slowly rubbing his head, 'I think you were a little keen there, Bobby. Maybe wait until you hear the tap on the test.'

'Yes, Mr Prosser.'

'*Hah, that'll teach him,*' Max added, looking at the red glow on the instructor's head.

'OK, pull over and park on the right side of the road, please,' Mr Prosser replied.

'*You may not learn how to drive, but blimey, you'll be a parking expert,*' Max moaned.

Bobby checked his mirrors, manoeuvred the car to the opposite side of the road, and parked.

'Well done, Bobby, you've mastered it. However, if I have one issue, it is that you're driving like you've been doing it for years which may come across as a little bit arrogant to an examiner,' Mr Potter said.

'*Oh, so now it's a crime to drive like you know what yore doing, is it?*'

'*Yes, he's said before the examiners like people to be cautious in their tests. It's all part of the game, like exaggerating head and eye movements when you use the mirrors,*' Bobby replied, adding, '*Hey, won't you need to pass a test with your new identity?*'

'*Not a problem. You've just witnessed some of my driving prowess.*'

'*Wait, you've not been controlling my body. I've been driving.*'

'*True, but without even realising it, you're picking up some of my basic skills.*'

Mr Prosser interrupted their thoughts. 'OK, Bobby, I think we'll do the twenty-minute independent driving part next. I've set the satellite navigation to take you to a destination. Remember, this won't sound the same as the official one, but it's close. So pull out when it's safe to do so and follow the navigation.'

As Bobby pulled out, the navigation started, 'At the end of the road, turn left.'

'*How did mankind ever find their way before sat nav?*' Max asked sarcastically.

Bobby ignored him.

'At the roundabout ahead, take the third exit,' the artificial female voice instructed.

'In a quarter of a mile, leave the roundabout at the first exit,' the voice continued.

'*Does it tell you when to stop for a pee too?*' Max asked.

'*It's the future cowboy. Just go with it. Hey, this is the way to Vicarage Road. Up the Hornets.*'

Everything was going smoothly. Bobby felt relaxed, Max stopped moaning, and Mr Prosser stopped rubbing the growing lump on his head. The navigation said they would arrive at their destination in 13 minutes, and if it weren't for the grey BMW driving close behind them, it would have felt like a relaxing drive.

'Bobby, what is the speed limit here?' Mr Prosser asked.

'Sixty, sir.'

'So why are you doing almost sixty-five?'

Bobby slowed the car to sixty, which meant the vehicle behind was now dangerously close.

'Mr Prosser, I shouldn't ask, but what about that idiot in the BMW behind us?' Bobby queried.

Mr Prosser checked his mirror and said, 'Their rush isn't your reason to break the law. They probably know this road will become a dual carriageway shortly, so they'll overtake us then. Just concentrate on your driving.'

'OK, sir.'

Max felt uneasy and tried to take a good look in the mirror, but the BMW's windscreen was picking up the sun's reflection and glaring. As the road widened, Bobby increased his car's speed to 70mph, but the BMW behind pulled out and started to pass them. Max glanced to the right and recognised the driver, but she was looking straight ahead, oblivious to his presence.

'*It's her, the waitress,*' he said to Bobby.

'*But how would she know we would be here? They don't even know who me and my mates are.*'

'In half a mile, prepare to exit the roundabout at the second exit,' the navigation informed them.

The BMW pulled in front of them and continued to accelerate.

'*Looks like it's just a coincidence,*' Bobby said.

'*Maybe, but I don't like coincidences. Although it does look like she isn't interested in us.*'

'See,' said Mr Prosser, 'I said they'd overtake as soon as we got to the duel carriageway, but why are they—' he cut his sentence short as the BMW braked hard.

Bobby did his second emergency stop of the day, although no heads were injured during the making of this emergency stop.

'Excellent reactions Bobby,' said Mr Prosser. 'Now indicate and proceed round that car when it is safe to do so.'

Before Bobby could do anything, the BMW started to reverse slowly.

Max peered at the rearview mirror of the BMW, and aside from seeing the driver looking back, he could make out an aura. He turned and said, 'Mr Prosser, where is the traction control button?'

'Just to the side of the steering wheel Bobby, and why are you talking like that?' Mr Prosser asked.

Max hit the button to turn the traction control off and put the car into reverse before saying, 'No time to explain, but hold on tight and under NO circumstances touch the pedals on your side.'

Any attempt by Mr Prosser to speak was cut short as the car lurched backwards. Whilst nowhere near rush hour traffic levels, there were enough cars on the road for Max to have to swerve left and right to avoid the vehicles travelling in the correct direction.

'Bobby, what is happening, and why is that car chasing us?' Mr Prosser asked, gripping the handle above the door with one hand and gripping his seat with the other.

'Long story. Tell you afterwards. Let me know if she is gaining on us or pulls out a gun,' Max replied in a staccato fashion.

'What do you mean a gun?'

'You know, a long metal tube with a trigger. If they pull the trigger, it goes bang. Or at least if you're lucky, it goes bang; if you don't hear the bang, it means the bullet hit you, and you're dead.' Max bellowed back as he looked over his shoulder for a break in the oncoming traffic.

Max spotted his opportunity and hoped he was going fast enough not to roll the car. He floored the clutch, hit the brakes and spun the steering wheel on full lock.

'I know what a gun is. But, I mean, why would she pull a gun on—' Mr Prosser stopped as he was flung from side to side in his seat.

As the car was halfway through turning, Max shot it into second gear and started to straighten up the wheel. Then, as the vehicle was nearly straight, he lifted the clutch and shot forward, widening the gap between them and the BMW, which was still travelling backwards.

Max could see the road narrowing back to a single lane and knew his options were limited. The BMW completed a 180-degree turn and was now starting to close the gap. Max swerved to the right hoping it would send some oncoming traffic into the BMW's path and slow it down.

'Turn around where possible,' the navigation voice decided to interject somewhat unhelpfully.

The BMW also darted right, but in the process, it clipped another car sending that one into a spin and pushing the BMW onto the grass verge.

The BMW pulled back onto the main road swerving from side to side as the driver tried to regain control. It had slowed them just enough to allow a small gap to open between it and Max, but the reduction back to a single-lane carriageway was rapidly approaching. So Max pulled to the right again, sending vehicles streaming past in the opposite direction on his left.

The symphony of car horns increased as Max slowed a little allowing the BMW to close up to them. The BMW driver opened her window and started shooting.

'Bobby, why the hell are you slowing down? She's gaining on us, and if you haven't noticed, she is also shooting at us.' Mr Prosser screamed.

'No, it's alright. I'm pretty sure she is just aiming at the tyres.'

'Oh, that's fine the—What!' Mr Prosser said, 'How is that alright?'

'Well, it just means she would like us to stop rather than wanting us dead.'

Then Max saw the opportunity he was looking for, a gap between the two cars heading their way, which he could squeeze between.

'Hold on,' Max shouted.

'I am,' replied Mr Prosser, who may have taught many police drivers pursuit techniques, but he had never been the one being pursued before and certainly not by someone shooting at him.

Max went as far right as possible and then, at the last second, hit the brakes as hard as he dared before releasing them, knocking the car into neutral and spinning the wheel to the left as the vehicle drifted between the two oncoming cars leaving it facing the other direction but on the opposite side of the road.

With cars in both directions now blasting their horns and swerving all over, Max accelerated away back in the original direction they were headed, but on the wrong side of the road.

'In half a mile, prepare to exit the roundabout at the second exit,' the navigation informed them helpfully again.

'Can you shut that up,' Max replied.

Mr Prosser lent across to mute the navigation, then realised he was still clutching the handle from above his door, which he must have torn off during the chase. But before he could turn the navigation off, he was distracted by a loud crash. Looking over his shoulder, he could see the BMW flipped onto its roof and being spun by cars swerving to avoid it but clipping it as they passed.

'Well, I don't think we need to worry about her for the time being,' replied Max, who settled back into swerving the oncoming cars.

As they approached the roundabout, the navigation piped up again, saying, 'Exit the roundabout at the second exit.'

Mr Prosser leant forward and cancelled the navigation. 'Just take the first exit, Bobby. I think that will do for today.'

'But what about my mock test?' Bobby challenged. 'I've got my real one in a few weeks.'

'I think you have demonstrated you can handle a car, Bobby. But I am not sure my nerves can handle you for today anymore. Maybe we try to do the mock test again next week, preferably without any mad drivers and guns?'

Bobby drove the car back to his house and got out. Mr Prosser exited from the passenger side, and they crossed paths at the car's rear.

Mr Prosser looked down to see several bullet holes dotted around the bumper. Shaking his head, he said, 'That's not good.'

'I know,' said Max, 'It's appalling. I've not seen shooting that bad in years.'

'I meant because my insurance will never cover that damage.'

'OK yeah, that too,' Max replied as he headed towards Bobby's house. He stopped and turned back to see Mr Prosser walking around the car, noting the damage. 'Mr Prosser, before I forget, if anyone asks whom you were teaching this morning, can you not give them my details, please?'

'Excuse me, young man, but as a former police officer, I am fully conversant with data compliance regulations. I would never reveal any of my pupil's details,' Mr Prosser replied indignantly.

'Thanks, Mr Prosser,' Bobby responded as he turned and headed indoors. Closing the front door behind him, Bobby threw his coat on a chair and strolled into the kitchen. '*I need a drink,*' he said.

'*Yeah, me too,*' replied Max before groaning when he realised Bobby was reaching for a can of pop rather than a bottle of malt whisky.

'*Malt whisky? How rich do you think we are?*'

Bobby's phone pinged. He pulled it out of his pocket and opened the message; 'Home now, come over whenever.' He hit the thumbs-up emoji and clicked send.

'*That reminds me, we need to change your phone,*' Max said, '*I need to see Catherine to sort out access to my money and the rest of my estate.*'

'*Oh great. What do you suggest? That new Android looks good, but then so does the iPhone.*'

'*Smartphones are out, sorry. There are way too many ways for you to be tracked and traced. It would be best if you had something like mine.*'

'*But that's like an antique.*'

'*It's for the best. Do you have tools like small screwdrivers, a soldering iron etc.?*'

Bobby picked up a set of keys off the hook by the back door and headed towards the shed in the back garden. Unlocking the door, he walked into an array of electrical testing equipment.

'*Wow, there's some seriously impressive equipment in here. What did your Dad do?*'

'*He was some sort of electrical mechanic. I think. He worked for a car company in Australia, and they transferred him to the U.K. a couple of years before I was born. That's when he met my Mum. She worked in the canteen.*'

Pulling out his immobiliser Max said, '*Well, this is going to make this job much easier. I'm assuming you're not the sort to carry a pen, so what do you normally have in your pockets?*'

Bobby pulled out some loose change, a key on a keyring, his battered smartphone, Max's old phone and a small sports wallet containing a bank card, a five-pound note and a picture of his parents.

'*Hmm, not much there. How about your watch? You never take that off.*'

'*No, it's my Dad's, and it works exactly as it always did for him. It's one of those that use your kentick energy to keep it going without winding.*'

'*Kinetic energy, I think you mean.*'

'*Yeah, that's it, but nobody is tampering with it anyway. What about the keyring?*'

Max picked up the keyring and looked at it.

'*It's a torch. Dad bought it for me the Christmas before he died, but it doesn't work anymore even though I changed the battery.*'

'*May I use it if I get it to work again and leave it looking the same?*'

'*Yes, please, I'd like that.*'

Forty minutes passed as Max took apart his old pen and then stripped down the small keyring light. He rummaged through some components and circuitry, surprised by how advanced some of it was. Picking some parts, he'd analyse them and then discard them as he found better alternatives. Finally, he sat back with a sense of satisfaction.

'*How does it work then?*' Bobby asked.

'*Click the button once, and the light comes on. Click it again, and the light goes off. But hold the button down and point it at a Deceptor, and they're immobilised for an hour or so. Some of your Dad's inventory is quite advanced, even by my standards. He was a bit of a genius. Using some of his components, I've extended the range to several metres and made it safer for other lifeforms.*'

Bobby glowed with pride, then said, '*So it can be pointed at anyone, and they're immobilised?*'

'*Well, nothing is guaranteed until we can test it, but if my equations are correct, yes.*'

Bobby's phone pinged. 'Hey Bobby, are you still coming over? I'm leaving in 25.' He replied that he'd be there in a few minutes.

Stuffing everything back into his pockets, he locked the shed door and ran back into the house and up the stairs.

'*Well, you can't go for a run in jeans and Doc Martens,*' Max said, '*You'd better put some shorts on and a pair of trainers.*'

Bobby slipped on an old black T-shirt, pulled open a drawer and grabbed a pair of white shorts. He removed his boots and swapped his jeans for the shorts thinking, '*Do I need to do this?*'

'*Yes, you do. We need to up your cardio fitness. Although in these shorts, it's not your heart I'm worried about rupturing. Maybe put your grey joggers on instead.*'

Bobby reached down for his joggers, and the ripping sound confirmed that a change in legwear was a good idea.

A few minutes later, Bobby was out of his front door, heading towards his friend's house. Using the cut-through behind the supermarket at the end of Hinton Court meant he was ringing the doorbell of 17 Witts Avenue just four minutes later.

Whilst Adam's house was built around the same time as Bobby's home, it was more prominent with a bay window to the ground and first-floor front rooms. Granny Mosley always called Witts Avenue the posh houses as they had always been privately owned and were never council houses.

Adam opened the door and stepped out wearing a white T-shirt, blue shorts and tight blue base layer leggings with white stripes running down to his white sports socks and black running shoes.

'*You seem to be paying a lot of attention to his clothing,*' Max said.

'*Shut it,*' Bobby replied.

'Hey Bobby, looking good considering you don't normally do sports,' Adam said. 'I did wonder if you'd turn up in a pair of school gym shorts.'

'Oh, heck no, there's no way you'd catch me wearing anything like that,' Bobby replied.

'*Liar,*' chuckled Max.

'Let's jog to the golf course to warm up, and then we can run around the perimeter a couple of times. We shouldn't take more than an hour and a half to two hours.'

'Yeah, sure thing,' Bobby replied, 'Just out of interest, how far is that?'

'Oh, about six to seven miles around,' Adam said as they started jogging.

'Wow, I thought it would be further than that if it takes almost two hours.'

Adam laughed, 'No, you silly moose, I mean, it's about six to seven miles around the course, and we're doing it twice, so around twelve to fourteen miles in total.'

'FOURTEEN MILES!' Bobby spluttered before composing himself and adding, 'Yeah, erm, that's not a bad start.' Then he thought for Max's benefit, '*I'm going to flipping kill you if this running malarkey doesn't do me in first.*'

'*Now that is one threat you'll find hard to accomplish, considering I am you at the moment, buddy.*'

Thirty minutes later and barely four miles into their run, Bobby stopped, sweating profusely, and bent over with his hands on his knees as he gasped for air.

Adam noticed his friend wasn't behind him and turned around. Then, seeing him bent over, he ran back and put his arm around him, asking, 'Are you all right, Bobby?'

Bobby shivered under the touch of his friend. He'd known Adam since they started high school, but apart from the occasional play fight, they'd never been physically close like this.

Bobby looked up at his friend's face as a million scenarios played out in his mind. Should he admit how he feels? What if he kissed him? Would Adam ever speak to him again? Would he be bullied and ridiculed by all his friends and others at college?

'*For crying out loud, just tell him how you feel,*' Max said exasperatedly.

'Yeah, I'm good; thanks, Adam. It's just been a pretty crazy day with my driving lesson,' Bobby replied as he straightened up.

Adam moved in front of him, rested his hands on his friend's shoulders and said, 'Look, bud, you've managed almost four miles which is pretty good for a first time. So why don't we go back to mine, freshen up, and you can tell me about your day.'

Bobby felt like his friend was looking deep into his eyes, and for a split second, he thought he might take the risk and kiss him.

Max interrupted his thoughts, saying, '*An unprovoked kiss is a high-risk strategy, my young friend. Maybe you should tell him how you feel before trying to pounce on him,*'

An image of Bobby pushing Adam to the floor and jumping onto him flicked through his mind, and he laughed loudly.

'What's so funny?' Adam asked.

'Oh, erm, Max just reminded me of the bullet holes in Mr Prosser's car and his reaction,' Bobby replied, then thinking for Max's benefit, '*Fairs cowboy, jumping him probably isn't the best way to approach this.*'

'Bullet holes? I need to hear this. Race you back to mine. The first one there gets the first shower,' Adam said, breaking into a jog.

'That'll be me then,' laughed Bobby racing after his friend.

Bobby saw Adam sitting on the step, laughing as he approached his friend's house.

'What's so funny?' Bobby asked.

'Avery just called to ask what I was doing and if I was around tomorrow as she's on study leave until the exams start for real in a few days. When I said we had just been for a run, she said to make sure I didn't kill you both!' Adam replied.

'Aren't you both comedians,' Bobby replied, gasping as he tried to catch his breath.

'Didn't you used to have a thing with Avery?'

'Uh, well, I guess, but that was over a year ago now; why?'

'She just seemed very interested in you and Max. I thought maybe you two might be becoming an item again. Come on, I need a shower, and so do you, by the looks of it. I've got some spare clothes you can change into as we're a similar build.'

Bobby noticed the silence as they entered the house, 'Where are your Mum and Dad?'

'Oh, they're on holiday for two weeks. They only left yesterday. So I've got the house to myself and some cash for a pizza if you want to stop for tea or even ring your Mum, and we can have an old-fashioned sleepover. Come on, let's go and freshen up,' Adam said, heading upstairs.

Even though Adam was an only child, his parents had considerably enlarged an already decently sized three-bedroom house. They built an extension on the back of the property to create a large kitchen diner and extended into the attic to create a plush master suite for themselves. This meant Adam could have the sizeable former master bedroom at the front of the house with the bathroom next door. The two bedrooms at the rear doubled up as spare bedrooms and a study for his Dad when he worked from home.

They walked into Adam's bedroom, and Adam started to undress.

'Aren't you going to shut your curtains?' Bobby asked.

'Nah, that tree obscures most of the view, and besides, it's only a dental clinic opposite, so it might help take their patients' minds off the drilling,' Adam laughed as he pulled off his socks and stood in his black underwear.

Bobby laughed awkwardly. It wasn't that he didn't find the thought of the dentist's patients spotting Adam half-naked as they were getting fillings amusing. It was more that he struggled to look but not look at his friend's body.

Adam wandered out of the bedroom and returned, throwing a towel in Bobby's direction. 'Here you go, and whilst you shower, I'll sort out some clean clothes for you. I'm going for my shower now, but I'll leave it going as it goes cold if you turn it off and back on again, so get ready to dive in.'

As Adam shut the bathroom door, Bobby just stood there.

'*Come on, buddy, you heard the man get ready to shower,*' Max piped up.

'*Yeah, OK, it's just,*' Bobby started to say.

'*It's just; you've been in this room so many times before, but somehow this time it feels different, sort of exciting and tingly but also awkward?*'

'*Yeah, that's it. Seeing Adam all hot and sweaty and then stripping down to his underwear, I'd never thought about Adam this way before.*'

'*I get it, Bobby. I do. Your hormones are raging; I've been in many hosts before, and yours are off the scale. So it's natural to find other people attractive.*'

'*But he's one of my best friends, and he's male, so that's not natural, right? Even seeing his sweaty clothes on the floor excites me, and that can't be right.*'

'*Bobby, it's all perfectly natural. As long as you're not doing anyone any harm or committing any crimes, relax and enjoy growing up. Whatever will be will be my friend. Now you'd better get undressed as Adam must be almost finished.*' Max said reassuringly.

'*Swear you won't out me to him as you did about going running, will you?*'

'*Getting fit is something you need prodding to do. Confessing your feelings for someone is your business, my friend. I would never tread on those emotions,*'

'*You know, you're pretty sound for an old cowboy.*'

'Just for once, I'll let the old tag slide by, buddy. I'll confess you're a pretty cool chap.'

'Chap?' Bobby blurted out, 'You really are ancient, cowboy.'

'Who's an ancient cowboy?' Adam asked, walking back into the room with a towel around his waist and drying his hair with another.

'Oh, sorry, Adam, I was talking to Max, and he called me a cool chap,' Bobby replied as he undressed.

'Fairs,' Adam said laughing, 'My Dad used to call me a cheeky chappie when I was about five. But even he never said, chap.'

Adam walked across the room and sat on his bed facing Bobby. Bobby cursed under his breath at not getting undressed earlier as it now meant stripping in front of his friend, which made him feel particularly awkward as he was still a little excited.

'Chuck your boxers on top of mine in the bathroom, and I'll grab them with our clothes and bung them in the washing machine when I'm dressed,' Adam said.

Bobby hadn't been in Adam's house since the bathroom had been updated, and the mix of glass, mirrors and marble was a little dazzling, especially as it meant Max's aura was flashing around the room. He pulled off his boxers, threw them on top of Max's by the sink, and then stepped into the bath, moving under the refreshing stream of warm water.

He poured some shampoo into his hands and started lathering up his hair. Even though he showered at home, Adam's shower felt more powerful, yet the water felt softer. As he began to rinse off the shampoo, he looked through the clear glass shower screen and saw the bathroom door open.

Adam walked in, bent down and picked up the two pairs of underwear, adding them to the clothes in his arms. 'Nothing beats a good shower after a run, does it?' he said, looking at Bobby.

'Yeah, it feels good. I love the bathroom, by the way. It looks sick.'

'Mum loves it. She said she wanted loads of mirrors to see her hair from all angles, as their ensuite isn't as big as this room,' Adam replied, looking directly at Bobby.

Bobby glanced around and noticed he could see almost his entire body from every angle, immediately making him realise that so could Adam. He quickly squirted some shower gel into his hands and tried to cover up strategic body parts with foam lather.

'I was going to order a pizza. How does a Margherita with some potato wedges sound?' Adam said, seemingly glued to the spot.

'Like I'm just about to regain the weight I lost running,' joked Bobby, adding, 'Yeah, that'll be sound, thanks.'

'OK, I've left some clothes on the bed for you. Just bring them back after your Mum next does the washing. I've got plenty of trackies and stuff, so no hurry,' Adam replied. He started to turn, then laughed, saying, 'Oh, by the way, you've missed a bit.'

Bobby followed the direction Adam was pointing and realised he hadn't entirely covered his bottom with foam. 'Hey, you shouldn't be looking,' he laughed.

'Couldn't miss it the size of that dump truck,' Adam laughed as he headed out of the bathroom.

'Are you convinced now that you might get a more welcome response if you tell him how you feel?'

'No, that's just Adam. I've already told you he's always been flirty, and he's had many girlfriends. He's one hundred percent straight.'

Bobby finished washing and walked into the bedroom to dry himself off. He could hear Adam downstairs ordering the pizza. Looking down at the clothes on the bed, he chuckled, *'Straight out of the Adam school of fashion.'* Adam had laid out some black tracksuit bottoms with a white stripe running down the side, a white T-shirt with the black sports logo, some white sports socks and a pair of designer black boxer briefs with a white waistband.

He quickly got dressed, texted his mum, telling her he was stopping at Adam's tonight and wandered downstairs.

He found Adam in the living room setting up the games console.

'Pizza on its way, so I thought I'd give you a thrashing at football. Loser has to clean up after dinner,' Adam replied.

Bobby looked at his friend and said, 'Hey, you're wearing almost exactly the same clothes.'

Adam looked up at Bobby and smiled, 'Oh yeah. Well, that's pretty much all I wear, so I didn't pay much attention when I pulled them out for you. It's about time I taught you all about sartorial elegance.'

'Sartorial?' Bobby chuckled. 'When did you swallow a dictionary.'

'I'll have you know I went to Dazza's electrocution lessons,' Adam replied

'I think you mean elocution lessons,' Max said, not understanding the joke.

Adam and Bobby looked at each other and burst out laughing.

As they played football on the TV, Bobby started to tell Adam about the driving lesson.

'You're certain it was the same woman who tried to kill Max?' Adam asked.

'No doubt about it, Adam,' Max replied.

'Yeah, it was her,' Bobby added.

'You know, if someone had said to me last week that I would be sitting here, having a three-way conversation with my best mate and another person in his body, I would have said they needed locking up,' Adam laughed.

'If someone heard you were conversing with the two of us, they probably would lock you up,' Max joked.

The pizza came, which they devoured before going back to the football.

'What time do you have to be at college tomorrow?' Adam asked.

'They said to be there for ten thirty with the exam starting at eleven,' Bobby replied. 'It's a two-hour exam, and then I'm done until the real thing starts in a few days.'

'What subject is it?' Adam queried.

'It's history and the English Revolution, you know Cromwell and that,' Bobby said

'Oh, not that snot-nosed jumped-up farmer?' Max interjected.

'Did you know him, Max?' Adam asked.

'Did I ever,' Max replied, 'A bad-tempered distasteful man who seemed to derive pleasure in denying it to everyone else.'

'Oh, so you were a Royalist then?' Adam shot back.

'Hardly,' Max spat back, 'They flipping shot me in the leg during the Battle of Worcester. I was only taking some chickens to flog to the Roundheads to make a bob or two. A man's got to earn a living even if there's a war on.'

'Sounds like you've got some inside knowledge there, buddy,' Adam smiled at Bobby.

'Yeah, I guess so, although I'm not sure describing him as a snot-nosed jumped-up farmer would get me many points in an exam,' Bobby laughed.

They played football for the rest of the evening before turning in just before midnight. As Bobby flopped into bed in the spare room, his phone pinged, 'Hey champ, hope you're in bed now, don't forget you've got an exam tomorrow. Love you.'

'Yeah, just settled down now. Not forgotten and love you more.'

5
MISSING

The early morning sun streamed through the gap in the curtains lighting up the room. Bobby yawned and opened his eyes, having that brief where am I moment before he remembered that he'd spent the night at Adam's house.

He lay in bed looking around the room. Before Adam's parents had moved into the attic suite, the bedroom he was in used to be Adam's. It still had a football-themed quilt cover on the bed, football player posters on the wall and even some of Adam's old trophies on the shelves.

He looked at the football-shaped alarm clock, seven thirty-two, '*Wow, this is early for you, buddy,*' Max said.

Stretching and yawning, Bobby replied, '*Yeah, I know, but I feel so relaxed. That's the best night's sleep I've had for ages.*'

Bobby flicked back the quilt, swung his legs out of bed and stood up. Pain shot up his legs. '*What have you done to me? I've got aches in places I didn't even know existed,*' Bobby groaned.

'*A few more runs, and you'll soon be fine.*'

Bobby groaned again, '*A few more runs, and I'll feel as old as you sound, cowboy. I need the loo.*'

Bobby opened the bedroom door and heard a noise downstairs which he presumed was Adam. Walking across the landing, he entered the bathroom, shut the door and lifted the toilet lid. He finished, flushed the chain and washed and dried his hands. Then, as he stuck out his hand to grab the door handle, it flew open, and a naked Adam walked in.

'Oh, sorry, Bobby, I thought you were still in bed,' Adam said, adding, 'I've just been for a run and need a shower.'

Bobby glowed bright red, 'Uh, no, I've just got up. A run; wow, what time did you get up?'

'I'm always up by six,' Adam replied, 'I love an early morning run. It gets the blood pumping.'

'You should have woken me. I'd have joined you,' Bobby lied as he tried to squeeze past his naked friend without making bodily contact. 'I'll go and get dressed whilst you shower.'

Twenty minutes later, Adam came downstairs to find Bobby cooking.

'Omelette with wholegrain toast all right for breakfast, Adam?' Max asked.

'Sounds great, but that is you cooking, isn't it, Max? Bobby tends to burn water,' Adam laughed.

'Excuse me, but I am here, you know,' Bobby replied with half-hearted indignance.

'I'll come with you to college if that's OK, Bobby? Avery finishes her last revision exam at ten-fifteen, so she said she'd meet me there,' Adam said.

'Yeah, no probs,' Bobby replied, 'I just need to pop home first to get my college bag.'

Max placed the omelette in front of Adam, who wolfed it down.

'Blimey Max, you defo know how to cook,' Adam said, sitting back and patting his stomach.

'Yeah, apparently, it was Caesar's favourite,' Bobby said as he sipped his mug of tea.

'One of his favourites,' Max corrected.

'Really? Wow, César was one of Brazil's best goalies,' Adam replied.

'What is it with your generation? Haven't any of you heard of Emperor Caesar?' Max said exasperatedly.

'Who?' Adam replied.

'See,' Bobby said triumphantly, 'It's not just me; you're out of date, cowboy.'

'But Bobby, you're even studying history,' Max retorted.

'Yeah, but not that ancient Roman stuff,' Bobby replied.

They cleared up and loaded the dirty plates into the dishwasher before getting ready to leave.

'Damn,' Adam said, 'Sorry, Bobby, I forgot to stick our clothes in the dryer. So they'll still be wet.'

'No worries, buddy. I can drop them at ours and hang them on the clothes horse.'

'Erm, well yeah, but I feel guilty for forgetting, so let me dry them, and I'll drop them off later or tomorrow.'

'OK, yeah, that's fine.'

Adam picked up his backpack, and they headed towards Bobby's house. Turning right into Hinton Close, they noticed a police car leaving Bobby's home. They watched it drive down the road before running down to his house. His Mum was coming out of the front door with Lily behind her.

'Morning, champ and hi there, Adam. Hope you had a great evening?' she said.

'Morning, Mrs Morris,' Adam replied.

'Hi Mum, yeah, it was good, thanks. So what did the police want? Was it to do with Max's accident?' Bobby asked.

'Who's Max?' Pat asked.

'Sorry yeah, someone said that was the name of the old guy we saw run over in town,' Bobby replied hurriedly.

'Oh, no, it was nothing to do with that. Mr Prosser reported an incident that took place during your driving lesson. They said everything was fine but that they just needed a statement from you to close the report. You never told me there had been a crash? I told the police you had an exam today, but we could go to the station tomorrow. I've got the rest of the week off as I was going to do some decorating. Mary next door said she'd pick Lily up from school if I need her to.'

'Oh, not Mrs Nobbs. She makes me do my reading,' Lily wailed. She looked at Bobby and said, 'Hey, Stinky. So you're still hanging around with that old man, then? Hi, Adam.'

'Come on, Lily, get in the car, or you'll be late for school,' Pat replied. Then turning to Bobby, she added, 'You can tell me about the accident later.'

'OK, Mum, I'll be home by about two. Did you get the car fixed then?'

'Yes, Mary's husband Dave fixed it for me, something to do with a blocked fuel line. It only took him about forty minutes. He's almost as good with engines as your Dad was. Anyway, got to go. See you later, champ and good luck with your exam. Bye, Adam.'

'Bye, Mrs Morris, see you, Lily,' Adam said.

Bobby kissed his Mum on the cheek and said, 'Thanks, Mum, see you later. Laters Lily.'

Lily scowled, 'Bye, Adam,' then stuck her tongue out at Bobby before getting into the car.

Bobby and Adam watched Pat Morris drive off, then turned towards the house.

As Bobby unlocked the door, Adam said, 'Can Lily see Max then?'

'Max thinks it sometimes happens with young children,' Bobby replied, 'Apparently, they lose their ability as they get older.'

'I think I've heard of that sort of thing, like imaginary friends or seeing ghosts.'

'Make yourself at home, buddy. You know where the drinks and snacks are,' Bobby said as he shut the front door and headed upstairs.

Adam flopped down on the sofa and turned on the TV. Breakfast television was always so banal to him, but it was almost nine o'clock, and he hoped there might be some sports coverage on the news.

Bobby plodded down the stairs and into the living room. He dumped his bag on the nearest chair. 'It's a bit early to head for college. Do you want a drink?'

'You got any green tea?'

'I've not checked recently, but my guess is no. But we've got some half-decent supermarket own brand. I could drop some green food dye in it if we've got any.'

'I'll pass; thanks, buddy. Just water will be fine.'

Bobby wandered into the kitchen and turned the kettle on. He pulled a glass out of a cupboard and filled it from the tap. Once the kettle had boiled, he made a cup of tea and walked back into the living room carrying both drinks.

'One glass of the finest rusty spring tap water north of the Thames. Why is the telly frozen? Is that stupid box playing up again?'

'Cheers, Bobby. Didn't you say Max's body had died, and that's why he moved into yours?'

'Yeah, why?'

Adam turned to face Bobby, 'Well, they've just done that appeal for witnesses again, saying the elderly gentleman has been identified as Maxwell Thomas. Look, he is stable but in a critical condition at an unnamed hospital.'

Adam pressed play on the remote. The television replayed the accident images and then cut to a picture of a man looking like Max, unconscious in a hospital bed covered in cuts and bruises with wires and pipes connected to him.

'No, that's not possible,' Max said, 'Without me inside, that shell would be dead, plus I never carry any identifying items unless necessary. So that can't be my old body, unless....'

'Michael!' Bobby shouted.

'Who's Michael?' Adam asked.

'Remember my friend Catherine with the large house?' Max said. 'Michael is her father, and he was my last host before Bobby. You all looked at the pictures on the bookcase and thought it was me.'

'Oh yeah. But what's that to do with Max's body in the hospital?' Adam looked puzzled.

'I think that's Michael in the hospital. It's the only possible answer,' Max replied. 'I need to speak to Catherine.'

Max pulled his phone out of his pocket and called Catherine. 'Flipping voicemail. Oh, hi Catherine, it's Max here. Can you call me when you get this? I need to ask you something about your Dad.'

'Why didn't you mention the news and what you've told me?' Adam asked.

'Because she might not have seen the news yet as she'd be working at this time, and I don't want her to worry,' Max replied.

'What about his wife, Agathe?' Adam said.

'Agathe rarely watches television, and she never watches the news. She says it's bad for Michael's blood pressure, so she won't have seen it,' Max answered. 'I need to find that hospital.'

'I get it, but I need to do my revision exam. The College said anyone not doing them would be excluded from sitting the finals,' Bobby replied.

'Let's walk to college. Maybe some fresh air will help,' Adam suggested.

Bobby's phone rang as they walked down the road towards Haywood College.

'Hello. Oh, hi, Mr Prosser. Yeah, Mum said you'd spoken to the police. So, I've got to go to the station tomorrow to give a statement. But, no, I can't go earlier because I have an exam today. Is there a problem? Yeah, I'll say she started chasing us, and yes, I can say you were telling me how to avoid her if you think it's best. Fine, bye.'

'Is anything wrong, Bobby?' Adam asked.

'It was my driving instructor. He seemed a bit agitated.'

'I'd say a lot more than just a bit agitated,' Max added. 'If I didn't know better, I'd swear someone was putting pressure on him.'

A car horn blasted behind them. They turned to see a blue Volkswagen Caddy with the driver frantically waving at them.

'What does that muppet want?' Max cursed, still fretting over Michael.

'That muppet is our mate Danny, but what the flip is he doing in that car?' Bobby replied.

Adam and Bobby jogged back to the passenger window, which was slowly opening.

'White's Wheels is open for business,' Danny said with a cheery smile.

'Danny, what the heck are you doing with this?' Adam asked.

'It's my mobility car. I applied when I passed my test in September, but they've only just finished the wheelchair conversions based on my designs,' Danny replied.

'Let me guess, rocket launchers, invisibility mode, anti-radar and anti-speed camera detection,' Bobby joked.

'Almost, buddy,' Danny laughed, 'Where are you guys heading anyway?'

'Just to college,' Bobby replied, 'I've got to be there by ten thirty for an exam, and Adam is meeting Avery.'

'Lit, I'm going there too. I've got a meeting with the College Principal. For some unbeknown reason, they aren't happy that I tried to make the Information Technology exam harder. What's the point of a two-hour exam you can do in forty minutes?'

'Lit? What kind of English is that?' Max grumbled.

Bobby apologised, saying, 'Sorry, Danny, that wasn't me. That was Max, a grumpy geezer who decided to take up lodgings inside me.'

'So it's true then,' Danny laughed. 'Avery and Abi came to mine yesterday afternoon to see how I was and tell me all about what went down. Well, that's what they said, but I think they just wanted to use the pool and the jacuzzi,' he added with a wink.

'Yep, it's all true, and it's getting crazier by the day,' Bobby said as he climbed into the passenger seat, and Adam got into the back seat.

'Well, we've got thirty minutes to spare, so why don't I show you what this baby can do, and you can tell me all about it,' Danny said.

Half an hour later, Danny parked in one of the disabled spaces in front of the college.

'That's nuts!' Danny said, shaking his head, 'So you reckon those Deceptors have kidnapped this Michael fella cos he's the dead spit of the old guy killed by that car?'

'I'm not dead,' Max corrected him, 'I'm just transmuting between bodies.'

'Sorry, but this is bonkers. I'm conversing with two different people in the same body,' Danny replied, adding with a laugh, 'I wonder if I'm technically breaking the law having two people in the front passenger seat?'

'Hey, look, Avery is heading this way. Do you want me to get your wheelchair out, Danny?' Adam offered.

'Nah, just sit there in awe and wonder at my genius,' Danny replied, pressing a button which raised the tailgate and lowered a ramp. 'Now for part two,' he said, opening the driver's door and picking up what looked like a small games controller.

The press of a few buttons saw his wheelchair spring to life, drive down the slope and appear by the side of the driver's door. Another press and the wheelchair seat rose level with the car's driver seat. A quick shuffle saw Danny slide into the chair, which then lowered down to its standard height.

'Well, come on, dullards, I need to lock up,' Danny said triumphantly.

'Hey, guys, what's up?' Avery said, giving air kisses to all three of them as they greeted her in return.

'Danny's just been showing off his new wheels,' Adam said.

'And his latest chair adaptions,' Bobby added. 'How was your exam?'

'It was maths, so do I need to say more?' Avery replied, adding, 'Although it was better than politics last week. I wasn't expecting such a big question on the Magna Carta.'

'Yeah, that caught me out, too,' Bobby replied.

'Signed on the Fifteenth June 1215 at Runnymeade,' Max moaned. 'Nothing but a power grab by the barons over that crooked King John. I never understood why we had to do it in a field near Staines when we could have used Windsor Castle. But then John had no intention of honouring it anyway.'

Avery looked at Bobby in astonishment, 'You were there then? Max.'

'Of course, I've always found it useful to be around the movers and shakers of the time,' Max replied.

'This is insane,' Danny said, 'Were you one of the barons?'

'Definitely not. If you rise to the top, there's always someone ready to chop you down. It's better to be sat near the power thrones rather than on them, in my experience.'

'I could have flipping done with you inside me last week,' Bobby moaned as his friends laughed. 'Oh heck, I need to go, or I'll be late. I hope Catherine doesn't call whilst I'm in the exam.'

'Pass me your phone, hun, and if she does, I'll explain what we saw,' Adam said. 'We'll see you here in a couple of hours.'

'Cheers, Adam,' Bobby replied, handing over his and Max's phones before rushing off.

Adam looked at Max's old-fashioned mobile with amusement before stuffing both into his pockets.

'Hun?' Avery questioned, looking at Adam. 'And when did Bobby start dressing like you?'

Adam ignored the first point and replied, 'Oh, he stopped at mine last night and needed some clean clothes after Max insisted he started exercising. Remember I told you yesterday that we had been running together.'

Two hours later, Bobby was standing by Danny's car, arguing. '*I'm telling you, Cromwell was a Puritan. Everybody knows it. He even banned Christmas.*'

'*He was a signed-up member of the Church of England. He only became a Puritan because he liked their bad-tempered intolerance of having fun,*' Max replied.

The debate was interrupted by Avery, Danny and Adam's arrival.

'Hiya Bobby, how did it go?' Avery asked, hugging him.

'Yeah, not too bad, although Max kept trying to give me his version of events,' Bobby replied.

'Well, I was there, you know.'

'That may be so, cowboy, but I have to put what is recorded as facts, not what your memory says happened.'

'Sorry to interrupt, but Catherine called,' Adam said.

'What did she say? Did she see the news?' Max replied.

'No, she hadn't seen or heard anything. She said she had the afternoon off if you're free.'

Bobby looked at his watch, 'It's one-fifteen already. It'll take us an hour and a half to get there on the tube.'

'The tube?' laughed Danny, 'Who needs the underground when you've got White's Wheels on standby?'

'Are you sure, Danny?' Max said.

'All aboard,' replied Danny.

'Thanks for helping, folks. You're all ace,' Bobby said. 'I'll text Catherine to let her know we're coming.'

Forty-five minutes later, Danny parked up in Glenthorne Crescent. 'And for my next superpower,' Danny said, pulling out his disabled parking permit.

They piled out of the car and headed towards number twelve. Catherine had been looking out for them and was already opening the door.

'Max, thanks for coming. I've not told Mama yet as I wanted to speak to you first to find out what you know,' Catherine said, 'Oh, where are my manners? Please, everyone, come in.'

'Thank you, Catherine. I think you've already met everyone else, but this is Danny, another of Bobby's friends and a bit of a computer whizz,' Max replied.

'Pleased to meet you, Danny,' Catherine said, holding out her hand.

'The pleasure is all mine, m'ladyship,' Danny responded, dramatically taking Catherine's hand, 'Please excuse me for not standing.'

'Do you need a hand getting up the step, Danny?' Adam offered.

'I fear no step,' Danny replied, hitting a button on his chair, which caused poles to lower, raising the chair off its wheels as it walked up the step by the front door.

'That's very impressive, Danny. I should get you to help with some of my disabled patients,' Catherine said, standing back to let him pass.

'Always happy to help, but you realise I'm not disabled?' Danny grinned wickedly, 'After all, which of us doesn't have to walk everywhere?'

'I love your attitude; that's so true,' Catherine replied. Then, joining the joke with a wink, she said, 'I assume the stairs hold no fear either?'

'Ha, I laugh in the face of stairs,' Danny replied.

'Don't tell me you can fly up stairs too?' Avery said, staring in disbelief.

'Oh, no, I don't stand a chance against stairs, but I still laugh at them,' Danny chuckled.

'Well, luckily, if you go down that corridor past the door under the stairs on the left and we have a lift so you can meet us on the first floor,' Catherine said.

After a trip in the lift, Danny came down the corridor and into the Drawing Room to see everyone sitting around. Looking at Catherine, he said, 'Nice pad. I saw from the lift that you even have a basement. I think I could easily make this my secret spy lair.'

Max laughed, 'You're too late, buddy. That basement is already mine.'

'I live; I mean, you live here?' Bobby said.

'One of dear old Uncle Max's many hideouts,' Catherine replied before saying, 'So what did they say in the news?'

'That my body, well, my old body was critical but still in hospital, and they showed an image of someone wired and tubed up,' Max answered. 'Have you heard from Michael in the last few days?'

'No, other than that text the other day, Papa has been quiet, but you know he's never been one to say much when he's away working,' Catherine replied, 'What are you thinking?'

'Well, without me in that shell, the body would die, so they're either using a stiff as a prop, or they've got Michael, and if that's the case, then they must be trying to flush me out.'

'But why do they want you, sweetie?' Avery asked.

'That is a good question,' Max replied, 'If you find out why, let me know, as I don't have a clue.'

'Which hospital is he in?' Avery queried.

Max replied, 'They never said.'

'I assume you guys have searched the NHS patient lists?' Danny interjected.

'Why didn't I think of that?' Catherine replied, 'Let me get my laptop, and I'll log in.'

After a few minutes of searching, Catherine said, 'No signs of a Maxwell or Michael Thomas or an M Thomas anywhere.'

'What about the private hospitals!' Danny asked.

'I've not registered to do any private practice yet, so I'm not on any of their systems,' Catherine replied.

'May I?' Danny asked, holding out his hand for Catherine's laptop. Is that TV connected to your wifi? I'll screen share so you can see what I'm looking at.'

Catherine turned on the TV over the fireplace as Danny clicked screen share.

'OK, so that's your NHS search. Now let's start digging. Nothing showing for M Thomas, Maxwell Thomas or Michael Thomas. Bobby, what was the name of the policeman you're seeing tomorrow?'

'DI John Fallon,' Bobby replied.

'Nope, nothing linked to him either. Let me try another option. Look at this, either we've got a high-profile person in critical care, or this may be what we are looking for,' Danny said, circling a record for U Male at the Oliver Clinic, Kensington.

'What does U Male mean?' Avery asked.

Catherine replied, 'Unidentified male. It's one of many terms used for a patient where we either don't know their identity or need to hide it.'

'But they said his identity was known as Maxwell Thomas!' Adam said.

'Come on, Adam, do you still believe what they tell you in the media?' Danny replied.

'So what's next?' Avery asked.

'Do you have any contacts at the Oliver Clinic?' Max asked Catherine.

'I've heard Papa mention it as very exclusive, but I've none personally,' Catherine replied.

'We need to get in there,' Max said, 'Could you pass as one of their clinicians?'

'I doubt it. Those places are very close-knit. Everybody will know each other in the clinical team. The only exception would be if they use agency nurses.'

'Why are you making it so difficult?' Danny replied, 'Mrs Janet Studerus is in the next room suffering from Alzheimer's, so let's just book someone as a relative to see her!'

'I'll do it,' said Avery, 'They'll never recognise me.'

'Are you sure, Avery? If they're on the ball, they'll quickly catch on to you not being there to see Mrs Studerus, and I don't want to put you at risk,' Max replied.

'Do it, Danny,' Avery said. Then, looking at Bobby, she said, 'Anything for you, sweetie.'

'You're not doing it alone,' Adam said, 'Make it both of us.'

Danny looked at Avery and Adam, 'OK, Alice and Paul Lee, you're off to see your Auntie Janet.'

'No, change the surname. Nothing linked in any way to us,' Max said.

'No probs, you're now O'Grady, don't forget Auntie Janet's flowers at two p.m. tomorrow,' Danny replied.

'Why tomorrow?' Avery challenged, 'Can't you do today?'

'Yeah, I could, but they've probably got trigger systems in their programming to spot last-minute bookings, so tomorrow is the quickest I can do safely without raising alarms,' Danny replied.

Max asked Danny, 'Are you sure you're not a Shadower? You're as cunning and suspicious as me.'

'I'll take that as a compliment,' Danny laughed.

Catherine turned to Adam and Avery, 'I really can't thank you, guys, enough for helping us.'

'Any friend of Bobby and Max is one of ours,' Adam replied.

The front door closed, followed by someone coming up the stairs.

'What are you all doing sitting around like this?' Agathe said, 'No drinks or nibbles? Catherine, have you no manners?'

'Sorry, Mama, we were just talking about a few things. Can we have a chat in Papa's study?'

Agathe looked around the room and recognised Adam as the boy who had helped her with the refreshments the last time. 'Adam, isn't it?'

'Yes, Mrs Tho... Agathe,' he said, remembering what Agathe had previously requested about how to address her.

'I'm sure you remember the way to the kitchen, so why don't you take your two friends downstairs and get some drinks and snacks? Feel free to have a rummage, and everyone, please help yourself. Mi casa es su casa,' Agathe said cheerily before following Catherine and Max into the study.

A minute later, Adam and Avery stood by the kitchen door, waiting for the lift to arrive.

'I need to reprogram this lift for them. I've aged three years going up and down in it,' Danny joked as he finally rejoined his friends.

'This kitchen is stunning,' Avery said, 'I love the minimalist look and the way they've combined different shades of grey on the cupboards and walls with the black granite.'

'Oh no, Avery's switched to design mode. I'll see if I can reboot her,' Danny said, grinning.

'Not a chance,' Adam replied. 'Once a designer goes into appreciation mode, there's no stopping them.'

'I mean, it's not like it's well coordinated; look, not one of the chairs matches,' Danny chuckled.

'You heathens wouldn't know about style if it came up to you, slapped you in the face, and handed you a business card with my name is Style on it,' Avery joked back. 'Look, there's even a glass-fronted fridge full of cans and bottles.'

'If there's some water in there, I'll have one,' Adam said.

Avery passed Adam a bottle of water and took one for herself. Then, turning to Danny, she asked if he wanted anything.

'No, I don't like to drink and drive,' Danny replied, tapping his wheelchair. 'Come and look at the garden and patio. It's impressive.'

Avery opened the French doors onto an immaculate raised wooden deck surrounded by a glass and chrome balustrade.

'And it's even wheelchair friendly. There's no lip on the doorframe,' Danny said appreciatively as he headed outside.

'Looks like that's as far as you're going, buddy,' Adam replied, pointing at the steps.

'No, there's a slope behind this plant pot,' Avery said, walking down the slope, quickly followed by Adam and Danny.

Looking at the back of the house, Danny said, 'It's not as big as my place, but it's impressive.'

Avery corrected him, 'You mean your parent's place.'

'You know what I mean,' Danny replied.

'That's quite a steep slope to push a wheelchair up,' Adam said.

'Nah, look, there's a button here. I assume it's for a lift mechanism,' Danny replied.

'What button?' asked Adam.

'I can't see a button either,' Avery said.

'Oh, you guys just prove who's disabled. It's here half hidden by this wooden leaf, as anyone at my height can see,' Danny replied as he pressed it.

Max's phone silently vibrated wildly in his pocket. He pulled it out. The message said entry eight - activated.

'Is something wrong?' Catherine asked.

'No, it's fine. I think the guys just found my spy cave,' Max laughed. He walked to the window and saw Bobby's friends in the garden.

The slope Avery, Adam and Danny had just walked down lifted into the air revealing another slope going under the patio.

'Press it again,' Adam said, 'We can't go down there; it's wrong.'

'Yes, it's definitely wrong,' Avery said.

'Guys, where's your sense of adventure?' Danny asked.

Avery's phone pinged, 'Feel free to explore, guys. I don't mind.' She looked up and saw Bobby waving from the window. She waved back and said, 'Bobby said it's fine for us to go down there.'

'Bobby or Max said?' Adam asked.

'Max, sorry.' Avery laughed.

'And now the heroes enter the villain's cave, ever vigilant for hidden death traps,' Danny said in his best deep and mysterious voice as he went down the slope, followed by Avery and Adam.

'If anyone is the villain, it's you with your gadget chair,' Adam chuckled.

'Yeah, he just needs a white cat and a fish tank full of sharks,' Avery added.

'They're coming tomorrow. Did you think that swimming pool you and Abi were in yesterday is really for humans?' Danny cackled in an evil voice, adding, 'Well, except for when I push them in to feed my new pets.'

They burst out laughing as they got to the bottom of the slope.

'Well, so much for the drama,' Avery said, adding, 'Some garden furniture on that side under the decking and just a rickety door over here, which opens to reveal, wow, an old bike.'

'Are you sure there's nothing else in there?' Danny asked, 'That seems like a very elaborate entrance for some storage, and it's a bit dark in that shed. Plus Bobby, I mean Max said he lived in the basement.'

'There's a switch here,' Adam said, pointing at a simple-looking light switch at the bottom of the slope. He flicked the switch, but nothing happened.

'Maybe the bulb has blown,' Avery said.

Danny had moved to the open shed door and flicked a button on his chair, resulting in a bright light shining from the front of it. He peered into the shed and noticed a recess on the right wall, directly opposite the bicycle.

He turned to Avery, 'Can you pass me your water, please?'

She handed it over and watched as he opened it and started pouring it in front of the lipped entrance to the shed.

'I thought so,' Danny chuckled, 'Max, you crafty devil. Adam, try flicking that switch again, but when you do it, press hard on the switch and hold it in.'

Adam did as he was told, 'Nope, still nothing.'

Danny looked at Adam, 'Oh yes, there is. You can probably let go now and come and look.'

Except for the door, the rest of the shed slid almost silently to the right to reveal a terraced area behind it. All three went through what was now a corridor leading to the terrace and saw a door to the right. A small screen flickered into life by the side of the door, showing Bobby's face.

'Well done, my enterprising friends. Nobody has ever worked out how to get through that quickly. I'll buzz you in. I suggest using the stairs or lift to return to the house,' Max said.

Back in the study, Max turned to face Agathe and Catherine. 'So first of all, we need to see if Michael is in the hospital and establish his condition. Then if it is him, we can find the best way to get him out safely.'

'But you said you and Adam saw him on the news. So why can't we get him out now?' Catherine asked.

'Just like her father, gung-ho,' Agathe said, 'If there's one thing I've learnt over the years, it's to trust Max's caution, dear.'

'Also, we can't be certain it is him on the news. They may have set up Maxwell's dead body, used a lookalike or even used artificial intelligence to make it look like him. That's all assuming that U Male in the Oliver Clinic is the person they showed on the news,' Max added.

'But Max, aren't you putting those lovely young people at risk?' Agathe asked.

'Everything in life comes with some risk Agathe. But there's no direct link between them and us as long as they don't use their real names. Sending Catherine might be risky if Michael wakes up and sees her, and they'd only need to catch my reflection to spot I'm a Shadower as that woman did on Bobby's driving lesson yesterday.'

'But how will we know for sure that it's him?' Catherine asked.

Max tapped the side of his nose, 'That would be telling, but the Oliver Clinic is less than a mile away, so if we can meet here at one p.m. tomorrow, I'll take everyone through the plan.'

Catherine stood up and walked towards the door, 'Let's see what Bobby's friends have found in your flat, and we can mention your plan, Max.'

'*Well, once I've worked out a plan, I can,*' Max thought.

'*What do you mean once you've worked out a plan?*' Bobby screamed, '*Are you making it up as you go along?*'

Max paused briefly, then replied, '*Of course I am. Do you think this is some book or film where the hero always knows what to do and has everything planned to the most minute detail?*'

'*Well, when it puts my friends at risk, I would hope you'd have at least a bit of a plan,*' Bobby bellowed back.

'*Of course, I have a bit of a plan.*'

'*Well, that's something at least, and it'll definitely work?*'

'*Definitely is such a powerful word, don't you think? Plus, in what way do you mean work?*'

'*As in it gets Avery and Adam in and out, confirms whether it's Michael and nobody gets hurt sort of way?*'

'*Hopefully, should do and not intentionally.*'

'*That sounds like a shallow threshold of hope. At least you're sure Adam, Avery and Michael won't get hurt?*'

'*Mind if I don't answer that?*'

'*Why?*'

'*Because I don't know the answer.*'

The three of them walked downstairs to the ground floor, opened a door that looked like a cupboard under the stairs, and Max pressed and held the light switch. The floor slowly dropped away, becoming a staircase they walked down, appearing in the corridor of the basement apartment. Hearing voices from the living room, they entered to see Danny inspecting a bookcase in the far corner of the room with Adam and Avery protesting with him to leave it alone; it's just a bookcase.

'Can I help you,' Max roared.

Adam and Avery turned and started to apologise, but Max just smiled, 'It's fine, I said feel free to explore. What do you think you've found, Danny?'

Danny turned in Max's direction, 'There must be something behind this bookcase. I've been into the kitchen next door and the pantry, so I know the footprint in this room is at least six or seven feet too short.'

'Not only are you very good with computers and gadgets, but I see you're also extremely observant,' Max said, leaning forward, pushing in several books, and pulling out a couple more. There was a click, and the bookcase opened to reveal a room behind it.

Max waved Danny forward, 'After you, my intrepid explorer. Welcome to my workshop.'

The room was racked out from floor to ceiling with various gadgets. At the far end was a workbench filled with equipment and, on one side, a large computer.

'Wow, I could live here and never come out again,' Danny said, examining components and tools.

'I'm happy you approve,' Max said, smiling.

Agathe ran a finger across a shelf, inspected the dust on her finger and said, 'Even I've never seen this room before.'

'And that's exactly why not,' Max replied, laughing.

'I'm surprised the place isn't rigged out with secret cameras,' Avery said.

'It probably is. Look at the size of this tiny camera,' Danny said.

'Avery, Danny, that's it. I could kiss you both,' Max said excitedly, 'That's how we can make tomorrow work.'

'I think I speak for both of us in saying if that was Max talking, we respectfully decline, and if that was Bobby, then easy, Tiger, not in front of the children,' Danny replied, nodding in Adam's direction.

Adam replied indignantly, 'I'm only a couple of weeks younger than Bobby.'

'Plus, I'm not so sure if I would refuse that offer,' said Avery winking at Max.

Catherine interrupted the banter, 'Guys, can we please remember we are supposed to be talking about getting my Papa out of that clinic.'

'Sorry, Catherine,' Max, Danny, Avery and Adam chorused.

Max took the camera off Danny, 'This could be the answer. If we put cameras on Adam and Avery and give them earpieces, we can direct them into Michael's room and get them to show us what we need. The only challenge is getting them to transmit from the hospital to here, almost a mile away.'

'Oh, come on, ask a difficult question, buddy,' Danny laughed, 'I could probably sort that with just my equipment at home, but let me take a few of these cameras and those earpieces home, and I guarantee by tomorrow morning, I'll have it sorted.'

'Thank you, Danny.' Max replied, 'OK, let's meet back here between noon and one o'clock tomorrow, and I'll go through the detail. Danny, grab anything you need.'

'White's Wheels ready to roll, guys,' Danny said, grabbing several cameras, earpieces and a few other components before they headed towards the lift and stairs.

As the car pulled away, Danny glanced at Bobby, 'I'll drop you and Adam off first, as Avery lives just down from me.'

'Cheers, bud,' Bobby replied.

'If you need more equipment, just message Catherine and go and get it. I've already told her and Agathe to let you have anything you need, and here are the books you need to press and pull,' Max replied, putting a piece of paper in the cubby on the dashboard.

Danny parked outside Bobby's house, and Bobby and Adam got out. 'I'll drop you at yours, Adam,' Danny said.

'It's fine, Danny. I can walk it in a few minutes,' Adam responded, 'Besides, I need to ask Bobby something.'

Avery climbed out of the car. 'I may as well enjoy the ride from the front.'

'OK, but no funny stuff this time,' Danny said, winking.

Avery laughed. 'In your dreams, chauffeur. Besides, I've only got eyes for one slightly older man,' she said as she turned, put her hands on Bobby's cheeks and gave him a quick kiss on the lips before getting into the car's front seat.

Bobby started to blush.

'Aww, look, he's gone red,' Danny laughed, then added, 'He won't be washing his face ever again. Shut that door, ma'am; it's time to leave these losers. Laters, guys.'

Avery shut the passenger door, and Danny pulled away as Adam and Bobby shouted, 'Laters loser.'

'See you in the morning, mate,' Adam said, walking away.

Bobby went to reply, paused and then said, 'Adam, I thought you wanted to ask me something?'

Adam turned back and looked at his friend, 'Yeah, erm, I did, didn't I? I can't remember now what it was.' His mind went into overdrive, and he felt awkward before he said, 'Oh yeah shall I meet you here tomorrow morning, and what time?'

'Better meet me at Catherine's as I've got my police interview in the morning, so I don't know how long I'll be,' Bobby replied.

'OK, mate, see you tomorrow,' Adam replied, walking away.

'Yeah, see you tomorrow Adam and thanks for helping,' Bobby said.

Adam crossed the road and started to head for home, but then he stopped and looked back to see his friend opening his front door and heard Bobby shout, 'Hi Mum, it's only me. Sorry, I'm late. Did you get my message?' Adam sighed and started walking again.

Bobby turned to shut the door, but he watched Adam walk away before he did.

'Shut the door! Were you born in a barn?' his Mum shouted, breaking Bobby's thoughts.

6
The Swerve

Bobby was sitting in the living room when his Mum returned after dropping Lily off at school.

'Morning champ, are you planning on going to the police station dressed like that?'

'I'm only giving a statement, not going to court.'

'Even so, I would have thought some tidy trousers and a shirt would look better than a T-shirt and those tracksuit bottoms. Where did you get them from anyway? I don't remember seeing them before,' Pat queried. 'I'll just put these groceries away, and then we can go.'

Before he could reply, his Mum wandered into the kitchen.

'*I wonder why you are still wearing those clothes when you've got your own upstairs,*' Max chuckled.

'*Whatevs,*' Bobby responded before going into the kitchen.

'Mum, what did the police say about today?'

Still putting some tins in a cupboard, Pat replied, 'Just that your driving instructor had given a full account of what happened and why but as you were driving the car, they did need to speak to you too. They did say it was nothing to worry about.'

They left the house, and Pat unlocked her car, 'Hop in. It'll take us twenty minutes to get there.'

'But the station is just in the High Street. So we can walk there in under five minutes,' Bobby replied.

'No, we have to go to the North West London Police Headquarters. That's where DI Fallon is based.'

Twenty minutes later and Pat pulled up outside the police station.

'*I've got a bad feeling about this,*' Max said, '*Why would a detective be interested in a traffic incident?*'

'Pat Morris with Bobby Morris to see Detective Inspector Fallon,' Pat said to the desk clerk.

The clerk told them to take a seat and that she would let DI Fallon know they were there. After a few minutes, a door opened, and a man in a casual grey suit walked out.

'Mrs Morris? I'm DI John Fallon. Delighted to meet you.'

Pat Morris stood and shook the outstretched hand of the officer.

'I presume this is our new future racing driver,' DI Fallon said, shaking Bobby's hand. 'Follow me. We just need to take a statement from you. It shouldn't take very long.'

Bobby indicated for his Mum to go first, then followed behind. The officer led them down a long double-height corridor with offices on both sides. Looking up, Bobby saw a line of windows on the left-hand side angled so that someone behind them could look down.

Max looked up at the large convex security mirror at the end of the corridor and saw DI Fallon, his mother and himself in it. But, to his relief, only he had an aura.

At the end of the corridor, the officer pulled open a door on the right-hand side and waved them inside, 'If you can both take a seat on that side of the table. I need to go and fetch my colleague.'

The interview room was sparsely furnished with a table, four chairs and a recording device on the wall.

'*No one-way mirror?*' Bobby thought.

'*That's normally just in the movies,*' Max replied, '*Although I wish there were a mirror or some other reflective surface in here.*'

'Mum, have you got a mirror on you?' Bobby asked Pat.

'Only this one,' she replied, rummaging in her bag and pulling out a compact.

Max took the compact and opened it. He pretended he was using it to brush something out of his eyes, but in reality, he had angled it to reflect the door, and he didn't have to wait long before it opened. DI Fallon entered, followed by another officer who introduced himself as Detective Sergeant Carter. Max checked Carter's reflection, then handed the compact back to Pat. '*No aura around him either,*' he mused.

The interview lasted about forty minutes, with Max being cautious not to allow Bobby to say any more than he had to.

'Thank you, Bobby, you have confirmed everything Ian told us,' DI Fallon said.

'Ian?' Pat queried.

'Sorry, Mrs Morris, I meant Ian Prosser, Bobby's driving instructor. He reckons Bobby is a natural behind the wheel and followed every move he said to avoid the woman's car.'

'So, have you arrested that woman? It sounds like she is a danger to everyone driving like that, plus surely all that shooting is against the law?' Pat added.

'Unfortunately, the lady involved has left the country using a diplomatic passport, so there isn't anything we can do,' DS Carter said.

'Can't she be extradited?' Max asked, already expecting a negative response.

'No, we do not have an extradition agreement with that country,' DI Fallon replied.

'Oh, that's not fair. Which country is it?' Max pressed.

'We are not at liberty to reveal that information, I am afraid,' DS Carter answered.

DI Fallon stood and opened the door, 'We've taken up far too much of your time already. Thanks again for popping in to confirm what happened. I'll show you back to the main entrance.'

'Don't I need to sign a statement or anything?' Max queried.

'No, that won't be necessary. As we said, we can do nothing about the incident anyway. The interview was merely to ensure we recorded everything officially. Besides, the tape machine records the whole interview if we need to recheck anything.' DS Carter said.

DI Fallon escorted them to the front desk, 'Mr Morris, I hope you don't mind me giving you some advice, but be careful about who you are getting involved with. Not everything is as it seems. Now I must dash. Have a safe journey.'

Fallon walked back down the corridor, and Bobby and Pat left the police station and headed to the car.

'You didn't tell me just how bad that incident was,' Pat said. 'I'm worried now.'

'It's fine, Mum. Besides, you heard them say she had left the country,' Bobby said, looking back at the police station.

'You're sure that is the same boy involved in the incident at Picadilly Circus,' the detective said to the woman standing by his side as they looked down at Bobby.

'Yes, no doubt about it,' the woman replied.

'And he has an aura?'

'He does. What do we do next?'

'We were told to confirm his identity and to keep him under observation. Nothing more at this stage. Is everything in place for this afternoon?'

'Yes, there are two of them coming, one male and one female. We have a backup plan if he isn't the male. So it should be possible to do what we have to.'

The detective turned to face the woman, 'Under no circumstances are you to mess this up. Do you understand?'

The woman went to protest but then dropped her head, 'Yes, I understand.'

'Mum, can you please drop me off at Catherine's house?' Max asked, using his Bobby voice.

'Oh yes, and who is Catherine, may I ask?' Pat loved teasing her son, 'Is she your new girlfriend, and where is her house.'

Bobby went bright red, *'Thanks, cowboy as if my life isn't complicated enough.'*

'Oops, sorry about that,' Max thought, then said, 'No, she's a friend of Danny, that's all. We said we would meet up there. The address is 12 Glenthorne Crescent. It's by Earls Court.'

'Danny is such a lovely lad. I wish I had half his parent's money, though. How come you have all these wealthy friends?'

'I wouldn't call Adam or Dazza wealthy, nor Abi, to be honest,' Bobby said, relieved that his Mum had dropped the girlfriend point.

'True, but Avery and Danny are both from wealthy backgrounds and now this friend in Earls Court.'

'Just proves gaming isn't all bad then,' Bobby replied, 'I met Danny online. As for Avery, we met at college.'

'I'm surprised she didn't go to a posh college.'

'You haven't met her Dad,' Bobby answered, 'He's always saying his Dad came to this country with nothing and put him through state education, so if it was good enough for him, it was good enough for anyone. Plus, to be honest, I think he's tight and doesn't like to spend money.'

Pat laughed at her son's honesty, 'That's exactly what your Dad would have said.'

'Which bit?'

'All of it,' Pat chuckled.

'Do you still miss Dad?' Bobby asked.

'Every single day. It's the little things like having someone to have a good moan with. Someone to curl up to and watch pointless television on a cold evening. Heck, I even miss his awful jokes and taste in music. How can anyone have a music collection with Mozart, Kenny Rogers and Metallica on shuffle?'

'I miss him too. I told Adam about him and how we watched the old Batman TV shows together.'

'You know your Dad always claimed to have met that guy who played the Joker in that show.'

'Yeah, I remember that. Oh, that's the house there,' Bobby said, pointing.

Pat pulled up to the kerb, and Bobby got out of the car, 'Thanks for the lift, Mum. Don't worry about tea for me. I'll probably grab something later.'

'OK, champ, have a nice time and behave yourself with Catherine. Don't do anything I wouldn't do,' Pat replied, laughing as she drove off.

Max spotted Danny's car a little up the road and was relieved, as this meant they should have the time to ensure everything worked. He walked up to the door and rang the bell. A few seconds later, Catherine opened it, 'Why didn't you just use your key?'

'I know I could have, but it still feels a little strange at the moment,' Max replied.

They walked upstairs and found Agathe and Danny in fits of laughter.

'What on Earth are you two up to?' Max said.

'Oh Max, your new friend is an absolute riot and so cheeky, too,' Agathe said.

'Hiya Bobby,' Danny chuckled, 'Don't believe a word Agathe tells you. I have been the epitome of discretion at all times.'

'Well, never mind that. Have you been the epitome of engineering genius?' Max asked.

'As if there was ever any doubt,' Danny replied in mock outrage, 'But these devices are just too small to get them to transmit as far as we need them, so I've rigged this up.'

Danny held up a small mobile phone-looking device about ten centimetres long by five centimetres wide. 'One of them keeps this on them, and the cameras and earpieces connect to it. The device will then stream directly to my car outside the Clinic, and from there, I can easily get the signal back to this device which connects directly to the TV. So you will be able to see and hear everything. You can talk to them using this microphone. Left button for the one, right button for the other, or both buttons to talk to both.'

'The only problem I see is that most hospitals make you turn off your mobile phone if it's in a critical care area,' Catherine said.

'No problemo, look, it's not a real phone. You can press a key, and it lights up, but it doesn't make calls or anything, and even if you turn it off like this, it is still working,' Danny replied.

The doorbell went, and Catherine headed downstairs to answer it. A minute or so later, she reappeared. 'Looks like we've got a full house.' She said as Adam, Avery, and Dazza appeared behind her.

'Hope you don't mind me tagging along, but I was at Adam's,' Dazza replied, adding, 'Hiya Bob, hey guys.'

'That's fine,' said Agathe, 'I've made plenty of food for everyone. Can't have you going to rescue my Michael on an empty stomach now.'

Agathe got up and headed off downstairs to the kitchen.

Max got everyone seated and asked Danny to take them through everything again.

Adam picked up one of the cameras and inspected it, 'You've made it look like a badge.'

'The easiest way to hide something is to make it visible,' Danny replied. 'If you try to make it look like a button or something, it stands out as it never looks the same as the other buttons. Make it look like a badge, and people assume it's a badge. I used one-way film, so whatever is on the badge doesn't interfere with the camera image. Neat, huh?'

'Very,' agreed Avery. 'Are we supposed to be archaeology fans or something, as they both say DIG on them?'

'Let me guess, it stands for Danny Is Great,' Dazza laughed.

'Wrong as always, big man. It's Danny Is Genius,' Danny said, flexing his biceps.

'Well, Mr Genius, let's see it in action,' Max said.

'Yes sir,' Danny replied, saluting Max. 'Stick this bit in your ear,' he said, handing two small round devices to Avery and Adam, 'and pin the badges on your jackets.'

As Adam and Avery did as instructed, Danny plugged a wire between his laptop and the small phone device. 'OK, it's scanning and bingo. There you go, two clear images from each camera.' Danny leant forward and pressed both buttons on the microphone, 'Repeat after me. Danny is king.'

Avery and Adam looked at each other and shook their heads.

'What!' Danny said worriedly. 'Couldn't you hear me? Don't say they've stopped working.'

'Oh, we heard you just fine, Danny. We just disagreed with you,' Avery replied, laughing.

'Oh, very funny.' Danny disconnected the mobile phone-looking device and threw it towards Adam, 'One of you needs to keep this with you. It boosts the signal to and from your cameras and hearing devices.'

Adam stuffed the device in his pocket.

'Try going out into the back garden to see how it performs through walls and at a distance,' Max suggested.

Avery and Adam walked downstairs, giving a cheery smile to Agathe, who was putting food onto some large platters, and then went out into the garden.

Max leant forward, pressed one button and said hello, to which Adam replied. He repeated the process with the other button, waited for Avery to respond, and then pressed both buttons and said they could return.

A few minutes later, they emerged carrying a couple of large platters.

'Where is Agathe?' Max queried.

'Right here, dear. I just used the lift to bring the trolley up. My word Danny you have made that lift work much better. Thank you.'

'My pleasure,' replied Danny with a smile.

'Well, it looks like we are ready to go Michael hunting. Thanks, Danny, you've done a great job on those devices,' Max replied, 'We've got about half an hour to demolish this food before the off.'

Thirty-five minutes later, Avery and Adam get out of Danny's car. Danny opened his window and said, 'Can you see and hear everything, Max?'

'He said yes,' Avery replied.

'Let's go hunting then,' Adam said as he and Avery headed towards the Clinic entrance.

Inside the Clinic, they walked up to the reception desk and said they were there to see their Aunt.

'What is your Aunt's name?' the receptionist asked.

'Auntie Janet,' Adam flustered.

'It's Studerus, Janet Studerus,' Avery said, squeezing Adam's hand to calm his nerves.

The receptionist typed the name into his computer and then looked up at them, 'Your names are?'

'Paul and Alice O'Grady,' Adam said, feeling slightly more confident.

'First floor, room W103. Use the lift over there and turn left as you exit the first floor. A nurse will be along to see you shortly.'

'Thank you,' said Avery as they headed towards the lift.

Once the lift closed, the receptionist picked up a phone and dialled a number, 'The guests for Mrs Studerus are on the way. No, neither of them matched the picture.'

Once on the first floor, Adam and Avery followed the sign pointing out rooms W101-W104. They glanced through the partially obscured glass as they passed the first two rooms, but both rooms were unoccupied.

'Here we are, room W103,' Adam said.

'Check the final room before going in there,' Max crackled through their earpieces.

They got to the room but couldn't see who was inside as the bed was in a different position than the other rooms. Deciding to explore further, Adam pushed open the door and stepped into the room when a male voice behind them said, 'Can I help you?'

He turned and saw a male nurse walking towards them.

'We're looking for our Aunt, Janet Studerus. I'm sure the man downstairs said room 104,' Avery said.

'It's room 103 you need,' the nurse replied, opening the door to the room. 'I'm here to update you on her condition. I'm Nurse Jon Willis.'

'I've managed to grab a frame from Adam's camera. Is this him?' Danny's said, his voice floating into the room at Glenthorne Crescent.

'That's Michael,' Max replied. 'How can we hear you, Danny?

'I put a third channel into the device connected to your telly with constant two-way microphones so that we can talk to each other,' Danny replied. 'I activated it once I knew you could hear Adam and Avery's devices when we parked.'

'I'm scanning this place for your bugs when we've sorted Michael out,' Max said, laughing.

Pressing the buttons on the microphone, Catherine said, 'Adam or Avery, can one of you try to get back into room 104, please?'

A thumbs-up appeared in front of Adam's camera.

'I'm afraid your Aunt isn't likely to make it through the night,' Nurse Willis said, looking at the array of screens.

'Oh no,' Avery replied, trying to look upset. Adam put his arm around her in mock consolation.

'You can stay with her as long as you wish. If you need food or something to drink, there is a restaurant at the other end of this floor. I'll leave you to it and pop back in about half an hour to see how you all are.'

Nurse Willis left the room, and they listened as his footsteps disappeared down the corridor.

Adam stood up, 'You stay here. I'll go next door to check on Michael. Guys, if that nurse returns, let me know, and I'll sneak out and fetch some drinks so my absence won't look suspicious.'

Avery grabbed and squeezed Adam's hand, 'Be careful.'

Adam opened the hospital room door and looked down the corridor. Then, seeing it was clear, he sneaked into room 104 and walked up to the bed. 'Hello, Michael, can you hear me? He's not responding. What should I do?'

'Do you know how to check for a pulse?' Catherine asked.

'Yes,' Adam replied, grabbing the patient's wrist. 'I can feel it, but it's slow and weak.'

'Show me his left hand,' Max said.

Adam lifted the patient's left hand towards the camera badge.

'Look, his fingers are all straight, so it's Michael without a doubt,' said Max.

'Why isn't he moving, though? What have they done to my Michael?' Agathe asked.

'Adam, look for his medical charts. They'll probably be at the end of the bed,' Catherine said.

Adam found the charts and held them up to the camera as Catherine guided him to move them around so she could read them. 'They've crossed out U Male and put Maxwell Thomas in. Can you slowly move the page up so I can read it, Adam? First, propofol was administered, and now midazolam has him in an induced coma.'

'Do you recognise the consultant's name?' Max asked.

Adam moved the charts so the doctor's name appeared on the screen.

'Mr R Mueller, that's Richard Mueller. He retired maybe fifteen years ago. I'd just started in medicine when he retired. So why would he still be practising now?' Catherine asked.

'Why indeed,' Max replied. 'Does he know Michael?'

'The name sounds familiar, so either Michael has mentioned him, or we've met at one of those medical conventions,' Agathe said, adding, 'but either way, most of the local senior consultants of that age tend to know each other even if it's only in passing.'

'If the doctor treating him knew him, why was he listed as an unknown male when they did that appeal on the news?' Dazza asked.

'That, my friend, is an excellent question. I wish I had an excellent reply for you,' Max answered.

'So, how do we get Michael out?' Agathe asked.

'Flumazenil would help bring him around, but you need the training to administer it, which means I'm the only one who could do it. Plus, we can't be sure how long he's been under. I need to examine him. Adam, show me his vitals?' Catherine said.

'His what?' Adam asked

'Sorry, Adam, go over to those machines and slowly move the camera across them so I can read the screens,' Catherine said as she got up and walked over to the television.

'What's happening?' Avery interjected, 'I don't feel comfortable sitting here with this poor lady.'

Max pressed the button and said, 'Sorry, Avery, we haven't forgotten you. We've confirmed it's Michael, but they have put him in a coma. Adam is showing Catherine his medical records.'

'Almost done,' Catherine shouted from her position by the television as she scanned the machines Adam was showing her. 'His output and levels are fine, which is good news.'

'I can hear footsteps,' Avery said, 'Quick, get Adam to come back.'

Max pressed both buttons and said, 'Adam, quick, someone is coming. Try to get back to Avery. We have enough for now.'

Adam cracked open the door and looked out, 'Too late, it's that nurse. Operation cup of tea is a go.'

'Sorry, Avery, Adam can't get back to you, so he's going to pretend to be fetching tea,' Max said, 'We'll keep watching and listening at this end.'

'Oh, you're alone,' Nurse Willis said, entering room 103.

'Yes, my brother has gone to get us some tea,' Avery replied, watching the nurse walking around the bed and checking the machines.

'That's very nice of him. My brother wouldn't get me a cup of tea if it were on the table in front of him. Were you and your brother close to your Aunt then?'

'Not really. We don't live near London, but as we heard she was in a bad way, we thought we should make an effort,' Avery lied.

'Adam, we can see the nurse has his back to the window, so if you're quick, he won't see you pass,' Max said into the microphone.

Avery watched Adam creep past quickly, then realised the nurse was talking to her. 'I'm sorry. What did you say?'

'I'm sorry, but I'm afraid this is the end for your Aunt. Her vital signs are failing fast. Maybe you'd like to hold her hand to comfort her,' Nurse Willis replied with a sad look on his face.

'Adam, it looks like the lady in the room with Avery is about to die. Get a move on,' Max said urgently.

'I can see the restaurant now. I'll grab one drink and run back,' Adam said, breaking into a run.

Adam's camera feed was jerky from his running, but Avery's signal suddenly started to break up and went blank.

'Avery, can you hear us? Unfortunately, we've lost your camera. Is everything OK?' Max said.

Danny's voice piped up, 'I don't think she can hear us guys. Adam's got the transmitter and is too far away from Avery. We didn't plan on them being so far apart.'

They looked at the screen and saw Adam standing behind someone who was paying.

'Adam, quick, get back to Avery. We've lost her signal,' Max yelled.

Adam was talking to the cashier, 'Here and keep the change. I'm in a hurry.' He dropped some coins on the counter and ran back up the corridor.

Avery's camera feed started to flicker and then came back to life. Finally, they heard Nurse Willis say, 'Just sit there. It's for the best. Your Aunt is at peace now.'

As the nurse finished talking, the door opened, and Adam walked in. 'What's happened,' he said, seeing the nurse sitting by Avery holding her hand.

'I'm so sorry, but I'm afraid your Aunt has passed away,' Nurse Willis said as she stood up. 'My condolences to you both. I need to go and get a doctor to certify the death, but you're welcome to stay if you wish?'

'Do you mind if we go,' said Avery. 'It's been a bit of a shock, and I need some fresh air.'

'Of course. Shall I call you a porter? He can bring a chair for you if you're not up to walking,' Nurse Willis offered kindly.

'No, it's fine. I feel a little overwhelmed,' Avery said.

Adam helped Avery stand, and they followed the signs towards the Clinic's exit.

The nurse picked up the phone by the side of the bed and dialled. 'Hello, is that Mr Mueller? Yes, Mrs Studerus has passed on. Her guests have left, so it's all clear if you wish to come and certify her death.'

Once Avery, Adam and Danny were back at Glenthorne Crescent, Agathe insisted on Avery eating something and having a sweet cup of tea, 'I don't care what anyone says, a warm cup of sweet tea is the best answer for all shocks.'

'I prefer a shot of single malt. But you do look shaken, Avery. Are you sure you're all right?' Max asked in genuine concern.

Avery sipped the tea, 'I've never seen a person die. Well, apart from you, but that all happened so quickly. It was like the world slowed down with that old lady as she slipped away. It was peaceful but shocking at the same time.'

'Would you like me to take you home?' Danny asked.

'Yes, please,' Avery replied.

'I'll come with you and ensure you're alright,' Bobby offered.

'Thank you, sweetie, but I'd rather be alone if you don't mind. Abi is coming around later for dinner, so I won't be alone all evening. I need to sleep and have some me time, if you don't mind?'

'Let's go, Avery. The last one to the car is a loser,' Danny said, 'Do you guys want me to come back and pick you up after?'

Catherine replied, 'It's fine, thank you, Danny. I can give the rest of them a lift home. Just take care of Avery for us.'

Avery stood facing the television as Bobby and the others hugged her before she turned and headed towards the stairs. 'Please, everyone, I don't want to make a fuss. You stay here and discuss the next steps. I'll see you tomorrow. Oh, Catherine, I'm so pleased we found your father.'

'We can never thank you enough,' Agathe said as she followed Avery downstairs to the car.

As they stood by the upstairs window and watched Danny drive away. Catherine said, 'I think she was more shook-up than she let on. I know I'm not her doctor, but I think I'll pop by her house and check on her after I've dropped you all off. Can someone let me have her address?'

Dazza grabbed some paper off the table, wrote down Avery's address and handed it to Catherine.

'Lychbar! That's a pretty exclusive area,' Catherine said.

'You should see Danny's house. It's just around the corner from Avery's, but it's much bigger,' Dazza replied.

'Come on, guys, let's park the game of who's got the biggest house. We need to work out how to get Michael out of that Clinic,' Max said

'We can't risk trying to resuscitate him in the Clinic as the time for the Flumazenil to react can vary, and he would still be very unstable even if he did wake up quickly,' Catherine said.

'So that means it has to be some form of medical extraction like a hospital transfer, but we'll need an ambulance,' Max replied.

'To do that, we will also need to get it onto their patient system, informing them of a patient transfer, which will give them advance warning of what we are doing,' Catherine said.

'What if Danny uploaded the transfer details as we entered the Clinic?' Bobby suggested. 'It'll be there when security checks, and then we get Danny to remove it to stop it flagging up. That way, if anyone noticed that it appeared and disappeared, it would make it look like someone hit the wrong button and then corrected it.'

'That could just work. But we still need an ambulance, a driver and some paramedic uniforms,' Max said.

'Leave that to me,' replied Agathe. 'I think Michael and I have fed and watered enough private ambulance drivers and paramedics over the years to call in some favours. What size uniforms do we need?'

'I'm going in as the escorting medic,' Catherine said firmly.

'Well, I don't have a licence yet, but as you saw the other day, I can drive,' Bobby added.

'Not a chance, my friend. I will not help you lose your licence before getting it. Besides, we can't go in there in case someone spots my aura,' Max replied.

'I have my licence,' Adam said.

'Me too,' replied Dazza.

'Looks like we have our ambulance crew then. Adam, we'll need to get you some disguise just in case that nurse is there,' Max said.

'Never mind a disguise. I can sort out some beanie hats or caps. But how tall are you, lad?' Agathe asked, looking at Dazza.

'Six foot four,' Dazza replied, 'Oh and large build.'

'At your height, you are an average build, dear boy. Oh well, it looks like I've got a busy day ahead of me,' Agathe continued. 'When are we looking to do this?'

'We shouldn't leave it too long. Let's source what we need tomorrow, meet up here the day after for a run-through and then we go for it the day after. I'll speak to Danny about monitoring the Clinic's systems to ensure they don't move him before we can,' Max replied.

'That's a Saturday,' Adam pointed out, realising he might miss a Watford home match.

'Even better,' Max replied, 'Lots of visitors to act as a distraction and hopefully less staff around. We had better be making tracks. There's a lot to do before then.'

'Mama, my car is a bit small for all of us. Can I borrow Papa's?' Catherine asked.

'Of course, dear, I'll just fetch the keys,' Agathe replied.

Forty-five minutes later, Catherine dropped them off near Bobby's house in Michael's Range Rover.

'See you on Friday all, and good luck with everything tomorrow. I hope you do well with your trial at Watford, Adam,' Catherine replied.

'It's only their reserve team, but I'm keeping everything crossed, and Dazza is coming as my lucky charm,' he replied, digging Dazza in the ribs.

'Lucky charm?' Bobby challenged. 'More like as your bouncer.'

'Nobody messes with my clients,' Dazza joked, puffing out his chest.

Later that evening, Bobby was lying in bed contemplating the day when Max's phone rang.

Answering it, they hear Catherine say, 'Hi both, sorry to disturb you, but I've just returned from Avery's house. She's a little better than earlier, but her temperature is up slightly. So I've advised her parents to keep an eye on her and let her rest for a few days. If she's no better by the weekend, I said they should take her to their doctor.'

'Thanks for letting us know. Avery did a cracking job today, and I'm sure that lady dying on her wasn't an enjoyable experience,' Max replied. 'Thanks to you as well, Catherine and see you on Friday. Goodnight.'

'Night, Max, night Bobby,' Catherine said and hung up.

'Wednesday is supposed to be humpday when the worst of the week is behind you,' Bobby thought.

'If it makes you feel any better, at least you don't have college again until your first exam next Wednesday,' Max replied.

'Thanks for that. Somehow it really doesn't make me feel even the slightest bit happier. Goodnight, cowboy.'

'Night, buddy and thank you for being a star this week.'

7
THE UPGRADE

Bobby woke up early, slipped on the tracksuit bottoms and t-shirt Adam had given him, and wandered downstairs to find his Mum in the kitchen.

'Morning champ, I'm just making Lily some bananas on toast. Do you want any?' Pat asked.

'Is that with chocolate spread too?' Bobby asked.

'Of course, unless you want the healthier choice with honey,' she said, kissing her son.

'*How is that healthier?*' Max grumbled.

'*It comes from bees, of course, pure and natural,*' Bobby thought, then out loud added, 'I'll go for the honey option, please, Mum.'

'Go and watch telly, and I'll bring it through. Fancy a cuppa with it?'

'Yes, please. I'm trying to cut down on sugar, so can I have..'

'One,' Max jumped in.

'No, make it two sugars, please,' Bobby finished saying. '*Nice try, cowboy.*'

Bobby walked into the living room, where Lily was staring at the television showing her favourite cartoon again. A few minutes later, his Mum walked in carrying two plates balanced on two mugs of tea.

'There you go, champ, one banana on toast with honey and a cup of tea,' she said, passing him a mug with a plate balanced on top. 'Lily, here's your chocolate and banana toast and don't forget your milk.'

Pat picked up the television remote and sat down, sipping her tea. She pressed a button on the remote and switched on the news channel.

'Mum,' Lily wailed.

'Breakfast now, young lady. We need to leave soon.'

'Any chance you could drop me off at Danny's?' Bobby asked.

'I could do later, Bobby, but I need to drop Lily off at school, and Mary next door asked if I could take her to the dentist as Dave had booked to play golf early this morning,' Pat replied.

'Never mind, I'll message Danny and see if he can pick me up, or maybe we can meet in town.'

'Hey Danny, are we still good for today and if so, could you pick me up?' Bobby messaged.

Bobby's phone pinged with a typical Danny reply, 'Bet bro, no problemo, see you in 30.'

Bobby replied, 'Lit, I'll meet you by the supermarket at the end of my road.'

'Over the last few days, I am learning to understand most of what you think and what you and your friends mean, but if there is one thing I still find difficult, it's your language,' Max said.

'Don't get you, Max? We speak English like what the King does,' Bobby added in a fake mocking accent.

'It's all this whip, lit, bet stuff. Well, I understand whip now means a limousine and some other words I can understand from the context. But some of the words seem like a jumble, and trust *me, after two-thousand years, I've become a bit of a polyglot, so words are normally easy for me.'*

'*Bet is, well, a bit like facts or sure thing. And lit is like dope, gotcha or cool. So why is that difficult?'*

'*When you say it so eloquently, I can't possibly imagine why I'm confused. Well, I know sure thing means yes or certainly, so I'm presuming if bet is like sure thing, and so is facts; then Danny said yes to you, asking if you were still meeting him today and if he could pick you up?'*

'*See, cowboy. It's not that hard,*'

'*Gotcha or cool, I know means I understand, or that's great, so you were saying lit means, err, it's great that he's picking you up?'*

'*Nice one, give the man a medal.'*

'*How come you don't have problems understanding anything I say?'*

Bobby laughed, '*Well, I guess you've made me a polyglot understanding multiple languages too. Just I'm better at it.*'

Bobby stood up, leaned over, and gave his Mum a peck on the cheek, 'Thanks Mum, that banana toast was great. I'm just going to go and clean my teeth, and then I'm shooting off. Danny's picking me up from the supermarket. I'll be home for dinner.'

'See you later, champ.'

'Laters shorty, have fun at school,' Bobby shouted to Lily, who was playing a game on her computer tablet.

'Laters stinky, and you cowboy Max,' Lily replied.

Bobby headed towards the stairs but heard his Mum ask, 'Is cowboy Max the game you're playing?'

Lily replied, 'No, he's the old man Bobby was talking to. He makes me laugh but don't tell them that.'

'*See, someone appreciates me,*' Max laughed.

'*I know you said young children can sometimes see you and that they grow out of it. But how does she know your name?'*

'I guess sometimes they can hear us too. But this is a first for me. Oh, by the way, I'm impressed with you. Home for dinner and not tea.'

'Well, I guess you're influencing the way I speak. I'll soon be talking about cricket and jolly hockey sticks with a silver spoon in my mouth, old bean.'

'You do realise I can make you give yourself a slap?'

Fifteen minutes later, Bobby stood outside the supermarket near the disabled parking area as Danny pulled up. He opened the door to get in, but Danny said, 'Do you mind if we go up the precinct first? There's a little tech shop behind the market, and they've rang to say my upgrade has arrived.'

'Upgrade?' Bobby queried.

'Yes, my friend, one day I will be able to use a BCI to control everything I want to, just by thinking about wanting to do it,' Danny replied.

'A BCI?' said Bobby.

'Yeah, a Brain-Computer Interface,' Danny responded with disdain.

'Is that viable given the current state of Earth's technological understanding?' Max challenged.

'Nyes, or is it Yno?' Danny replied, adding, 'In other words, a lot of the technology is there with artificial intelligence, neural profiling, BCIs using EEGs or ECoGs etc., which is the yes part. But making them all work perfectly is still a work-in-progress, which is the no-bit.'

Bobby looked puzzled, 'So it's all theoretical at the moment?'

Danny looked at his friend and shook his head, 'Of course not. Some medical conditions relating to tremors or nerve damage already use BCIs, but it's still minimal.'

'But you are going to try it?' Max asked.

'Heck no, I'm no guinea pig. There's no way I'm wearing a chunky headset or some dumb-looking pair of AI glasses which is the non-invasive way the EEG or electroencephalogram solution. But there is also no way I'm getting things stuck inside my head which is the ECoG electrocorticography way,' Danny replied, shuddering.

'I'm lost,' Bobby said with a blank look.

'To be fair, so am I,' replied Max, 'What exactly is your upgrade.'

'Why am I the only genius around here?' Danny laughed. 'Look, I want to get to the point where I can control things through thought in the same way you walk by subconsciously thinking it, understand?'

'Yeah,' Bobby and Max tried to say simultaneously, resulting in a garbled 'Yyyeaeahh.'

Laughing, Danny said, 'OK, maybe for you guys, even talking isn't the easiest thing to do with your combined minds. So anyway, until we can get away from the insert or stick-on solution, I'm taking the cheaper route using eye control. But I'm debating the better solution, electrooculography or infrared reflection.'

'OK, let's stop at eye control,' Max chuckled, 'I used to think being inside Michael was bad enough with all the medical terms he had, but I've got a headache now.'

'*And to think you thought whips and lit were hard to grasp,*' Bobby thought, '*Imagine if it had been Danny, you had woken up inside!*'

Max shuddered.

'In the meantime, back to the controller,' Danny said as he brought his wheelchair from the boot to the door and climbed into it.

Danny and Bobby left the supermarket car park, crossed the High Street, and headed towards the pedestrian precinct. On the way, Max explained the plan for Saturday, including the need for precise timing for uploading and deleting the patient transfer.

'Sounds easy enough,' replied Danny. 'If we park up facing the ambulance entrance, we can activate the transfer as they enter, and if I give them a trigger device, they can signal as soon as they have Michael, and I can remove it. Then we follow the ambulance out.'

'You make it all sound so simple.' Max said. 'I have lived through the Industrial Revolution and the computer age. Not to mention all my technical and engineering skills from my former planet, and yet in your short life, you can do more than I ever could. So how do you do it when you're....'

'Don't you dare say it,' Danny said aggressively.

'Say what?' Max replied.

'The D-word. I am not disabled. I am abled in different ways.'

'I was going to say, how do you do it when you're so young? You've learnt more in seventeen years than I have in over two millennia.'

'I'll let you off then,' Danny said, punching his friend in the arm. 'and I'm eighteen, not seventeen. My birthday was last September, as the bone head you're body sharing with knows, so there with knobs on.'

They arrived at the aptly named TechTwo shop and entered. They heard a little buzzer going off in the back of the shop and headed towards the counter between the rows of components and gadgets.

'I expect Mr Bowles is in the back. He can take a few minutes to appear if he's concentrating on something,' Danny explained. 'That sensor you heard going off means he'll know we are here.'

Bobby's mind wandered. He had heard Danny mention Mr Bowles before. He had always envisaged him to be a tall, skinny mad scientist wearing a head mirror and at least two pairs of glasses simultaneously.

'It's me, Mr Bowles, Danny. I've come to collect my order,' Danny shouted.

'Danny dear boy, how marvellous to see you,' said Mr Bowles emerging through a doorway to the side of the counter. 'I'm sorry I was engrossed in something.'

'*Well, you were way off the mark,*' Max thought. '*Five feet four at the most and on the comfortable side of normal weight.*'

'*Well, he is at least wearing one pair of glasses, and you must admit that wild wavy grey hair is a bit eccentric,*' chuckled Bobby.

'I couldn't get some of the more expensive and unusual equipment through my usual suppliers. However, I did track everything down and asked them to send it directly to you. They said they should deliver it later today or tomorrow at the latest. But everything else is in here,' Mr Bowles said as he handed Danny a small package the size of a shoe box from behind the counter.

Danny opened the box and peered inside, 'Perfect, Mr Bowles, just add it all to my account.'

'Already done, dear boy. Just settle at the end of the month as normal,' he replied with a wink. 'Have you got a new apprentice?' he added, looking at Bobby.

'No, I'm just a friend,' Bobby replied. 'But it is nice to meet you.'

'You too, young man. Any friend of Danny's is always welcome here. Now I must dash. I think I've left my soldering iron on my desk,' Mr Bowles said, scurrying back through the door he'd come through.

'Is he always like that?' Bobby asked.

'Yep,' Danny replied. 'He's as mad as a box of frogs. He set fire to the shop once. He went out for some fish and chips but left his laser going. Look over there, and you can still see the hole where it burnt through the wall. Despite that, if Mr Bowles can't fix it or find it, nobody can.'

Danny and Bobby left the shop and headed back toward the supermarket.

Danny sighed, 'I hate to say it, but Freddie Fallon is heading in this direction with two of his buddies.'

'Is it too late to go that way instead?' Bobby asked.

'What's the problem?' said Max.

Bobby explained that Freddie was the school thug and had disliked Bobby since primary school. He also pointed out that Freddie behaved like he was better than others because his Dad did an important job, claiming it was top secret. However, since going to college and Bobby becoming friends with Avery and Danny, Freddie's dislike for Bobby has become almost hatred because of his two wealthy friends.

'Well, if it isn't the freak with his little disabled rich playmate,' Freddie sneered.

'What do you want, Freddie? Hiya Tom, alright Paul,' Bobby answered.

Tom and Paul mumbled a greeting as Freddie started walking around Bobby and Danny.

'*This kid is asking for a slap,*' Max said.

'*Not now. Mum always taught me never to provoke a fight and be the better person.*'

'I hear you think you're some sort of rally star,' Freddie said, almost spitting the words in Bobby's face.

'*I'm going to land this thug on his ass,*' Max growled.

'I don't know what you mean,' Bobby lied.

'I hear you tore up the bypass, swerving, doing U-turns, and risking people's lives just because you were chasing someone. That's not nice, Robert,' Freddie snidely continued.

'It's Bobby, and we were the ones being chased,' Bobby replied.

Freddie kicked Danny's wheelchair and, turning to Tom and Paul, said, 'Well, he certainly wasn't involved driving this crate.'

'Oi, don't touch my wheels, buddy,' Danny shouted.

'Or what little rich boy? Will you run home to Daddy and ask him to buy you another? Oh yeah, sorry you can't run, can you,' Freddie laughed at his sick humour.

Max was near breaking point as he said, '*Please let me take him down, Bobby.*'

'*Don't underestimate Danny. Freddie will regret messing with him,*' Bobby replied.

Turning back to Bobby, Freddie said, 'Why would anyone want to chase a sad git like you anyway. My Dad said you were scared stiff during the interview.'

Bobby said, 'Your Da...' then stopped as he realised that Freddie Fallon's father was DI Fallon. 'Your Dad's a copper.'

'Yeah, what of it?' Freddie sneered.

'You always claimed he did a top-secret job,' Danny chipped in.

Freddie paused, caught out, before replying, 'He's on an undercover assignment.'

Danny burst out laughing, 'What with the traffic police? Yeah, sure.'

Tom snickered, which resulted in Freddie turning to look at him with contempt. Freddie composed himself, turned back towards Danny and said, 'Shut it, wheels,' before kicking his wheelchair again.

'Final warning, you will regret it if you touch my wheels one more time,' Danny said surprisingly calmly.

Freddie laughed, 'Here that lads, wheels boy is threatening me. Oh, I'm so scared. What should I do?'

'Push him back towards the precinct Freddie,' Tom said, laughing.

Paul added, 'Yeah, it's downhill, and he'll go flying backwards.'

'Good thinking, lads,' Freddie replied as he turned towards Danny.

Danny looked into Freddie's eyes, 'I wouldn't if I were you.'

Freddie leant forward, putting one hand on either side of the metal armrest supports, 'Or waaaaaaaa....' He screamed as he flew through the air, landing on his back a few feet away with his hair sticking up and sizzling.

Danny laughed, 'Hey, look, it's southern fried Freddie.'

Max looked at Danny with surprise.

'What's the point in sitting in a metal chair with rubber wheels, rubber armrests and a rubber-coated seat if I can't stick the occasional electrical charge through it?' Danny said with a broad grin.

Freddie stood up with smoke gently rising from his hair and looked at Tom and Paul, 'Get them.'

Danny looked at Bobby, 'I think now might be a good time to test my speed module.'

'Stay right there, Danny. Now it's my turn to do some charging,' Max replied.

After just witnessing Freddie going flying, Tom and Paul hesitated.

Freddie raised his voice, 'I said get them, the freak first.'

Tom and Paul looked relieved they didn't have to go near Danny's wheelchair and moved towards Bobby.

Max stood there, slowly moving his gaze from one to the other, 'Now it's my turn to say I wouldn't if I were you.'

Tom and Paul paused, making Freddie scream, 'Now.' He charged forward, grabbing Tom's arm as he passed him, heading towards Bobby. The movement inspired Paul to join the attack just behind them.

Before he reached Bobby, Max had dropped down and swung his leg around, sweeping Freddie's legs from under him. As Freddie crashed to the ground, Tom lunged towards Bobby, but he barely moved before Max grabbed Tom by the shoulders. Next, Max flipped over Tom's head, kicking Paul in the chest as he completed the somersault sending Paul flying backwards.

As Max landed, he spun around and crouched, grabbing Tom by the ankles and flipping him forward, making him land face down on the floor.

Feeling satisfied with his work, Max stood up and moved back beside Danny, saying, 'Danny one, Max three, I reckon.'

Freddie, Paul, and Tom slowly stood up, bruised and battered. They looked at each other and ran off away from Bobby and Danny.

Danny shouted after them, 'Freddie, just remember I'm a differently abled rich playmate, not a disabled one.' Then looking up at Bobby, he asked, 'What just happened?'

Max replied, 'I did a few martial arts moves on them. Did you like the somersault move?'

'Well, it was impressive, but how did you move so fast?' Danny asked, 'It was like watching a kung-fu movie on fast forward.'

'It felt like normal to me. Although now you come to mention it, they seemed a bit slow,' Max replied.

'It was incredibly fast. One minute Freddie was shouting now, and within seconds they were all on the floor, and you were standing by my side saying one three,' Danny said.

'I don't understand. I know I can optimise the human body beyond what you humans do with it, but that normally needs training.'

'Well, I can guarantee if there is one thing Bobby doesn't do, and that's training,' Danny laughed.

'I am here, and I'll have you know I went for a run with Adam on Monday,' Bobby protested.

'And how far did you go?' Danny enquired.

'That's not the point,' Boby replied. 'Anyway, Max, could your alien powers be making you so quick?'

'Well, I know I can fight quickly. After all, I've had quite a few years of practice, but not this quickly in a new host,' Max replied, 'I'm confused.'

'It looks like I'm not the only one getting upgraded,' Danny laughed, patting the box on his lap.

Bobby and Danny returned to the supermarket car park and headed for Danny's home. The route took them past Avery's family home.

'Should we call in and see how she's doing?' Danny asked.

Bobby noticed Abi's battered yellow Fiat 500 on the drive and said, 'Yeah, come on.'

Danny parked up, and they headed to the front door. They rang the doorbell, and Avery's voice said over the intercom, 'Hey guys, lovely to see you. I'll be there in a sec.'

The door opened, and Avery greeted them with a smile. She bent forward, hugged Danny, turned to Bobby, threw her arms around him, and kissed him, 'Hey, babe.'

'Well, someone is pleased to see you,' Abi laughed from behind Avery. 'Hey Danny, hiya Bobby.'

Danny and Bobby returned greetings, and they went through to the kitchen. Avery got them both drinks, and they went out onto the patio.

The friends chatted and chilled in the early summer sun for a while.

'How are you doing?' Bobby asked.

'Yeah, I'm great now,' Avery replied, 'I feel like a new person. That woman dying was a surprise, but we all must go some time.'

Bobby exchanged a glance with Abi.

'*Is it me, or is Avery remarkably upbeat?*' Max asked.

'*I thought that, but I guess it's maybe a reaction to the shock,*'

'*Shock can make people behave strangely.*'

'*You seem to have a soft spot for Avery,*' Bobby teased.

'*She reminds me of the first human I partnered with on Earth.*'

'*Oh wow, Max has a crush.*'

'*Whatevs,*' Max replied.

'*Now, who's getting down with it,*' Bobby laughed.

Danny interrupted Bobby and Max's thoughts, saying, 'Why don't we go back to mine? It's a lovely warm day, and our pool and jacuzzi are calling.'

Abi replied, 'Yeah, that sounds great.'

Avery sighed, 'You guys go if you want, but I'm OK here. What about you, babe?'

'I'm easy,' Bobby replied.

Danny laughed, 'So I've heard, buddy.'

Abi joined in, saying, 'Oh, the rumours spread so fast.'

Avery jumped to Max's defence, saying, 'Come on guys, you're better than that.'

Danny, Abi, and Bobby looked at each other.

'We need to shoot Danny. You need to be home for that delivery,' Bobby said.

'Heck, yeah, I need those components,' Danny replied.

They got up and headed towards the door, leaving their empty glasses in the kitchen.

'What time Saturday are you meeting to rescue Michael?' Avery asked.

'We're aiming for....' Bobby started to say before Max replied, 'Noon.'

'*We said eleven*,' Bobby thought.

'*And we are going for eleven, but something feels wrong here*,' Max replied.

Avery said goodbye to Abi and Danny but grabbed Bobby's arm, 'Sorry, Bobby, I hope you don't feel weird, but I just realised that I think I'm falling in love with Max,' she said, kissing him on the lips. 'I think it's because he's so mature and kind.'

'I think you're a wonderful person, too,' Max replied, smiling.

'*What happened to it feels wrong*?' Bobby said.

'I've got to go, but I'll message you later,' Max replied.

'OK, babe, have a nice time at Danny's,' Avery replied as Bobby walked to Danny's car.

At Danny's home, they grabbed some drinks and headed out to the pool, spending the rest of the afternoon chilling by the swimming pool and jacuzzi. At one point, the doorbell rang. It was a delivery man with several large packages. Danny had the parcels put in his garage workshop and thanked the delivery driver with a tip. When he returned to the pool, Bobby, Max, and Abi were discussing Avery.

'She was so upset when I first got to her house. She barely touched the meal her Mum cooked for us, and we were in bed by nine,' Abi said.

'So she only cheered up this morning, then?' Bobby asked.

'No, she was down all day until about an hour or so before you arrived. She'd gone for a nap, and when she woke up, it was like the dark cloud had lifted from her,' Abi replied.

'They say trauma can make you behave strangely,' Max said, 'I think we just underestimated just how traumatic it was seeing that poor lady dying.'

Bobby's phone pinged, 'Hey, champ are you still home for tea?'

'Oh, heck, I forgot I told Mum I'd be home for tea,' Bobby said, panicking.

'I can drop you off if you want?' Abi offered, 'I need to go soon anyway.'

Bobby accepted Abi's offer, and before long, they were heading back to Haywood whilst Danny went off to his workshop.

'Does Danny ever stop inventing things?' Abi laughed as they were pulling into Hinton Close.

'I hope not,' Bobby replied, chuckling, 'I think one day he'll find a cure for everything.'

'I'd bet on that too. Do you need Avery or me tomorrow or Saturday?'

Bobby shook his head, 'No, it's fine. I think the fewer of us involved, the better.'

Max butted in, 'Maybe you could keep an eye on Avery instead. I'm a bit worried about her.'

'Yes, of course I will, Max. Good luck, guys. I look forward to meeting Michael,' Abi said as she drove off.

After finishing his dinner, Bobby announced he was going to Adam's to see how he got on with his football trial. A few minutes later, he was walking into Adam's home.

'Well, come on, how did you get on?' Bobby asked Adam excitedly.

'I scored the winning goal, and they seem to like me.'

'Oh, stop teasing. Did they offer you a contract?'

'Well, the money isn't great, but there are appearance bonuses, and yes, they've offered me a one-year development contract with a first-refusal renewal clause,' Adam replied with a massive grin.

Bobby lunged forward, hugging Adam, 'That's fantastic news, Adam. I'm so pleased for you.' He pulled back slightly, looking into Adam's eyes and then down to his lips, and then he leaned forward and kissed his friend.

'Err, thanks,' Adam said stiffly.

Bobby released his hug and stood back.

'Evening Bob,' Dazza said, walking into the living room. 'Has Adam told you his good news?'

Bobby blushed, 'Yeah, he just told me.'

'We've ordered a takeaway to celebrate, but there's plenty to share if you want to stop,' Dazza said cheerily.

Bobby looked at Adam, standing still and not saying anything, 'Uh, no, it's OK. I've just eaten and only popped in to see how the trial went. So I'll leave you guys to it.'

The atmosphere in the room was decidedly chilly as Bobby headed towards the front door.

'What time shall we come to yours tomorrow morning, Bob?' Dazza asked.

Bobby turned, holding back his tears, 'Oh, whenever.' He slammed the door behind him and started running home.

Dazza looked from the door to Adam and back to the door, 'Did you guys have an argument or something?'

'No, it's all fine. Maybe he's just tired,' Adam sighed.

Dazza looked at Adam. They had known each other since they were babies, and he knew when Adam was lying, 'Well, if you need to talk, I'm always here for you, pal.'

'Hey, chill bro, that food is on the way, so how about I thrash you at football?' Adam said with a weak smile and waving a game controller.

At Hinton Close, the front door flew open and slammed shut. Bobby shouted, 'Night,' as he ran upstairs and slammed his bedroom door.

Pat looked towards the stairs. She hadn't spent the last almost eighteen years as a mother without knowing when her son was upset or when he needed space. Yet, despite this, it still made her sad and helpless, knowing he was suffering.

8
PLAN AND EXECUTE

Pat knocked on her son's door and peeked inside. 'Morning Bobby, fancy a cuppa?'

'Thanks, Mum, yes, please,' Bobby replied.

Pat walked in and placed a cup of tea by Bobby's bed, 'Forget the diet; I've put three sugars in.'

'Mum, can I ask you something?'

'You can ask me for the moon, and I'd give it to you if I could.'

'But you'll hate me.'

Pat looked at her son in a way only a parent can look, 'Bobby, whatever you may have done, you could never make me hate you.'

'It's Adam.'

'What about him? What has he done to you?'

'Oh heck, no, nothing. It's not him. It's me.'

'What do you mean?'

'I love him, I'm sorry, I'm so sorry, I know it's wrong, but....'

Pat grabbed her son in a vice-like grip, 'Don't you dare ever say sorry, son. We love whom we love. How does he feel?'

'I thought he felt the same, but I kissed him last night, and he was so cold. Oh, Mum, I'm so scared I've lost him, even as a friend. I just well...' Bobby said as tears ran down his face, his emotions raw.

'Oh, Bobby. You've been friends with Adam for so long. Maybe he was just shocked. If you think he felt the same, then maybe he needs time to think about it,'

'*You humans are awful about your emotions, Bobby. Your Mum is right,*' Max said.

'Do you want to know what I think?' Pat said.

Bobby nodded.

Pat looked at her son, she loved him so much, but her heart was breaking seeing him like this, 'I think a bacon sandwich, a shower and a shave will make things a bit better, but maybe not in that order.'

'Yeah, I guess a bacon sandwich in the shower might be a bit soggy,' Bobby said half-heartedly.

'That's my champ.'

Twenty minutes later, Bobby was downstairs wearing clean jeans and a sweatshirt, freshly washed and shaved, tucking into a bacon sandwich.

Lily was watching the television, but she turned to her brother and smiled, 'Love you, Bobby. But you're still stinky, though.'

Bobby looked at his sister, realising even she had noticed that he was feeling down. 'Well, you're not so sweet either, shorty,' he said, smiling back.

Bobby felt so down, but he realised they needed to sort out the Michael situation. So he texted Dazza, 'Ready when you are.'

'On the way,' Dazza replied.

A few minutes later, there was a knock at the door. Bobby opened it to see Dazza and Adam. 'Hi,' Bobby said as he grabbed his coat. He shouted back to his Mum and Lily that he loved them and would see them tomorrow, as he was staying at Danny's house.

The underground ride to Earls Court and the short walk to Glenthorne Crescent passed in relative silence. Several times Adam tried to start a conversation with Bobby only to be met with silence or a one-word reply. In the end, Adam and Dazza began talking to each other about the previous day's events at the football ground.

'*You need to talk to him,*' Max said.

'*How can I? You saw the way he reacted when I kissed him. I've ruined everything,*' Bobby replied.

'*I saw a young man in shock when one of his best friends unexpectedly gave him a kiss.*'

'*But he didn't respond or say anything.*'

'*You didn't give him much opportunity. You were out of that door like an Olympic sprinter.*'

'*Whatevs.*'

Danny, Agathe and Catherine were already in the lounge when Bobby, Adam and Dazza arrived. A few minutes later, Max was discussing the plan.

'So park up in one of the ambulance bays, and as Danny and I watch you go through the ambulance entrance, Danny will send the patient transfer details,' Max said. 'Catherine, you go to the reception desk to say you are there for the patient transfer. As soon as reception confirms it and tells you where to go, you press the trigger button on that little device Danny gave you, and we will cancel the transfer to avoid raising any alarm.'

Danny said, 'If you need the details to appear again at any time, double-click it, OK?

Catherine nodded, 'This is my area of expertise now. Adam, as you've been there before, you lead the way pulling the trolley behind you and Dazza, you push it. I'll follow behind, looking for anyone acting suspicious.'

'You mean apart from us?' Dazza laughed.

'Yes, apart from us, Dazza,' Catherine replied. 'Once in the room, I'll check Papa's vitals, and if he is stable, we can transfer him onto the trolley. Getting him out of there before worrying about any medication will be best. So if they have him hooked up to any drips, we will need to take them with us and deactivate any machines he is wired to. We can't afford to have any alarms going off.'

'Then it's back down in the lift and get him into the ambulance,' Adam said. 'Who is driving?'

'Who's the better driver?' Max replied.

'I am,' Dazza and Adam replied in unison.

'I think we will let them both have a test drive in the ambulance,' Agathe said. 'Kurt promised to drop it off sometime around lunchtime, and he said we can keep it over the weekend as it's due to go for refurbishment on Monday, so it's officially out of action.'

'Perfect, Agathe. How did you get on with the uniforms?' Max asked.

'I've left them in Michael's study for the boys to go and try on.'

'Let's go and give them a fashion show, buddy,' Dazza laughed as he and Adam headed towards the study.

A few minutes later and they were parading around the Drawing Room. 'Here we have that world-famous fashion model Darius Turner proudly turned out in this year's hottest combination of yellow and green,' Dazza said, laughing.

'Haven't you forgotten me?' Adam laughed.

'Oh yes, let's not forget our range for short people as modelled by that, not world-famous model Adam Lee,' Dazza replied.

'Very fetching guys,' Catherine said. 'I could almost believe you were real, even if Dazza is possibly the tallest paramedic I've ever seen. How did you manage to get them, Mama? They look brand new.'

'Mr Winsel, the procurement man at the hospital your Papa mainly worked at. He's always had a soft spot for me, and as soon as I said I was hosting a fancy dress event, he was happy to lend me them,' Agathe replied.

Adam and Dazza went off to get changed as the doorbell sounded.

Agathe stood and said, 'That'll be Kurt with the ambulance. He said he'd show the boys how to drive it.'

A few minutes later, Adam, Dazza, Catherine and Agathe were outside as Kurt showed them the various ambulance controls. He then got Dazza in the driver's seat as the five of them went for a drive. When they returned, they came into the Drawing Room excitedly.

'What's the verdict then?' Max asked.

'Dazza is driving,' Catherine replied.

'That steering is so heavy it was an unfair contest given his size,' Adam protested.

'Don't worry, pal, maybe one day when you're all grown up,' Dazza chuckled as Adam punched him in the arm.

'I think we are all set then,' Max replied, 'Let's head home and get back here in the morning for around ten. Getting to the Clinic for eleven should ensure plenty of visitors to keep the reduced weekend staff busy.'

'You are all welcome to stay if you want to. After all, it seems a shame to go all that way home just to come back again in the morning,' Agathe replied. 'Plus, I've made my Mama's beef pepperpot, and there's plenty to go around.'

'What's that?' Dazza asked, his ears pricking up at the sound of food.

'It's a thick and rich beef stew,' Max replied. 'Does it come with your cornmeal dumplings?'

'As if I would ever serve it without them,' Agathe laughed. 'Catherine, why don't you show Adam and Dazza to the spare bedrooms upstairs and Max, you and Danny can use your two bedrooms in your basement.'

The rest of the evening went by with laughter, some hearty food and Max regaling them with some of his exploits over his two thousand years on Earth.

The following day, Agathe was cooking breakfast with Catherine, Danny, and Bobby, drinking tea, when Dazza and Adam wandered in.

Dazza sniffed the air, 'Something smells good.'

'Do you ever think about anything else but food?' Danny laughed.

'Occasionally, but when I do, it makes me hungry,' Dazza replied.

Catherine interrupted the exchange by offering Dazza and Adam a drink before pouring a cup of tea for Dazza and handing a bottle of water to Adam.

After devouring the full English breakfast that Agathe had prepared, they went up to the Drawing Room to go through the plan again.

Bobby's, Danny's, Adam's, and Dazza's phones pinged, 'Good luck, guys. Tell Catherine and Agathe that Avery and I are thinking about you today.'

'Thanks, both. We are setting off in about 15 minutes,' Dazza replied on the group chat.

'*The Pick'n'Mix? What sort of group name is that*?' Max asked.

'*Can't you tell it's a Dannyism? Well, with a dash of Dazza added*,' Bobby replied.

'Talking of setting off, you guys go and get changed, and Max and I will head off to the Clinic,' Danny said. 'See you there, and good luck.'

Danny pulled up at the Clinic and positioned his car so they could watch the ambulance entrance.

'Looks fairly quiet from this end,' Danny said.

'I guess not many private patients are admitted at the weekend?' Max replied, 'The main entrance looked busy as we passed, which is what I was hoping for.'

Bobby handed Danny his laptop, which he opened and started logging in, 'Right, let's make sure he is still in the same room. M Thomas room W104. Yep still there. Now I need to set up the transfer details so they are ready to upload. Catherine said to do it to the Royal Free Hospital, didn't she?'

Max replied, 'Yes, it's far enough away to give us forty minutes just in case they track the transfer. But, of course, by the time we don't turn up there, it'll all be too late....'

Max paused and nudged Danny, 'Why is Freddie Fallon here?'

Danny looked up, 'Where?'

'Over there, look just past the entrance,' Bobby replied.

'I don't know, but he is walking away. Did he come out of the hospital? Perhaps he was visiting someone,' Danny said.

'I'm not sure I was watching you and glanced up, but he was already past the entrance heading away,' Bobby replied.

'Well, he either didn't see us, or he's not interested in us since he's heading towards those art studios and the main road. Perhaps he is just using the land and car park as a cut-through,' Danny added before returning to his laptop.

'As long as he doesn't come back. Today is too important for him to mess up,' Max added.

Just as Danny finished getting everything ready, Dazza pulled up in the borrowed ambulance. Adam and Dazza got out and opened the back door. They helped Catherine out and then unloaded the patient trolley. Looking around, Catherine spotted Danny and Bobby and just nodded briefly in their direction. Catherine walked into the Clinic with an air of authority, followed by Adam at the front of the trolley and Dazza behind.

'Adam may be average height, but Dazza makes him look tiny. It's like looking at a comedy routine on the telly,' Danny chuckled.

'Hmm,' Bobby replied.

'OK, it's showtime,' Danny replied, hitting the upload button on his computer.

Inside, Catherine approached the medical desk, 'I've come to do a patient transfer, Mr Michael Thomas.'

The nurse behind the desk looked up and said, 'OK, just give me a second it's all a bit crazy here today,' as she rushed off.

Catherine waited for what seemed like an eternity but was really just over two minutes.

The nurse came back. 'Sorry, love, what name did you say?'

Catherine made a show of looking down at the fake patient transfer form on her clipboard, 'Michael, no, sorry, my mistake, it's Maxwell Thomas.'

'Where's he supposed to be going, love,' the nurse replied.

Again for effect, Catherine looked down, 'It says here the Royal Free.'

'Oh, yes, that all ties up with on here. If you wait there, love, I'll get someone to take you up,' the nurse replied.

'Oh, there's no need for that. Just point me in the direction, and we can make our way there,' Catherine said.

'Not in the Oliver Clinic, you can't love. Apart from the visitor routes, all other doors and the medical lifts are card operated,' the nurse replied.

Catherine glanced at Dazza and Adam and rolled her eyes.

Outside, Max sighed, 'They are taking a long time. I hope everything is OK.'

Danny looked at Bobby, 'Talking of OK. What gives, bro?'

'About what?' Bobby replied.

'You and Adam. You've always been as thick as thieves, but yesterday and this morning, you could cut the atmosphere between the two of you with a knife,' Danny said.

'It's difficult,' Bobby replied.

'He told you how he felt about you, didn't he?' Danny said.

Inside, the nurse reappeared with a familiar face behind her, 'Nurse Willis will take you through.'

Adam moved back to Dazza, simultaneously pulling his cap down over his eyes, 'Hey, big man, take the front.'

'Why, what's up?' Dazza asked a bit too loudly for Adam's liking.

'Keep your voice down. That's the nurse who Avery and I saw on Wednesday. We can't let him see me,' Adam whispered.

Dazza stepped forward, trying to put his whole body between Adam and Nurse Willis.

Nurse Willis smiled at Catherine, 'This way,' he said, tapping his card against a reader and opening the door into a corridor.

Outside, Bobby went to ask Danny what he meant about how Adam felt when there was a tap on the driver's window.

Danny turned to see a police warrant card and lowered the window.

'Excuse me, sir, is this your car?' the police officer asked.

'Sort of,' Danny replied.

'What does that mean?'

'Well, it's given to me by the government,' Danny answered obtusely.

'So it's a company car then, sir?'

'Nope,' Danny replied with a smile.

'Looks like we've got a comedian here, Carter. Would you step out of the car, please, sir?'

Danny's phone buzzed once, meaning Catherine had pressed the buzzer on her device. Danny went to press a button on his laptop when the officer opened the driver's door, 'Do not touch your devices, sir. I've asked you nicely, but now I must insist you step out of the car under section 163 of the road traffic act 1988.'

Danny looked at the police officer, 'Well now, officer, sorry, what was your name?'

'Detective Inspector Fallon, sir.'

'Well, now, Detective Inspector Fallon, I'd be thrilled to step out of the car if you could have a word with the big man upstairs and ask him to make me able to walk again,' Danny stated, thumping his leg.

Bobby opened the door, and DS Carter shouted, 'Get back in the car now.'

Bobby ignored him and got out, turning to face them and saw DS Carter pointing a yellow device at him and shouting, 'Police! Stop, or I will use my Taser. Put your hands up, now.'

Bobby raised his hands, 'DI Fallon, DS Carter, it's me, Bobby Morris. Don't you remember me?'

DI Fallon stretched out his hand and pushed Carter's Taser down, 'Well, I never, if it isn't Haywood's budding Max Verstappen.'

'Considering how he drove, I'd say he's more a rally driver than a formula one driver personally,' Danny interjected.

Fallon glanced down at Danny, 'You really need to learn not to let your mouth run away with you, sir.'

Inside, Nurse Willis said, 'Rooms W101 to 104 are down this way. What was the name of the patient you're collecting?'

Catherine did her routine with the clipboard again, 'Maxwell Thomas.'

'Oh, he was in this room,' Willis said, opening the door to room W104. 'Such a lovely man, and apparently, he was a doctor too.'

Catherine looked inside to see an empty room, 'Which room have they moved him to?'

'He's no longer in the hospital. Mr Mueller discharged him this morning. Mr Thomas woke from his coma on Thursday morning, and by this morning, the doctor said he was fit to be discharged as an outpatient.' Willis replied. 'You seem to have been sent on a wasted errand.'

'What time did this happen?' Catherine asked, trying to mask her emotions.

Willis lifted his computer tablet and tapped away, 'According to our records, he was scheduled for your transfer at 10:56 this morning, and Mr Mueller discharged him only a minute or two later. That's such unfortunate timing for you.'

'And he was definitely discharged?' Catherine challenged.

The nurse turned his tablet to show Catherine, 'Yes, look, there's his signature at the bottom of the patient release form.'

Catherine recognised her father's signature on the digital copy of the form. 'But it's only ten past eleven, fourteen minutes ago.'

'Yes, that's right. Funnily enough, I passed Mr Thomas heading towards the taxi rank as I arrived to start my shift at eleven. He seemed very happy,' Willis replied. 'Is there anything else I can do for you, or shall I take you back to the ambulance area?'

'Oh, perhaps you could take me to the taxi rank. He might still be there,' Catherine replied.

'No, I'm afraid he'll be long gone. There were several taxis there, and nobody was queueing. Now if you could follow me, please, because I need to get on,' Willis said firmly.

'I don't suppose I could see Mr Mueller?' Catherine asked.

'I'm sure they can make an appointment if you contact his secretary. Now please, this way,' Willis snarled.

Outside, Danny went to say another wisecrack but changed his mind saying, 'So how can we help you, officers?'

'We have had reports of a person or persons acting suspiciously outside the hospital,' Carter said.

'We didn't see anyone did we, Bobby?' Danny replied.

'I think they were talking about you, sir,' Fallon said, looking at Danny. 'Would you mind explaining why you are outside this hospital?'

'Well, I thought I'd check out some private clinics which might be running tests for people with special abilities like me,' Danny said with an earnest look.

From the corner of his eye, Bobby saw Adam, Dazza and Catherine coming out of the hospital with an empty patient trolley.

'Do you not think it might be easier to check them out by going through the main entrance and talking to the staff?

Rather than looking at the patient entrance,' Carter asked, looking towards the medical staff getting into an ambulance.

'I always like to do the unexpected,' Danny replied. 'Keep on messing, keeps them guessing, is my motto.'

The ambulance drove off.

Fallon looked unimpressed by Danny's attempt at humour, 'You've still not explained whose car this is, sir.'

'Why didn't you ask that in the first place? I'd have told you,' Danny smiled. 'It's my mobility car. You know, the one you're entitled to if you are on certain benefits.'

'Thank you, sir. See, that wasn't difficult now, and you could have saved us a lot of time if you had said that in the first place,' Fallon sighed.

'I would have done it if you had asked me that initially. But, instead, I presumed you wanted to play a guessing game to see if you could work out whose car it was,' Danny replied, smiling.

'We should just arrest them for wasting police time,' Carter said before his phone rang, stopping any further comment. He answered his phone and walked off. Then, after a brief conversation, he returned and whispered something to DI Fallon.

'It seems that the hospital has called back to say the situation has been contained, and the persons have now left,' Fallon said. 'Given the circumstances, I'm minded to let you both go.'

'That's very kind of you, considering we haven't done anything wrong,' Danny replied.

Fallon crouched down so he was in line with Danny, 'You need to be very careful, sir. That mouth of yours will get you into a lot of trouble if you do not learn to control it.'

'Yes sir, sorry sir, thank you, sir,' Danny replied with more than a bit of sarcasm.

Bobby got back into the car and closed his door. He leant over towards the driver's side of the car and said, 'Thank you, DI Fallon. We appreciate your and DS Carter's time.' At the same time, jabbing Danny in the ribs to make him shut up.

'Just get on your way,' Fallon said, adding, 'I don't want to see you around here again.'

'What? You mean I'm not allowed to park in a public place? Am I allowed to drive down this public highw—Ow,' Danny said.

'Will you shut up and drive off before we spend the rest of the day at His Majesty's pleasure,' Max hissed, digging Danny in the ribs for a second time.

'Well, as long as someone is having pleasure,' Danny replied.

'I suggest you take your friend's advice before this escalates,' Fallon added.

Danny opened his mouth, but Max said, 'No! Shut up and drive. We need to get back.'

'I was only going to thank the kind officers for their interest,' Danny giggled as he pulled away.

'We need to get back to Catherine's to find out what has gone wrong. I don't know if you noticed, but they loaded an empty trolley into the ambulance,' Max replied.

'Yes, I saw that. Did you notice Carter clocked them getting into the ambulance too?' Danny said.

Across London, a phone rang. Answering the call, the recipient heard a voice say, 'Thank you for the timely information. We have been able to relocate the package. Is your situation secure?'

'Yes, it seems fully secure and accepted,' the person replied.

'You need to confirm the reaction and the possible next steps. J will be with us in a week or so and has said that everything needs to progress quickly on arrival.'

'Understood. I will start making enquiries and feedback on my findings,' the person replied before hanging up.

Max said in Danny's car, 'I'm still confused about why two detectives are involved?'

'Involved in what? Buddy,' Danny asked.

'Everything. First of all, why would they be carrying out statement gathering for a driving incident and then why were they here following up on a minor suspicious person report?' Max continued.

'Well, you did say the woman chasing you on your driving test was a diplomat.'

'That could explain them being involved in that incident, but why were Carter and Fallon here for a suspicious person? Also, the fact Freddie had walked past a few minutes earlier is too coincidental,' Max mused.

At Glenthorne Crescent, Catherine angrily stormed around the Drawing Room as Danny and Bobby entered.

'What happened?' Max asked.

'It's all my fault,' Catherine said in frustration.

'What do you mean? How could it be your fault?' Max replied.

Adam said, 'She accidentally said we were there for Michael Thomas when we first went in, and she thinks that tipped them off.'

'It must have done. You know the timeline. The five minutes that one nurse took to fetch Nurse Willis coincides with the period when they discharged Papa,' Catherine replied.

'I think it's clear they moved him rather than discharged him,' Agathe said. 'If Michael had been discharged, he'd have come straight home.'

'Your Mum is right,' Dazza added. 'That Nurse Willis looked well dodge, and did you notice how agitated he got when you kept pushing, Catherine?'

'Catherine, there was a catalogue of events that just don't make sense. For example, the police stopped us from cancelling the patient transfer when you pressed the trigger,' Max said, 'or at least they kept us busy so we couldn't cancel it.'

'And why were the police and Freddie even there?' Bobby added.

Max, Bobby, and Danny explained what had happened outside the Clinic, and then Catherine, Dazza and Adam went through the events inside.

'What are they after?' Bobby asked.

'That's what I don't understand,' Max replied. 'If they want me, they could have taken me when I went to give a statement after the driving lesson and again today outside the Clinic.'

'But why are they keeping my Michael?' Agathe asked.

'And where are they keeping him, too,' Max added.

'*You're worried, aren't you,*' Bobby thought.

'*I'm confused more than anything. Aside from that waitress, I've seen no signs of other Deceptors or Shadowers. But this is not the work of someone acting alone. I don't want to worry them.*'

'Danny, have you got any ideas?' Max asked.

Danny looked up from his laptop, 'I've been thinking about it. If I could get into the police or emergency services network, I might be able to find out why your police friends were involved.'

'They're no flipping friends of mine,' Bobby said.

'As for Michael. What's the best way to quickly smuggle someone out of a hospital?' Danny asked.

Everyone looked from one person to another before Adam said, 'In disguise?'

'Well done, Adam,' Danny replied.

'Wow, I was right, so how did they do it?' Adam said.

'No, you are wrong. I said well done because you at least managed to think of something,' Danny laughed. 'The best way to smuggle someone out in a hurry is not to move them out but keep them there until the fuss has died down.'

'You think he's still there?' Catherine asked.

'I don't know,' Danny replied, 'but I reckon he was whilst we were there.'

'Nice theory, buddy, but how can we prove it?' Adam asked.

'The Clinic's CCTV should help with that,' Danny said.

'But how can we get access to that?' Catherine asked.

Danny looked at Catherine and said, 'You need to ask?'

9
LOVE IN THE AIR

A while later, 'How did it go?' flashed up on the Pick'n'Mix group chat from Abi.

'Awful,' Bobby replied.

'What happened? Didn't you get Michael?' Avery said.

'Probably be easier if we call. Are you both together?' Bobby said.

Abi replied with a simple 'Yes.'

'I'll call them on my phone and stream it to the TV,' Danny said.

Agathe excused herself, saying she would go and get some refreshments whilst they were briefing Abi and Avery. A few seconds later, Abi and Avery appeared on the television.

'Hi there, can you see us all?' Danny asked, moving his phone around to try and get everyone in the shot.

'Hi Danny, yeah, it's fine. We can see Bobby, Dazza, Catherine, Adam, and you,' Abi replied. 'So what happened?'

Over the next twenty minutes, they briefed Abi and Avery about what happened at the Clinic.

'But why was Freddie there?' Abi asked.

'That is anyone's guess,' Bobby replied.

Danny sat back and mused, 'Guys, run with me on this, but what if Freddie's Dad sent him down there to see where we were?'

'Why would he do that? They had the call that we were outside, so they only had to walk down, see us, and have the conversation they did have,' Bobby replied.

'But we had only just arrived when Freddie went past. I was still completing the hospital transfer form, so a minute or two at the most after we parked up,' Danny continued.

'So the police didn't have enough time to receive the call, get to the Clinic and send Freddie to check us out. So that isn't what happened,' Max replied.

'Hang on, Max. Danny might be on to something,' Abi said as Avery turned to look at her. 'You said the police told you they had received a call about someone acting suspiciously outside the hospital, right?'

'Yeah, that's right,' Max replied.

'So, how long after you parked up did Catherine and the guys go into the hospital?' Abi continued.

'Freddie had just gone out of sight when the ambulance arrived. So maybe a minute or so,' Max answered.

'Catherine, how long were you inside before you activated the buzzer to remove the transfer details?' Abi persisted.

Catherine paused momentarily, then said, 'I think I see where you are going with this. We waited two minutes for the nurse. It felt like forever, but I kept looking at my watch, so it couldn't have been more than three minutes between entering and pushing that buzzer device.'

'Don't forget the nurse disappeared again to get Nurse Willis, so that was maybe one more minute,' Adam added.

Abi had been scribbling as Catherine, Max, and Adam were talking. Those sitting in Glenthorne Crescent watched the television as Avery and Abi had a heated debate about what Abi had written down.

Avery said, 'That's wrong. You must add that time, so the real-time is higher.'

'It's not wrong. Remember, Bobby and Danny, were already talking to the police when Catherine pressed the buzzer. So guys, how long had the police been there when the buzzer went off?' Abi asked.

'About three of Danny's sarcastic answers,' Bobby said.

Danny turned towards Bobby, 'Moi sarcastic? How very dare you.'

'Come on, guys, this is serious,' Catherine said.

'A minute or maybe a little more,' Max answered.

Abi looked down, scribbled something, and said, 'So the gap between your parking to Freddie passing and I'm being conservative is, say, two minutes. Another minute for Catherine to arrive makes three minutes. It's another three minutes waiting to be seen and another minute for Nurse Willit to arrive and Catherine to press the buzzer, so that's now seven minutes.'

'Nurse Willis not Willit,' Adam corrected her.

Abi dismissed the interruption and said, 'OK, Willis, Willit, whatever. We are at seven minutes, but the police were already talking to Bobby and Danny—'

'And Max,' Avery said, breaking her friend's train of thought again.

'Look, will everyone just stop interrupting for a second,' Abi said, getting irate. 'We are at seven minutes, but we lose a minute because the police had already arrived and were talking to you when the buzzer went off. Which means there are just six minutes between Danny parking outside the hospital and the police arriving.'

Avery shook her head, 'No, you need to add that minute, so you're at eight minutes.'

Abi looked at Avery, paused, and said, 'No, that's the wrong way round. You have to subtract it as it's an overlap of events.'

'Excuse me, but I'm the one doing A-Level mathematics, thank you,' Avery replied.

'Well, you'd better do some more revision because you are wrong,' Abi spat back.

Catherine raised her voice to interrupt the argument brewing at Abi and Avery's end of the call, 'Both of you, let's not get bogged down too much. What you are saying, Abi, is that somewhere between six and eight minutes elapsed between when Danny parked and the police arrived, right?'

'Yes, that's right, and it is six minutes,' Abi replied, glowering at Avery.

'So what's the point,' Dazza asked.

'The point, Dazza, is that let's assume they were at the nearest Police Station. How far away is it from the Clinic?' Abi continued.

'Thirteen minutes if you walk and seven minutes by car, according to Maps,' Danny shouted, adding, 'Hey, hang on, Bobby. Do you remember seeing Fallon and Carter get out of a car?'

Bobby sat back, thinking, then replied, 'Nope, they just appeared from nowhere. Did you see where they went as we pulled away?'

'I did look in my mirrors, but they stood there watching us until we turned the corner,' Danny replied.

'Let's be kind and assume they did have a car and were at the nearest Police Station for some reason. How can they make a seven-minute journey when you only parked six minutes earlier?' Abi asked.

'Eight minutes,' Avery said.

'Six!' Abi snapped.

Max jumped in, saying, 'Either way, that seven-minute journey is the time from point to point. It doesn't include the time to get in the car, pull onto the road, park at our end, and walk up to the car.'

'They would have had to have been sitting in the car as the Clinic called in and left immediately to investigate, and even then, it's cutting it fine,' Adam said.

'The timing is just too precise. How did Fallon know we would be there exactly at that time?' Max said, scratching Bobby's head.

Agathe said, 'There's some food and drink on the table. I didn't want to interrupt whilst you were talking. You realise there is another explanation for what you've just been discussing?'

Avery looked at Abi, who shrugged her shoulders, 'Guys, we didn't hear that.'

'In a second,' Max shouted, adding, 'Agathe, what do you mean?'

Agathe sighed, walked over to a sofa, and sat beside Dazza, 'I don't know how, but what if they knew you were coming?'

'You mean we were set up?' Catherine said.

'Set up, spied upon or else someone here let slip about our plans,' Agathe replied.

'There is a fourth option,' Avery said. 'It could just be they were driving nearby and were the closest police car to the Clinic as the call came in. Surely that's more likely than some cloak and dagger thing?'

'If it had been any other Police Officer, that is the most plausible answer, Avery. But the fact that it was Fallon and Carter triggers every red flag I can think of,' Max replied. 'I think Agathe is right.'

'Do you want me to get RF detectors to check the house and cars for listening devices?' Danny asked.

'Good idea Danny,' Max replied.

'Freddie has appeared twice now when we didn't want him around. Could he be spying on us?' Danny said.

'Freddie Fallon a spy?' laughed Dazza, stuffing his face with some of the food Agathe had laid out.

Adam nodded, 'Freddie is a lot of things, and none of them good, but he couldn't be a spy. I'm not even sure if he would know which end of a pair of binoculars to use.'

'Has anyone noticed anyone following them in the last few days?' Avery asked.

There was a chorus of shaking heads and different ways of saying no.

'The only person I've seen who looked suspicious was Nurse Willis, but I've not seen him anywhere except in the Clinic,' Adam replied.

'So we can park the idea of being spied on, although just to be sure, Danny will do some bug sweeping of any cars used and any houses since we agreed on the plan,' Max said.

'I'll give you a hand if you want with the higher places,' Dazza said.

'Cheers, Dazza,' Danny replied before adding, 'Hang on whilst Avery and Adam made the reconnaissance trip on Wednesday, and we said we would aim to get Michael out on Saturday. We didn't confirm the plan until Friday, and we all stayed the night here.'

Agathe nodded in agreement, 'He's right, Max. We only had all the uniforms, the ambulance and everything sorted yesterday. Since then, nobody has left the house.'

'And we weren't even there,' said Abi.

'*We, correction, you even told Avery an hour later than we were planning because she was having that funny moment after the lady's death,*' Bobby thought. '*So if anyone let it slip, it must be someone in this room.*'

'*Or one of them isn't what they seem. I regret asking Michael not to put up any mirrors so I don't keep seeing my aura now.*'

'*Don't reflections in glass work? Oh, right, they do but not as well. But that's still better than nothing. Just switch the television off and stand by it. Then, you should be able to get a half-decent reflection of everyone.*'

Max chuckled, '*You realise you've just had a complete conversation with yourself?*'

'*Oh great. I'm officially losing the plot as if my life wasn't bad enough.*'

Dazza was waving like crazy, 'Hello, Earth to Planet Max or Planet Bob. Are you receiving us?'

'What? Oh, sorry, were you talking to us?' Bobby asked.

'We were saying, where do we go from here?' Adam said.

'We need to find a clue about where they might have taken Michael,' Max said. 'Only when we've worked that out can we plan how to get him.'

'Well, I've missed the match, so I'm free for the rest of the day and tomorrow if you need help,' Adam said.

'Oh, sorry, Adam, I know your football's importance. You weren't due to play today, were you?' Max asked.

'No, my contract doesn't start until well after the exams. So I've got a few weeks yet,' Adam replied.

'You've got a football contract, Adam? That's fab news. Which club?' Abi asked.

'Watford FC. I can't believe I'll be playing for my home team after following them all these years,' Adam replied.

'That sounds like a reason to celebrate,' Agathe said. 'How about we open a bottle of wine or two and some beer?'

'You're all welcome to stop the night again if you want to, of course,' Catherine added. 'Plus, we can throw some ideas around about getting Papa.'

'Sounds good to me,' Danny replied. 'It's Sunday tomorrow, so I've nothing special planned.'

'Are we invited?' Abi asked.

'Well, there will need to be some doubling up in beds or some sofa surfing but of course. The more, the merrier,' Agathe replied.

'As long as I can change out of this uniform, I'm up for it, too,' Dazza laughed.

'Max, I don't suppose you have any sports clothes I could change into?' Adam asked. 'I could do with a run, but I don't want to get sweaty in the clothes I'll wear all night.'

'Yeah, sure, Adam, I used to keep fit when I was Maxwell, so I'm sure I've got something to fit. But, how about if I—' Max started to say.

'If you think I'm ever going running again, I'm serving you with an eviction notice,' Bobby laughed.

'We'll see you in an hour then,' Abi said as she and Avery waved and hung up.

Max walked over to the television and turned it off. He looked at the reflections in the darkness. Dazza and Agathe are both normal; Adam and Danny are fine, but I can't see Catherine. 'Where is Catherine?'

'She nipped to the loo,' Adam said.

'*Well, I think Catherine is the last person we need to worry about,*' Max thought.

Danny looked at Bobby and said, 'How powerful is that computer in your workshop, Max?'

'About the most powerful tower you can get at the moment,' Max replied. 'Why?'

Danny winked and said, 'I've got a few ideas, but I'll need a lot of processing power, and I presume you have access to encrypted and obfuscated servers via a VPN?'

'Why do you need a virtual private network to hide what you're doing?' Adam asked.

Danny laughed, 'Now, why would our resident footballer know what a VPN is and does?'

Adam blushed, 'Erm, Dad uses one for work.'

'Seriously though, what have you got planned?' Max asked.

'I'm going spoofing,' Danny said, pulling up an image on his laptop of when DI Fallon held up his warrant card.

'How did you? No, on second thoughts, I don't need to know, but let's get this show on the road,' Max replied. 'Come on, Adam, I'll sort some clothes out for you while Danny gets himself set up.'

As Catherine returned to the room, Agathe looked at Dazza and said, 'Why don't you help me clear up Dazza? I've got some

Rum Cake downstairs that you might like to test for me. You too, Catherine.'

Dazza stood up, 'That sounds good to me. Are you coming, Catherine?'

Catherine was still mulling over the day's events and looked troubled, 'I think I'll stay here.'

'Come on, let's go and have some Rum Cake; everything looks better eating Rum Cake,' Agathe teased.

'OK, I'll come,' Catherine said, smiling. 'I guess it'll stop me fretting about earlier.'

'We can prepare some food for later whilst we are down there,' Agathe added.

'Wicked, I'll just change out of this uniform and be down in a sec,' Dazza replied, saying to Catherine, 'I like your Mum.'

'Her food is quite good, too, isn't it?' Catherine laughed, giving Dazza a playful jab.

Danny, Adam and Max exited the lift into the basement. 'Can you remember the code for my workshop Danny?'

'I never forget anything,' Danny replied, heading in that direction.

Max escorted Adam to his bedroom. 'If you go through that wardrobe, you'll find plenty of sporting clothes, and if you need socks or underwear, check out those drawers over there. I'll be with Danny if you need anything.'

'Cheers, Bobby, sorry, I mean Max,' Adam said.

'Don't worry about it. I get confused about which of us is thinking or saying what, and I've done this before,' Max said as he walked out of the bedroom towards his workshop.

'Hey, Danny, have you got yourself set up?' Max asked. Then, realising Danny was already tapping away on his keyboard; he said, 'How did you access my computer? It has Special Intelligence grade multi-factor authentication.'

'That may be true, but it also has an ID ten T loophole,' Danny laughed without looking away from the screen.

'That's a new one on me. Can you show me?' Max asked.

Danny said sure, picked up a pen, and wrote out ID10T. 'There you go, ID ten T. Multi-factor authentication is only effective if you log out of your computer or at least lock it rather than just turning off the screen.'

'I guess I've become a little lazy with my IT behaviour inside my lair,' Max laughed. 'So what are we accessing first?'

'Why work in sequence when you can work in parallel?' Danny asked. 'That's old school, Chief. So we are going full steam with a multi-pronged approach.'

Danny explained that he was using a multi-hop VPN chain through distributed servers in various locations, 'We then hit a heavily encrypted exit node in Northern India, so anyone who tries to track us will think it's just some hackers.'

'Well, you are a hacker,' Bobby laughed.

'Excuse me. I am conducting a very sophisticated investigation for a friend in need. I have principles, you know,' Danny replied in mock indignation.

'But in effect, you make the trail cold in India?' Max asked.

'If they get that far. I'm also tunnelling it through the Tor network to add another layer of encryption and obfuscate everything.'

'Fascinating, but how do we pick up the trail on Michael,' Max queried. 'The way I see it, we have three or four questions to answer. First, did Michael leave the hospital? If Michael left the hospital, then how? Whatever they used to get him out of the hospital, where did it go? And finally, what is going on with Fallon and Carter, and are they involved?'

'I can use spoofing with Fallon's warrant card details to access the police records database without arousing suspicion. That way, we can check the timing and allocation of the Clinic's call. I'll probably use a reverse shell and then run my password cracker. But I'm not expecting much resistance. I'll go in via either the Greater London Police website or else the links via the government pages. A touch of cross-site scripting with a heavy dash of server-side request jiggery-pokery, and we should be in.'

'OK, that deals with the Fallon issue, but what about the main challenge, finding Michael?' Max asked. 'How about accessing the CCTV network in the hospital? I'm guessing they will have deleted the patient records after this morning's failed rescue attempt.'

'Yeah, I've already tried the hospital records route using my laptop and M Thomas or U Male no longer exists as a current or past patient. I'm still not clear about how they found out about us going in that way, though,' Danny mused. 'As for the CCTV route, I'm going for the hospital and the London Transport Authority. That way, we should be able to follow Michael out of the hospital and track wherever they have taken him.'

'I'll catch you guys later. Good luck with the hunt,' Adam shouted as he used the lift to return to the main part of the house.

'Have a good run,' Bobby shouted back.

'You two back to normal now, then?' Danny asked.

'It seems so,' Bobby replied, 'That reminds me, what were you saying in the car about him telling me how he feels?'

'I assumed that's why you fell out,' Danny said, concentrating on the computer screens.

'How he feels about what?' Bobby pushed.

'About you, you melt!' Danny laughed.

'Oh, yeah, he made that clear when I kissed him,' Bobby replied, then, realising what he had said, added, 'accidentally. We were hugging over him securing his football contract, and he sort of turned his head at the wrong time. So it was more like a peck than a kiss.'

Danny turned away from the screen and looked at Bobby, 'I've known you for almost three years and hung out with you guys for at least the last two years. In all that time, well apart from when you were dating Avery briefly, you and Adam have totally had the hots for each other.'

'I, we, um. That's not true,' Bobby spluttered.

'Of course it is. Don't sweat it, bro. It's no big thing. When Adam told me he fancied you a few weeks back, I thought you would make a great couple. Oops, here we go, we are in.'

Danny turned back to the computer screens. The one on the left was still scrolling line after line of computer code, while the one on the right now displayed a large Greater London Police logo.

'Adam said what?'

'Shh, I need to concentrate,' Danny hissed back.

He minimised the software displaying the logo and called up another piece of programming code. Looking from his laptop to the larger desktop screen, Danny said, 'The name is John Fallon, and his collar number is DIJFCID4659.' Danny pressed enter on the keyboard and sat back. 'Now it's time to see how quickly my little password finder can work.'

'I always thought I was pretty talented on a computer, but how did you learn all this?' Max said in admiration.

'Boredom mainly. When your ability to move is constrained, and the technology and equipment available were designed by people who don't have the challenges you face, you soon learn the best way is to develop it yourself. That leads to research which becomes practice, and before you know it, you've accidentally downloaded the tax returns for every politician in the country!' Danny laughed.

'You didn't. Did you?' Max chuckled.

Danny smiled, 'No, the files were humungous, but I may have had a sneaky peak at a few and let's say some were well dodge.'

'I bet dodgy is a definite understatement,' Max replied, pointing at the screen; he added, 'Hey, look, something has happened.'

Danny started tapping on the keyboard, 'We are in. Now we need to be careful. They will have intrusion detection and audit tracking. We don't want to set any alarms off, nor do we want Fallon to notice strange activity on his history log. Write this down. The event time is 14:55 this afternoon. The event requires NFA. Presumably, that means no further action.'

'That's getting close to two hours ago. Why do we need to know that?' Bobby asked.

Danny sighed, 'Because my not-so-tech-savvy buddy, when we come out of the system, I will use a data wiper to remove all events after that point, so they will never know we were here.'

'Look, the other screen is up now. It looks like the live feed from the Clinic,' Max said.

'One hack at a time, buddy. That can wait until we've finished with the police system. Now we were at the Clinic just before eleven this morning. But according to this log, Fallon and Carter were attending a diversity course in Barnet from ten in the morning until two-thirty,' Danny said

'That's well over an hour away. So even if they had maybe an early break or something, there is no way they could have got to the Clinic and back,' Max replied.

'Maps is saying it's 93 minutes each way,' Danny added.

'Can you check the course records to confirm they were there?' Max asked.

'Already on it, Chief. Yep, according to this, Fallon and Carter both registered and were there for the full course,' Danny replied. 'Oh, look at this, Fallon even commented on how much he enjoyed the course, and it's made him think about things differently.'

'Funnily enough, it has also made me think differently about him. Or, more precisely, it has confirmed my suspicions they, or at least Fallon, are not honest,' Max said, leaning back. 'They were not assigned to investigate the incident when the Clinic called in to report us outside.'

Danny laughed, 'It gets better, Chief. I'm cross-referencing the emergency services phone logs around the time we were at the Clinic to phone calls made from the Clinic. No calls were made from the Clinic to the police, and no log was raised regarding an incident at the Clinic.'

'How did they know we would be there today and at precisely that time?' Bobby asked.

'That is my biggest concern,' Max replied. 'Someone in this house on Friday must have informed Fallon. I can't think of any other way.'

'If you rule us out, that just leaves Agathe, Catherine, Adam or Dazza,' Danny said.

'There is no way Agathe or Catherine would risk Michael. So that leaves us with Dazza or Adam,' Max mused, 'but neither of them are Deceptors. So are they working for Deceptors, or did they talk to one without realising it?'

'Of those two, Adam is the only one who has behaved differently in the last couple of days,' Bobby replied.

'There has been a cold atmosphere between you and Adam, but I thought that was because he fancied you,' Danny said.

'He's a funny way of showing it, ain't he' Bobby retorted.

'Come on, buddy, tell your Uncle Danny the full story,' Danny said, leaning forward.

'It was Thursday after I found out that he had got his contract with Watford,' Bobby sighed.

'And?' Danny prompted.

'When he told me, I hugged him, and everything seemed so perfect, well I....' Bobby trailed off.

'You kissed Adam, didn't you? And it wasn't an accidental kiss,' Danny laughed.

'It's not funny. He just froze like I had tried to; well, I don't know what, but he didn't move or respond.'

'And then you ran out of his house without giving him a chance to explain,' Max added.

'Blimey, I thought my love life was complicated. Well, actually, it isn't complicated because I don't have one at the moment, but that's next-level awks,' Danny replied. 'No wonder you two have been acting strangely around each other.'

'Either way, Dazza or Adam seem the most likely source of the leaked plan. I'm not saying they did it maliciously, but we must be careful. Whatever we discuss down here stays between us two, agreed?' Max asked

'Us three,' Danny corrected. 'Don't forget that bonkers, lovestruck boy whose body you're currently inhabiting.'

'Oi, I am here, you know,' Bobby said. 'Now, get back to work. We still have the CCTV to check.'

'Yes sir, of course, sir,' Danny laughed, returning to the computer screens.

'Right, unlike Mr I-Only-Turn-My-Screen-Off here, let's cover our tracks and shut down the police link properly. Data wiper running followed by audit log file shredder,' Danny said before turning to look at the left screen. 'Now, let's see what we can discover about Michael's disappearance.'

Danny quickly accessed the files for that morning and fast-forwarded the film to the point where they saw Catherine and the rest walking towards Michael's room. Danny then put the film into reverse, and there nineteen minutes and five seconds before Catherine came into the shot, there was a flurry of activity with Michael's bed being wheeled out of the room with him in it.

'So they knew we were on the way about twenty minutes before Catherine walked down that corridor,' Max started. 'Can you follow where they take that bed?'

'Keep watching,' Danny replied, switching from camera to camera as the Clinic staff pushed the bed down the corridor. They watched as a door opened, the bed wheeled inside, the door was closed, and the team returned to Michael's original room.

'So he was still there when Catherine arrived,' Max said. 'We need to keep watching the camera on that room.'

Danny increased the speed of the film as they watched Catherine, Adam and Dazza arrive and then leave. Five minutes elapsed which accounted for an hour on the CCTV image in front of them, before they saw more staff entering Michael's new room and exiting with someone in a wheelchair.

'Zoom in and enhance that image,' Max said.

'I don't think I can. The CCTV system seems quite dated,' Danny replied.

'Here, let me,' Max replied, grabbing the mouse. 'This little program here should, yep, look, it grabbed a screenshot and is enhancing it.'

'That sure looks like the images I've seen of Michael,' Danny nodded.

'There is no doubt about it. It's Michael. Let's follow where they take him,' Max replied.

The images continued to flicker across the screen as Danny took back control and kept switching cameras until the wheelchair-bound Michael was outside the ambulance entrance that Danny, Bobby and Max had been sitting outside only a few hours earlier. They watched as Michael was pushed into a minibus.

'OK, I've got the registration number, L4 MAS. I'll search to find out who owns it,' Danny said, scribbling down the number.

'I have a sneaking suspicion it'll be the Lamasery Spa and Well-Being Centre in Richmond-Upon-Thames,' Max replied.

Danny turned to Max, 'Wow, that's impressive. How do you know that from just the number plate?'

Bobby laughed, 'Don't be fooled, Danny. It says it on the side of the minibus.'

'Well, it's impressive, I noticed,' Max replied.

'Let's switch to the LTA's road cameras,' Danny replied.

'Can't we just do an ANPR track on where it goes?' Max asked.

'OK, that's an automatic number plate recognition track, but what does it mean?' Bobby asked.

'In simple terms, we use their systems to highlight every time that number plate passes one of their cameras,' Danny said. 'The downside is it creates a sizeable pull on their systems which could raise the alarm. So it's safer to track it visually. Plus, even though the same operator runs multiple systems for the police and other authorities, they are very disjointed.'

Panning through the CCTV, they follow the minibus to the Lamasery. Danny tried to log into the Centre's systems with limited success. 'This is going to take some time. They seem to have some very sophisticated intrusion detection and network segmentation. I can access the public area cameras, but getting into their other systems will take some time.'

'OK, in the meantime, do a screen print of Michael in that chair. I want to check something with Catherine,' Max said.

They watched Michael being removed from the minibus and taken into the reception area. After a few minutes, a nurse appeared and pushed Michael away.

'That's as far as I've got access to currently,' Danny sighed.

'Can you go back to that nurse, please? Use my software to zoom in on her face,' Max said.

'No need, Chief, this system is state of the art, unlike the Clinic's state of the ark,' Danny replied.

As Danny enlarged the image, a familiar face appeared.

'At last, it's starting to make sense,' Max said.

Danny looked at Max with a puzzled look.

'She is the Deceptor that tried to kill me as Max Thomas in Picadilly Circus and again on Bobby's driving lesson,' Max replied.

'Let's take a break and join the others,' Danny suggested. 'I'll come back down in an hour and give you a shout when I've accessed their systems.'

'Good idea,' Max agreed, 'but if anyone upstairs asks, we are pretty sure he's still at the Clinic, but we don't know in which department they've got him.'

'Got who,' Adam asked from the doorway.

'Oh, hi, Adam. How long have you been there?' Max asked.

'I've just got back from my run, so I thought I'd come and grab my underwear and the ambulance uniform before going to my room for a shower,' Adam replied. 'So who has got whom?'

'It's Michael,' Danny said. 'It looks like they lied about him leaving the Clinic. But we haven't worked out yet where they've put him.'

'Sneaky,' Adam replied. 'See you guys upstairs.'

Ten minutes later, Bobby and Danny entered the Drawing Room. Music was playing quietly in the background. The table was stacked with food, and to the side were opened bottles of red and white wine with some cans of beer and lager nearby.

'I need a scotch,' Max replied as Agathe asked if they wanted a drink.

'I'll have a coke, please,' Danny said.'I don't drink and drive,' he added with his usual wheelchair tap.

'Oh, not that old joke again.'

Bobby turned to see Avery behind him laughing.

'Hello, Max babe,' Avery said, planting a big kiss on Bobby's lips.

'Hi, Avery. Lovely to see you again,' Max replied.

'Hey Avery, you OK?' Bobby added.

'Oh, hi Bobby, it's still so weird talking to two people in one body,' she replied.

'Trust me, it's even stranger being one of the two people inside one body,' Bobby chuckled.

'Oh, Bobby, you're so funny. Why did we ever split up?' Avery asked.

Bobby just stared at her, 'Well, I think you saying you fancied Tommy, the rugby team captain and that you felt more like my sister had something to do with it.'

'Oh yes,' Avery giggled.

'Have you found where Papa is,' Catherine asked.

'We think he's still at the Clinic,' Danny replied.

'Here's a picture of him being moved in a wheelchair. Do you think that means they are weaning him off the coma-inducing drugs?' Max asked.

'Well, it's a positive sign that he can be moved safely without them, but I'd still want to check him to be sure,' Catherine replied.

Over the next couple of hours, everyone chilled out. Danny disappeared downstairs to continue trying to hack the Centre's systems, whilst Bobby stayed upstairs with his friends, chilling and drinking.

'Adam, can I talk to you?' Bobby asked.

'Yeah, of course,' Adam replied.

'I want to apologise for kissing you,' Bobby said.

'I should be the one saying sorry,' Adam replied. 'I'd just got a professional football contract, then had my crush show me he felt the same as I felt about him.'

'I'm your crush?'

'Of course, I thought you knew that.'

'But you froze when I kissed you.'.

'Well, you made me realise I've got a lot of thinking to do. I could be with you or be a professional footballer,' Adam replied. 'Anton Hysén, Jake Daniels and a handful of others like Zander Murray have come out, but nobody in the top flight is out.'

'Oh, Adam, I never want to stand between you and your talent.'

'But I never want to be without you either. I'm determined to make it work.'

'Hey guys, you're missing out on Adam's party. Come on, babe, let's dance,' Avery said, pulling Bobby away from Adam.

10
PLAN AND EXECUTE PART 2

Max was confused. Where was he? Why did his head hurt and his body ache? He could only remember parts of what had happened last night, and what was that awful noise? Had he transmuted again, and why? What could have killed 'Bobby!' he said, sitting up quickly. The noise turned into a grunt, and Max looked to his right, 'Dazza, what the heck are you doing in my bed?'

'Huh,' Dazza grunted in reply.

Max got out of bed and walked to the bathroom to look in one of the few mirrors in the entire property. Looking back at him was the familiar face of Bobby surrounded by Max's aura. He washed his face and brushed his teeth. It didn't stop his head from pounding or resolve the gurgling sickness in his stomach, but it made him feel slightly more human.

'*What happened last night*?' Bobby asked, looking at his reflection, '*I'm covered in bruises.*'

'*I don't have a clue,*' Max replied, '*I remember Avery dragging us off to dance, but after that, it's a blur.*'

Bobby returned to the bedroom where Dazza was sitting, drinking from a water bottle. 'Morning, Bob. I hope you're feeling better than you look,' Dazza laughed.

'Morning, Dazza. I feel awful. What happened last night?'

'You got very drunk and started telling Avery and Adam that you loved them both,' Dazza replied. 'Well, I think it was Max telling Avery and you telling Adam, but it got very confusing.'

'Oh, that's cringe,' Bobby replied. 'How much did I drink?'

'We can't be certain, but Agathe reckons you had two small whiskies with ice,' Dazza said.

'But I've drunk some serious partygoers under the table over the years,' Max replied. 'I'm in a lightweight.'

'You might have, but I don't drink alcohol. I've never liked the taste,' Bobby said. 'After this, I may never drink again. Did anything else happen because I'm battered and bruised?'

'Well, you challenged Abi to an arm wrestle and lost,' Dazza laughed. 'Which was when you decided to go to bed, except instead of walking to the lift, you got to the top of the stairs and fell down them.'

'Talking of going to bed, Dazza, why are you in my bed?' Max asked.

'Don't you remember Avery and Abi stopped over? So they had my bed, and Catherine suggested I double up with you to make sure you were OK,' Dazza replied as he got out of bed. 'I'm going for a quick shower if that's alright? Then I reckon it's time to see if Agathe has rustled up some brekkie. Are you coming?'

'Yeah, go right ahead. There are some clean towels on the side. I'm just going to check on Danny,' Max replied, grabbing his dressing gown from the back of the door.

'I'm never showing my face again,' Bobby moaned, then added, 'Especially in this dressing gown, it's like an old man's.'

'*That's because it was until eight days ago,*' Max growled.

Walking into the workshop, they saw Danny slumped over the desk. Bobby shook him, 'Danny, are you OK?'

'Waa. Uh, what time is it?' Danny said groggily.

'Just after eight,' Max replied. 'Have you been here all night?'

'Looks like it,' Danny said, rubbing his eyes and looking up. 'Blimey, have you been in a car accident?'

'Not for a few days,' Bobby said with a half-hearted smile. 'I'm thinking of giving them up.'

'Looking that rough, I don't blame you,' Danny chuckled.

'How have you got on?' Max inquired.

'Not very far, to be honest. The security is first-rate,' Danny sighed. 'But during a moment of boredom, I have upgraded the software on the sensors you've got around the building upstairs, so now they also monitor for bugging devices whenever you do a sweep. The good news is this building is clean.'

'I guess with all the high-profile guests and celebrities going through the Lamasery, it needs good security,' Max replied. 'Thanks for doing those sensors; you're a little genius. I've been meaning to do that for ages.'

'It took longer to do the first sweep than write the code, Chief. As for the Lamasery, it's looking like we may have to resort to good old-fashioned breaking into the place.'.

Bobby held his sides, 'The way I feel, the only breaking I'm doing is to my ribs.'

'Come on then, what did happen last night after I came down here?'

Bobby told Danny the little he could remember and the rest that Dazza had told him.

'You realise I'm never letting you forget this, although, to be fair, the rest of them probably won't either. It was good of Dazza to look after you, even if his snoring woke you up.'

'I don't snore,' Dazza shouted from the door, trying not to laugh. 'And to think I was going to ask if you fancied some breakfast.'

'Hey, Dazza, Bobby told me you were his hero last night,' Danny responded.

'Not so sure about that. But he was certainly entertaining. Did he tell you about losing his arm-wrestling contest to Abi?' Dazza laughed.

Danny looked at Bobby, 'Funny that it seems to have slipped his memory. Maybe it's the hangover.'

Dazza looked at the computer screen, 'Is Michael at the Lamasery?'

'We're not certain, but it's possible,' Danny said, trying not to say too much to one of their two leak suspects.

'How did you recognise the place from that angle?' Max asked.

'I've been there often enough,' Dazza laughed.

'Oh, it's not your alcohol addiction again, is it?' Danny said with a wink.

'Shh, you promised not to mention that alcohol issue,' Dazza laughed.

'Please, stop mentioning alcohol, or I'm going to vom,' Bobby said, putting his hand over his mouth.

Dazza looked at Bobby, 'Sorry, Bob, I promise not to mention alcohol, alcohol-based products or anything containing alcohol again today.'

Danny couldn't resist joining in, 'Nor will we mention any specific alcoholic drinks, especially whisky or whisky mixers.'

'If I puke on you, it's your fault,' Bobby replied, looking decidedly green.

'Seriously though, how do you know it's the Lamasery?' Danny asked Dazza.

'My Dad is the Head of Maintenance, and he got me a part-time job there,' Dazza said, pulling his staff card out of his wallet.

Danny looked at Max and said, 'Are you thinking what I'm thinking?'

'If it's, shall I go and throw up? Then yes, I am,' Max replied.

Danny turned to Dazza, 'If you're involved in maintenance does that mean you can log into their computer system?'

'Of course, I can. The guests or staff record any maintenance issues online, so we have to log on to see any faults raised, in what locations, and when the rooms are free.'

'So if I load the system, you can log in?'

'Yeah, it's called MaintRep. But you won't get me or my Dad in trouble, will you?'

'If you can get me in, then I can eliminate all traces as I go along,' Danny replied.

'Great, but can we grab some brekkie first? I'm starving.'

'I need five minutes to grab a shower and get dressed,' Bobby said.

'I'll be up with Bobby. But first, I need to shut down the secure link,' Danny replied.

'I'll go with Bob as I've not cleaned my teeth,' Dazza said.

Several minutes later, they entered a quiet kitchen. Agathe was standing by the stove poaching some eggs for Catherine, who was drinking a black coffee.

'Well, look what the cat dragged in, Mama,' Catherine chuckled.

Agathe turned and belly laughed, 'Oh my word, I've not seen anyone look that bad since Michael and Max had that late-night poker game with those two actors from Wimbledon and Ireland in 1995.'

Catherine stood up, 'Take a seat, guys, and I'll get you some drinks. Tea Max?'

'Yes, please and four sugars, please,' Bobby replied.

'*I'm not even going to protest.*' Max thought.

Danny and Dazza asked for cold drinks. Agathe said, 'Well, I'm sure my boy Dazza wants a full English, but what about you two?'

'Defo, Mrs T,' Dazza replied.

'Could I have a bacon buttie, please?' Danny asked.

'I'll pass, thanks,' Bobby replied, gulping the tea Catherine had passed him.

'No, I won't pass, thank you. Could I have some scrambled eggs, bacon and toast, please, Agathe,' Max insisted. 'Where are the others?'

'Abi and Avery are upstairs watching some reality show called Bonkers in Birmingham, and Adam has gone for a run,' Agathe replied.

'We think we've found Michael again, but we can't tell anyone else,' Max said, feeling the benefit of the sugary tea.

Dazza looked shocked, 'What, not even Adam? I've never had a secret from him.'

'Sorry, Dazza, not even Adam,' Max replied. 'Whoever accidentally let slip about us last time, we need to do everything to stop it from happening again.'

'Stop what from happening?' Adam asked, coming into the room drenched in sweat.

Danny looked at Bobby, then turned to Adam, 'Oh, we were saying we need to stop Dazza eating all the breakfast.'

'Now that sounds harder than breaking Michael out of the hospital,' Adam joked.

'Yeah,' they all laughed.

'Hiya Bobby, feeling better this morning?' Adam laughed, kissing him on the cheek.

'Oh, don't. I feel awful. It sounds like I humiliated myself in front of you all,' Bobby replied.

'Well, I've never had someone swear undying love before doing cartwheels down the stairs. So I'd say entertaining rather than humiliating,' Adam chuckled.

'Do you want some breakfast?' Agathe asked Adam.

'I'd love some scrambled eggs on toast, please, Agathe, but can I have five minutes for a shower?' replied Adam.

'Of course, Adam. I've got some smoked salmon as well if you want it?'

'You're spoiling me, Agathe. That would be lovely. See you guys in a bit,' Adam replied, heading towards the door.

'It's nice to have a houseful to spoil again,' Agathe smiled.

Danny, Bobby and Dazza finished their breakfasts and returned to the workshop. Danny reactivated the obfuscated route into the Lamasery computer system. After a few frustrating searches, he finally found the login screen for MaintRep.

'You promise this won't get me into trouble?' Dazza asked nervously, tapping in his user ID and password. As he pressed enter, an alarm went off, and the screen changed to show 'Darius Turner, illegal login, contract terminated.'

'You said...' Dazza started before realising Danny was laughing hysterically. 'Oh, very funny, you numpty.'

'Sorry, Dazza, you were just so paranoid about getting into trouble.'

'Come on, Danny, we bow to your skill, but we need to see if Michael is there,' Max said.

'Yes, Chief,' Danny replied, 'Now I'm in; I can start searching. Since yesterday morning, we have 1003 as a PA, 3326 marked as NA, 3016 flagged as code 16, room 1102 as pending, and 2112, 1103, 5420, 3136 and 1117 as code 2.'

'Well, code 16 is a substance sweep, like alcohol or other substances, so you can ignore that, and code 2 is a blown bulb, so I don't think they're relevant,' Dazza said. 'An NA means not available, which is normally a trashed room. The last time we had that was when the lead singer of The Great and Good went loopy when his phone was confiscated. The pending means there is an issue, but it has yet to be confirmed what the problem is.'

'What is the PA?' Max asked.

'Patient Arrival. New guests are more demanding, so they get flagged for several days. We try to visit at least once during that period to ensure they are OK,' Dazza replied.

'So we've got three options. Either Michael is in 1003 as a new arrival, or they've blocked 3326 and put him in there, with 1102 a possibility depending on what they put as the problem,' Max said. 'Can you check the CCTV?'

'Nope, the network is so segmented, Dazza's access doesn't include the cameras,' Danny replied.

'Nah, we don't maintain the camera system. That bit is outsourced,' Dazza said.

'Are those rooms close to each other?' Max asked hopefully.

Dazza shook his head, 'Sorry, Bob, but the first digit refers to the wing, the second one is the floor, and the last two are the room. If it's any help, there's five wings and four floors, so it could be worse.'

'So one room is on the ground floor in wing one, the second one is the same wing, but the first floor and the third is in wing three on the third floor?' Danny queried.

'Yep, you got it,' Dazza nodded.

'Can you get me in there?' Max asked.

'I'd need to ask Dad, but possibly.'

'What about the CCTV company Dazza? Do you know who they are?' Danny asked.

'It starts with a K, or is it an N?'

'I'll take that as a no,' Danny laughed.

Dazza picked up his phone and rang his Dad, 'Alright, Pops? Are you at work today? Great, I'm after a favour. A mate of mine wants to look around as he's always hearing about the celebrities going there. Yes, Pops, I totally trust him to keep anyone or anything he sees confidential. No, he won't ask for autographs. A code 13? You don't really want me .... Fine, I'll do it. He can help me.'

'Are we in then?' Bobby asked.

'Yeah, but Dad said I have to clear up a code 13 in exchange, and I'm not doing that alone,' Dazza replied.

Bobby gulped, 'The way you're talking, it sounds unpleasant. Are we talking about vom or the brown stuff?'

'Yes,' Dazza answered.

'Max, you owe me so much for this,' Bobby growled.

'I know, bud, but think of the bigger picture,' Max replied.

'I'm busy thinking of a pile of stinking—' Bobby started to say.

'Come on now, boys, remember Michael,' Danny laughed.

'How many entrances and exits are there, Dazza?' Max asked.

'There's the main entrance at the front and the staff entrance at the rear with a delivery entrance near the kitchen. There is also a fire exit on every floor and each wing, so that's um,' Dazza said as he started to count on his fingers.

'Twenty fire doors and three other entrances,' Dazza chipped in.

'Only three doors not alarmed then. That's going to make it challenging,' Max mused.

'Oh no, all the doors are alarmed except for the main entrance,' Dazza said. 'You need a security pass, like my staff card, or someone to buzz you in or out; otherwise, the alarms go off.'

'Are they all wheelchair-friendly doors?' Danny asked.

'Only the main entrance and the delivery entrance,' Dazza replied.

Max asked Dazza to show them where the two entrances were, and they discussed the alternative ways to get Michael out of the building. Max and Danny then got into a detailed debate about deactivating the cameras and the fire alarms and letting them use the fire doors to escape.

'Why don't we just wheel him out of the main entrance?' Dazza said, looking from Bobby to Danny.

'What do you mean?' Danny replied with a confused look.

'Well, the main entrance also leads to the sun terrace, the guest's garden and the outdoor swimming pool,' Dazza said, 'People are constantly wandering in and out. It's not like a prison. Only the visitors are vetted, and that's to protect the guests.'

'Why did you let us spend the last half hour debating how to get Michael out then?' Max asked.

'Well, you guys seemed to be having fun thinking up clever ways to do it,' Dazza laughed.

'Let's get going then. I'll ask Agathe if we can use the Range Rover,' Max replied.

'Aren't you forgetting something?' Danny asked, winking at Dazza.

'Yeah, I reckon he has,' Dazza chuckled, 'Are you going to remind him?'

'Why spoil the fun? He'll work it out in a minute,' Danny laughed.

Max looked from Dazza to Danny and back again, 'What?'

'You, or more precisely Bobby, hasn't passed his test yet,' Danny replied.

'Hey, I can still drive,' Bobby protested.

'We've had this discussion, and it's not happening,' Max replied.

'White's Wheels it is then,' Danny smiled. 'I can be the lookout.'

Danny shut down the computer, and they headed upstairs. As they got out of the lift, they bumped into Adam and Catherine carrying some mugs of tea.

'Hey guys, how's the hunt for Michael going?' Adam asked.

'Slow, unfortunately,' Danny replied.

'It looks like you guys are off out. How come?' Catherine inquired.

'Dazza's Dad called and asked him if he could work today. Danny offered to give him a lift, and I need a break,' Max replied.

'Give me two minutes to take these up to the girls, and I'll come for a ride,' Adam suggested.

'Sorry buddy, but I'm picking up a package on the way back, so I need the space,' Danny replied. 'But we should be back in an hour.'

'That's a shame, but OK. Take care of my new man,' Adam said, kissing Bobby quickly. Then, turning to Dazza, he said, 'Don't work too hard, big man.'

A few minutes later and Danny was heading towards Richmond Upon Thames. 'Should be there in about twenty minutes.'

'I hated lying to Adam,' Bobby said.

'Yeah, me too,' Dazza agreed.

'But you heard him joking about getting Michael out of the hospital, and he's seemed to be eavesdropping a few times,' Max replied.

'I know what you're saying, but I still don't believe it, not my Adam,' Bobby replied.

'Oh, get you,' Danny laughed, 'It's my Adam now. It wasn't that long ago when you two were barely talking.'

'That was just a misunderstanding, as you well know,' Bobby protested.

'Guys, I don't want to worry you, but I think we're being followed,' Danny said.

Max grabbed the rearview mirror, 'There are no Deceptors in there, and it's not Fallon and his buddy. Are you sure they're following us?'

'They've been behind us for ten minutes ever since we went through Chiswick,' Danny replied.

'But nobody knows where we're going,' Dazza said.

'Yes, they do?' Max said, burying his face in his hands.

'Catherine and Adam,' Bobby replied, 'We told them we were taking Dazza to work.'

'But Catherine wouldn't know where I work,' Dazza protested.

'Maybe not, but Adam knows, doesn't he?' Danny said.

'Yeah, I didn't think of that,' Dazza replied.

'Nor did I,' said Max

'False alarm, guys, they've pulled into that supermarket,' Danny said.

Dazza punched Danny in the arm, 'Don't do that to us.'

'No interfering with the driver,' Danny replied, 'Especially when they're as sexy as me.'

'In your dreams, Danny,' laughed Bobby.

'It's showtime, guys,' Danny said as he pulled into the Lamasery car park. 'Bobby, stick this in your ear. If you need to talk, press it. Let go, and you'll hear me. Here is the transmitter.'

Dazza and Bobby got out of Danny's car and headed to an outbuilding to the side of the main building.

'Hiya Pops, this is my mate, Bobby,' Dazza said.

Bobby held out his hand, 'Pleased to meet you, Mr Turner.'

'You too, Bobby,' Mr Turner replied, 'There are some spare overalls over there. I trust my lad, so please don't let him and me down.'

'I won't, sir,' Bobby said.

'Room 1102 is the code 13, son,' Mr Turner told Dazza.

'OK, Pops.'

'That's one room off our list of possibilities,' Max said.

Five minutes later, Dazza and Bobby walked into room 1102. 'It looks spotless,' Dazza said.

'It does, but that smell says otherwise,' Bobby replied.

Bobby and Dazza walked around the room trying to find the problem before Bobby opened the bathroom door and then put his hand towards his mouth about half a second after his stomach decided it needed emptying.

'Well done, Bob, like we don't have enough to clean up,' Dazza scowled.

After thirty minutes of cleaning, gagging and more cleaning later, the bathroom was habitable again.

'You don't have to do this regularly, do you?' Bobby asked.

'Not very often, I'm pleased to say.'

'As we are in this wing, let's start with room 1003,' Max suggested.

They took the stairs down to the ground floor. Dazza looked at his tablet and knocked on the door. 'Mr Perry, maintenance here.'

The door opened. 'Yes, can I help you?'

'Hello, Mr Perry. I'm from the maintenance team. I just wanted to make sure you've settled in and everything is OK with your room, sir,' Dazza said.

'Yes, fine,' Mr Perry replied.

'And check-in showed you how to report any issues, sir?'

'Yes, thank you, is that all?'

'Thank you, sir. I hope your stay with us at the Lamasery is a refreshing one,' Dazza said, nodding slightly.

The door slammed shut.

'That's Ju—' Bobby started to say.

'Yes, it's Mr Perry,' Dazza replied. 'We only ever refer to them by their checked-in name.'

'You bowed to him!' Bobby exclaimed.

'All guests get the same respect, Bob,' Dazza replied.

'Let's head to room 3326,' Max said.

'Are Bobby, Danny, and Max still trying to find Michael?' Abi asked in Glenthorne Crescent.

'They are. They're struggling to trace what happened to Papa at the Clinic,' Catherine said.

'Maybe they need some refreshments,' Avery suggested.

'They've gone out,' Adam said, 'Dazza's Dad asked him to do a shift at work, so Danny offered to drop him off.'

'Oh, Danny is so sweet sometimes, despite his ego,' Abi laughed.

'They won't be long, though. Danny said they'd be back in an hour. Just in time for lunch, Agathe,' Adam laughed.

'Where does Dazza work then?' Avery asked.

'That swanky spa place in Richmond Upon Thames,' Adam replied.

'Not the Lamasery?' Abi asked.

'Yeah, that's it,' Adam replied.

'Oh, I would love to go. They have so many famous people there,' Abi said, 'I bet it's amazing meeting all those celebrities.'

'Dazza says it depends. He says the real stars tend to be incredibly humble, but some reality stars are awful. Apparently, the reality stars act like, don't you know who I am?'

Bobby and Dazza entered room 3326 to find a man sitting in a wheelchair with his back to the door.

'Michael, is that you?' Max said, running forward,

Michael was slumped forward in his chair and grunted.

'Let's get him out of here,' Max said.

A small black mobile phone is picked up, and a number dialled. 'They have gone to the Lamasery,' the voice said.

'When did they go there?' the other voice responded.

'From what I understand, maybe forty minutes ago,' the voice said.

'Thank you, we'll neutralise the issue,' the other voice replied.

'You're sure we can just wheel him out like this?' Max queried.

'Guys, what is happening in there? I'm feeling rather awkward just sitting here. I've already had one person ask if I needed help,' Danny said in Max's ear.

Max pressed the device in his ear, 'We've found Michael, so we should be with you in a few minutes.'

Dazza wrapped a blanket around Michael's legs and put another around his shoulders and over his head, leaving just part of his face visible. 'There you go; if anyone stops us, we were just asked to take him to the garden for some fresh air. Now let's get going.'

Max pushed the wheelchair into the corridor. 'This is too easy. I can't believe they don't have him under guard or something. Which way was the lift?'

They reached the lift and stood waiting for it to arrive. 'Why are all the lifts in this place so slow?' Max grumbled.

'They don't want to spend the money replacing them,' Dazza replied.

Finally, the lift arrived, and the doors crept open. They wheeled Michael inside and pressed the button for the ground floor.

'Hold that lift,' a female voice shouted.

Max leant forward and saw the female Deceptor running up the corridor as the door started to close. It would be tight as he watched her hand lunge forward to try to stop the lift, but the doors closed just in time.

'I almost think it would be quicker to carry him,' Max moaned.

Finally, the lift stopped on the ground floor, and Max and Dazza pushed Michael as fast as they could towards the main entrance. They heard a door fly open behind them, and Max glanced back to see the female Deceptor gaining ground.

'Here, take Michael out to Danny and get him in the car,' Max blurted out. 'I'm going to try to slow her down. Get Danny to tell me when you are ready.'

Max pulled the key ring out of his pocket, pointed it towards the rapidly approaching Deceptor and held down the button, but he missed her and hit a fire extinguisher sending it flying off the wall. The Deceptor tried to avoid it but tripped herself up in the process. Max took the opportunity to start running towards the entrance again.

'*Are you sure you calibrated your immobiliser correctly?*' Bobby thought.

'*Of course, I have. I was aiming for the extinguisher,*' Max lied.

'You can't escape, Max. We know all about you, that boy Bobby Morris and all his friends,' the Deceptor shouted as she got up and started chasing again.

Max turned and aimed his immobiliser again as the Deceptor stopped running and stood staring at him.

'We've been trying to catch you since you killed my partner. He never got to see our child grow up,' she said. 'But now we don't want to kill you. You're going to suffer instead.'

'Who was your partner?' Max asked, keeping his immobiliser pointed at her.

'Max, come on, we're ready to go,' Danny said through the earpiece.

'The man you brutally killed in Bredwardine. You knew it was isolated at the top of that hill, so he wouldn't be able to transmute,' she snarled.

'Ah, the guy who tried to steal the Mappa Mundi, that was fourteen years ago,' Max replied. 'It was his choice to try to escape by heading somewhere remote.'

'Max,' Danny screamed. 'I can hear police sirens.'

'Sixteen years, actually, and we are looking forward to handing you to my Daxson,' she sneered.

'Well, it's been a blast catching up with you, but I've got to go now,' Max replied, firing his immobiliser again.

Max turned and ran without looking to see if he had hit her. Danny had pulled in front of the main entrance and opened the front passenger door. Max dived into the car and slammed the door shouting, 'Drive.'

Danny sped down the driveway of the Lamasery and skidded out onto the main road. Ahead of them, they saw a black unmarked police car heading towards them with its lights and sirens going.

'Look, it's Fallon,' Danny shouted.

'Slow down. We don't want to call attention to ourselves. How's Michael doing back there, Dazza?' Max asked.

'He's making the occasional grunting noise, but he seems to be breathing OK,' Dazza replied.

'*She knew my name*,' Bobby thought.

'*Yes, buddy, I heard her*,' Max replied, trying to sound reassuring.

'*But if she knows my name, she probably knows where I live, which means Mum and Lily are at risk.*'

'*We need to plan what to do to protect them, and let's not forget your friends, too.*'

'What happened in there, Bobby? We were beginning to think she'd got you,' Dazza asked.

'I'll explain when we get Michael home,' Max replied.

'Can you guys have a shower too? Don't take offence, but you guys stink of a bad night in a pub toilet,' Danny gagged.

'Spent much time in them, have you, buddy?' Dazza asked.

'No, and that smell is why,' Danny replied, opening his window.

The rest of the journey back to Glenthorne Crescent was spent discussing what had happened in the Lamasery. After parking near the house, Max rang the doorbell, and Catherine answered it.

'You might want to give Danny a hand with his package. I'm just going to get that old wheelchair Michael used when he had his hip operation,' Max said.

Catherine ran to Danny's car. 'Papa, is it really you?'

'I think he's still heavily sedated,' Dazza replied.

'But how, where?' Catherine said, with a million and one questions going through her mind.

Danny said, 'Let's get him inside first, and you can check him over. Here's Bobby with the wheelchair.'

'Yes, they have just arrived with him,' the voice said into the mobile phone. 'I don't know what they've discovered yet, as they are still getting him out of the car.'

'We believe the information regarding the Daxson may have been leaked. Try to find out if they are aware of him. J is aware of the leak and very displeased. Make sure no more mistakes are made,' the voice at the other end of the phone replied.

'Is my sibling OK?'

'He immobilised her, but she'll live. No more slip-ups, understand?'

'Yes, sir.'

'Avery, have you seen they've got Michael back,' Adam said, returning from the toilet.

Avery turned away from the window, 'Yes, I've just been watching them get him out of Danny's car. Isn't it fantastic news?'

11
TIME TO HIDE

'How is Michael?' Adam asked as Catherine walked into the Drawing Room.

'I don't want to give him anything to help him wake up as I can't be sure if they've used a benzodiazepine or propofol sedation, but his vitals are strong, and he's comfortable,' Catherine replied. 'It's been a few hours now, and he is starting to come round. Mama is staying with him in case he wants anything.'

'We have another problem,' Max said, looking from face to face. Max tells them the Deceptor knows Bobby's identity and claims to know all about the friends.

'Did she name us?' Adam asked.

'No, Bobby was the only name she mentioned. But I think it's safe to assume Fallon and Carter are involved, so they probably got his name that way,' Max replied.

'If those two are involved, then they have my name as well,' Danny said.

'They'll know me too because I work at the Lamasery, which means my Dad could be at risk,' Dazza wailed.

'That means it won't take them long to track me down, too,' Adam added.

'What about us?' Abi asked, indicating herself and Avery.

'Look, we need to keep calm about this. The Deceptor made it clear that it was me they were after. I killed the Deceptor's partner some time ago, and she seems to want revenge,' Max said, trying to reassure everyone.

'But they did make it very clear they knew about me. And let's face it, Max, you and I are one person. So getting you means getting me,' Bobby replied.

'It's probably worth letting your parents know they should be careful. Just tell them Bobby's had some crank threats, and the police are investigating,' Max said.

'If it helps, you're all more than welcome to stay here as long as necessary,' Catherine suggested, 'I know Mama would be happy.'

'As I'm in an empty house at the moment, I'd like to stay,' Adam replied.

'I need to go home tonight to finish working on my upgrade. But my place has so much security I'll be fine,' Danny added.

Abi said, 'I think I'd rather be home tonight.'

'Me too,' Dazza said, 'I want to see what Pops has to say. Any chance of a lift, Danny or Abi?'

Danny nodded to Dazza to confirm he could take him home.

'What about you, Avery?' Abi asked, 'Do you want a lift home?'

Avery looked at Max, 'Have you told us everything? What are we going to do next? I'm not deciding anything until I know the facts.'

'Bobby is right. To get to me, they have to take him as well, and that means we need to protect his Mum and sister,' Max explained.

'In which case, I'll come with you. I can help, babe,' Avery smiled.

Max shook his head, 'I'm sorry, but I need to do this alone. It will be hard enough to persuade Mrs Morris as it is without a group of us there.'

'*Babe?*' Bobby queried.

'*Hmm, she does seem very fond of me,*' Max replied.

Avery grabbed Max's hand, 'Well, if you're sure, babe, please let us know when they're safe. I'll stay here with Adam then if that's OK, Catherine?'

'Honestly, I'd welcome the company,' Catherine replied.

'*Why haven't you mentioned the Daxson?*' Bobby asked.

Max paused, then replied, '*Partly because I don't believe there is a Daxson here. They were left behind when we evacuated Zephyrion. But, also, why worry everyone about something they would have no control over.*'

'*What do you mean they have no control over?*'

'*A Daxson is like a wild tormented beast. They have no loyalty to anything except those that feed them. But, even then, they would devour that energy soul if they could. You can't trust Deceptors, but a Daxson is totally reliable. It will always kill, given the opportunity.*'

'*That sounds like a pretty important piece of information.*'

'*It's only important if they came across a Daxson, and it's not something they are going to meet walking down Haywood High Street.*'

Bobby added, '*And you still don't trust Adam or Avery?*'

'*I'm not sure who I trust now, apart from you, Danny, Agathe, Catherine, and probably Dazza.*'

Max looked at Danny and discreetly nodded towards the stairs, 'Do you still want to borrow my spectrometer?'

'Oh, yeah, please, if that's OK?' Danny replied.

A few minutes later, they were sat in Max's workshop. Max leaned over the desk and pressed a button, activating an array of proximity alarms. 'Just making sure nobody gets within earshot of us this time without warning.'

'What's up, Chief? You're beginning to worry me,' Danny replied.

'I need your help, Danny. At the moment, you're the only person I trust with transport apart from Agathe,' Max said.

'Wow, it must be bad,' Danny joked.

Max went through some of his concerns about the other friends and then started to discuss the Daxson. 'They were genetic mutant Shadowers. As far as I know, what caused the mutation was never discovered, but when one was born, they were incredibly powerful. As they matured, they could tear apart normal Shadowers with their bare hands.'

'And they consumed vast amounts of energy?' Danny asked.

'Yes, that's why we had to leave them on our planet. There were only around a hundred alive when we evacuated the planet, but they consumed so much energy when we first tried to send one through an Exodus machine; it fully drained the machine halfway through the process. To this day, I'll never forget the agonised scream as it was ripped into atoms,' Max replied.

'If that's the case, how can one be on Earth?'

'Good question. I suppose someone may have developed technology capable of sending them, but I heard Zephyrion imploded less than five years after we left.'

Danny sat back and thought about what Max had told him, 'Could any of your species have bred on Earth? You did say it was a genetic mutation.'

'Theoretically, I suppose. I did hear reports of a case on another planet. A Daxson was reportedly born only a few months after the parents were evacuated there, but even as a newborn, the baby quickly started to use up so much energy it didn't survive more than a few days, or it might have been weeks. With Earth's light atmosphere, I can't imagine it surviving even that long.'

'What about some form of incubator?' Danny challenged.

'I'm no biologist, but it could work in theory. Some form of chamber from which the Daxson could draw energy. I can't imagine how they would know the right amount of energy to supply it, though.'

'Wouldn't they just give it an unlimited supply?'

'It's not that simple. Too little and it would dissipate like a Shadower without a host or a shell, and too much would make it disperse dramatically, resulting in the same net result.'

'Perhaps it's still young, and they want your help controlling those levels. You certainly seem very knowledgeable for someone not into biology.'

'Technology is my expertise, so I guess there's an overlap of sorts. But the Deceptor made it sound like the Daxson was an adult. She said I would suffer,' Max said, leaning forward.

'What can I do, Chief?'

'I'm going back to Bobby's tonight. I want to be there in case anything kicks off and to try to persuade Pat and Lily to go to a safe house.'

'So you want me to drop you off when I take Dazza home?'

'Well, yes, but will you come and pick us up in the morning on your own and drive us to one of my safe houses?' Max asked.

'One of your safe houses? How many have you got?'

Max tapped his nose, 'Enough, my genius friend. I'll let you know which one in the morning. Say about ten a.m.?'

'No problem.'

'Oh, and Danny...'

'Yeah, I know, not a word to anybody,'

'You know, for a cocky little genius, you're a nice guy,' Max laughed, slapping Danny on the back as he stood up.

'Nice? Ha, you wait until I show you my bad side?' Danny chuckled.

Max leaned back over and deactivated the proximity alarms, 'Let's rejoin the others.'

'Forgotten anything?' Danny asked.

'Oh, sorry, please excuse my manners; thank you, Danny, for all your help.'

'Not thanks, you numpty, the spectrometer. It might look a bit sus if we go back up without it,' Danny laughed.

'Good point,' Max replied, face-palming himself before passing the spectrometer from a nearby shelf and picking up some keys by the desk.

As they returned to the Drawing Room, Avery said, 'You were a long time down there, babe.'

'Sorry, Avery, that was my fault. Max tried to fob me off with his cheap spectrometer,' Danny replied.

'You missed the big event,' Adam said, 'Michael is awake. He's a bit groggy but otherwise fine, according to Catherine.'

'Has anyone been up to see him?' Max asked.

'No, Catherine said he needs to rest, but she did say you could pop in,' Abi said.

Max knocked on the door to Michael's bedroom.

'Come in,' Agathe said.

Max walked in and sat on the side of the bed, 'Hello, old friend, how are you feeling?'

'Like I've been beaten black and blue, drugged up into a stupor, carted halfway around London, then chased out of a luxury spa by a crazed alien,' Michael replied.

'Oh, fairly normal then,' Max laughed.

'So how is it you're the one they wanted, and yet I'm the one laid here bruised and battered, and you've lost several pounds and forty-odd years?' Michael asked.

'Just lucky, I guess,' Max chuckled. 'By the way, I should introduce you to Bobby, my new host.'

'Pleased to meet you, Bobby. I hope Max is treating you better than he treated me when I hosted him,' Michael joked.

'Nice to meet you too, Mr Thomas. So far, I've been in a car chase during my driving lesson, shot at, almost killed with exercise, helped break into two medical centres and been questioned by the police,' Bobby replied.

'How many weeks have I been gone?' Michael asked.

Agathe patted Michael's hand, 'Only nine days, my love.'

'Good grief, that's a record even for you, Max,' Michael roared. 'And call me Michael, Bobby. I'm only Mr Thomas when I'm working.'

'It even gives my first transmute in the Americas in April 1861 a run for its money,' Max nodded. 'What can you remember about what happened!'

'I'd got a call Friday morning saying Rich Mueller was asking for me. The person claimed to be his secretary, and they mentioned a celebrity I used to deal with occasionally,' Michael started.

'Didn't you think it strange, Papa, as Mr Mueller retired years ago?' Catherine asked.

Michael laughed, 'You should know, my dear, surgeons never retire; they just hand over the needle and say suture-self. Seriously though, most of us do some private work for as long as we can.'

'What happened next?' Max asked.

'Well, they asked me to go to one of the hospitals I used to use, but the ward they sent me to was empty. Before I could do anything, I felt a needle going into me. When I woke up, I was in a hospital bed in a private room. They kept calling me Max and demanded I show them how to build an Exodus machine,' Michael said.

'Why would they want one of them?' Max looked puzzled. 'Sorry, I interrupted you.'

'They even hooked me up to a polygraph, and of course, I couldn't deny knowing about them after hosting you,' Michael said. 'But even though it said I was telling the truth about not being you, they started getting violent. I'm sorry, but in the end, I blurted out that I was due to meet you that evening with Catherine.'

'No need to apologise, old friend. What happened next?' Max asked.

'They must have drugged me again because until I woke up here, I don't remember a lot. I remember being moved to a different hospital with the change in light and the movement of a vehicle. I think they moved me again because I can vaguely remember this ginger ogre of a man who smelt of vomit and excrement,' Michael groaned.

Catherine looked at Max with a puzzled look.

Max replied, 'Dazza.' As Catherine and Agathe burst out laughing.

'What did I say,' Michael asked.

'It's OK, my love, as well as this charming young Bobby, we've got a few other new friends to introduce you to,' Agathe said.

'Did they mention a Daxson to you?' Max inquired.

'Not that I recall. I thought you said the Daxson were wiped out when your planet collapsed?' Michael groaned wearily.

'It seems that may not quite be the case,' Max replied.

'Well, that's my side of things. So what the heck happened to you? The last I heard, Catherine was going to be your next host unless, of course, you need some new DNA,' Michael said.

'I was chasing a Deceptor through Piccadilly Circus and had a slight altercation with a car,' Max laughed, 'Bobby and his friends came to see if I was OK, and nature took its course.'

'It certainly looks like you've had a good upgrade,' Michael laughed, then started coughing.

'Sorry, Max, but Papa is getting tired. Unfortunately, the drugs aren't totally out of his system, so he needs to rest,' Catherine said.

'I'm fine, Catherine, don't fuss.'

'Now then, Michael, just do as the good doctor instructs you,' Max joked, 'I've got to go anyway. Bobby's family need to move to a safe house.'

'Which one?' Michael asked.

'Not sure yet, but definitely one outside of London. Anyway, my friend, I'll hopefully be back tomorrow or Tuesday at the latest.'

After saying their mutual goodbyes, Max opened the bedroom door to see Adam and Avery in conversation.

Avery turned to Max and asked, 'How is Michael?'

'He's doing well, thanks.'

'I've just asked Abi if she would mind popping me home and then back, as I need some clean clothes,' Adam said. 'So I needed to get my door keys from the bedroom.'

They wandered down to the Drawing Room to find Abi waiting to take Adam home and Danny waiting with Dazza for Bobby.

'Michael's doing well, thanks to you guys,' Max said, 'I really couldn't have done it without all yours and, of course, Bobby's help.'

'Where do we go from here?' Avery asked.

'Well, we've done what we needed to do regarding getting Michael back. But I think the safest thing is for everyone to return to their normal lives,' Max replied.

Abi looked at Max with incredulity, 'Uh, hello. We've just kidnapped an old man out of a care home after previously trying to break him out of a hospital. Not to mention there's this killer alien who knows who Bobby and the rest of us are, and you think we can just return to normal?'

'It's a Spa and Wellness Centre, not a care home,' Dazza replied. 'But Abi has a point, Max.'

'I understand why you're all worried, but I have been doing this for a long time. The Deceptor made it very clear that I was the one they wanted, and after talking to Michael, he's confirmed I'm their target, not you,' Max answered, trying to allay their fears.

'So we just go back to doing our exams and whatever whilst we wait for this Deceptor to come and kidnap you and, therefore, our friend Bobby?' Adam said. 'I'm sorry, Max, you seem like a nice and well-meaning guy, but Bobby means too much to us, especially to me, to let that happen.'

Bobby grabbed Adam's hand, 'Look, everyone, I know precisely what Max is planning, and I can say that literally for once. He isn't about to put anyone at risk, and he is also not going to sit back and wait for the Deceptor to kidnap us.'

'So what are you going to do?' Avery challenged.

'I'm taking Bobby's Mum and sister down to Brighton. I've got a little cottage there where they will be safe,' Max replied, 'Then I'm going Deceptor hunting. We know she was at the Lamasery as a nurse.'

'I'm guessing Pops will soon make it clear who she is and how much trouble I'm in when I get home,' Dazza said. 'I'll let you know as soon as I can.'

'What'll you do when you find the Deceptor?' Adam asked.

'Thanks, Dazza. And I'll do what I always do, and that's take them out of action.'

'You mean kill her?' Avery said.

'That is the most likely scenario, I'm afraid.'

'You're sure she is the only threat? You're not hiding anything else from us, are you?' Avery challenged.

'When do we start the hunt?' Adam asked, 'Tomorrow?'

'We don't. I need to do this on my own for now. I've put you all in danger at times over the last few days. Tomorrow is too soon. By the time I get Mrs Morris and Lily safe and settled in, it'll have to be Tuesday or, more likely, Wednesday.

'Look, those of you staying here tonight, keep an eye on Agathe and the family and let's stay in contact. I'll let you know when I have found something and how you can help.'

'Come on, gang. It's been a long day for all of us. Putting Max through the Spanish Inquisition isn't helping anyone,' Danny said.

'I don't want to be a party pooper, but we have exams starting this week. Avery and Abi, we've got Politics Wednesday morning, and I've got History that afternoon with Economics on Thursday morning,' Bobby said.

'Oh, heck. With everything going on, I'd forgotten about our exams. I definitely need to go home. I've got Media Studies tomorrow afternoon, then Photography and Business Studies on Tuesday,' Dazza replied.

'We're in that Business Studies exam too, Abi,' Adam added, 'It's my first exam with Sports Science Wednesday morning.'

'Yeah, we are. As well as that and the Politics exam, I've also got Spanish Thursday afternoon,' Abi sighed.

'I've got two on Wednesday and one Thursday morning,' Danny said, 'Assuming I'm still allowed to sit them. What about you, Avery?'

'Mine are Maths on Tuesday morning, Politics on Wednesday and Art and Design Thursday morning,' Avery replied.

'That settles it. There is nothing we can do together this week until Friday at the earliest,' Bobby said. 'Adam, Avery, are you still going to stop tonight?'

'Yeah, I think I will,' said Adam, 'The company will be a distraction. Besides, there's not much point in trying to do last-minute cramming. Since I have to go home tomorrow, don't worry about running me around tonight, Abi. I'll make do in these clothes.'

'I'll still stop tonight, too,' Avery said. 'We can catch the tube together in the morning Adam.'

'I'll just pop up and let Catherine know,' Max replied. 'I'll see you and Dazza in your car Danny.'

The other friends said farewell to each other as Max went to Michael's bedroom to tell them what was happening.

After watching their friends enter Danny's car and waving Abi off, Adam turned to Avery and said, 'I'm just popping to the toilet. Don't let Bobby go without me saying goodbye.'

'OK, Adam. Don't be long.'

A phone rang in north London. 'Hello, what is happening.'

'Max is planning to hunt for my sibling.'

'When?'

'Not until Friday. They are all busy with exams.'

'That is most fortuitous. Do they know about the Daxson?'

'No. It would appear that the noise at the Lamasery during their escape meant that Max didn't hear it mentioned. Is J still coming at the end of this week?'

'That has not been confirmed at this stage. It was only an indication of when they might arrive. Is there anything else I need to know?'

'Max is moving the boy's family to a safe house in Brighton tonight or tomorrow.'

'We appear to be getting a run of good news. As long as he is busy running pointless errands, sitting exams and then chasing your fool of a sibling, we can monitor him until we need to trap him again. J was very unimpressed that we captured his old host instead of him last time. They have said we only take him this time when we are ready to get started.'

'Yes, sir.'

Bobby walked into the Drawing Room to see Avery standing by the window, 'Where's Adam?'

'Right behind you as always,' Adam replied, wrapping his arms around Bobby's waist.

Max jumped instinctively, then turned to face Adam. 'I'm sorry, Adam, that was Max reacting. He doesn't do sudden surprises,' Bobby said, kissing Adam.

'Hey, babe. Don't I get one of them too?' Avery asked, walking over to him.

'Of course, you do,' Max replied, kissing Avery. 'I've told Agathe, Michael and Catherine you two are stopping tonight and heading home in the morning. Catherine has to go to work, but Agathe has said she will drop you both back home.'

'Oh, that's so sweet of her,' Avery replied.

Bobby and Max said their goodbyes and headed to Danny's car.

'Let's go, guys,' Danny said. 'So we're off to Brighton tomorrow, then?'

'No, we're going to Cambridge,' Max replied.

'So you still don't trust everyone, then?' Dazza asked

'I'm unsure if it's trust or just me being overcautious. The less that know, the fewer who can leak. Don't you find it strange Adam and Avery are the only two who wanted to stop?' Max asked.

'Adam is on his own at home at the moment,' Bobby replied. 'But Avery staying seems weird.'

'We also caught them both outside Michael's bedroom. It was like they had been listening in,' Max said.

'Come on. Adam was going to pop home for some clean clothes. He had a reason for being there, unlike Avery,' Bobby protested.

'Guys, chill out. Is it possible for two people to fight when they are in one body?' Danny laughed, trying to lift the mood.

The rest of the journey back was quiet. Dazza was worried about what his Dad would say whilst Bobby and Max were thinking about the best way to persuade Mrs Morris that they needed to leave the house for a while. But, ultimately, they decided to be honest and tell her all about Max. Danny dropped Dazza off first, then drove to Hinton Close.

'Is ten a.m. still OK, Danny?' Bobby asked as he got out of the car.

'Sure thing, bro. See you in the morning. Good luck with your Mum,' Danny said before driving off.

'Is that you champ? I was getting worried and was just about to text you,' Pat shouted from the kitchen.

'Yeah, sorry, Mum, I lost track of the time. It's been a hectic day,' Bobby replied.

Pat walked in carrying a plate and a mug of tea, 'I've just made myself a sandwich. Do you want one?'

'No, I'm OK, thanks,' Bobby replied.

'Are you sure? I've got some bananas and a fresh bottle of salad cream,' Pat replied, knowing her son's weakness for a banana and salad cream sandwich.

Bobby knew what his Mum was doing, and he loved her for it, 'OK then, you've convinced me. I'll come with you, though, as I need to talk to you about something.'

'Sounds ominous,' Pat laughed, putting her plate and tea on the coffee table.

As they walked into the kitchen, Bobby replayed in his mind everything he and Max had discussed in the car and then decided to ignore it totally, 'Mum, do you remember that incident on my driving test? Well, some not-very-nice people were involved in smuggling that diplomat out.'

'What does that mean? Do the police want to see you again?' Pat turned with a concerned look on her face.

'No, it doesn't involve the police. Well, not directly. But it has been suggested that we should go away for a couple of weeks. You know, like a holiday.'

'Sorry, champ, but I really can't afford it. Work says I've got to take two weeks holiday before the end of next month or I lose them. So how about I book them for after your exams finish, and we have some days out?' Pat said, ruffling Bobby's hair.

'Mum, not the hair!' Bobby protested. 'Do you remember that friend who lives near Earls Court?'

'Oh, your new girlfriend, yes, what about her? Is she coming too?' Pat teased.

'No. Her uncle has a cottage in the countryside with a pool, and he said we could use it for a couple of weeks. Free of charge.'

'That's very nice of him, but why would he do that?'

'He said we would be doing him a favour as he's not had a chance to use it this year, so it's been mothballed for a few months.'

'Oh, he wants a free cleaning lady to tidy it up, does he?' Pat laughed.

'No, it's not that,' Bobby stuttered.

'I'm teasing dopey. Where is it?'

'It's near Cambridge, so not too far.'

'That sounds perfect. I can ask at work tomorrow, and we can go Thursday after your last exam. I'm sure I can swing it with Lily's school as it's almost half-term.'

Bobby panicked, 'No, we need to go tomorrow. Danny will follow us up and bring me back for my exams.'

'What's going on, Bobby? Why are you so keen to get rid of me?' Pat asked as she passed him his banana and salad cream sandwich.

'It's Adam,' Max replied, taking a bite of his sandwich to give himself time to think.

'*What are you doing, cowboy?*' Bobby thought.

'*Trying to save your skin, buddy. I said we should have been honest.*'

'Are you two still not talking!' Pat said, hugging Bobby.

'It's the opposite. We are seeing each other,' Max replied as Bobby blushed.

'As in, he's your boyfriend?'

'Mum, that's so cringe. Nobody uses words like boyfriend or girlfriend now, but yes, we are a couple,' Bobby replied.

'Oh, Bobby, that's wonderful. So that's why you want us out of the way. Well, I hope you're being careful,' Pat laughed, giving Bobby a huge kiss.

'Mum,' Bobby protested.

'Tell you what, I'll email my boss and the school tonight, and if they reply by the morning saying it's OK, we will go to this cottage,' Pat replied.

'What if they don't?' Bobby replied.

'Then I'll ring them in the morning and tell them we are going. After all, how often does a two-week free holiday in the country with a pool come along? Now eat up; you're dripping salad cream everywhere. Let's go and sit down, and I'll do those emails.'

'*I want to hate this sandwich, but it's actually quite tasty*,' Max thought.

'*It's a classic. My Dad got me into them*,' Bobby replied.

'*It's like cold sweet, and sour in a sandwich*,' Max said, taking another large bite.

'Careful, champ. I don't want you choking before our holiday. It'll be, what's the phrase, so dope?' Pat laughed.

'Mum, that's so not even last year,' Bobby groaned, 'You mean it'll be lit.'

'*Glad I'm not the only one struggling with modern slang*,' Max chuckled.

Pat sat on the sofa and started eating her sandwich while typing her emails. Bobby checked his phone and saw a message from Dazza 'Pops is fine. He said she was a private nurse who shouldn't have even been on the premises.'

'Awesome, Dazza, what happened to her?'

'Those coppers arrested her and took her away. So hopefully, it'll be the last we see of her for a while.'

'*Bet they released her as soon as they left the Lamasery*,' Bobby thought.

'*Undoubtedly, Fallon and Carter are so heavily involved, and I just need to work out in what way*.'

Bobby sent a thumbs-up emoji back to Dazza and another to Danny thanking him and confirming the plans for tomorrow. He then sent 'Goodnight x' messages to Adam and Avery with a B at the end of Adam's message and an M at the end of Avery's.

'I'm off to bed, Mum. Love you,' Bobby replied, kissing her.

'Love you more, champ,' Pat replied, watching him heading towards the stairs. She thought I wish your Dad could see what a wonderful man you're becoming.

Lily shattered the early morning peace by jumping up and down on Bobby's bed. 'Bobby, Bobby, wake up, come on, sleepy head, we're going on holiday.'

'Yeah,' Bobby groaned, glancing at the time on his phone.

'*We really should get up,*' Max thought, '*Danny will be here in just over an hour.*'

'Danny's coming. Oh, cool,' Lily replied.

'*Can you hear me, Lily?*' Max thought.

'That's silly. Course I can. You're talking,' Lily giggled.

'*Can you hear me talking?*' Bobby thought.

'You two are silly. Mummy is cooking bacon. See you down there, stinkies,' Lily laughed, running down the stairs.

'*This doesn't make sense,*' Max said, '*How can she hear us thinking?*'

'*You tell me, cowboy. I'm new to all of this. You've got a two-thousand-year head start on me,*' Bobby said, puzzled.

Bobby shaved, showered and headed downstairs, almost tripping over the suitcases in the hallway. He walked into the kitchen and caught his Mum singing along to the radio, 'Someone sounds happy.'

'Oh, morning, Bobby. My boss sent an email this morning saying I could have the two weeks off, and a quick call to the school sorted them out too,' Pat smiled, 'Bacon butty?'

'Yes, please and ketchup,' Bobby replied. The doorbell rang, 'That'll be Danny. He's early.'

As Bobby opened the door, his Mum shouted from the kitchen, 'Ask Danny if he wants a bacon sandwich. There's plenty.'

'Yes, please, Mrs M,' Danny shouted back, then to Bobby, he said, 'Your Mum is talking my language.'

'How come you're early? And why are you wearing tinted glasses?'

'Because, my not-so-genius friend, I wanted to show you something. Watch this and look no hands,' Danny replied, raising his hands. He blinked twice, then looked past Bobby. His wheelchair shot forward, hit the doorstep and stopped. 'Flip, I forgot about that step.'

Danny blinked again, looked down at the step and then into the hallway. This time the wheelchair lowered its legs and walked up the step and into the house. He repeated the blinking process and looked into the living room, and his wheelchair took him into the room.

'You've got your upgrade working then,' Bobby said.

'It's still a little temperamental, as you saw, but as a prototype, it's well on the way,' Danny said proudly. 'Hiya, Lily.'

Lily turned and said, 'Hey, Danny,' before returning to watching her cartoon.

'What sensors are you using on it?' Max asked.

'I've got the cameras mounted and some radar, but I need to add lidar, geolocators and GPS,' Danny replied, 'If I'm right, I shouldn't need to do those separate processes to come in a house.'

'Impressive,' Max replied.

'Who's impressive?' Pat asked, carrying a large plate of sandwiches. 'Here you go, guys, tuck in. There's the tomato ketchup.'

'Thanks, Mrs M. Don't suppose you've got any brown sauce, do you?' Danny asked.

'Of course, I'll get some. And call me Pat, please.'

As Pat returned to the kitchen, Max looked at Danny, 'Brown sauce on a bacon sandwich? Are you sure you're not from another planet too?'

'I've just got a refined palate,' Danny laughed, squirting the brown sauce Pat had just given him inside a sandwich.

'Are you OK, champ? Your voice sounded a bit croaky,' Pat asked.

'That's just Max, Mummy,' Lily said without breaking her gaze from the television.

Pat furrowed her brow in confusion.

'It's a voice I sometimes jokingly use with Lily,' Bobby whispered.

'Well, don't overdo it. Lily seemed convinced Max was real yesterday,' Pat said quietly.

An hour later, they were on their way following a debate about whether Bobby should go with his Mum and Lily or keep Danny company.

'Are we there yet?' Lily asked.

'Twenty minutes, sweetie,' Pat replied, looking at the sat nav Bobby had bought her for Christmas.

Pat's phone rang, and she pressed the answer button on her headset.

'Hey, Mum, There's a dual carriageway coming up, so Danny will overtake you. However, don't overtake after that, as we need to turn down a lane soon, and the property entrance is not very visible from the road,' Bobby said.

'You sound like you've been here before.'

'*Fudge, I didn't think about that,*' Max thought.

'No, it's just Catherine's uncle, Mr Thomas, who told me to view it on Planet Maps before coming so I'd know what to look for,' Bobby lied. Then, he thought, '*Another fine mess I've got you out of, cowboy.*'

'OK, champ. I've got to admit I'm looking forward to the holiday in a relaxing little cottage,' Pat replied, 'See you when we get there.'

'See you in a bit,' Bobby replied before hanging up.

After driving down a narrow, twisting country lane twenty minutes later, Max tells Danny to turn right.

'That's just a farm gate,' Danny said, 'Look, it's just a mud track on the other side.'

Max pressed a button on the keys he'd picked up from his workshop, and the gate swung inside to the right.

'As soon as you start to enter the field, turn left onto the gravel driveway,' Max replied.

Two minutes later, they parked outside a grand-looking 4,700 square-foot Lincolnshire limestone house.

'Bobby, you said it was a cottage,' Pat said, getting out of her car, 'It's huge. Look, it's even got three garages.'

'It's only got two. The other is a false front for my workshop. I mean Catherine's Uncle's workshop,' Max replied.

'*Cowboy, will you please stop talking, or it'll be game over with Mum,*' Bobby thought as he walked over and unlocked the front door. He walked back to his Mum's car to help with her luggage.

'Good job I upgraded to four-wheel drive and all-terrain tyres last year,' Danny muttered as his wheelchair rumbled across the gravel drive spitting stones in various directions.

'Where's the swimming pool, Mummy,' Lily said, excitedly running between the car and the house.

'Be careful, munchkin. Don't go near the pool until I'm with you,' Pat replied.

'It's OK. Mr Thomas said the pool room is locked, but there's a key here so you can keep Lily safe,' Bobby said, handing his Mum the keys.

They deposited the luggage in the master bedroom, and Bobby gave his Mum a house tour.

'Anyone would think you lived here, champ,' Pat laughed.

'Mr Thomas showed me the floorplan from when he bought it,' Bobby lied.

'Mummy, Mummy, look, there's the pool. Can I go in?' Lily said, jumping up and down.

'Let's finish unpacking first. Then you can put your costume on and swim.'

'I'll put these groceries away in the kitchen. Do you want a cuppa, Mum?' Bobby asked.

Twenty minutes later, they sat in the pool room, drinking tea while Lily splashed around in the water.

'OK, champ, what's going on?' Pat asked, giving her son a look that only a parent can.

'About what?' Bobby replied, trying to give his best innocent face.

'You know exactly what I mean. Who lets virtual strangers have free access to a beautiful place like this?' Pat said, 'Maybe you know Danny?'

Danny squirmed in his seat, 'It's like Bobby told you, Mrs, err, Pat.'

'Which was Danny?' Pat challenged.

Danny looked beggingly at Bobby, 'Well, uh....'

Bobby looked from Danny to his Mum, 'It's like I said, Mum. Catherine's Uncle heard about that diplomat and the advice to go away for a while and—'

'Uncle SchmUncle,' Pat retorted. 'I want the truth right now, gentlemen.'

'Fine, but I'm not sure you'll believe me,' Bobby sighed.

An hour passed as Bobby told his Mum everything that had been happening. He was backed up several times by Danny chipping in.

'Well, you were right,' Pat replied, swigging her cold tea. 'It's a crazier story than some stranger handing over the keys to his luxury country house.'

'It took me a while to believe it even though Max is inside me,' Bobby laughed.

'I believed it straight away,' Danny laughed. 'Bobby couldn't wire a plug, never mind holding a sensible debate about engineering concepts.'

'Oi, you cheeky git,' Bobby replied, thumping his friend in the arm.

'So, how does it work? You know me having a conversation with you or this Max?' Pat asked.

'If you're talking to Bobby, you're also talking to me,' Max replied. 'The only distinguishing element is Bobby's voice sounds slightly different when I talk.'

'So that's why I thought you sounded croaky this morning. Max was talking?' Pat said.

'Yes, I'm sorry about that. Oh, where are my manners? I'm very pleased to meet you properly, Mrs Morris,' Max replied, putting his hand out for a handshake.

Pat looked at Danny and laughed, 'You're right, Danny. Once you start talking to Max, you can tell he's a different person. Pleased to meet you too, Max.' She shook his hand and said, 'Shaking my son's hand is certainly one of my stranger experiences.'

'Trust me, since Max came along, weird has become the new normal,' chuckled Danny.

'Well, this changes everything. I guess we can stop tonight, but I'm not leaving you alone in London,' Pat said.

'No, please, Mum. I need to know you're safe,' Bobby pleaded.

'Keeping you and Lily safe is my priority. So that's what needs to happen,' Pat responded resolutely.

'How about Bobby stays with me whilst he's doing his exams? You've seen my parent's home, and we've got so much security nobody can get near the place without us knowing,' Danny suggested.

'Well, it certainly looks like Fort Knox from the outside,' Pat agreed.

'Please, Mum?' Bobby begged.

'You promise me you won't leave Danny's place except to do your exams?'

Bobby hugged his Mum, 'I promise,' he replied, winking at Danny and showing his crossed fingers.

'OK, we'll stay. But you ring me every night, and I want messages during the day,' Pat insisted, 'And as soon as the exams are over, you had better come back here, with or without your friends.'

'Yes, Mum.'

'Yay, we're staying,' Lily said excitedly.

12
EXAM TIME

'Yesterday and this morning have been great,' Bobby said as Danny drove them back to London.

'Yeah, it felt normal, and who knew your Mum was such a wicked poker player,' Danny laughed.

'Dad taught her to play. Mum says he used to go and play in some semi-professional competitions occasionally.'

'I think I would have got on with your Dad.'

'I know you would have. He was an engineer in the motor industry,' Bobby said wistfully. 'And his sense of humour was even worse than yours.'

'You only mock because you're jealous of what you don't have,' Danny laughed as he pulled over and parked. 'Right, hurry up and grab what you need for college and some clean clothes.'

'Yes, Mother,' Bobby laughed as he exited the car.

A while later, after dumping his bag in one of the spare rooms in Danny's house, they went to Danny's garage workshop.

'How's your combined love lives going then, guys?' Danny asked, swapping out of his wheelchair into his simpler workshop wheelchair.

'Complicated,' Bobby replied, 'I had a one-hour call with Adam last night with Avery constantly texting Max. Then Max had a one-hour call this morning with Avery. I wouldn't mind, but she rang at six am. I didn't even know that time existed.'

'I do my best thinking in the morning. Any more than four or five hours of sleep, and I'm grumpy all day,' Danny chuckled as he started working on his wheelchair.

'You're grumpy every day,' Bobby laughed. 'Talking of Adam and Avery, what do you have regarding bugging equipment?'

'Blimey, that's a bit of a drastic way to see if they're cheating on you, isn't it?' Danny laughed as he attached more sensors to his wheelchair.

'I need to find out what they are saying to other people. One must be the leak, so if I can hear or see who they are talking to, I might find the Deceptor,' Max replied.

'There's a box of devices and sensors in that green plastic box. The transmitter and the camera badges are on that bench, and help yourself to any other components or tools. Oh, there's your spectrometer. You could have at least lent me a decent one,' Danny smiled.

A few hours later, Max sat back, admiring his handiwork. 'That should do it.'

Danny looked, 'They're certainly discreet. They look like a small box of mints, but what do they do?'

'They've got a GPS tracker in them so I can see where they are and a recording device,' Max replied. 'And if you pop the top off, they've got a few mints in them too.'

'No camera?' Danny asked.

'As I can hardly ask them to wear them. I assumed they'd be in bags or pockets, so I'd be unlikely to get any images, thus making a camera pointless. It'll help with the battery life anyway, and I can use the space to increase the storage capacity,' Max replied.

'Good thinking, Chief,' Danny replied. 'What's the transmitter range for the sound?'

'They're digital devices which can piggyback wifi for the GPS tracker, and I can upload sound files to this device whenever I'm within thirty to forty feet of them if I hold down this button. It's about the same range for getting a live stream, too,' Max replied.

'Cool,' Danny nodded. He slid across from his workshop wheelchair to his main one, put on his glasses and said, 'Now it's my turn to show off.'

He moved slowly across the garage using his double-blink technique and then looking at where he wanted to go. Then he tried it again but moved his eyes quicker, and the wheelchair moved back faster. He then tried looking up, and the chair raised. Next, he tried looking higher, and the legs lowered, taking him up to the highest shelves in the workshop. Finally, glancing to the left resulted in the chair ambling in that direction.

'Very impressive, buddy. Should we try the doorstep test instead of using the other entrances back into the house?' Bobby suggested.

'Good idea. I'm ready to call it a night anyway.'

Danny locked the workshop, and they went to the front door. He pressed a button to open the door, blinked twice and looked into the hallway. His chair rolled forward, stopped at the doorstep, lowered its legs, walked up the step into the hallway, and lowered itself back onto its wheels.

'Ta-da,' Danny said triumphantly.

'I knew you'd do it,' Max said.

'Well done, buddy,' Bobby added.

Danny's father came down the hallway carrying a glass of water, 'I just saw that, son. Amazing. I think I need to start trading shares in you.'

'Thanks, Dad. But it would crash the stock market if I was floated,' Danny chuckled.

'Hello, Bobby. Danny said you were stopping with us for a while.' Mr White said. 'Make yourself at home. I'm off to bed, son. Your Mum turned in an hour ago.'

'Hi, Mr White. Thanks, and I think I'm off to bed too. I've got my first exam tomorrow,' Bobby replied.

'You lightweights. I'll go online then. I fancy a bit of gaming,' Danny said. 'Night both.'

The following morning Danny parked up at the college. As he and Bobby exit the car, they spot Abi and Avery chatting.

'When are you planning on giving them their mint bugs?' Danny asked.

'As soon as possible,' Max replied.

'Hi, Bobby. Hey there, Danny,' Abi greeted them as they approached.

Avery turned and smiled, 'Hiya, Danny and Bobby and hi, babe.'

'Good morning, ladies,' Danny replied, doing a mock bow.

'Ready for politics this morning?' Bobby asked as he opened the small tin in his hand and took a mint out. He offered Abi and Avery a mint which they both accepted.

'Here, Avery keep the tin as there's only a few left, and I've got some more,' Max said.

'Thanks, babe,' Avery replied, putting them in her pocket.

'I thought Adam had an exam this morning?' Bobby queried.

'Yeah, you just missed him. His exam starts fifteen minutes before ours,' Abi replied.

Danny wished his friends good luck as he headed off to start his Computer Science exam, and Abi, Avery and Bobby trudged off to their exam room.

'You may now turn over your exam paper and begin,' the Exam Invigilator said.

'*I'm dreading this,*' Bobby thought.

'*We will smash it,*' Max replied as they read the first question.

What are the primary sources of power for the Prime Minister, and how has this evolved in recent years?

'*What do they mean by recent?*' Max asked, '*I mean, Walpole started it all, really, so I guess they mean from 1721?*'

'*Shh, I need to think,*' Bobby snapped.

'*What's to think about?*' Max replied, '*The first part has to be things like the royal prerogative, the legislative agenda, party leadership, cabinet appointments, and of course, the use of PR and the media to influence the public.*'

'*Will you shut, uh, what did you just say, and think it slower,*' Bobby replied.

The following two and a half hours flew by with an exam room full of sighs, groans, frustration and scribbling.

'Please stop writing now,' the Invigilator shouted. 'Only once we have collected all the papers will we say you can leave.'

A few minutes later, Avery, Abi and Bobby walked out of the exam room, and Avery asked, 'How did you get on? I struggled to get into that first question.'

'Oh, I didn't mind that one, especially the second part, as that's all about the changes like using mainstream and social media to influence or even coerce,' Abi replied. 'It was that last one on the impact of globalisation on the state that I struggled with. What about you, Bobby?'

'I quite enjoyed it,' Bobby said smugly. 'That last question had to be about the International Federation for Fiscal Security, with their future commander programs and everything.'

'Yeah, I went down the IFFS route as well, plus the way some of those trade agreements operate for the benefit of some elite businesses,' Avery replied.

'Oh, you two are so switched on,' Abi moaned. 'I'll be lucky to get a grade C.'

'Have faith in yourself, Abi. I bet you'll do well,' Max reassured her.

'Yes, just listen to my babe. He's so wise,' Avery replied.

'Who's wise,' Adam asked from behind the three of them.

'My Max, of course,' Avery said, grabbing Max's arm.

'Excuse me, but Max is just the squatter. That's my arm, and it belongs to my man Adam,' Bobby joked, pulling his arm free.

'Shh, not so loud,' Adam said to Bobby as he looked around.

Max pulled out his other tin of mints, 'Anyone want one? How about you, Adam?'

'No chance. Have you seen how much sugar they contain?' Adam replied.

'But they're sugar-free ones,' Max said.

Adam shook his head, 'I'll still pass, thanks. The sugar alcohols in them disagree with me.'

'I didn't know there was alcohol in mints?' Abi said with a puzzled look on her face.

'There isn't,' Adam replied.

'But you just said the sugar alcohols don't agree with you,' Abi protested.

'It's the name for low-calorie sweeteners. They aren't sugar or alcohol in the normal sense. They are naturally occurring carbohydrates in some fruits and vegetables. We cover them in Sports Science because they cause digestive problems in some athletes,' Adam replied.

'I'll take your word for it,' Abi laughed.

'*Flip, how do we get him to take the bug*?' Bobby thought.

'*Traditional bugging techniques*,' Max responded.

'*Which is*?'

'*This*,' Max replied, carefully dropping the mints in Adam's bag.

'Student canteen or Mike's Café?' Danny asked as he approached his friends.

'Got to be Mike's,' Abi said. 'I need some comfort food after that exam.'

A few minutes later, they were outside the café. Adam pushed open the glass door and said, 'Ladies after you.'

Abi and Avery entered, followed quickly by Adam, who held the door open for Danny. Bobby followed, keeping the door open until Danny had cleared it.

Danny looked back at Bobby, who stood by the door, still holding it open and staring at it. 'Are you joining us, Chief?'

Danny's voice snapped Max out of his thoughts. 'Oh, yeah, sorry, I just thought I, well, err, it doesn't matter.'

'Reckon that exam burnt out the last of your brain cells,' Danny laughed as Bobby joined them at the counter.

It wasn't long between orders being placed and the friends sitting at a table eating their lunches.

Danny asked Adam and Avery, 'How was Michael when you left yesterday?'

'He was pretty good, all things considered,' Adam replied.

'He even joined us for breakfast,' Avery added before turning to Max, 'any more sightings of that Deceptor babe?'

'No, it's been very quiet. Almost too quiet,' Max said.

'Well, I guess it's better than being chased.' Avery replied. 'Talking of being chased, has Bobby's family settled into your safe house in, err, Buckingham, wasn't it?'

'Brighton,' Danny corrected her.

'Oh, yes, that's right,' Avery said.

'Anyone heard from Dazza?' Bobby asked.

'Yeah, he did his last exam with Adam and me yesterday, Business Studies,' Abi said. 'I think I did a lot better in that than I did today.'

'He told us there was no problem with his Dad or work?' Adam replied. 'Apparently, the nurse wasn't even authorised to be there. Do you know what happened to her?'

'Dazza said that Freddie's Dad and that other copper arrested her and took her off,' Danny said.

'Those two policemen are very suspicious, don't you think?' Adam asked.

Bobby looked at Danny and frowned.

'Yeah, maybe,' Max replied, trying to sound indifferent.

'But I thought you agreed? Especially after they were at the Clinic and turned up again at the Spa,' Adam queried.

'I know, but maybe I'm just being overly suspicious,' Max replied.

'Hey, bro, we'd better make tracks. Unlike these lucky devils,' Danny told Bobby, 'We've both got exams this afternoon.'

'Good luck, guys,' Abi shouted after them as Bobby and Danny left the café.

'Is it me, or did Max and Bobby's attitude about Freddie's Dad and that other policeman seem very strange compared to how he talked about them over the last few days?' Adam asked.

'I thought that,' Avery agreed.

'Maybe it's just the exam stress getting to him. I know it's getting to me,' Abi replied.

The friends finished their lunch and went their separate ways. A couple of hours later, Danny was sitting in his car waiting for Bobby when the passenger door opened.

'Max Janus getting shot by the Royalists at the Battle of Worcester was not a turning point in the Civil War,' Bobby said.

'Well, it was a turning point about who I was supporting,' Max grumbled.

'Are you still complaining about that?' Danny laughed. 'You realise that was over 370 years ago.'

'Exactly, it's almost yesterday,' Max chuckled.

'So you're a Republican now?' Danny asked.

'No, I became a Republican in 1651, then a Royalist in 1660,' Max replied.

Danny started laughing, 'What happened in 1660? Did a Republican shoot you as well.'

'Don't be daft,' Max scowled. 'Charlie the Second reclaimed the throne. Always staying close to the power without taking power is the secret to surviving and thriving.'

'Fairs,' Danny replied, starting his engine and heading onto the road.

'Talking of staying close to the power,' Max said, opening the Pick'n'Mix group chat on Bobby's phone.

A minute or so later, Danny's phone pinged, and he told his phone to read the message. 'Max suggested we meet at Catherine's on Friday around 11 am. He'll know where the Deceptor is. He's going to check tomorrow afternoon after my last exam.'

'How did you know that?' Danny asked in surprise.

'I messaged Catherine earlier and asked if it was OK to meet up, of course,' Max replied.

'Not that you numpty. You know what I mean. How did you find out where the Deceptor is?' Danny protested.

Max looked puzzled at Danny, 'I don't. We haven't even started looking yet.'

'OK. Now I'm confused. You've just said—' Danny started to say.

'I said I will know where the Deceptor is on Friday. OK, it might not be the Deceptor from the Lamasery, but there will be one inside Glenthorne Crescent,' Max interrupted.

'You think they'll try to break in?' Danny questioned.

'They won't need to break in,' Max replied. 'Catherine, Agathe or Michael will welcome them in.'

'My ears heard what you said, but my brain refuses to turn it into logic,' Danny frowned.

'In what order did we enter Mike's café earlier?'

'Erm, I think Abi was first, then Avery and Adam, and then you kept the door open for me. So you were last. Actually, you were a bit weird, if I remember. You just stood there.'

'Spot on. When Avery and Adam entered, I caught the flash of an aura in the door's glass.'

Danny braked and turned to Bobby, 'Which one?'

'I wish I knew. But, unfortunately, because they walked through at almost the same time, and it was a chance set of angles between where I was standing, the door and where they were, and I couldn't work out whose aura it was,' Max replied, shaking his head.

'Why didn't you try to check when we left?' Danny asked as he started to drive again.

'I did, but all the window posters and signs made getting a reflection from the inside of the window and door impossible, and because we sat by the wall in line with the door, I couldn't get the angle when we opened the door either.'

'Why mention checking tomorrow afternoon?' Danny queried.

'To quote a rather clever friend of Bobby's, it's because my not-so-genius friend I don't want to risk flushing them out on Friday in a house with everyone there unless it becomes a last resort. It's my backup plan. But I'm hoping they'll panic tomorrow and go and visit the other Deceptor and we can track them with the mints.'

'But you can't follow Adam and Avery,' Danny said.

Max looked at Danny and raised an eyebrow.

'What're you looking...ah. You want me to follow one, don't you?' Danny realised.

'Almost. You, Avery and I all have exams in the morning, but Adam has finished his.'

'Yeah, and?'

'Well, we can't know if Adam goes to see the Deceptor in the morning. So I need you to get close to him with this receiver to download the voice recordings, please,' Max replied.

'I'd come with you, Max, but I've got my final exam tomorrow afternoon,' Abi replied in the group chat.

Over the next minute, Dazza, Adam and Avery all replied, offering to go with Max on Thursday afternoon to look for the Deceptor.

'Flip,' Max muttered.

Danny started laughing, 'You weren't expecting everyone to offer to help, were you?'

'Why not get Adam and Dazza to go with Danny? Then we need to make an excuse for Avery?' Bobby suggested.

'That's not a bad idea, buddy. It'll give me a chance to download the voice files from the bug in Adam's bag,' Danny replied as he pulled up on his driveway.

'How can we sort out Avery, though? I can't follow her if she's with me,' Max sighed.

'I have a plan,' Bobby replied, picking up his phone.

<u>'Thanks, guys. Max and Danny have built an aura detector. Max has some locations where he thinks the Deceptor is. One is in town, and the others are a bit of a distance. Adam and Dazza, can you go with Danny and Avery and I can do the town centre place. Sound good?'</u>

The Pick'n'Mix group lit up with thumbs-up emojis from Dazza and Adam and a heart and kissing face from Avery.

'I hate to burst your plan, but there is no such thing as an aura detector. I've tried to build one many times, but they don't work,' Max said.

'We could try,' Danny replied. 'Let's look at exactly what we are trying to detect. Is it a certain frequency or light emission?'

'I tried those options. I even looked at gamma rays.'

'I've got it. What about a light or heat detector which looks for a peripheral emission beyond the physical body?'

'That's an interesting idea. Let's do some testing.'

'Guys, you're overcomplicating this. We don't need an actual detector, just a simple device which Danny can wave around as if it's one,' Bobby said, interrupting the discussion.

'Huh?' Danny said, looking perplexed.

'Max and I will be with Avery. Now we know either Adam or her is a Deceptor, it'll be easy in town to get her reflection to see if it's Avery,' Bobby explained.

'Ah,' Danny said. 'And if she isn't one, it must be Adam.'

'Good grief, I think he's got it, cowboy,' Bobby laughed.

'Not bad, Bobby, you're becoming as cunning as me. How good an actor are you, Danny?' Max chuckled.

'Excuse me, they don't call me the Tom Holland of Haywood for nothing, you know,' Danny preened.

'More like Tom and Jerry than Tom Holland,' Babby laughed.

'Seriously though, if we make a device that bleeps or something, you could jokingly set it off in Adam's presence and see how he reacts,' Max replied. 'You can always claim it was in test mode if you need to.'

Danny pauses briefly and then replies, 'That might be risky. What if he is the Deceptor and gets violent?'

'Good point. Perhaps stick to pointing it towards buildings and pretending it's doing a sweep,' Max said.

'Probably the better option. I can always get Adam to take it nearer a building, too, and that should give me a chance to scan the voice recordings from the bug you planted in his bag.' Danny replied, then added, 'Just a thought, Chief, but once we've identified the Deceptor, what next?'

'Generally, I would then kill th....' Max stopped.

'I thought you might say something like that, but we're talking about our friends Adam or Avery. Putting aside the fact we can't just go around randomly topping people,' Danny replied.

'There must be a way to kill the Deceptor without harming the host?' Bobby asked.

'It's not something I've ever had to consider. The only way to force a Shadower out of a body is for the body to die. It's the same whether it's a shell body or a host,' Max replied.

'There's no way you can just rip it out? Isn't it a Deceptor, not a Shadower anyway, so are you superior or something?' Danny asked.

'Deceptor is just the name for a Shadower operating on the bad side of the law,' Max replied, 'We are the same species, so no, there is no way to rip them out. Well, unless you have a pet, Daxson. They are powerful enough to do it. That's why we used to call them the Chief Executioners.'

'So let's take Adam or Avery to that Daxson the Deceptor mentioned. Then they could rip them out?' Danny suggested.

'What are you suggesting? We knock on the door and say excuse me, Mr Daxson, could you please pull this baddie out of our friend without hurting them, and if you do, we'll give you a nice cup of tea and a biscuit?' Max chuckled.

'OK, smarty pants, at least I'm trying to think of a way to kill the Deceptor without killing our friends.' Danny laughed, then added, 'What about Catherine?'

'No, she wasn't with us at the café, so she is not a Deceptor,' Max replied, shaking his head.

'You know, for an old intelligent guy, you really can be a twit sometimes,' Danny replied. 'I meant, what about asking Catherine if there is a way we could make the Deceptor believe our friend was dying so they leave their body, but we don't kill them for real?'

'Oi, not so much of the old, thank you, I'm eighteen again now,' Max laughed.

'Seventeen, actually, cowboy,' Bobby corrected.

'Almost eighteen then. But actually, that's not a bad idea, Danny. Let me text Catherine and see if she is in. Fancy a trundle to Earls Court?'

An hour later, they sat in Glenthorne Crescent's kitchen, drinking tea.

'Let me get this right. You think either Adam or Avery is a Deceptor, and you want to convince the Deceptor that the body they are in is dying, so they leave the body, and then you can kill the Deceptor?' Catherine asked.

Max replied, 'Well, sort of. The body must die for a few seconds, or the Deceptor will reenter it.

'What about using a cardioplegic solution? That would stop the heart,' Michael suggested.

Catherine shook her head, 'It would need flushing out of their system, so we would need a heart and lung machine and a specialist cardiologist in the room, as that's not your or my specialism.'

'Good point. I can't say I've ever had to think about how to kill someone without killing them,' Michael mused.

'I should hope you've never thought about killing anyone full stop,' Agathe laughed.

'Only Colin at the golf club, but then you can't stand the man either,' Michael chuckled.

'I forgot to say. When we do this, there can't be anyone else in the room apart from me and the Deceptor. In fact, you need to be around 200 feet away,' Max interjected.

'Why so far away?' Danny asked.

'Because it takes about 5 seconds for a Shadower to vaporise in Earth's atmosphere. So if it can reach another living thing in that time, it can use them as a new host,' Max explained. 'If I've immobilised them, they are highly unlikely to be able to move and certainly not at full speed, but even at half speed, that would be around 100 feet.'

'We could use that abandoned ward the Deceptor tricked me into,' Michael suggested, 'It would seem quite poetic in a way.'

'Is it in a single-storey building?' Max asked.

'No, but it's only three floors. They are winding down the place in preparation for relocating near Twickenham,' Michael replied.

'We can't use it then. A Shadower can pass through solid objects in its energy soul form. If the immobiliser starts to wear off and it can escape the dying body, or if it is one of those anomalies where the immobiliser doesn't fully work on it, then it would drop down to a lower floor and into a new host,' Max sighed.

'Are they moving to the new St. Ethelbert's Hospital?' Catherine asked.

'That's the one,' Michael nodded.

'They've got a bit of a wait. I'm the clinical liaison on the Greater London Property Trust Board. Their board meeting overrunning was why I was late meeting you at the Willow Max,' Catherine said. 'It's built and kitted out, but it can't be signed off due to some planning dispute and an issue with building regulations.'

'The answer is right there, Chief,' Danny replied. 'If the new building is built, but they can't move in, then why not use that?'

'It's a university hospital, so one of the operating theatres has a viewing gallery,' Catherine said. 'That's got to be around 100 feet to the back of the gallery, if not a bit more.'

'Well, it sounds good, but we still haven't worked out how to trick the Deceptor out of our friend's body,' Bobby said.

Michael leaned back in his chair, 'The way I see it; we can't do anything that involves surgery, but what if we went down the route of either anaesthetics or antiarrhythmic medication?'

'You mean to induce a cardiac arrest?' Catherine asked.

'Woah there guys, well doctors or whatevs,' Danny said, holding his arms out. 'Are you suggesting we make Adam or Avery have a heart attack? I know Avery's addiction to the word babe is annoying, and Adam's main conversation always involves a football, but these are our friends.'

'It's a cardiac arrest, not a heart attack,' Michael said. 'There is a difference, dear boy. A heart attack is generally caused by a blockage or something reducing blood flow. We are discussing deliberately causing the heart's electrical system to stop working.'

'But the net result is they would still be dead?' Danny queried.

'Yeah, come on, there has to be another solution,' Bobby added.

'The body dying is the only solution. Unless we lock the Deceptor up for six months until they finish transmuting,' Max replied.

'Then that's what we will have to do. Could we pretend they've gone on a backpacking holiday or something so their parents don't worry?' Danny suggested.

'Are you kidding? Avery or Adam backpacking? There's more chance of me winning the lotto than that happening,' Bobby laughed.

'Gentlemen, calm down. The advantage of inducing a cardiac arrest is we should be able to restart their heart after the Deceptor has gone,' Michael said.

'If we make sure there is a defibrillator in the room, then as soon as it's safe, we can hopefully shock them back to life,' Catherine added.

'You both mentioned two words I don't like the sound of,' Danny said, 'Should and hopefully.'

'Well, yes, it carries risks, but they are manageable,' Catherine replied.

'But they might die?' Danny queried.

'We can connect the defibrillator pads up so Max can fire it up the second the Deceptor has gone,' Michael said reassuringly.

'But they still might die?' Danny asked firmly.

'Papa and I will rush straight down as soon as Max gives us the all-clear,' Catherine said soothingly.

'But, they could still die?' Danny insisted.

'Yes, there is a small, and I mean a minimal, risk we might not bring them back,' Michael confirmed.

'Max, you told us you can help regenerate our bodies and effectively make us last forever. So if something goes wrong, can't you go into their body to resuscitate them?' Bobby asked.

'If you had thought about that question, you'd already know the answer, Bobby,' Max sighed. 'A Shadower cannot enter a dead body, nor can we bring it back to life. We can repair damage to a degree but not recreate life.'

Danny looked from Catherine to Michael, then to Agathe before finally staring at Bobby, 'So this is literally our only option?'

'I'm afraid so, Danny,' Max replied. 'I can see how torn you are, and trust me inside this head, Bobby has just been giving me a lesson in English words, some of which I haven't heard in centuries.'

'When do we do it then?' Catherine asked.

'I've suggested we all meet here on Friday around eleven a.m.,' Max replied, 'By then, we should know, plus I'll have a mirror here to confirm who the Deceptor is. I can then use my immobiliser on them, which gives us an hour to get them to that hospital you mentioned.'

'That's going to be tight timing. I reckon it's about forty minutes from here,' Catherine replied, 'Plus, how do we get in? I can get the plans so we know where to go, but I'm unaware of any keys.'

'As it's a new hospital, won't it have digital access controls?' Danny asked.

'You mean like swipe card access? Yes, I would assume so, but I don't think they'd have downloaded any health service data to it yet, so my key card wouldn't work,' Catherine replied.

'Who needs key cards when you've got a Danny?' Danny smiled as he pulled out his laptop.

'I'll go and get mine from the study and see what I can find out from my health service access and the Trust Board meeting minutes,' Catherine said, heading towards the study.

An hour or so later, they had the hospital layout from the planning meeting records, and Danny had identified the access software and hardware suppliers.

'Typical Brinkswell Construction using cheap suppliers whenever possible. They might just as well tie the door handles together with string,' Danny grumbled.

'Do you know the builders then?' Michael asked.

'I know of them rather than know them,' Danny replied, 'My Dad was going to invest in them, but when he did the due diligence, he discovered they've got a track record of building places full of faults and issues that they never fix, so he backed out of the deal.'

'But if they are that bad, how did they get the contract to build a new hospital?' Agathe asked.

'Good question. I guess having a minority shareholder who used to be a Health Secretary and is now the Deputy Chair of the IFFS might help,' Danny smirked.

'You mean?' Agathe said in shock.

'Yep, that's the one. That's the other reason Dad pulled out. It seems most of their major contracts came via that route,' Danny replied. 'If they lose that connection, they would fold.'

'Shocking,' Agathe responded.

'If you think that's bad, guess whose family trust owns the firm providing the hardware and software, NetDat Ltd,' Danny said, crossing his arms.

'Not the same person?' Michael asked.

'Close. It's his husband's family trust,' Danny replied. 'We'll have no problem getting in. The first time I hacked one of their systems was when I was nine, and they're still using parts of the same code even now.'

'We'd better get off, Danny. It's getting late, and tomorrow will be a busy day,' Bobby said.

13

CONFIRMATION

'Morning, buddy. All ready for the big day?' Danny asked cheerfully.

'Morning, Danny. Not really, I'll be glad to get this morning over with,' Bobby groaned.

'Hello, Bobby. Would you like some breakfast?' Mrs White asked. 'I'm just doing some scrambled eggs on toast for Danny.'

'Good Morning, Mrs White. I don't suppose you happen to have any bananas and salad cream, do you?' Max replied.

'Oh, sorry, Bobby, I've not done the shopping yet, so I don't think we've got much fruit in, but we have some mayonnaise if that is any use?' Mrs White replied.

'*No way. Banana and mayonnaise sandwiches do not work EVER. It's salad cream or nothing*,' Bobby thought indignantly.

'Scrambled eggs on toast would be lovely. Thank you, Mrs White,' Bobby said to Danny's mother.

'Cup of tea, bro?' Danny asked, passing a mug and the teapot to Bobby.

'I think I might need something a lot stronger to get through today than tea, but it's a start, thanks,' Bobby replied, filling his mug from the teapot.

Mrs White put a plate of scrambled eggs on toast in front of Danny and then turned back to the stove to start making some for Bobby, 'What have you boys got planned after your exams today?'

'Oh, we thought we might do some undercover spying, capture an alien terrorist and kill one of our friends with a heart attack,' Danny replied, winking at Bobby.

Bobby's mouth dropped open at hearing his friend saying it out loud.

'Oh, that's nice. Hope you boys have fun,' Mrs White replied, having clearly not listened to what Danny said.

Danny leaned across to Bobby and whispered, 'Does your Mum do that?'

'Do what?' Bobby whispered back.

'Ask you questions but then totally ignores the answer? Mine's always doing it, and my Dad,' Danny replied.

Bobby just shrugged his shoulders in a half-hearted, I guess, motion.

'Morning, all,' said Mr White entering the kitchen and kissing his wife on the cheek.

'Morning dear,' Mrs White replied. 'Can I get you any breakfast since I'm cooking for this pair anyway?'

Mr White shook his head, ' No thanks, hun. I've got a breakfast meeting in the City, and they love to lay on the bacon rolls for these things. So what are you lads up to today?'

Mrs White put Bobby's breakfast on the table and winked, saying, 'They've got exams this morning, then apparently, they're capturing an alien spy before killing one of their friends.'

'A normal day at the office then,' Mr White said, laughing loudly.

Danny's mouth dropped open as Bobby whispered, 'It seems your mum hears more than you think.'

'What exams are you doing, Bobby?' Mr White asked.

'History, politics and this morning is economics.'

'That's a good mix. Any idea what you want to do after college?'

'I've not really thought about it, but maybe something to do with finance. I don't think I'll be able to afford university, though.'

'Well, if you decide to skip university, even if just taking a gap year, let me know. I've got a few contacts in the City who are always looking for bright lads like you.'

'*So have I, and I bet I've got more of them than he has,*' Max retorted.

'*Easy cowboy, it's not a competition, you know.*'

'Thank you, Mr White. I might take you up on that offer,' Bobby smiled.

'Hey, what about me, Dad?' Danny said in mock indignation.

'I'm not letting you loose on any of my friends' computer systems,' Mr White chuckled.

'Why? Afraid I might crash them?'

'No, I'm afraid you might upgrade their security and make industrial espionage even harder,' Mr White laughed.

'Fairs,' Danny replied, laughing along.

A short while later, they set off for college.

'I've been thinking. If we meet with Adam and Avery for lunch, why not download the voice files from their bugs at lunchtime? Then, you could always nip to the loo to listen to them,' Danny asked.

'Because your not-so-genius friend Max set them both to the same frequency,' Bobby chuckled.

'Ah, so if he tried to download both simultaneously, they'd—' Danny started to say.

'Yes, they'd corrupt each other. I know rookie error level one,' Max replied.

'We could take a mirror with us and check them out that way?' Danny suggested.

'I don't want to risk them knowing we've found them out. Being as blunt as just using a mirror threatens them spotting it, and they could turn violent and possibly use one of you as a hostage,' Max replied.

'You just like controlling the situation, don't you?' Danny laughed.

'You've all asked a few times whether I was the person in power or at the top in previous lives, but the truth is that being at the top isn't where the power lies. The power sits with the ones who control and influence. Everything else is just pretence,' Max replied.

After plenty of banter during the rest of the journey, Danny pulled up outside Haywood College and was greeted by Avery.

'Hello, Danny and Bobby and how's my babe this morning?' Avery said as she kissed Bobby.

Danny, Bobby and Max responded with similar pleasantries, although in Bobby and Max's case, what came out was 'Morning Averyhun.'

Danny laughed, 'You two still need to work on not trying to speak simultaneously whilst you are body sharing.'

'We are not body sharing. Max is squatting,' Bobby chuckled.

'Well, if you want to squat somewhere else, babe,' Avery winked.

'Avery, do you mind? I've only just had my breakfast!' Danny said indignantly.

'We had better get moving. The exams start in a few minutes. See you both after. How about Mike's Café again?' Max suggested.

'Sound good to me, Chief,' Danny said as he headed off.

'Me too, babe,' Avery replied, kissing Bobby again and heading towards her exam.

'I know I used to go out with Avery last year, but she's changed so much in the last few months. I will be so glad when you have

your own body, so she's kissing you and calling you babe instead of me,' Bobby shuddered.

'*She's sweet. I guess she is just finding her adult personality,'* Max replied.

'*We'll find out if she is hiding another personality later.'*

'*Hang on a minute. It could equally be Adam. You said yourself he has changed over the last few weeks. Plus, he knew the time we went to the Clinic to try to rescue Michael the first time, whereas Avery was with Abi and didn't know until after.'*

'*It's not Adam. As Granny Mosley used to say, I can feel it in my water. Whatever that means.'*

'*I've got one word to say to you, Bobby.'*

'*And what's that cowboy?'*

'*Economics.'*

'*Oh, flip,'* Bobby responded, running to his exam room.

Just under three hours later, Bobby walked down to Mike's Café. '*You were very quiet in there today, cowboy.'*

'*That's because I'm an engineer, not an economist. However, I have used regression analysis to predict complex systems' behaviour and understand the effect of different variables on the system in the past. But, being honest, I think you did rather well. I didn't detect rising stress levels, and you answered every question.'*

'*Thanks, cowboy. Fudge, they are all here. I was hoping to be able to open the door for at least Adam or Avery.'*

Bobby walked into the café and exchanged greetings with his friends before ordering food at the counter.

'Can I have a banana and salad cream sandwich on white, please?' Max asked.

'Do we look like some bleedin' hipster deli?' Mike, the proprietor, replied. 'It's what's on the board or any mixture thereof. I recommend the fry-up.'

'You always recommend the fry-up,' Bobby laughed.

'Course I do. No matter what ails you, it'll always look better after a nice plate of sausage, beans, bacon, eggs, fried bread, black pudding and toast, with optional mushrooms for an extra

50 pence,' Mike laughed, holding his sides, which hinted at his own fondness for more than the occasional fry-up.

'I'll just have a ham and cheese toastie, thanks,' Bobby replied.

'Sure I can't tempt you? Your mate over there is having one,' Mike replied, nodding towards Dazza.

Dazza looked up and gave Bobby a thumbs-up. 'It's grood,' he said with a mouthful of beans.

'Cheers, Mike, but I'm fine with just the toastie, thanks. Oh, and a water, please,' Bobby replied.

'Still or sparkling?' Mike asked.

'Oh, erm, I didn't know you did sparkling. I'll have one of them, please,' Bobby replied.

'We don't, but as you thought we were a friggin' deli, I thought I'd give you the option,' Mike laughed again before turning to a serving hatch, 'Carol, one jam and knees toastie with a glass of tap water, please.'

'Aight, Mike,' came the voice from the kitchen.

'So what's the plan then, Bob,' Dazza asked, wiping his plate clean with a slice of toast as Bobby sat at the table.

'Well, I'm sure I've seen a Deceptor in three places. First, one is here in Haywood, then there was the one at the Lamasery, but I reckon that was a temporary location while they were holding Michael,' Max replied.

'Where is the third location?' Avery asked.

Max turned to face her and said, 'The final location was in Eaton at the Nort West London Police Headquarters.'

'Why there?' Avery asked, looking blankly.

'Well, I guess it makes sense, given how crooked Fallon and the other copper are,' Danny replied.

'Oh, yes, I forgot all about them,' Avery said, smiling at Danny.

'What do you think, Adam?' Max asked.

'*Leave him alone. I'm telling you it's not him*,' Bobby protested.

'*Easy, buddy. We will soon know for sure*,' Max replied.

'Well, they are the only locations you've seen anything so far, but last time we spoke about it, you were cold on the idea of police involvement,' Adam said, adding, 'Plus, I've got a question. You can see a Deceptor's aura, but how will we know?'

'Good question. Danny, the Deceptor detector, please?' Max asked, holding out his hand.

'I thought you had it,' Danny replied.

'But I'm sure I saw you pick it up last night,' Max said desperately.

'Just kidding, Chief,' Danny laughed, pulling it out of a pocket in his chair.

Danny proceeded to wave it around the room away from Adam and Avery before pressing a discreet little button as he pointed it at Bobby setting off an alarm and flashing a red light.

'Bobby's a Deceptor?' Dazza asked, confused.

'No, but Max is a Shadower. The detector picks up Shadowers; it can't distinguish Deceptors separately as we're the same species, remember,' Bobby replied as Mike slapped down his toasted sandwich and a glass of water.

'What's the range on it?' Adam queried.

'Should be about 150 feet, so we might need to get out of the car to get closer to the buildings,' Danny replied.

'That's OK, Danny. You can stay in the car, and Adam and I can sweep the buildings, right?' Dazza replied, looking at Adam.

'Yeah, no problem,' Adam responded.

'What about us? Babe,' Avery asked.

'With that Deceptor being on the bypass when we did that driving lesson, I think it must be based around here, so we can go for a walk through town to see if we can see anything,' Max replied. 'Danny, how long do you reckon it'll take to get down to Richmond, then up to Eaton?'

'Allowing for some time to sweep the front of the buildings, it's going to take two hours before we can be back here,' Danny replied.

'OK, let's get cracking then,' Max replied, chewing on the last of his toastie. 'Let's meet at Danny's place in around two hours. Is that OK, buddy?'

'Yeah, it's fine. Dad's in the City all day, and Mum is out shopping. She generally stops by my Nan's on the way back, so the place should be empty,' Danny replied,

'I can't stay that long as I promised my Mum I'd meet her for a post-exam celebration in Covent Garden. So I'll go with you, babe and check out Haywood, then leave you to brief everyone afterwards. Is that OK, babe?' Avery said, looking at Bobby.

'Uh, yeah, sure. I wouldn't want you missing out on a treat,' Max replied.

'Follow me, team,' Danny said, using his eye controls to head towards the door.

Unfortunately, Danny was sitting at the height where his eyes looked through a gap in the posters and out into the street, and his chair took off, ploughing straight into the glass door, smashing it.

'*Fudge, I was going to use that to check Adam and Avery for auras,*' Max grumbled.

'Hey, that's my frigging door,' Mike shouted, running across the café.

'Good to see your first concern is your customer's welfare, my good man,' Danny replied sarcastically as he brushed the fragments of tempered glass off his arm.

'You look flipping fine to me, which is more than can be said for my door?' Mike replied defiantly.

Danny handed Mike his Dad's business card, 'I'll message my Dad now, and if you get the quote, he'll transfer the money over straight away for the repairs.'

'Sounds like you've done this before,' Mike replied.

'Once or several times to be honest,' Danny laughed.

'Well, OK, and I'm glad you're alright, lad. I don't want to lose any good customers,' Mike chuckled back as he studied the business card.

'Don't think I'd call someone smashing up your front door a particularly good customer,' Dazza laughed as they all tried to step over the glass to leave the café.

Bobby looked down at the glass shards where he saw aura flashes, but it was impossible to tell who they were coming off. Some reflections may have even been his aura.

After checking Danny was alright, Bobby, Max and Avery headed off downtown.

'Are you sure you're OK, Danny? You hit that door at one hell of a rate,' Adam asked.

'I think my pride was hurt more than my body, buddy,' Danny laughed, still brushing glass off him as they headed towards his car.

'Where are we going first, Danny boy?' Dazza asked.

'I thought we'd pop to the cop shop first in Eaton before doing the long trek to the Lamasery,' Danny replied.

'Adam, you sit up front, and Dazza can stretch out on the back seat,' Danny said as they got into his car.

'So how does that thing work then?' Adam asked.

'You point it at the building and slowly sweep it across, trying to keep a steady distance between you and the building,' Danny lied as they set off on the short journey to Eaton. 'If the alarm sounds and it lights up, then we know a Shadower is in the building.'

'Sounds simple to me,' Dazza replied.

Adam sat silently, then said, 'Yeah, it does sound simple. Too simple for you and Max, to be honest.'

'Uh, yeah, well, we didn't have much time to work on it. Oh, and Max had been trying to develop one for a long time, so it was the best we could come up with for now, but of course, we will improve it,' Danny panicked.

'I wonder how Avery and Bob are getting on?' Dazza queried.

Back in Haywood, Avery smiled and said, 'Babe, carry on, and I'll catch you up. I need to ring my Mum. It might be a long call.'

'It's OK, I can wait,' Max replied.

'Uh babe, it's a woman thing,' Avery said.

'Oh, OK, I'll just be down there on the benches,' Max answered, pointing to some seats.

The traffic was light, and soon Dazza and Adam got out of Danny's car and walked towards the police station with the Deceptor detector.

'Remember to walk slow but steady, guys,' Danny shouted out of his window.

'Yes, I've already explained I can't stay here long. I know we agreed to meet this afternoon, but I just needed to do this first,' Avery said into her phone.

Max leaned forward and looked around at the shop windows. No matter how he looked, he couldn't find a single reflection of Avery.

'*Why are so many shops all stone and Greco-Roman when this place was a tiny village until the train arrived at the end of the Victorian era,*' Max grumbled.

Danny picked up the voice recorder receiver Max had given him and pressed the download button. The device bleeped once, but then a red light came on.

'Come on, device, I need two bleeps and a green light,' Danny muttered as he pressed it again.

'It's not doing anything,' Adam moaned as they started walking along the length of the police station.

'Pass it here. It's probably an operator error,' Dazza laughed.

Danny leant across, trying to get closer to Adam's bag and pressed the download again, resulting in another single beep and a red light. 'Thirty feet, he said the range was. It can't be more than three feet. Flipping amateur,' Danny cursed as the receiver failed again.

'Either this place is Shadower-free, or Danny has finally developed a device that doesn't work,' Dazza grumbled, shaking the device to try to make it work.

'Maybe we need to get closer to the police building?' Adam suggested.

'Well, it can't hurt, although what do we say if a copper stops us?' Dazza asked.

'We can't tell them the truth; they'd lock us up. Perhaps we can claim we're testing a new type of, oh erm,' Adam started to say.

'Good idea, it's a new type of metal detector,' Dazza agreed, 'That'll work.'

***

'Yes, I understand, but I said I needed to do this with Max first. He claims he knows. I have to look like I'm supporting him but stop worrying. I'm fine,' Avery said.

'*Maybe if I move over there, I might be able to get a reflection,*' Max thought, walking across to another bench and waving at Avery.

Avery waved back and smiled.

'Flipping heck. How can it be so far down in the passenger footwell,' Danny complained as he stretched across, trying to reach Adam's bag.

The Deceptor device's red light illuminated, and the alarm sounded. 'See, I said it was an operator error,' Dazza said triumphantly.

'You were just lucky you had it when it found a Deceptor,' Adam said. 'Now, where exactly were you pointing it?'

'That way,' Dazza replied, pointing it back in the same direction.

'Well?' Adam asked, crossing his arms.

Dazza started waving it left and right, but nothing happened. 'I don't understand. You heard it go off, didn't you? Can they move so fast that they've now gone?'

'OK, but I can't just leave now. Give me thirty minutes at least,' Avery said in desperation.

'*Well, that was a pointless move, cowboy. All we can see now is the reflection in that shop back to Mike's Café.*' Bobby said

'*Ladies and gentlemen, let me introduce Bobby Morris, Professor of the flipping obvious.*'

'*Oh no, I don't believe it,*' Bobby moaned.

'*What, what did I miss? I was thinking about Danny and the guys. Did you see an aura?*'

'*No, it was an advert on the side of that bus for that flipping whisky I drank at Agathe's. Just seeing it makes me want to puke. I'm never drinking again,*' Bobby groaned.

'About flipping time,' Danny sighed as he finally got his fingers around a part of Adam's bag and pulled it towards him. 'I'll grab the bug, and Max can download the files manually.'

'Pass it back here,' Adam said, snatching the detector off Dazza.

'Snatchers be nimble, snatchers be quick, but the manners they haven't as they're about to get hit,' Dazza replied, punching Adam in the arm.

'Oww,' Adam replied as he rubbed his arm, and the detector went off again.

'Hang on, that was pointing at you,' Dazza replied, stepping back.

'I'm not a Deceptor,' Adam protested, pointing the detector at himself as the alarm went off again.

'Oh, for crying out loud, Adam, why have you got sweaty sports gear in your bag? You've been doing exams this week, not running a marathon,' Danny muttered as he tried to find the mint tin. 'This is gross.'

'OK, in thirty minutes, message me, and I'll make my excuses and come to you. Are we still meeting in Covent Garden?' Avery asked into her phone.

'*Why don't we try walking around? At least the angles will keep changing, so we might finally see Avery's reflection,*' Bobby suggested standing up.

'I swear, Dazza, we've been mates our entire lives. I would never lie to you. I swear I'm not a Deceptor,' Adam pleaded.

'Pass me the detector,' Dazza demanded.

Adam passed the detector over. Dazza grabbed it and pointed it at Adam, and it went off again.

Adam started getting emotional, 'I'm not a Deceptor, I'm not.'

'Well, Danny and Max's device says otherwise,' Dazza replied, dropping his arm down as the alarm went off again.

Dazza looked at the device and frowned. He pointed it at Adam again, but it stayed silent. Then he dropped his arm again, and it went off briefly.

━━━━━━━━

'Look, am I mistaken, or is there a bit of an aura showing behind that column reflection?' Bobby asked.

━━━━━━━━

'If I ever touch another pair of sweaty socks or underwear in my life, it'll be too soon,' Danny moaned. 'Ah, what's that hard thing?'

'What's going on?' Adam looked puzzled at Dazza.

'I don't know,' Dazza replied, pointing the detector at himself and then at Adam without the alarm activating.

'Let me look at it again,' Adam insisted, wiping his eyes.

'Oh, at last. Max, you owe me so bad for getting this for you,' Danny grumbled.

The detector alarm went off, and then it stopped. It went off again and then stopped.

'This thing is fake,' Adam snarled. 'Look, if I press this tiny button, it triggers the alarm.'

'Let me try,' Dazza said, holding out his hand.

'Sorry, babe. Mum was a bit angry with me,' Avery said as she walked up to Max and kissed him.

'That's OK, hun,' Max replied. 'Let's go down this way towards the indoor precinct.'

Danny was annoyed, 'I should not be having to stuff a mate's sweaty clothes back into a bag because someone can't make their devices work prop—'

The passenger door flew open.

'Oh boy, if I wasn't angry enough already, why have you got my sports socks in your hand and what are you doing in my bag?' Adam demanded.

Avery and Max walked into the precinct with glass-fronted shops surrounding them.

'*I knew it,*' Bobby said.

'Sorry, Adam, I err, dropped my mints, and as I was trying to get them, I knocked your bag over,' Danny tried to explain.

'And I guess this detector being fake was caused by what? Some dropped mints as well?' Adam growled. 'Hang on, that's the mint tin Bobby offered me at college.'

Adam grabbed the tin of mints off Danny, 'This is the same one, but why has it got a connector jack in the base?' Adam tipped out the remaining mints and started examining the tin before finally prising it in half, 'And why is there a circuit board inside it?'

Danny started to explain why Max had been concerned about Adam and Avery.

'So this man that claimed to love me also didn't trust me?' Adam snapped.

'Bobby did trust you, but Max said either you or Avery had to be the leak.'

'So what's this piece of trash all about then?' Adam sneered, throwing the detector towards Danny.

'Max wanted me to keep you guys busy whilst he checked out Avery.'

'It's true, mate. Max was the one who suspected you. Bobby was convinced it was Avery,' Dazza said.

'Hang on, are you saying you knew about this too, Dazza?' Adam screamed angrily. 'I thought we were best friends. We grew up together.'

'*Avery's got an aura*,' Bobby said.

'*Yes, I can see*,' Max replied, '*We need to let the guys know.*'

Danny's phone pinged.

'Adam, please. Max asked me to stay quiet until he was sure. I'd never ever betray you,' Dazza pleaded.

'But you never even thought to speak to me in private? You even pretended I was a Deceptor and let me beg when that stupid detector toy went off.' Adam challenged. 'Some friend.'

'Adam, I swear I knew nothing about this. I knew about Lamasery by accident and how Max was suspicious about you and Avery, but I was as much in the dark about this as you were,' Dazza replied.

Danny tried to plead with Adam, 'Be angry with Max and even with me, but please don't take it out on Dazza or Bobby. Today was Max's idea, and I was the only other person who knew what was happening.'

Dazza's phone pinged.

'Guess that'll be your friend,' Adam sneered.

'Please, Adam, nothing will ever come between us,' Dazza said.

'Nothing except that alien freak,' Adam replied.

'Max has just said Avery is a Deceptor,' Danny said.

'Well, frigging bully for him,' Adam replied.

'We need to go back to Haywood. He'll need our help,' Danny said.

'You go. I don't want to see him ever again,' Adam snapped.

'I'm with Adam,' Dazza replied. 'As much as you guys are my friends, Adam comes first.'

'Doesn't flipping sound it,' Adam snarled.

'Adam, we watched the school swimming pool being built as five-year-olds. We've shared laughs and everything growing up. I don't care what this alien dude says or does; you are my best friend forever,' Dazza replied.

'I'll drop you guys back home then,' Danny replied.

'Just go, Danny, we'll make our own way home,' Adam replied.

'But,' Danny said.

'Scram, Danny, save your pal Max or whatevs,' Dazza replied.

They watched Danny drive off and start walking.

'Any idea where the tube station or bus stop is, buddy?' Dazza asked.

'Haven't got a clue,' Adam shrugged.

'Look, I understand why you are angry, but honestly, Bobby was totally against this; we both were. We only went along because Max was trying to protect us all.'

'Really? How does lying and deceiving me protect anyone? What have I done to deserve any of this other than love a man and jeopardise my professional career by being with him?'

'It wasn't you that he saw as a threat. He thought maybe you or Avery were talking to someone linked to the Deceptor.'

'So what was all this rubbish about Deceptor detectors then?' Adam answered, feeling the rage slowly subsiding.

'Honestly, mate, I don't have a clue, but the fact that Avery is a Deceptor proves Max was right to be suspicious, doesn't it?'

'I guess, but I wish he or any of you had just asked me. I'd have walked over hot coals if that's what it took to show them the truth.'

'I know you would have Adam. But be honest, if you suspected someone was well dodge, would you ask them or try to prove it first?'

'I'd ask them, of course,' Adam said, smirking.

'Do you take me for a mug?'

Adam looked at his friend and smiled, 'Nah, I'd say more like a three-course meal than just a mug.'

'I'll give you that just this once,' Dazza laughed as he did the ceremonial punch in the arm. 'Hey, look, there's a bus stop.'

'Reckon, we should go and help Max and Bobby?' Adam asked, adding, 'Danny's still got my bag in his car.'

Dazza nodded, 'I think we should. Today has been so over the top that I'm not sure I could cope if something awful happened to them. And maybe we overreacted a little bit, although understandably.'

'I could accept a little awfulness for Max, but I don't want anyone else hurt. Oh, and you're right. I overreacted again.'

'No, buddy, you reacted perfectly normally under the circumstances. So please don't beat yourself up over it. But I am putting a note in my diary of the day you admitted I was right,' Dazza replied. 'It says we need the number 142 for London Zoo. I wonder if it's too late to ask Danny to come back and pick us up?'

'London Zoo, how appropriate. It feels like we're all a bunch of animals at the moment,' Adam chuckled half-heartedly. 'And what do you mean you'll make a note in your diary? When did you learn to write?'

'Max, if Avery is a Deceptor, then not only can we see her aura, but she can see yours,' Bobby thought.

'Yeah, but she already knows I'm a Shadower,' Max replied.

'You're missing the point. If we can see your aura and, of course, hers, then so can she see both of them and that means....'

'Oh fudge, that means she'll know we know. Flipping heck, that's why I don't blatantly use mirrors.'

'Hang on, hun, let's go back outside. I need to call Danny,' Max said.

'OK, babe, shall I wait here? We've only just walked inside,' Avery replied.

'No, let's both go back into the main square; the signal is better,' Max lied, trying to find any excuse to leave the corridor of glass.

Max pulled out Bobby's phone, scrolled to Danny and hit dial, 'Hey Danny, we're drawing a blank here, how's..... Woah, slow down, buddy. Adam's what?'

'Babe? What's up?' Avery asked, putting her arm around him.

'It's Adam. He doesn't want anything to do with me anymore,' Bobby wailed.

'Oh, Bobby, why would he say such a thing?' Avery queried.

'I messed up, Chief, sorry. That download device didn't work, so I tried to extract the recorder, and Adam caught me,' Danny said. 'I'm on the way to you now. How's it going? Ah, I'm guessing she's by you? OK.'

'How do you feel about Bobby then?' Dazza asked as the bus trundled along.

'I'm angry with him, but I still love him,' Adam replied, 'I know he's got Max inside him, and that means he's not behaving as he normally would, but he could have still spoken to me.'

'But it wasn't my choice,' Bobby said to Danny. 'Max said we had to do this.'

'Do what, babe? What has Max made you do?' Avery asked.

Bobby looked at Avery and realised she had just called him babe instead of Max. 'I'm, uh, I love, uh, well, I'm in love with Adam,' Bobby blurted out, trying to find something dramatic to say.

'Well, we know that, Bobby. You said it the other night at Agathe's house,' Avery replied, 'But what did Max make you do?'

'He insisted we split up to search for the Deceptor. If we'd stayed together, Adam might not have decided to end it with me,' Max replied, trying to sound like Bobby.

'*That's true too. This is all your fault, Max,*' Bobby thought, '*The sooner you're gone, the better.*'

'*Of course, Bobby. It's not fair on you or your friends to be dragged into my life,*' Max replied. '*As soon as I can, I'll go.*'

'Adam, you know how I feel about you, don't you? We are good, aren't we?' Dazza asked.

'Err, sorry, Dazza, but I love Bobby. I'm not looking for more. Besides, I didn't know you liked guys,' Adam replied.

'Say what? Sorry buddy, no, no, no, I didn't mean it like that. I meant you know you're my best friend forever, and no matter what, I've got your back,' Dazza replied, 'Anyway, I fancy Abi.'

'I'm coming into Haywood now. Where are you?' Danny asked.

Avery's phone pinged, 'Come on, it's time to meet.'

'We are near the precinct,' Max replied.

'You fancy Abi?' Adam said in shock.

'Yeah, but she wouldn't look twice at me,' Dazza replied, looking down.

'Why not? You're a good-looking guy Dazza.'

'Course I am. Everyone fancies a fat ginger giant, don't they,' Dazza said forlornly.

Adam grabbed Dazza, 'Don't you dare say that, Dazza. First of all, you're not fat. Blimey, for your height, you're the perfect build. I'd love to be your build instead of being scrawny.'

'But I'm still ginger.'

'I like ginger nuts,' Adam replied with a wink.

'I said I'm not that way,' Dazza laughed.

'In your dreams,' Adam interrupted, adding, 'Do you think we should call Danny or Bobby?'

'I tried,' Dazza replied, 'But both their phones were engaged. I'll send them a message.'

***

Danny's phone pinged then Bobby's pinged.

'I need to go, babe. Mum's just messaged,' Avery said.

'What? Oh yeah, OK, Avery. Have a nice time,' Bobby replied distractedly.

Avery kissed Bobby on the cheek, 'See you tomorrow, babe. Good luck hunting that Deceptor. See you too, Bobby.'

Avery headed off towards Haywood underground station with a smile.

'I've just parked up, Chief. I'll be with you shortly. Oh, Dazza's messaged,' Danny said.

'Yeah, I saw it flash up, but I'm not sure I can take it,' Bobby replied. 'I'll see you in a few minutes.'

***

Dazza looked at his phone, 'Strange, neither of them has read the message.'

'I've blown it, haven't I,' Adam said. 'Why do I have to be so headstrong sometimes?'

***

Danny opened the message from Dazza, 'We've caught the bus. See you in a bit.'

A few minutes later, Danny saw Bobby standing outside the precinct, 'Hiya bro, how are you doing?'

'I've been better,' Bobby sighed. 'I just don't think Max and I are compatible.'

'I think my lifestyle is too chaotic for you guys,' Max confirmed.

'I'm staying out of that debate, although I would say you're both amazing guys,' Danny replied. 'What happened to Avery?'

'She left not long ago. She's off to meet her Mum for a post-exam celebration,' Bobby sighed.

'Excuse me, but wasn't this setup about proving who was the leak and a Deceptor and following them?' Danny asked.

'Oh fudge, yes it was, and now I've let her wander off,' Max replied angrily.

'Sorry, Max, it's my fault. I agreed to help, but things turned out bad so quickly,' Bobby said.

'Bobby, I should have realised this wouldn't work. I'm so old and set in my ways, and you're young and still exploring life. I should never have entered you,' Max replied.

'Ifs, buts, and maybe guys. You are where you are. Let's focus on the positive and get that Deceptor,' Danny said.

'The positives? Let's see. The Deceptor is getting away again. Our friend is that Deceptor and the love of my life is on the way here to say to my face that he never wants to see me again,' Bobby groaned. 'Why don't I just end it now?'

———

'It's OK, they know we're coming now they've both read my message,' Dazza said cheerily.

'I am so embarrassed about how I spoke to Danny,' Adam said.

'Oh, he'll be fine. You know how focussed he gets. I bet he's not even mentioned our fallout to Bobby or Max.'

'I hope so.'

'You could not make it up,' Avery laughed into her phone. 'I was seconds away from thinking they'd discovered me when that fool Bobby had a domestic with his boyfriend.'

'So you're still in the clear?' the voice replied.

'Amazingly, yes. We were in the precinct with our combined auras dancing in the shop windows like crazy when he had to make a call, and his world unravelled,' Avery chuckled.

'Well, I'd better get the cocktails in.'

'About time you paid. I'll have a long island iced tea, sis.'

'How much longer before we get back to Haywood,' Danny sighed.

'One more stop, I think,' Dazza replied.

'I can't wait. First, I need to apologise to Danny and then throw my arms around Bobby. I feel such a fool for reacting as I did.'

'What next then, Chief?' Danny asked, 'Do we try the GPS tracker in those mints you gave her?'

'I'd forgotten about the tracker. Have you still got that download device?' Max asked.

'It's useless, Chief. I clicked it, but it didn't work.'

'I said hold the button down until it bleeps twice and the light goes green.'

'No, you, erm, well, may not have done,' Danny faltered.

'Just pass it here, and I'll connect Bobby's phone to it. Maps will then show where she is.'

'Guys, I really don't want to face Adam, but we can't just run off if he's coming here,' Bobby said.

'Haywood next stop,' Dazza said.

'I'm so scared,' Adam replied.

'It's chill, bud. They know we're coming. I'll check where they are,' Dazza answered.

'Where are you? We'll be in Haywood next stop.' Dazza messaged Bobby and Danny.

'Oh no, I'm scared,' Bobby replied, 'Where's Avery? We need to get on.'

'What happened to we can't run off?' Danny asked.

'Reality, bud, just reality. I don't want to hear Adam end it,' Bobby replied.

'According to Maps, she is heading southeast, which ties into her saying Covent Garden,' Max said.

'We're pulling into Haywood now. Where are you ?' Dazza messaged Danny.

Danny read the message and said, 'Guys, we can't ignore them. I saw how angry Adam was. Surely we at least owe him the chance to tell you face to face?'

'We are by the precinct, and I'm sorry,' Bobby messaged back to Dazza.

'They're by the precinct. See, I said it would be OK,' Dazza said.

'I hope so,' Adam replied.

'My whole life is about to end,' Bobby said.

Danny wondered how to reply. Should he try to be positive, maybe affirm Bobby's view but put a bright perspective on it but in the end, said, 'It is what it is.'

'Is that the best you've got, Mr Genius,' Bobby replied.

'They're over there,' Dazza said as he and Adam walked towards Haywood town centre.

'Oh fudge, they're here,' Bobby sighed.

Adam ran the final few metres and flung his arms around Bobby, 'I'm so sorry I got angry with you.'

Danny frowned at Dazza, and Dazza winked back.

'But I, well, I thought you....' Bobby started.

'You thought I never wanted to see you again,' Adam replied, 'But I was angry. I'm still angry with you and Max, but thanks to Dazza, I also understand.'

'That's why I told you to go,' Dazza whispered to Danny. 'I've known Adam my entire life, which means I know when he needs space and time.'

'I hope I'm lucky enough to find a friend as true as you one day,' Danny replied.

'You already have my friend,' Dazza replied with a wink.

'So we're still?' Bobby asked.

'Yes, my gorgeous, wonderful man. We are still,' Adam replied. 'So whatever else is going on, let's save Avery and get back to normal.'

'Normal?' Danny queried, 'When have we ever been normal?'

'He's got a point,' Dazza laughed.

14

TERMINAL OPTION

'Are you sure this is such a good idea?' Adam asked.

'What do you mean?' Max replied.

'We know Avery is a Deceptor, so why follow her?' You've already explained what will happen tomorrow when we're at Agathe's house.'

'That's a good point, but I need to find out who else she is working with.'

'What if she sees us? Won't it look strange us all being in Covent Garden simultaneously, especially as we are supposed to be Deceptor hunting,' Dazza reasoned.

'The big man is right, Chief,' Danny chipped in.

'Because once we find out where Avery is meeting her Mum or whoever, we need to make sure we've got all the exits covered, and I can follow the other person,' Max replied.

'Almost there, Chief. Anywhere specific you want me to park?' Danny asked.

'The tracker has stopped at one of those external seating areas facing the Opera House,' Max replied. 'Park in one of the side streets a couple of streets away somewhere like Tavistock Street?'

'Cheers, sis. I so need this,' Avery replied, sipping on her cocktail.

'You're welcome,' the Deceptor replied, 'I've got to say you rock that teenage look. Do you think you'll stay like that?'

'Are you kidding me, Claudia?' Avery replied, 'This girl does nothing but whine. There's no way I'm spending six months inside her, even if I like the look. I want you to kill her so I can go into another body as soon as possible.'

'Talking of which, I spoke to Jon Willis earlier, and he's happy for you to transmute in him still,' Claudia replied, 'By the way should I call you Avery or Sabina?'

'Sabina, please. If I hear this girl's name one more time, I may get violent,' Sabina laughed before lifting her glass, 'A toast to Jon. I quite fancy being a man again. I think the last time I was one was in 1891.'

'You did rather get carried away back then,' Claudia replied.

'I'm not proud of it, you know. That laudanum you gave me for the migraines I had in that body made me a bit crazy,' Sabina chuckled.

'Crazy for three years? Well, that's one way of looking at it, although I'm not sure the people of Whitechapel would agree.'

'I've missed this so much. Just chilling out with you. Hey, how about we take turns transmuting in Jon? We had fun looking the same as women until I had to go in this body.'

'Oh, that could be interesting,' Claudia laughed, then she spluttered, 'I picked the wrong drink. This one tastes awful.'

'Here, have a mint. They're alright for peppermint,' Sabina replied, handing the tin of mints over.

'I love peppermint.'

'Keep them. This girl's taste buds make everything taste a bit overpowering.'

Danny found a disabled parking spot, and they piled out of his car.

'OK, Chief, how do you want to handle this?' Danny asked.

'If we approach from different angles, then when they split, hopefully, one of us will be in the right place to start following the other person until I can get there,' Max replied. 'Flip, I've messed up again.'

'What's up, Max,' Adam asked.

'I should have brought some walkie-talkies,' Max groaned.

'No problem, let's set up another group chat, and we can use that,' Danny proposed as he tapped into his phone.

'The Tooty-Fruities?' Dazza sighed, looking at his invitation to join the new group.

'It'll do for now,' Max said. 'Now, Danny, you approach from the south. Dazza, you stand out, so you head towards St Paul's church, then cut through the Apple Market and Central Avenue to mingle with the crowds. I'll cut round to James Street, then stroll towards the Opera House, and Adam, you can—'

'I can come with you. I'm not letting you loose again on your own,' Adam replied defiantly. 'Besides, Avery thinks we've fallen out, so if she sees us, we can say we've come somewhere neutral to talk about it.'

'When did you become so cunning?' Dazza laughed.

'It's mixing with these guys,' Adam said, waving towards Danny and Bobby. 'They've corrupted me.'

'I've not had a chance yet,' Bobby laughed.

A few minutes later, they were circling Covent Garden.

'I can see her. She's sat at a table with a blonde woman near the Opera House. I'll grab a table by the Jubilee Market Hall,' Danny typed into the Tooty-Fruities group chat.

'I'll have a lemon iced tea, please,' Danny said to a passing waiter.

As Bobby, Adam and Dazza neared the church, Dazza turned and headed inside the market. Adam turned to Bobby and said, 'Stay there a minute. I've spotted something I need to get.'

'But Adam, we've not got time,' Max started to say.

'Stay there, don't move and do as you're told,' Adam snarled with a smile.

'I'm lost,' Dazza messaged.

'You've only been in there a minute,' Bobby replied.

'I know, and I've passed the same hoodie stall three times already,' Dazza answered.

'They appear very relaxed. They've just toasted something,' Danny messaged.

'Hold out your hands,' Adam said as he returned to Bobby.

'Why, what have you got? We are busy, you know,' Max replied.

'Yes, I realise that which is why I've bought you some hi-tech surveillance equipment to avoid the mistakes of this afternoon,' Adam laughed as he handed the object to Bobby.

'It's a compact mirror,' Bobby chuckled.

'Yes, it's so much simpler as a Shadower for checking out baddies,' Adam said with a smile.

'OK, I'll give you that,' Max replied. 'Now, let's get over to where Avery is.'

'It's OK. I've worked out where I am, and I've spotted Avery. She's with that nurse from Lamasery,' Dazza messaged.

'You're in Covent Garden, Dazza. No need to thank me.' Danny replied, adding, 'Hey, look to your right. I can see you. What are you eating?'

'A chilli and cheese burrito, it's so good,' Dazza said.

'How the heck can you stand there calmly eating a burrito when we're spying on Avery?' Danny asked.

'Well, I can't eat it excitedly, can I? The filling would go everywhere,' Dazza replied.

'Will you guys knock it off? I've just spotted Avery from this end. That's the Deceptor from the Willow, Lamasery and Bobby's driving lesson,' Max messaged.

'You're sure that's the Deceptor?' Danny asked.

'Yeah, I used Adam's hi-tech detector, and she and Avery are both Deceptors,' Max smiled, winking at Adam.

'Have you tried connecting to the bug you gave her?' Danny asked. 'And when did Adam go hi-tech?'

'How's your Daxson?' Sabina asked.

'Getting worse by the day. He'll be seventeen soon, but he's already totally out of control. I don't think even I am safe with him anymore,' Claudia replied.

'But the magnifying transmitter is still keeping him alive?' Sabina asked, 'That must be some comfort.'

'It is, and if J is right about the Technician, then we can get an Exodus machine and send him to a denser planet so he can be free,' Claudia sighed.

'Have you ever met J?' Sabina asked. 'I know you are friendly with that copper who seems to speak to J regularly.'

'No, I've never met or even spoken to J. I just get given instructions. Well, we both do. That's why you are in that stupid girl.'

'Who are they talking about?' Adam whispered to Max, 'The first thing I heard was worse by the day.'

'I'm unsure. If I had to guess, maybe the Daxson or another Deceptor. But the fact they are talking about using a magnifying transmitter makes me think it might be the Daxson,' Max replied.

'Why, what is it?' Adam asked.

'In simple terms, it's a way to discharge high voltages of electricity through the air. Remember all those old Hollywood films with mad scientists and electricity arcing like lightning,' Max explained.

'But how is that of use to the Daxson?' Adam continued.

'There is a voltage drop as the electricity goes through the air. When Tesla invented his coil, he proved that the energy could illuminate the light bulb in his hand and using the magnifying transmitter intensified it to even work over distances of a kilometre or more,' Max replied, 'I'm assuming they've got it rigged somehow so the Daxson can draw on that airborne power.'

'Tesla? You mean the car guy invented this?' Adam looked puzzled.

'No, Nikola Tesla. He was a genius inventor and engineer. He only died in 1943 and was responsible for some huge advances in electrical and mechanical equipment. The car firm is named after him. Now, shh, we need to listen.'

'So, who is J? Is it the name of the Daxson?'

Max sighed and looked at Adam, 'If we listen, we might hear.'

'They are on the move. It looks like Avery is heading your way, and the other one is heading towards me,' Danny messaged.

Max looked over and could see Avery heading towards them. 'Quick, behind this column, and kiss me,' Max said urgently.

Avery passed Max and Adam without noticing them hiding behind the column and headed toward the underground station. As soon as they thought it was safe, Adam and Max ran down to Dazza.

'Which way did that Deceptor and Danny go?' Max asked.

Dazza, with a mouth full of the remains of his burrito, pointed down the alleyway between the London Transport Museum and the Jubilee Market. Adam and Max set off in that direction, with Dazza following. They emerged into Tavistock Street, but there were no signs of Danny or the Deceptor, so they started strolling northwest in the general direction of Drury Lane.

'Danny, where are you?' Max typed into the group chat.

'On the Strand, heading towards the posh hotel,' came the reply.

'With you in a sec,' Max messaged back.

Adam, Bobby and Dazza broke into a run, down Burleigh Street and onto the Strand.

'Danny's over there by the hotel entrance,' Dazza replied.

The three of them crossed the road and caught up with Danny.

'Where has she gone?' Adam asked.

'She's gone into the hotel,' Danny replied.

'You guys wait there. I'll go in and see if I can spot her,' Max said.

'Excuse me, but if you are going in, so am I,' Adam replied, grabbing Bobby's hand.

'Oh my word, it's awash with marble and wood,' Adam said in awe as they entered the hotel.

'A bit over the top for my tastes,' Max grumbled.

'I agree with Adam. It's gorge,' Bobby replied, looking around the reception area.

'Can I help you, gentlemen?' said a man in a tailored black suit, adorned with a gold lapel badge and neatly groomed receding silver hair.

'Yes, we were looking for a friend who was supposed to meet us here. She said she had just arrived a minute or two before us,' Max said in the most refined voice he could muster.

'Of course, sir. What is their name?' The butler asked.

'She's about five foot ten, blonde hair and wearing a plum-coloured jacket, jeans and a grey top,' Max replied.

'I'd say it's more mauve than plum,' Adam interjected.

'Fascinating, sir, but does this mauve jacket-wearing lady have a name?' the butler enquired again.

'She came in a minute or two ago, so I'm assuming if you were stood there, then you would have seen her passing,' Max insisted.

'Indeed I may, sir. But without a name, I am afraid I cannot assist you. We take the privacy of our guests very seriously,' the butler replied.

'Could I just go through to the foyer and restaurant to see if I can see her?' Max asked.

'If you were due to meet her, I presume you have a booking. Is it in your name?' the butler responded.

'Err, no, we don't have a booking. It was just an informal catch-up,' Max replied.

'In which case, gentlemen, I wish you a safe onward journey. The exit is that way,' the butler said, indicating how they had come in.

'May I just use your loo, please?' Adam asked.

'Of course, sir. Just behind me and down there on the left,' the butler replied.

Adam strolled in the direction indicated, looked back and then rushed to the foyer lounge. After failing to see her, he followed the restaurant signs, and at the far end of the room, he recognised the Deceptor. Adam pulled out his phone, hoping to take a picture of her and the man she was with but from where Adam was, he could only see the back of the man's head. So he went to walk into the restaurant but was stopped by a hand on his shoulder. He turned to see the dignified butler standing behind him.

'Excuse me, sir, but you appear lost coming back from the gentlemen's conveniences,' the butler said. 'It is this way,' indicating the main entrance.

'Did you see her?' Max asked as they walked out of the hotel.

'Not only did I see her, but look, I got a picture of her with the man she was with,' Adam said proudly, pulling up the picture.

'Well done. Oh, well, I guess it could be worse. But, at least we know it's a man, even if we don't know who he is,' Max replied.

'What's the news then?' Dazza asked as Max and Adam rejoined him and Danny.

'We've got a picture of her eating with a guy, but we can only see the back of his head,' Adam replied, showing them the picture.

'I was going to say that could be Fallon or Carter as they have similar colour hair, but to be honest, it could be just about anyone,' Danny said.

'There's a pub and a sandwich place over the road. Do we sit it out in one of those, waiting for them to come out?' Adam asked.

'Sounds good to me,' Dazza answered.

'No. They could be in there hours, or they might even have a room booked. But, at least we now know there are two Deceptors and a man involved,' Max replied.

'Don't forget the bungling bobbies,' Danny laughed.

'How could I ever forget Fallon and Carter,' Max laughed.

'Hey, that sounds like a good name for a restaurant,' Dazza added.

'Only you could think like that, big man. Never change, my friend,' Bobby said.

'Think I might have to change. Look, I've got chilli on my top,' Dazza laughed, trying to wipe it off.

'Do you think that guy in the restaurant is the mysterious J?' Adam asked.

'Who's J?' Danny looked puzzled.

'They referred to a J a few times. Fallon or Carter talks to J regularly, they said. Hang on, I'll play the voice recording,' Max replied, pulling out his receiver.

'Oh, you managed to get it to work, did you?' Danny sneered in jest.

'To quote my esteemed friend, it has always worked. It was just an ID ten T issue,' Max replied, pressing play.

'Cheers sssssssss isnees,' The receiver garbled out.

'It's probably had trouble connecting to start with. So I'll forward it a little,' Max said, jabbing at the device.

'Igotsly teenage lodyslthat,' the receiver spluttered.

Max jabbed it again and was rewarded with 'gldo whine.'

'OK, It doesn't work, well, except as a tracker,' Max sighed. 'But Adam and I did get some of their conversations.'

'And now, thanks to your super gadget, we know they like wine; say cheers and have a teenager involved. So the plot has gone deep,' Danny laughed. 'You must have used a left-handed screwdriver when you built that receiver.'

'Back to plan B tomorrow, then,' Bobby said.

'I didn't know there was a plan A or B?' Dazza frowned.

'Meeting up at Catherine's at eleven tomorrow,' Danny said.

'Is that when we confront Avery?' Adam asked.

Bobby and Danny exchanged glances, and Max said, 'Yeah, that's right. We've got a plan to free Avery from the Deceptor, but we won't know until tomorrow if everything is ready.'

'Are you guys hiding something from us?' Dazza challenged.

'It's an idea Catherine and Michael came up with. Let's get heading for home, and I'll explain on the way,' Max replied.

Thirty minutes into the drive home, Max finally finished explaining the plan to Adam and Dazza.

'So if I had been the Deceptor, would you be arranging to give me a heart attack,' Adam asked angrily.

'We don't need to think like that because you're not, so it's all OK,' Bobby replied.

'To be honest, Adam, yes, we probably would,' Max added, 'I've known the Thomas family for generations, and they are some of the most experienced medics I know. So if they are sure this will work, I totally trust them.'

'It's not your life they are risking, though, is it?' Adam continued.

'But it sounds like the only option, Adam,' Dazza replied.

'I was like you, Adam. I challenged Catherine and Michael. I pushed them several times about how Avery could die,' Danny said.

'And what was the answer?' Adam asked.

'That it was a risk, but they could make it a tiny risk,' Danny replied.

'Is there no way you could extract the Deceptor out of Avery, Max?' Adam asked.

'Only a Daxson can pull energy souls out of bodies. They can even tear an energy soul apart. But a normal Shadower can't voluntarily leave our hosts or shells,' Max replied.

'But you and Bobby said you weren't compatible, so I assumed that meant you would just go into someone else,' Danny said.

'Not that simple, buddy,' Max replied.

'I'm sorry, but you're not killing Bobby just so you two can split,' Adam said firmly.

'Relax, Adam. I wouldn't do anything to hurt any of you and especially Bobby deliberately,' Max replied.

'You'd better not,' Dazza replied. 'Anyone who tries to hurt my friends has to answer to me.'

'I can vouch for Dazza after what happened earlier this afternoon,' Dazza laughed.

Danny dropped Adam and Dazza in Haywood, then returned home with Bobby.

'I never knew Adam had such a temper,' Danny said.

'Nor me,' Bobby agreed, 'I don't think I've ever seen him get annoyed, let alone angry.'

'Mum said she's left some casserole in the oven for us,' Danny said as they parked and headed towards the house. 'She's gone to meet Dad in the city for dinner.'

'That's nice,' Bobby replied.

'Are you thinking what I'm thinking?' Danny asked.

'Pizza?' Bobby suggested.

'Exactly. Stuffed crust meat feast, here I come,' Danny laughed.

'Bolognese Italian thin crust for me. Besides, I think we'll need the energy for tomorrow.'

'Bolognese ragu on a pizza?' Max gasped. 'Mama Mia!'

The following morning Danny and Bobby arrived at Glenthorne Crescent early.

'So, is everything ready?' Max asked.

'I've got my old wheelchair in the study, and I've parked the Range Rover right outside so we can load Avery into it,' Michael replied.

'I checked NetDat this morning whilst you guys were snoring,' Danny laughed. 'I was right. The security at St Ethelbert's is just a rehash of old code they've used in other buildings.'

'I do not snore,' Bobby replied.

'Well, Max certainly used to,' Agathe replied, 'Every bit as bad as Michael. We could hear the walls rattle from the basement.'

'Is this pick on Max and Bobby day?' Max huffed.

'Oh, no, we don't need a special day for that,' Catherine joined in. 'So Danny, have you hacked it to give us access or what?'

Danny waved a credit card attached by a cable to his laptop, 'No need to hack anything. This little card connected to my laptop will get us into the entire hospital.'

'The gang will be here soon. I should do some nibbles,' Agathe said.

'Actually, Agathe, my immobiliser is more effective if the Shadower hasn't just eaten,' Max replied.

'Also, I'd prefer it if Avery hadn't just eaten with our side of the process,' Catherine replied.

The Pick'n'Mix group chat pinged from Adam, 'Earls Court is our next stop. See you in a bit.'

'We're just coming down the A3220. Should only be a couple of minutes,' Avery messaged.

'Flip, I was hoping Abi would come with Adam and Dazza so they could have briefed her on the way,' Max cursed.

'Catherine and I will find a distraction to get her away from Avery so we can brief her,' Agathe said.

'I should do it, really,' Max replied.

'Come on, Chief, she's acting like she loves you. She'd follow you if you went,' Danny said.

'Yeah, I guess so,' Max replied.

'Besides, if any of us know what needs to be done and knows what having a Shadower inside you means, it's us,' Agathe stated.

'Looks like it's about to be showtime,' Danny said.

'Doesn't anything phase you, Danny?' Michael asked.

'Before yesterday, I'd say nothing. But I never want to see an angry Adam again,' Danny chuckled.

Over the next few minutes, Adam and Dazza arrived, followed shortly afterwards by Abi and Avery.

'Hi, babe,' Avery said, throwing her arms around Bobby's neck. 'And hey to you too, Bobby.'

'So what happened yesterday then?' Abi asked.

'Why don't we get some drinks first?' Agathe suggested. 'Abi, could you and Catherine give me a hand? I'll never remember what everyone wants.'

Everyone placed their orders, and the three went down to the kitchen. Catherine and Agathe took Abi through the plan. As anticipated, there followed an argument about why Abi believed what they were about to do was too high a risk, followed by Agathe and Catherine trying to persuade her that there was no other option.

'And Max is positive Avery is a Deceptor?' Abi asked.

'One hundred percent. He saw her aura, and Adam, Dazza, Danny and Bobby followed her yesterday afternoon when she met up with the Deceptor who tried to kill Bobby on his driving lesson,' Catherine replied.

'And Bobby confirmed the other one?' Abi challenged.

'Yes, Abi, I'm afraid there was no doubt about it,' Agathe nodded.

'You promise Avery will be OK?' Abi asked, looking at Catherine.

'My Papa and I will do everything to make her safe,' Catherine answered.

'We need to get these upstairs before anyone starts asking questions,' Agathe said.

A few minutes later, they were all in the Drawing Room.

'Come on then, babe, what did you discover yesterday?' Avery asked.

Max sat beside Avery and pulled out Bobby's keys, 'It was a crazy day, to be honest, hun.'

'In what way? Babe,' Avery continued.

'Well, you see, I put so much planning into the day that I ended up mistaking what I knew was true with what I knew couldn't possibly be true,' Max said, smiling at Adam.

'Oh, babe, I know that feeling so well,' Avery said.

'I risked upsetting so many people I love,' Max sighed, 'Just because I let myself be blinded by my emotions.'

Avery put her hand on Max's knee, 'Don't worry, babe, we are all right behind you, aren't we guys?'

Everyone in the room nodded or expressed their agreement. Max looked at Abi, 'Are you all really behind me.'

Abi dropped her eyes but nodded in confirmation.

'That means more than I could ever say,' Max said as he stood up with his back to Avery and moved the innocent-looking torch into his hand. 'My friends, I have been on a very long journey through life's twists and turns, and I want you to know that your safety and well-being mean everything to me. I will stand by the side of every one of you, unwavering and strong, with a watchful eye, a caring heart and an outstretched hand to catch you should you fall. The friendships I had before and the new friendships I have been blessed with are treasures dearer to me than I can ever deserve to have, and I will go to any lengths to safeguard them. I hope we can use courage and loyalty as our guiding lights always to do what is right for each other and, through adversity, find the love and strength to forge ahead.'

Max turned to face Avery holding the torch discreetly down by his side.

'Oh, babe, that was beautiful,' Avery said, standing up.

'Avery, I hope you can hear me when I say we love you and will save you,' Max replied as he pressed and held the button on the torch. A flash shot out of the immobiliser, hitting Avery full in the chest and sending her back onto the sofa.

'Come on, we need to move fast,' Max said.

Nobody moved for a moment until Danny said, 'Chief, I have to admit those were possibly the most moving words anyone has ever said to me or us.'

'I meant every word, but will you get a shift on? We need to get Avery to that hospital,' Max shouted.

Max's shouting brought everyone back into action.

'I'll fetch the wheelchair,' Michael said.

'No, Michael, I'll get the wheelchair. You go and start the car and open the back passenger door,' Agathe commanded. 'Catherine, check that Avery is still alive and OK.'

Catherine checked Avery's pulse and breathing, 'Her vitals are slow but steady. She seems perfectly fine, just asleep.'

'Exactly how she should be. More importantly, the Deceptor is immobilised. It can't control her or do anything, although it will be aware of what is happening around it,' Max warned.

Catherine returned with the wheelchair.

'Dazza and Adam help Bobby with Avery. Abi, can you call the lift up, please?' Agathe said, taking complete control of the situation.

Within a minute or two, they got Avery into Michael's car along with Abi, Catherine and Agathe. Next, Danny, Bobby, Adam and Dazza piled into Danny's car and set off to the hospital.

'*I hope you know what you are doing, cowboy,*' Bobby thought.

'*So do I,*' Max replied.

'Where is Michael going?' Danny asked, 'It looks like he's heading for the M4.'

'I guess that's the shortest route,' Bobby replied.

'But I've never driven on a motorway,' Danny replied.

'What happened to the cunning genius and the man of mystery and intrigue?' Dazza shouted from the back.

'He's gone on holiday and said he's not sure when he'll be back,' Danny replied, gripping the steering wheel. 'Why's he going so fast?'

Bobby glanced at Danny's speedometer, 'You're doing seventy. That's the speed limit.'

'I know it's a crazy speed,' Danny replied. 'Why couldn't he just stick to the A4?'

'Never mind that, buddy. It'll help if you speed up. Michael is pulling away,' Dazza said.

'It's OK. Look, Michael's indicating to pull off,' Adam replied.

'About time, too,' Danny muttered.

'How's Avery doing, Catherine?' asked Agathe.

'Still stable,' Catherine replied. Then, she turned to Abi, 'Considering you've had very little time to think about this; it was brave of you to agree.'

'I didn't feel like I had much choice, to be honest,' Abi replied. 'But the more I think about how she's changed recently and been getting snappy with everyone except Max, it started to make sense.'

'I've known Max for as long as I can remember,' Michael said, indicating to leave the motorway, 'And before anyone says it, no, that wasn't when dinosaurs were alive. I would trust him with the life of any of us.'

'That speech he gave just felt so genuine,' Abi replied.

'I've no doubt it was genuine, but I also think he was saying it for Avery's benefit,' Agathe said.

'But that was the Deceptor in Avery's body,' Abi challenged.

'It was, but Avery is still inside there too. The Deceptor is just keeping her suppressed. But, remember, I've been a host like Avery is. Even on the rare occasion when Max suppressed me, I was still fully aware of every sensation, sight and sound,' Michael replied.

'Hang on, does that mean Avery will know when we kill her?' Abi asked anxiously.

'No, I've given her something to make her drowsy, so she shouldn't feel anything. It'll be like a dream until she wakes up Deceptor free,' Catherine said.

'Hospital straight ahead,' Michael said.

'Park outside the accident and emergency entrance. I checked the plans. That is the shortest route to the operating theatre.' Catherine replied.

Danny parked behind Michael as they got out of the vehicles and bundled Avery into Michael's old wheelchair.

'Dazza hold this against that black pad, please,' Danny asked before typing away on his laptop. Within a minute, the door slid open.

Catherine grabbed Avery's wheelchair, 'Follow me. It's this way to the operating theatre.'

The rest rushed through as Danny and Dazza closed the doors behind them.

'How long have we got before your immobiliser thingy wears off?' Adam asked.

Bobby looked at his watch, ' I reckon fifteen minutes at the most. This is going to be tight.'

The wheelchair crashed through the operating theatre doors. Abi held Avery's head steady as Adam, Dazza, and Bobby lifted her onto an operating table and then strapped her down.

'Is that necessary? Chief,' Danny asked. 'I can't see the Deceptor doing much damage in that state.'

'It's about protecting Avery from the Deceptor more than anything.' Max explained. 'If she starts to wake up midway through this, she could make a run for it, which could be the end for Avery.

A couple of minutes later, Catherine had hooked up an intravenous line in each arm with a syringe attached to each. At the same time, Michael had brought over a defibrillator from the corner of the room and began wiring Avery up to it, with Agathe helping him wire Avery to a heart monitor.

The steady beep in time with Avery's heart filled the operating room.

Michael asked Max, 'Are you sure you understand what you must do?'

'Yes, I need to empty this syringe into her and wait. Then, once I see the Deceptor dissipate, I need to empty the other syringe to offset the first set of drugs and hit that button there to defibrillate Avery.'

'Remembering not to touch her or any part of the table simultaneously,' Michael added. 'And soon as she is shocked, start CPR.'

'Yes, sorry, of course,' Max replied. 'Now, you guys need to hurry up to that gallery.'

'And don't start until Catherine and I can see you. If anything goes wrong, we need to be able to see what it is,' Michael added, leaving the operating room with everyone else except Bobby and Avery.

'Avery, I'm not sure you can hear me with the drug Catherine has given you. But please know that I will never stop fighting for you. Bobby here knows it, but the others don't, but I want you to know that I've grown very fond of you,' Max said, holding her hand.

'*Tell her the truth, cowboy. This is your moment*,' Bobby thought.

'I think I love you,' Max said as a tear rolled down his face.

'*I swear that heart monitor just got a little faster for a second or two*,' Bobby said.

A couple of minutes later, Michael's voice boomed over the loudspeaker, 'OK, Max, it's time.'

'See you shortly,' Max whispered as he emptied the first syringe.

'Nothing's happening,' Abi said.

'It can be almost instant or take a few minutes,' Catherine said, clutching Abi's hand. This started a chain reaction of hand holding with Abi holding Danny's, Danny grabbing Adam's, and Adam squeezing Dazza's hand. Then, finally, Dazza looked to his right and saw Michael.

'It's OK, dear boy. We need to support each other,' he said, taking hold of Dazza's hand and Agathe's on his other side.

The bleep of the heart monitor slowed, and then an alarm sounded as it flatlined. Avery's body went limp.

'OK, Max, Do the other syringe now,' Abi said.

'Not yet, Abi, we—' Catherine started to say as a yellow energy cloud of light floated out of Avery's body. It hung in the air for a second, and then there was a blood-curdling scream as it headed straight towards the viewing gallery. Everyone leapt back, but it scattered and disappeared before it reached them.

Michael hit the button on the microphone, 'Inject the second syringe count to five and then hit the defibrillator button. We're on our way.'

Max emptied the second syringe into Avery. The defibrillator had detected her heart had stopped, and it went into charging mode. Max counted to five, paused until the defibrillator confirmed it was charged, and then hit the button.

Avery's body convulsed as the controlled electric shocks passed through the pads attached to her chest.

Max started CPR as the heart monitor continued to flatline. Then, the operating room doors flew open as Michael and Catherine led the group back into the room.

'She's still flatlining,' Bobby said pleadingly to Catherine and Michael.

'Keep going, Max. Everyone else, please stand back. Charging,' Michael shouted urgently. 'Everyone clear?'

'Clear,' they all replied.

'Shocking,' Michael said as he hit the button again.

Avery convulsed again, and then Max resumed CPR. Catherine felt Avery's pulse.

'It's not working. You promised us,' Adam shouted.

'She can't die,' Abi screamed.

'You said the risks were minimal,' Dazza snarled.

'Shh,' Catherine replied, 'I think, yes, I'm sure there's a faint pulse.'

The heart monitor flickered, and slowly the pulse of the beeps strengthened and got more regular.

'She's alive,' Catherine sighed as Dazza, Abi, Adam, and Danny rushed to be by the operating table, and Max stopped the CPR.

Michael pulled across the oxygen canister nearby and put the mask over Avery's face.

'Good work Max. I couldn't have done it any better,' Michael said.

'Looks like my six months inside a doctor wasn't entirely wasted,' Max smiled.

'Excuse me, I'm a consultant, not a doctor,' Michael replied, laughing.

'Not back then, buddy. You were just a struggling, overworked junior doctor,' Max replied.

'I hate to rain on your backslapping parade, but Avery isn't waking up,' Danny interjected.

'Give it time, Danny. It can take a few hours to wake up after a cardiac arrest, but the fact that this was a controlled situation and treatment was delivered quickly, I'm hopeful it will be more like a few minutes,' Michael replied.

'There's that word I hate hearing from doctors again, hopeful,' Danny replied.

'How long before we can move her?' Abi asked.

'Ideally, we want her to wake up, and once Papa and I are satisfied her vitals are stable and acceptable, we can consider moving her,' Catherine replied.

'How long will that take?' Danny asked nervously.

'Hard to say, Danny. Why'd you ask?' Michael replied.

'Well, even though I deactivated all the alarm systems and NetDat and Brinskwell couldn't organise a rave in a nightclub, I'm sure they must at least have someone on security with a timetable for checking whether systems are active or not and if not should they be,' Danny explained.

'How will we know?' Max asked.

'Either the alarms start going off because they've reactivated them remotely, or we suddenly see some security guards,' Danny replied.

There was a groan from the bed, and everyone turned to see Avery's head slowly moving.

Abi grabbed Avery's hand, 'Avery, it's Abi. Can you hear me?'

Avery's hand reached up to pull the mask away, but Catherine held it firm, 'Just leave that there for now, Avery, just for a while.'

'Danny, could you check the alarm system and surveillance cameras? Whilst I'm sure it makes life exciting in the movies when the bad guys suddenly turn up, I prefer the ones where they don't and the good guys get away,' Max laughed.

'No problemo, Chief,' Danny replied, tapping away into his computer. 'The good news is the dullards have still not noticed the alarm system is off.'

'And the bad news is?' Max asked expectantly.

'A lot of the cameras appear to be offline. In fact, none of the cameras inside the building are working, and the only ones operating outside are those around the perimeter,' Danny replied.

'What happened to me?' Avery groaned.

'We've managed to free you from the Deceptor, Avery,' Adam replied, holding her hand.

'You'll feel weak for a while, but that's perfectly normal. I'm just monitoring your vital signs, and once I'm happy with them, we can move you,' Catherine replied.

'Where are we going to move her to?' Dazza asked.

'Ah,' Max replied.

'We didn't discuss that bit,' Danny added.

'We have some basic medical equipment at our house,' Catherine proposed.

'I could text Avery's mum and say we are having a sleepover,' Abi suggested.

'It is Friday night. How about a little social gathering at our place,' Agathe suggested. 'Michael missed out on the last one.'

'If anyone suggests malt whisky, I will not be responsible for my actions,' Bobby stated.

'But you love a glass of malt,' Michael replied.

'Maybe so, but my new host makes a Granny look like a heavyweight drinker,' Max replied.

Danny chuckled, 'You haven't seen my Nana and Mum when they get together on the gin and tonics. Bet they could drink all of you under the table.'

'Can we stop talking about alcohol,' Bobby replied.

'Uh, Bob, didn't you say your agreement with your Mum was that you would return to her today? Now the exams are over,' Dazza asked.

'I'll message her and say I'll go over tomorrow,' Bobby replied.

15
THE TRUTH

'Hey, Mum, I hope you're enjoying the break. We're having a post-exam party at Danny's. Love you.'

'OK, champ. See you tomorrow and have a nice time but be careful,' Pat replied.

'OK, love you.'

'Love you more.'

Dazza and Abi also contacted their parents to explain that they would stay out overnight.

'What about you, Adam and you, Danny?' Bobby asked.

'I've already learnt to plan ahead since Max arrived,' Danny laughed. 'My folks aren't expecting to see me until Sunday at the earliest.'

Dazza turned to Adam, 'And you, Adam?'

Adam blushed and looked at Bobby, 'Well, I was just hoping we could maybe.'

'Spend some time together?' Max interrupted, trying to ease Adam's embarrassment.

'Oh, yeah, bro. So how long have you told your folks you're having a romantic break for?' Danny teased.

'Don't be such a silly moose, Danny,' Bobby scowled.

'It's alright, Bobby. I told Mum and Dad we'd probably spend the weekend together,' Adam replied.

'Bob and Adam, aww, it's so sweet. Did you notice our Bob is even copying Adam calling people silly moose,' Dazza chuckled.

The laughter was interrupted by an alarm going off.

Danny grabbed his laptop, 'They've reactivated the intruder alarm. Unfortunately, it's connected to the local police station too. I'll deactivate it and send a false alarm report via the system to the police.'

The alarm went silent.

'I think we've overstayed our welcome,' Max said. 'How's Avery doing?'

'I think Avery's vitals have recovered enough for us to move her,' Catherine replied. 'Papa, what do you think?'

'Her heart rate seems strong and stable, and her oxygen saturation levels are good enough. Although I think we need to borrow this oxygen tank.'

'The monitoring station is repeatedly trying to reactivate the alarm,' said Danny. 'I'm only guessing, but I think we'll soon be getting a visit from their security team.'

Dazza, Adam, Bobby, and Abi helped lift Avery off the operating table and into the wheelchair.

'Let's get going,' Max said, pushing the wheelchair towards the theatre doors.

They wheeled Avery back to the cars and manoeuvred her into the back seat of the Range Rover.

'Can someone get in the other side so I can pass the oxygen tank over?' Michael asked.

Abi climbed in beside Avery and took the tank off Michael as Agathe got into the front passenger seat.

'Guys, I don't want to worry you, but there's a security van entering the grounds,' Danny said, watching the perimeter CCTV on his laptop.

'How long have we got?' Michael asked.

'About thirty seconds.'

Michael threw his car keys to Dazza, 'You drive them home, dear boy. Catherine, or should I say Miss Property Trust Board member? You're about to show a consultant around this new hospital.'

'Sounds like a plan. I'm not sure it'll work, but it is a plan,' Max said. 'Adam, you go with Dazza and the others. The fewer here, the better.'

'But—' Adam started to protest, but Bobby kissed him and said, 'Please, hun. I'll be safe.'

'If Avery appears to be struggling, call Catherine or me straight away,' Michael shouted after them.

As Dazza drove off, Michael looked at the others, 'I'm here to check out the clinical side. Bobby can be my assistant, so I guess that makes you the I.T. inspector, Danny.'

'You're not the first person to call me IT, Michael,' Danny smiled cheekily.

'I think you're missing two letters off the front of that,' Bobby laughed.

As the security van drove around one side of the roundabout, Dazza drove the Range Rover around the other side. The van stopped outside the entrance, and a security guard exited the vehicle.

The guard is dressed in an ill-fitting, navy blue security uniform with Cranside Security emblazoned. His shirt is unbuttoned at the top, revealing a hint of a coffee-stained vest. His trousers are a tad too tight around the waist, straining against his expanding girth. His scruffy beard and dishevelled hair add to the air of disinterest exuding from him.

'Can I 'elp you folks,' he asks casually, reaching for a packet of crisps from his pocket.

'Ah, good day to you, sir. My colleague here is a Health Service Property Trust member, and she was just about to show me around these new facilities,' Michael smiled.

'Not open, mate,' the guard says absentmindedly, munching on his crisps.

'That's why we've come, to look at everything before the hospital opens,' Catherine explained.

'How'd you get the door open?' the guard asked, peering around them and spitting out crisp crumbs as he spoke.

'That's an excellent question,' Danny replied. 'I've been checking the Health Trust systems to see if we had had an illegal entry as the doors were open when we arrived. You may have passed my colleagues as you came up here. They are heading back to base to check out our mainframe.'

'Dunno 'bout that. We run the security systems 'ere.'

'Yes, I know, but my colleagues have returned to the data centre to perform an extensive diagnostic analysis on the core infrastructure to investigate a complex systemic anomaly affecting the network architecture.'

'Oh, OK, I guess,' the guard replied with confusion and disinterest. He walked past Danny, Michael, Bobby and Catherine, his steps slow and lacking enthusiasm and his belly slightly protruding as he shuffled along.

He peered into the hospital, scanning the surroundings with indifference and annoyance. The flickering fluorescent lights added an eerie atmosphere, casting long shadows on the walls. He yawns audibly, revealing a glimpse of yellowed teeth and unimpressed by the situation, he said, 'You seen anyone 'ere?'

'Only you,' Bobby replied.

The guard raised his doughy hand, waved a keycard against the entry pad, and the hospital doors closed. Then, pressing a button on the walkie-talkie attached to his uniform, he said, 'All clear. Try reactivating the alarm now.'

There was a single beep as the alarm reset, followed by silence.

A voice crackled over the guard's walkie-talkie, 'Reset looks fine now.'

'Waste of flipping space these systems,' the guard muttered before pressing the walkie-talkie button again, 'Roger, everything secure 'ere.'

The guard slouched back to the others with a demeanour that suggested this was just another mundane task he'd grown tired of, 'Gunna 'ave to ask you to leave.'

'But we haven't seen inside yet,' Michael protested half-heartedly.

The guard gave a half-hearted shrug, 'Not my problem, mate.'

Michael turned to Catherine and said in mock disgust, 'Well, thank you for wasting my time. We need to leave.'

Danny unlocked his car, and Michael climbed into the front passenger seat. Catherine and Bobby clambered into the back of the vehicle as Danny slid into the driver's seat and sent his wheelchair around to the boot of his car.

'Flash git,' muttered the guard with a final bite of his crisps. He turned and returned to his van with a distinct lack of urgency. The building may be secure, but his enthusiasm and motivation clearly clocked out long ago.

'Well, that went better than expected,' Michael chuckled as Danny pulled out of the hospital grounds.

'Given our luck, I'm amazed we didn't have Fallon and his buddy turn up,' Max agreed.

'The spy amongst us has been eradicated. So we should be free of them for now,' Danny replied. 'Unless, is there any way a Deceptor can communicate with others before they evaporate?'

'No, we don't possess any telepathic powers. Or at least if there's any that do, they're rare, and I've never met any,' Max replied.

'Why was that disabled boy and, I assume, others at St Ethelbert's?' The man's voice asked.

'I don't know, and I've not heard from my sister for a few hours,' Claudia replied.

'I do hope she hasn't messed up.'

'Everything was fine yesterday, as I told you over dinner.'

'You need to keep her under control. I've seen her records, and she has a history of getting out of control.'

'I'll speak to her as soon as possible.'

'J will be here this weekend. Are we ready?'

'Yes, sir. I've checked the safe house near Cambridge, and we can swoop in as soon as you tell us to. I've contacted that military group you recommended, and their leader has agreed to provide fully armed support.'

'I'm pleased you took my advice about using the Captain and his men. His team are very experienced at cleaning up if there are any casualties.'

'But why don't we just take Max instead of using bait to bring him to us?' Claudia asked.

'Because if we try to grab him, there will be a fight, and he might be killed. Ideally, we need him to surrender to us. Once he does, we can inject him with the treatment, and he will be fully compliant.'

'So then he will have to build the Exodus machine to save my Daxson?'

'Yes, of course. But remember, nobody dies until we have him secured.'

'And afterwards?'

'We can't have any loose ends. Besides, your Daxson needs some new toys to play with,' the man laughed before hanging up.

'How's Avery,' Catherine asked as Agathe opened the door at Glenthorne Crescent.

'She seems to be picking up. I've just taken her a cup of tea, and the others are sitting with her,' Agathe replied. 'I've put her in the bedroom opposite ours.'

'Guys, I'll go with Catherine to check on Avery. See you in the Drawing Room,' Max said.

'Hello, Avery. How are you feeling?' Catherine asked as they entered the bedroom.

'Like I've been crushed under a huge weight for a week, and now it's suddenly been lifted, but it's damaged every bit of me,' Avery replied.

'That'll be the after-effects of the Deceptor suppressing you,' Max said. 'You may feel euphoric over the next few days due to the sudden release and regaining control of your body.'

'The cardiac arrest will make you feel strange for a while too. You may be a bit confused and disorientated as well as being tired and weak,' Catherine added.

Avery looked at Adam, Abi, and Dazza, 'Guys, can you give us a few minutes? Oh, and thanks again, you've been mega.'

'Of course, we can. You need to rest anyway,' Abi replied.

'Just take it easy, Avery,' Adam said, kissing her on the cheek.

'I wonder if Agathe has any of her Mum's beef pepper pot on the go?' Dazza wondered.

'Dazza!' Adam, Abi, and Bobby chorused.

Avery grabbed Dazza's hand, 'Dazza ignore them and don't ever change. I've missed you, well, all of you, to be honest.'

'Especially your babe?' Abi joked.

'Oh, don't. Every time she said that word, I cringed. I will never say babe ever again.'

'You just did,' Dazza chuckled.

The friends went down to the Drawing Room, leaving Catherine, Avery, and Bobby behind.

Avery sat up, 'Catherine; I will be OK, won't I?'

'You should be fine. You've got a strong body, and we artificially induced the cardiac arrest. It wasn't due to any weakness in your body. Don't get me wrong, what we did was dangerous, and we will need to monitor you for a while to ensure no long-term damage, but there is no reason to believe you won't fully recover.'

'Do I still need to wear this mask?'

'Please just indulge me a little bit longer. Even though your brain was only starved of oxygen for a few minutes, I want to err on the side of caution.'

'And I don't want you to take any risks either,' Max added.

Catherine checked Avery, saying, 'You seem to be recovering well. I think you might even be alright to get up soon, but no physical exertion for two to three days. I'll leave you and Max, well, Bobby and Max and see how Dazza is getting on with Mama's food.'

'Thanks, Catherine,' Avery replied.

Catherine closed the door, and Avery grabbed Bobby's hand.

'Max, I heard what you said before you shot me with that zapper thing, and I'm not sure, but I think you said something in the hospital too.'

'I wanted you to know before I immobilised you just how important you are and that we would rescue you.'

'What about at the hospital?'

'Oh yeah, I said see you shortly.'

'*Tell her, cowboy,*' Bobby thought.

'*Butt out, Bobby, remember how you didn't want me to out you to Adam,*' Max snapped.

'*I'd never do that, Max, but you admitted in the hospital; you love her.*'

'Max?' Avery queried.

'Sorry, Avery, I was just thinking what an emotional day it's been.'

'*You criticise us, humans, for not being honest about our emotions, but you're as bad,*' Bobby said.

'But it's complicated. I've had partners in the past, and losing them tears you apart.'

'Do you want her to be a part of your life or not?'

Max looked at Avery and said, 'I may have also said I love you.'

'Really?' Avery asked.

'Yes.'

Avery flung her arms around Bobby, 'Max, I don't know how this will work, but I love you too.'

Avery pulled her mask off, 'Come on, I've spent a week not being me with my friends. Let's go downstairs.'

'But Catherine said,' Max started to say.

'Look, there are two doctors downstairs if I feel dodge.'

'Well, if it isn't the lady of the hour,' Michael said as Avery and Bobby walked into the room.

'There's some food on the table if you're hungry. Or our Dazza has requested some beef pepperpot, but it'll be a while,' Agathe chuckled.

'I am a little peckish,' Avery replied, heading to the food table.

'Maxwell, it's been a long day. How about a nice malt?' Michael asked, standing up.

'I'll have a diet cola, please,' Bobby replied.

'My new host doesn't do alcohol, remember' Max replied.

'I thought you were joking. The man who took on Reed and Harris has finally been tamed,' Michael laughed.

'Did you turn the oxygen tank off?' Catherine asked, wandering over to Avery.

'Yeah, I did.'

'Well, take it easy and put it back on tonight when you go to bed. I'll check your vitals in the morning, and hopefully, that should be the worst over with.'

'You and your Dad risked your medical careers today to help me, and I'll never forget it,' Avery replied, hugging Catherine.

'Wow, I wasn't expecting that but thank you.'

'Well, I bet that lot haven't considered the risks you both took.'

'My family promised Max generations ago to help him. So there is no way we'd ever turn our back on him or anyone who helps him.'

'Come on then, Avery, how was it being a baddie?' Danny asked as Avery sat down on a sofa.

'Absolutely awful,' Avery replied, 'She never let me take control and be myself except during the exams.'

'So was the whole Max and babe thing just a front?' Adam asked.

'No, that was one of the worst things. She took my inner thoughts and used them to get information.'

Adam glanced at Bobby sitting beside him and clutched his hand, 'So you do fancy Max then?'

'I do feel, well, I do like, or maybe yes, I find Max very attractive,' Avery tried to explain.

'And how does Max feel?' Adam questioned.

'I am very attracted to Avery, but Bobby loves you, Adam. Until I transmute, Bobby is in charge of the physical side,' Max replied.

'Not quite, cowboy. When it comes to a fight, you're in charge,' Bobby chuckled.

'So, who's in charge of arm wrestling?' Abi laughed.

'Depends if I've been drinking,' Bobby smiled.

Agathe wandered downstairs to check on her beef pepperpot.

'Did you learn anything from the Deceptor?' Dazza asked as he tucked into a plate of food.

'Oh, yeah, so much,' Avery replied. 'The other Deceptor is her sibling. And they think of each other as sisters.'

'But we don't have genders anymore,' Max said. 'Once we became energy souls, the whole gender thing became irrelevant. We are what we are.'

'You may not have, sweetheart, flip I almost said, babe, but Claudia and Sabina definitely act like sisters rocking it,' Avery replied.

'Claudia and Sabina?' Danny queried.

'Yeah, the Deceptor in me was Sabina, and her sister was Claudia,' Avery said.

'Oh my word, Sabina and Claudia terrorised Rome when I first came to Earth,' Max replied.

'So you know them then, Chief?' Danny asked.

'I never actually met them. I assume they are the same couple, but they weren't what I'd call Deceptors back then. They just lived a raucous lifestyle. They were well-known for living the high life.'

'How many of you are there on Earth?' Adam asked.

'I have no idea.' Max replied, 'I've dispatched so many over the last couple of thousand years, but they keep appearing. Unfortunately, they also seem to have corrupted many humans like that Fallon copper.'

'What was it like with her inside you?' Abi asked.

'Very weird,' Avery replied, 'I'm not sure how it is for you, Bobby, but having someone else controlling everything you do and you can't stop them is horrid.'

'I guess I'm lucky. Max has only taken control a couple of times,' Bobby replied. 'Most of the time, he's like my hidden voice advising or directing me, if that makes sense?'

'I'm privileged to have someone agree to host me, so I would never control someone unless I need to resolve something. Well, excluding a handful of hostings,' Max said.

'You're so lucky,' Avery replied. 'Sabina dominated me. She decided what I'd eat or drink, what I'd say, everything.'

'I'm confused about one thing?' Dazza said.

'Blimey, big man, things are on the up if you're only confused about one thing,' Danny laughed.

'Very funny, oh, I can't breathe from laughing. Seriously though, Max, how come when Avery died, we saw that Deceptor come out of her, but there was nothing when you died and went into Bob?'

'That's because Sabina was looking for a new host, but in my case, Bobby was touching me so I could just slip straight into him,' Max replied.

'That sounds so wrong on every level,' Abi laughed.

The laughter was interrupted as Agathe walked into the Drawing Room, pushing a trolley with a large dish on it, 'Who wants some pepperpot?'

Before long, the group sat feeling bloated and content.

'I hope you don't mind, but I think I'll head off to bed,' Avery said. 'I'm feeling a little drained.'

'I'll come with you just to check you're OK,' Catherine replied.

'Where do we go from here?' Dazza asked.

'That's a good question,' Max replied. 'Once Claudia knows Sabina is dead, she'll want revenge.'

'On whom?' Adam queried.

'Do you want the nice answer or the right one?'

'Both,' Abi replied.

'Well, the nice answer is she'll want revenge on me as I'm an Enforcer.'

'And the truthful one?' Michael asked, sipping his whisky.

'All of us,' Max replied. 'Claudia and Sabina are, sorry, were so close. Claudia will want revenge on everybody involved in the death of Sabina.'

'When do you think she'll find out?' Adam asked.

'Hard to say. It's not like there's a body to discover. I guess they had some form of communication routine, and when Sabina misses that routine, Claudia will start to panic.'

'How can we find that out?' Danny asked. 'I could try hacking Avery's phone to see who she's been calling.'

'I think Avery has had her privacy invaded enough. But we need Avery to tell us everything she can remember when Sabina was inside her,' Max said.

'Avery is not telling anyone anything this evening, Max. She is very weak, so I've just given her something to help her sleep,' Catherine said, walking into the room.

'Avery is free of that, Sabrina, isn't she?' Dazza asked.

'You mean Sabina, and yes, that light you saw in the operating theatre was Sabina dying as her energy soul dissipated,' Max replied. 'But just to be safe, I used Adam's hi-tech Deceptor detector.'

'Oh yes, you mentioned that yesterday. So when did our football star become a techie? Let's see this gadget,' Danny demanded.

'Don't you dare try to steal my design, Danny,' Adam laughed. 'I've already got patents pending.'

Max reached into Bobby's pockets, pulled out the compact mirror, and passed it to Danny.

'OK, this looks innocent enough. How do you activate it?' Danny asked.

'See that little button on the side,' Bobby replied with a smile.

'Shh, Bobby, don't give away my trade secrets,' Adam laughed.

Danny pressed the button, and the mirror popped open, showing a standard mirror and a magnifying one in the other half, 'It's a mirror!'

'To you, it's a mirror, but to me, it's an aura detector,' Max laughed.

'They got you good and proper, Danny,' Abi chuckled as the room burst into laughter.

The rest of the evening was spent trying to avoid discussing the growing risk of a Deceptor on the prowl seeking revenge.

'Come on, Michael, I think it's time we went to bed,' Agathe said. 'Are you all OK to sort out the sleeping arrangements?'

Catherine turned to Abi and said, 'I think we should take the two bedrooms on the top floor and let the lads fight over who is sharing with who in the two basement bedrooms.'

'Looks like it's you and me again, Bob,' Dazza laughed.

'Excuse me, but I think you'll find you're sharing with Danny. I'm with Bobby this time,' Adam said firmly.

'Agathe, how can you agree to run such a house of ill repute,' Danny laughed, 'They're not even married.'

'I'm sure they'll behave,' Agathe replied with a wink.

'Besides, there's three in that bed. Don't forget Max,' Catherine laughed. 'Definitely the gooseberry and passion killer.'

Michael looked at Agathe before saying, 'Night all.'

Before long, they were all in their respective beds.

'I just need to message Mum, sweetheart,' Bobby said to Adam.

'Night, Mum, see you tomorrow. It will probably be late afternoon.' Bobby said.

'Goodnight, Bobby, sleep well.'

'Love you, Mum.'

'I love you too.'

Bobby put his phone on the bedside table, turned over and curled up to Adam.

The next morning followed what was rapidly becoming the norm in Glenthorne Crescent. Agathe was standing by the cooker taking and delivering breakfast orders, Adam had gone for a run, and Catherine was on drinks duty.

Abi walked into the kitchen, 'Avery is awake, but she said she might stay there and rest for a bit.'

'I'll pop up and see if she wants anything to eat and see how she's doing,' Catherine replied.

'Oh, she's already asked if there was any chance of a bacon sandwich and a cup of tea,' Abi laughed.

'On the way,' Agathe replied.

'Can't you cope with being apart from Adam for even an hour whilst he goes for a run?' Danny teased Bobby.

'I'm just messaging Mum to see if she wants us to bring anything later,' Bobby replied.

'Morning, Mum. How're things, and do you need us to bring anything?'

'Morning, Bobby. Everything is fine, and Lily sends her love. No need to bring anything, just yourself x,'

'OK, love you.'

'And we love you.'

'Are you OK, Bob? You look a little puzzled,' Dazza queried.

Bobby shook his head, 'No, everything is fine. I'm probably just imagining things.'

'Imaging what?' Abi asked.

'Well, Mum and I have this thing we've always done where one of us says I love you, and the other always replies with love you more.'

'And?' Dazza said.

'Well, I didn't pay much attention last night. But when I said I love you to her last night and again just now, she just said I love you too,' Bobby frowned.

'Maybe she's just busy getting things ready for when you arrive?' Abi suggested.

'Yeah, I'm sure you're right,' Bobby replied. 'Besides, we need to decide what to do about Claudia first.'

'Avery's bacon sandwich is ready. Does anyone know what sauce she wants, if any?' Agathe asked.

'Brown,' Danny replied.

'Get that weirdo out of this kitchen now,' Dazza laughed, pointing towards the back door.

'See, Danny, I said brown sauce on a bacon sandwich wasn't right,' Max laughed, 'It has to be tomato ketchup.'

'Actually, she said no sauce, please,' Abi interjected.

'I'll take it up. I can check how she's doing,' Catherine said.

'Mind if I come with you?' Max asked.

'Not at all. You can carry the tea,' Catherine replied.

'How are you feeling this morning?' Catherine asked Avery as she entered the bedroom after knocking.

'A bit weak still but much better than last night. Did I miss anything?'

'Only Danny being tricked into believing Adam was some hi-tech genius,' Bobby laughed as he explained about the compact mirror.

'Mr Gadget outwitted by a mirror is something I would have liked to see,' Avery replied.

'Your pulse certainly feels strong and healthy, and the rest of your vital signs seem good,' Catherine said, putting her stethoscope back on a nearby table.

'Is it OK if I get up then?'

'I don't see why not, but you're certainly not ready to start doing anything too strenuous for a few more days.'

'Talking of doing things, do you think you can manage to answer a few questions?' Max asked.

'Ask away. I'll try to answer what I can, but Sabina is already starting to feel like a bad dream,' Avery replied.

'That's what I feared. Once a Shadower leaves a host, the shared memories start to fade. Of course, they don't all go, but it's like our powers or skills. Sometimes the host gets to retain part of those skills, and other times the ability goes away quite quickly,' Max explained.

'What do you want to know then?' Avery asked.

'Max, let her enjoy her bacon sandwich and get dressed. Surely half an hour won't make much difference,' Catherine scolded.

'I'm sorry. Yes, of course, Avery. When you're ready, we can chat then. See you downstairs in a bit,' Max replied, kissing her.

'How is she?' Danny asked as Catherine and Bobby walked back into the kitchen.

'She's fine. She's getting up after breakfast so we can find out what she knows about Claudia and the Daxson,' Max replied.

'By the way, Chief, I tried to access that hotel's CCTV this morning to see if we could work out who the man having dinner with Claudia was on Thursday, but their security seems as well guarded as their reception was by that butler,' Danny sighed.

'That's a shame. What about the public CCTV on the street?' Max asked.

'The cameras right outside seem faulty as big chunks of time are missing like they have some type of intermittent fault.'

'Or could someone have deleted the footage?' Adam asked, walking into the kitchen.

'How do you do that?' Bobby asked.

'Do what, sweetie?' Adam asked as he bent to kiss Bobby.

'You always seem to enter a room mid-conversation without anyone hearing you.'

'If a footballer can't be light on his feet, who can be? Plus, football is all about timing, too,' Adam laughed.

'You're right, Adam. Someone could have deleted or tampered with the camera data,' Danny agreed.

'Could that someone be a Detective Inspector or his colleague?' Max asked.

'They do seem to be regularly involved in traffic incidents, so yes, quite possibly,' Danny nodded.

They finished breakfast and gathered in the Drawing Room, where Avery sat, sipping her tea.

'Carry on without me,' Michael said, 'I need to sort out some urgent emails, but if you need me, just shout. I'll be in my study.'

'What do you know about this Daxson then?' Max asked. 'Is it real?'

'Oh yes, very much so. I haven't seen it, but Sabina has,' Avery replied. 'I'm not sure, but I think it is somehow related to Claudia. I'm struggling to remember, but the Daxson is somehow connected to them.'

'Where is it? Can you remember where they are keeping it?' Max queried.

'I'm sorry, I can't. I thought you would ask, and I've been trying to think, but I don't know,' Avery sighed.

'Hey, that's OK, you're doing brilliantly,' Max said, holding Avery's hand. 'Is there anything you remember about it?'

'I'm trying to remember, but as I never went there, I only have some of Sabina's memories. There were fields, and I remember a massive metal cage inside a warehouse and electricity-like lightning everywhere.'

'Sounds like a Tesla experiment,' Danny replied.

'What the car guy?' Dazza asked.

'No, don't be a silly moose, Dazza. Everyone knows the car firm was named after the genius engineer Nikola Tesla, but he died years ago,' Adam replied, giving Bobby a conspiratorial wink.

'And the cage is just a giant Faraday Cage to keep the energy contained,' Max added.

'What does this Daxson thingy look like?' Abi asked.

'It's tough to remember. I can see a human shape, but it is so bright it's almost like the sun but in human form but not as bright. Maybe like if a human was a bright spotlight. Sorry, I'm not helping much, am I?'

'No need to apologise. That proves it is a Daxson, as that description was pretty good,' Max replied. 'What can you tell us about Claudia? Do you know where she is living?'

'Claudia and Sabina used to have a flat in Islington together, but Claudia said they moved her for her protection after Sabina became me.'

'Who are they?' Catherine asked.

'I don't know. Claudia seemed to be in charge of everything. I know the police were involved in whatever they were up to.'

'Yes, we know all about Fallon and Carter,' Danny said, crossing his arms.

'Yes, I remember those names. Or am I remembering them because you mentioned them when Sabina was in me? I'm so confused.'

'So we know the Daxson is real. We also know the police are involved and that there is another Deceptor called Claudia.

But we have no clue where they are except maybe Fallon and Carter, who were at the North West London Police Force HQ in Eaton,' Adam summarised.

'That's about the size of it,' Max agreed.

'Sounds like we need to put trackers on Fallon and Carter,' Danny suggested.

'Shame you didn't put ones on them when you put them on me and Avery,' Adam replied sternly.

'Huh, what do you mean? Was there a tracker on me?' Avery asked.

'Oh, didn't they tell you? Max was so convinced either me or you were traitors they bugged us both,' Adam pouted.

'That's not exactly fair, Adam. After all, Avery was an actual Deceptor,' Dazza replied.

'Well, even so, it still hurts to think you slipped those mints into my bag to track me,' Adam said.

'Oh, well, it wouldn't have worked tracking me. I gave my mints to Claudia.' Avery laughed, then added, 'That reminds me, they've also been tracking you guys.'

'What? How?' Adam asked.

'Not all of you, just Danny,' Avery replied.

'How, where?' Danny said frantically, looking at his chair.

'Did you have a run-in with Freddie Fallon? Hey, didn't you say one policeman was called Fallon? Are they related'

'DI Fallon is Freddie's Dad, and yeah, we saw Freddie at the Oliver Clinic last Saturday,' Max replied.

'Don't forget we had that little fight with him the Thursday before, Chief,' Danny added.

'That's right, he kept kicking your chair until you gave him a light southern fried Freddie action,' Bobby laughed.

'No more than he deserved,' Danny chuckled.

'Well, that was when he planted the bug on you, Danny. He was supposed to put one on you too, Bobby, but he said something went wrong,' Avery continued.

'I'll tell you what went wrong. Old Max here gave him a pasting so fast he couldn't even twitch,' Danny replied. 'After that, they just ran off. But never mind that, where is this bug on me?'

Bobby and Adam walked over to Danny's chair and started inspecting it. After a minute or so, Bobby pulls a small silver disc about the size of a watch face out of a pocket on the back of Danny's chair.

'Is this one of yours?' Max asked, passing it to Danny.

'No, it is not. I'd never make something that bulky. I'm a craftsman,' Danny scowled as he pulled a screwdriver from another chair pocket and started prising it apart.

'So that was how they got to the clinic so fast they were tracking us,' Max said.

'Partly,' Avery replied, looking down, 'Sabina also contacted them to say what time you would be there.'

'But we never told you what time we were going. Well, Max told you a time, but that was an hour later than the actual time,' Bobby protested.

Avery picked up her phone, opened the Pick'n'Mix group chat, and held it up for the others to see, 'When I wished you luck, Dazza told me you were leaving in fifteen minutes.'

Dazza put his hand to his mouth, 'I'm so sorry. I never thought.'

'Don't worry, big man, none of us noticed it either,' Bobby replied.

Danny threw the Deceptor's tracker on the table in bits, 'Nothing there to help us find them, but at least that's stopped them from knowing where we are now. I'm going to nip down to your workshop Max and give this chair a quick bug scan if you don't mind.'

'No problem, buddy. Help yourself,' Max replied.

'Hey, big man, could you please give me a hand scanning the back of my chair?' Danny asked.

'Let's go,' Dazza replied as they headed for the lift.

'They didn't get you to try to bug anyone else, then?' Max asked.

'After you and Danny said you were sweeping the house for bugs, they decided it was too risky. They were surprised Danny's wasn't detected when you did this place,' Avery replied.

'I'm not,' Max answered, 'Danny did the sweep from downstairs using the detectors I have up here. So he wouldn't have shown up. Note to self to upgrade even more of my systems.'

'None of this gets us any closer to finding them or what they want,' Bobby grumbled in frustration.

'If we can follow those policemen, and they are linked to Claudia, that has to be the best place to start,' Abi said.

'I think it's our only option,' Max replied as he started thinking of the best way to track Fallon and Carter.

'It still doesn't explain what they want with us all,' Abi said.

'Abi's right. They kidnapped Michael and then invaded Avery. So what do they want?' Agathe agreed.

'Now that is something I do remember,' Avery replied, 'They want Max.'

'Why?' Adam asked.

'They think he can build an Exodus machine to send the Daxson to a safe planet,' Avery replied.

'I can't do that,' Max replied. 'Putting aside the fact that we don't have the technology and some particular minerals.'

'*You do know how to do it, don't you? I can see you're lying,*' Bobby thought.

'*No, of course, I don't,*' Max replied.

'*Max, I can see you are deliberately trying to hide it. It's like you're imagining a solid black wall to mask it.*'

'*That isn't possible,*' Max growled.

'*What is? The fact that you're doing it or that I can see you're trying to do it, and it isn't working?*'

'It took centuries of Enforcer practice, and I've been doing this for millennia. Nobody has ever been able to get through my black wall?'

'Well, I guess you've met your match,' Bobby laughed.

'The light is staying green,' Dazza said, running the bug detector around Danny's wheelchair.

'I can't believe Freddie got one over me,' Danny grumbled.

'It must be weird to think someone has been following your every move for over a week?'

'Yeah, I feel like I've been violated. I understand why Adam got so angry.'

'Hope you behaved yourself and didn't get up to anything bad,' Dazza laughed.

'Apart from the Clinic and Lamasery, I was just going to and from college. Oh, and taking....' Danny stopped mid-sentence, 'We need to speak to Bobby, now!'

'So what happened to the bug Max planted on you?' Adam asked.

'I've already told you,' Avery replied, 'I gave it to Claudia.'

'Say that again,' Max said as he finished his internal discussion with Bobby.

'I gave that tin of mints to Claudia.'

Max smiled broadly, 'Avery, I could kiss you.'

'Well, about time you did,' Avery laughed.

'Bobby, Max, I think we've got a problem,' Danny said as he and Dazza flew into the room.

The previous evening near Cambridge, DS Carter turned to Pat Morris and said, 'Well, now, Mrs Morris. I think you and Lily need to come on a little journey with us.'

'Where to and where is DI Fallon?' Pat asked.

'He's waiting at the other end to meet you,' Carter replied. 'Don't worry, my colleague PC Rossi will take care of you both.'

'But why do we have to go with you?'

'As I said earlier, it relates to that diplomatic incident involving your son. We have other Greater London Police officers on their way to pick up Bobby for you.'

'But I'll need to pack a few things.'

'It's OK, Mrs Morris. We have some officers on the way who can sort out some spare clothing etc., but we need to get you away from here as soon as possible. Oh, and I will need any mobile phones and communication devices,' Carter demanded.

'Can't I ring Bobby first?'

'That would be too high a risk as we suspect they are tracking his phone. If you called him, they would know your number and be able to track your phone. Just pass them to PC Rossi; she will care for them until you and Bobby reunite. In the meantime, I have arranged for armed security guards to patrol the grounds of this house in case there are any untoward incidents. The Captain in charge is a competent man.'

'Just call me Claudia,' PC Rossi smiled, 'I've got a child aged seventeen as well. They are such a worry at times. But it'll be alright.'

16
THE HUNT

'They know where your Mum and Lily are,' Danny said.

'What are you on about?' Max asked.

'They were tracking me. So they know we went towards Cambridge.'

'My safe house!' Max exclaimed.

'Exactly, and you said earlier you thought your Mum was a bit strange with her messages.'

'We have to go there now,' Bobby insisted.

'I'm afraid Danny is right,' Avery replied, 'they knew the Brighton ploy was a lie.'

'Hey, Mum, I'm leaving soon. Hope everything is OK?' Bobby messaged.

'Hi Bobby, all good here and I can't wait to see you?'

'How's Lily?'

'Missing you so much,'

'That's not Mum messaging,' Bobby said.

'Are you sure, Bobby?' Catherine queried.

'She doesn't speak like that, and there's no way Lily would admit to missing me.'

'Danny, can you call up my tracker? The one I gave to Avery?' Max asked.

'Sure thing, Chief,' Danny said, tapping into his laptop.

'Why are you using your laptop, not my receiver?' Max asked.

'Because my not-so-genius Chief, your gadget is about as much use as a chocolate teapot. Anyway, your tracker appears to be in a power plant twelve miles from your safe house.'

'Mind if I use your laptop, buddy?' Max asked Danny.

Danny passed over his laptop, and Max typed in an IP address, user ID, and password. The screen changed to show CCTV images outside his safe house.

'Look over there,' Danny said, pointing to the corner of one image.

Max clicked on the image to make it full screen, and you could see several armed individuals watching the back of the house. Max minimised it and clicked on another shot showing the front of the property. At first, it seemed empty, but then they spotted two or three more armed people dressed in black standing well back from the driveway entrance and just on the edge of the camera image. Max swung the camera further in that direction, and there was a black van and more people dressed in black.

'It looks like they are getting ready to swoop,' Max said.

'What about inside?' Danny asked.

Max clicked a button on the screen, and the images changed to show views from inside the house, 'There's nobody there. Where's Pat and Lily?'

Max pulled Bobby's mobile phone out of his pocket, 'Hey Mum, we're leaving shortly. Put the kettle on if you're home. How's Lily?'

'OK, Bobby, Lily's in the swimming pool. Message me when you are close, and I'll put it on.'

'Well, now we know that's not your Mum. Look, the pool is empty,' Danny said, pointing at the screen.

'Can you triangulate her mobile phone's location if I tell you her network provider?' Max asked.

'Probably, but if I know Mrs M. Ah, I see Bobby is already doing it,' Danny laughed as Bobby took control of the phone and opened the Find My app.

'Sometimes the simple ways are the best,' Bobby replied. 'According to this, she is, oh no, she's in the same power plant as Claudia.'

'If they've already got your Mum and Lily, then those armed individuals must be a welcome committee for you,' Adam said.

'I think I need to activate my intruder deterrents,' Max growled.

'Hold on, Max. If you do that, won't they know you've rumbled their trap?' Dazza said.

'The big man has a point, Max,' Danny agreed.

'If you let them think you are still going to the house, then that's what fifteen to twenty armed individuals standing around doing nothing instead of guarding your Mother,' Agathe said.

'That leaves us with the challenge of how to get into the power station,' Abi said.

Danny used the TV remote to turn on the television and paired up his laptop. Then, using Planet Maps, they looked at the site from above and from the road views.

'Can you tell where Bobby's Mum's phone and Claudia are?' Adam asked.

Bobby looked down at his phone and said, 'Mum's phone is at the northern end of the site by that building site.'

Danny flicked to the tracker tab on his screen and confirmed the tracker was in the same location.

'Danny, can you get a roadside view of that big warehouse building you are saying Claudia and Mrs Morris are in, please?' Avery asked.

'The trees are masking it from the road, but the buildings here have been captured using artificial intelligence, so hang on a second. There you go,' Danny said as an AI image of the building appeared on the screen.

Avery approached the television, 'Can you rotate it to the right a little bit? A large warehouse roller door and a pedestrian doorway should be on that side.'

Danny moved the image, and Avery's predicted doorways appeared on the screen.

'How did you know that was there?' Abi challenged.

'That's it. That's the place where the Daxson is,' Avery replied.

'Are you sure?' Bobby asked.

'Definitely. You go through that door, and there is a long corridor with some old offices on the right-hand side. There is another doorway at the end of the corridor leading back outside, but there is an internal doorway to your left before you reach it. Go through that door, and that is where they are keeping the Daxson. His cage takes up most of the length of the building and almost half of the width. I can see it clearly.'

'Anything else you can tell us?' Max asked.

'The noise was like a mind-numbing buzz, and the electricity arced inside the cage with a crackling sound. There was a lot of equipment inside the cage, which seemed to produce the electricity, but from what I remember, the controls were all outside the cage.'

'How come Avery was allowed to see so much of Sabina's mind? Surely she would have tried your black wall trick to stop her from seeing all this and telling us,' Bobby thought.

'It could be that Sabina never learnt how to black wall, but I suspect Avery living to tell us was never part of their plan.'

'That part looks like it hasn't been used for some time. How do you get to it?' Catherine asked as Danny returned to an aerial view of the end of the power station incorporating the warehouse.

Danny moved the image on the screen, 'They've got a two-metre barbed wire fence around the front and one side.

There's the building site on the other side and an embankment and railway line at the rear with a wooded area in between. It seems like the only route is via the main gate into the power station, or there is a secondary access point over that footbridge from the subsidiary site across the road. Either way, they've got barriers and security guards at both entrances.'

'Does it say how old these images are?' Max asked.

Danny clicked on the screen, and the data showed the image providers and the dates, 'Some are this year and the rest last year, Chief.'

'Can you show the main entrance again, please?' Max asked.

Danny went back to the roadside view and zoomed into the main entrance.

'Cranside Security, wasn't that the—' Catherine started to say.

'The firm operating St Ethelbert's Hospital security, exactly. And I bet if Danny goes down to that building site,' Max said, then paused, waiting for Danny to change the screen image.

Danny whistled, 'Brinkswell Construction. Oh, look at the signs protected by Cranside Security and NetDat. Well, give me the keys. Danny is coming home.'

'Call me stupid, but how does your ability to crack NetDat's security systems help us get into the power station next door?' Adam asked.

'OK, as you asked stupid, I'll tell you,' Danny chuckled. 'Look at the site. See how the banking goes around the power station and the building site?'

'Yeah, and I guess I did ask you to call me stupid,' Adam laughed.

'That says to me that once upon a time, the whole site was part of the power station, and now they've sold off part of the no longer used land for development,' Danny explained.

'So?' Dazza challenged.

'Well, big man, my betting is the barriers between the building site and the power station are only temporary until they've finished the development or at least got it well underway. Look, you can still see the internal roads from the power station extending onto the building site.'

'That'll be how they get in and out of the power station,' Adam surmised.

'Bingo, give that man a straw hat and a bag of popcorn,' Danny replied.

'With Cranside monitoring both sites, they probably don't even care about internal divisions currently,' Max mused.

'How can we be sure?' Abi asked, studying the screen intently.

'Only one way to do that,' Max replied, 'I'm going to have to go there.'

'You keep forgetting, Max. We've told you before, and I'll repeat it: if our friend or his family needs help, you are going nowhere without us,' Abi replied, turning away from the television.

'We do this, and we do this together,' Dazza added as the rest agreed.

'OK, but we need to develop a plan. Avery, I'm sorry, but you will have to stay here. You've just had a heart attack and—' Max started to say.

'It's a cardiac arrest Max, not a heart attack. But you're right; there is no way Avery can take the risk. You're still recovering,' Catherine agreed.

'Danny, you stay here, and we will wear body cameras and headsets so you can coordinate it,' Max continued.

'No way, boss. I'm happy to get the equipment ready and working, but there is no way I'm staying here,' Danny insisted.

'But Danny, come on, you're in a wheelchair that gives you a distinct d—' Max replied.

'A distinct advantage is the word you're grasping for,' Danny growled. 'I can easily carry tools. Most people tend to ignore someone in a wheelchair, and let's be honest; there will be systems controlling that Tesla Coil and Faraday Cage, as well as security systems restricting access. As good an engineer as you might be, you are not the hottest computer hacker.'

'Fine, and yes, you probably will be more useful to us there than here. Is anyone else going to disagree with me?' Max muttered.

'Depends on the rest of your plan,' Dazza smiled.

Max took them through the rest of his plan. Catherine, Abi and Danny were going to go through the building site in Danny's car, and Adam, Dazza and Max were going to park up nearby and use the wooded embankment to try to get onto the power station from the rear. Avery and Agathe would monitor and coordinate everything from Glenthorne Crescent.

An hour later, Danny had everyone going to the power station fitted up with bodycams and earpieces.

'Don't we need transmitters to get the signals to and from here?' Adam asked.

'We have one, and it's already in my car from when we tried to rescue Michael from the Oliver Clinic,' Danny replied. 'I've boosted these devices so they'll easily transmit far enough to reach my car even if we have to leave it on the building site.'

'Avery and Agathe, I've labelled each button with our names. Press and hold down the one you want to talk to. You can also hold down more than one button if needed. If you press the button marked all, well, I think that's self-explanatory,' Danny explained.

'Adam, take my Mini, it'll be easier to park up than Papa's Range Rover, and if it gets damaged, then it doesn't matter too much,' Catherine said, throwing her car keys.

Before long, Adam was parking Catherine's car in a car park by some shops.

'It says ninety minutes maximum wait,' Dazza said, getting out of the car.

'Flip, I wonder if we should have found a long-stay car park?' Adam replied.

'Guys. I think a parking ticket is the least of our worries. Besides, ninety minutes is plenty of time to get in, save the two fair maidens and get back out. We'll probably have enough time to grab some fish and chips from that chippie on the way back,' Max joked.

'Really?' asked Dazza excitedly as he put on some sunglasses.

'I was joking,' Max replied, 'and why are you putting on sunglasses?'

'Everything looks better in sunglasses,' Dazza replied. 'I thought everyone knew that.'

Max sighed as they circled the shops and scrambled up the embankment behind them.

'They haven't even bothered to put up any fence on this side of the building site,' Adam said, 'You could walk straight down onto the site.'

'Danny's just arrived at the security barrier,' Dazza said, pointing towards the road.

Eric Williams was a thin and chirpy security man, proud of his twenty years of service with Cranside Security and its previous iterations. He took his latest role in charge of the entry barriers of this building site with an air of enthusiasm. Clad in his navy blue security uniform with a vibrant orange hi-viz vest, he radiated an infectious energy that contrasted starkly with the surroundings.

Eric approached the car, ready to exercise his duties to the full. His neatly combed hair and perfectly groomed appearance hinted at a meticulous nature, determined to maintain order amidst the site's controlled chaos.

'Good morning, sir. Oops, I'm sorry, it's afternoon now,' Eric said, glancing at his watch.

'Good afternoon, Mr uh...' Danny replied, hanging the end of his sentence.

'Williams, sir, Eric Williams. How can I help you?' Eric asked.

Danny held out an official-looking card, 'I'm from Cambridge Borough Council, Building Regulations.'

Eric studied the card and then asked Danny, 'Mr Thomas Witts, isn't it a little early for building regs to do an inspection?'

'Not at all, Eric. I can call you Eric, can't I?' Danny smiled, 'and please call me Thomas.'

'Thank you, Thomas, and yes, of course, Eric is fine,' Eric replied. 'It's just they only finished clearing the site a couple of days ago, and they've barely started on the foundations.'

'They're on the foundations already? My word Eric they've got some quick workers on site. But I bet you work twice as hard as any of them,' Danny said, winking.

'Well, I do what I must, Thomas,' Eric grinned.

'I know it's not easy looking after security on sites like this, and yet guys like you, Eric, rarely get the appreciation you deserve.'

'Thank you, Thomas,' Eric beamed, 'Oh, I almost forgot, who are your passengers? I need to enter them in the visitor's book.'

'This is Melanie Ting,' Danny smiled, then leaning out of his window half-whispered, 'I need to make a good impression. She's my boss.'

'No problem, Thomas, and who is your other colleague?'

'Ah, she's from Spain studying how we do building regulations in the U.K.,' Danny replied.

'Hola, mucho gusto. Por favor, déjanos entrar,' Abi said.

'I understood, hola,' Eric said proudly, 'Pleased to meet you, miss. Sorry, I didn't catch your name.'

'Sorry, Eric, how remiss of me. It's Jacinto Balde,' Danny replied.

'If you turn right and go to the end, turn left behind those huts, and you can park there. You'll see them working on the foundations in that top corner under the embankment,' Eric said, lifting the barrier before whispering, 'Good luck.'

'What did you say to him?' Danny asked Abi.

'I just said, hi, nice to meet you, and please let us in. But I can't believe he didn't twig the names.'

'Yes, Danny, you're impossible,' Catherine laughed as they headed in the direction Eric indicated.

'What do you mean?' Danny asked, feigning innocence.

'You're T Witts, and I'm Mel Ting!' Catherine chuckled, 'And I dread to think what you called Abi.'

'Oh, I never escaped being Dannyied,' Abi laughed, 'In English, Danny just introduced me as Hyacinth Bucket.'

'Hmm, being Dannyied, I might trademark that,' Danny chuckled.

'OK, they're past the front security guard. Let's get moving. We want to coordinate our move to the warehouse,' Max replied, heading towards the woods at the back of the power station.

Max, Adam and Dazza headed across the top of the embankment towards the woods fighting through the dense foliage until they arrived at the edge of the woods. Unfortunately, the trees added another layer of a deterrent to the unruly undergrowth and thorns, causing them to slip and slide and utter one or two less polite phrases as the thorns tore at their clothes and skin.

As they moved deeper into the wooded expanse, the sunlight struggled to penetrate the dense canopy overhead, adding an eerie ambience to their journey. The chirping birds and rustling leaves filled the air, heightening their senses and sharpening their focus. Suddenly a loud horn blasted through the woods.

'What was that?' Bobby jumped.

'Relax, Bob, it was just the train sounding its horn as it passed,' Dazza replied.

'Who's flipping idea was it to come this way?' Bobby grumbled as he stumbled forward.

'Yours. Well, Max's, which technically makes it yours as well,' Adam replied. 'Come on, we need to get past this building to the clear area where we can jump down behind the warehouse.'

'It's alright for you, short guys. I have to duck with every step,' Dazza moaned.

Bobby turned to Dazza and replied, 'Try taking your sunglasses off. You might see better.'

'No chance they've stopped me being poked in the eye several times already,' Dazza griped.

'I'll poke you in the eye if you don't get a move on,' Max said.

Adam continued to lead them through the tricky terrain with the crack of twigs and the occasional stumble on the way. As they approached the embankment's edge overlooking the power station, the ground beneath their feet grew steeper.

Finally, they reached the edge and looked across the vast expanse of the power station. In front of them was an open concrete area at the back of the warehouse. To their left, they could see the power station's main buildings, steel structures and towering chimneys standing like industrial sentinels, dwarfing their presence. The hum of machinery filled the air as a reminder of the station's vital role in powering the area.

'Did you notice the armed guard stood by the entrance the others will go through?' Dazza asked.

'Yeah, I'm not sure how they will manage that,' Max replied.

'We need to get down there first, and that looks like a good five to six-foot drop,' Adam said.

'Move a bit further along. Then, at least, we will land on the grass rather than concrete,' Max suggested.

'Dazza hold our hands, and we can lower you down, then you can help each of us down,' Adam said.

The sight of Dazza slowly lowering himself down with Bobby and Adam holding his hands to stop him from slipping and falling wouldn't have looked out of place in a slapstick film of the 1920s. All it needed was the jaunty piano playing in the background.

'Woah, easy big man, you're almost pulling us down with you,' Bobby shouted.

With almost prophetic timing, Dazza slipped the last two feet of the drop, just enough to send him sprawling and pulling Adam and Bobby down on top of him.

'When you guys said I can help you both down, I didn't think you meant to use me as a landing mat,' Dazza grumbled as he stood up.

Adam looked down at himself and then at his two friends and started laughing.

'It's not funny,' Dazza complained. 'You guys are flipping heavy from that height.'

'No, sorry, Dazza, I'm not laughing at you. I'm laughing at us. As my Mum would say, we look like we have been dragged through a hedge backwards,' Adam chuckled.

'We virtually have been, but in our case, we pushed ourselves through the hedge,' Bobby muttered.

Danny, Catherine and Abi exited Danny's car and headed to the fencing between the power station and the building site.

'They haven't even tried to make this difficult, cowboy builders,' Danny muttered. 'Just temporary mesh fencing panels with no clips holding them together. Would you both mind lifting one out of the way, please?'

Abi and Catherine lifted the end of one of the panels and swung it open like a door, leaving enough room for them and Danny to pass through.

'We'd better pull the fence back in place so it's not noticed,' Abi said to Catherine.

'Abi, Danny and Catherine, it's Avery here,' Avery said over the earpieces.

Danny tapped his earpiece and replied, 'Yes, Avery, we can hear you.'

'Dazza, Bobby and Adam have made it to the back of the warehouse, but they spotted an armed guard outside the entrance you are heading towards,' Avery continued.

'Was it just the one?' Abi asked.

'Yes, just one guard. From what I could see on the bodycams, it looks like you are by an old building which faces the side of the warehouse. So if you move to the corner of that building, you should be able to see the guard without being spotted,' Avery told them.

Abi, Catherine and Danny moved to the corner of the disused building and took turns looking at the warehouse.

'Avery, can you ask one of the others if they could throw something towards the other side of this building towards the embankment? I've got an idea, but I need to get closer to the door before he intercepts me,' Danny said.

'Danny, what are you doing?' Catherine asked.

'This will work, and then you can run over and join me,' Danny said as he turned a dial on his wheelchair and pulled out a cable connected to his joystick controller.

'You should hear a noise shortly, so keep an eye on the guard,' Avery said.

'Dazza, Avery said they wanted a noise to distract the guard. Unfortunately, I don't think a small stone will be very effective over the sound of this power station,' Adam said.

'Got a better idea?' Dazza huffed.

'Yeah, throw this brick as hard as you can towards those rusting filing cabinets and then duck behind these bins with us,' Adam replied.

A moment later, the brick collided with one of the filing cabinets with a loud clatter.

Danny watched as the guard headed towards the sound before dashing towards the door.

Dazza, Max, Bobby and Adam saw the guard reach the filing cabinets and look behind them before stepping down the side of the building to see if anyone was hiding there.

'Avery, tell them the guard is coming back,' Max said, tapping his earpiece.

'Guys, Max or Bobby, well, whichever they've said, the guard is coming back,' Avery said to the others.

'Danny, get out of there,' Abi shouted.

Danny raised a finger to his lips to tell Abi to stay quiet. Then, as the guard came into view, he started racing forwards and backwards near the door with the occasional spin for good measure.

'Oi, you, stay where you are,' the guard shouted, raising his gun and running over to Danny.

'Oh, thank goodness. My chair has gone crazy, and I can't stop it,' Danny said, doing another theatrical spin with his arms flailing.

The guard lowered his gun, and Danny used the opportunity to run over the guard's foot.

'Blimey mate, that thing really is out of control,' the guard said. 'Doesn't your joystick thing do anything?'

Danny flapped the joystick around whilst using his eye control mechanism to send his chair in opposite directions, 'Look, whatever I do, it just goes crazy. I had this problem with my old chair. I think all the electricity interferes with them. I ran over the boss in the office last time.'

'What can I do?' the guard asked, leaning his gun up against the wall by the door.

'If you could grab the chair and stop it spinning, that might help.'

The guard reached out and got a hand on one of the handles on the back of the chair.

'Flip,' Danny muttered, increasing the speed of the spin to dislodge the guard.

The guard sprawled across the concrete, 'Wow, that chair has got one hell of a kick.'

'Try grabbing it from the front. All the power is in the back wheels, so it might be easier to stop it from the front,' Danny lied as he went from spinning to shooting backwards and forwards again.

'OK, it should be easier to grab when it's not spinning,' the guard said as he lunged forward and grabbed the front of the chair. 'Hey, how's that? I think I've got it.'

'Yes, you certainly have,' Danny replied as he discharged an electric shock through the chair, sending the guard flying across the concrete and knocking him out.

Danny waved for Abi and Catherine to join them.

'We need to tie him up,' Catherine said.

'Put him over my lap. We can dump him behind those cabinets, and there's some rope in one of the back pockets of my chair,' Danny replied.

Once they'd secured the guard, they returned to the door, where Abi picked up the guard's gun.

'Abi, what are you doing?' Catherine asked.

'I'm taking his gun. We might need it.'

'But do you even know how to work it?'

'Of course, Avery's Dad is a member of the GBRA, and he got me into competition shooting,' Abi said as she inspected the rifle.

'You go, girl,' Avery said over the earpieces.

'GBRA?' Catherine queried.

'The Great Britain Rifle Association,' Avery said.

'And I thought I was the one with all the surprises,' Danny laughed. 'We'd better take a look in that corridor.'

At the other end of the warehouse, Adam, Bobby and Dazza were peeking around the corner in a stack like some comedy trio in a cartoon.

'That Carter bloke is talking to the guard,' Dazza said.

'Yes, thank you for telling us that, big man. We wouldn't have realised otherwise,' Adam sighed.

'All right, sarky,' Dazza muttered. 'So what's the plan? Should one of us distract Carter whilst the other two charge the guard?'

'That is definitely a plan,' Max said. 'Admittedly, one that would probably see two, if not all three of us, shot as the guard is armed.'

'Oh yeah. I don't fancy getting shot,' Dazza replied.

'It does tend to have some rather terminal consequences,' Max agreed.

'Avery, you should warn the others to be careful. Carter and another armed guard are outside the door at the other end of the corridor,' Adam said as he tapped his earpiece.

'I don't fancy taking on the two of them. Carter might well have a gun too. Let's watch for a minute and see if Carter goes inside,' Max said.

Avery's voice crackled over the earpieces, 'They said they would wait for your signal to go.'

'Carter is doing a lot of pointing inside and then back towards the main entrance,' Max noted.

As they watched, Carter stopped pointing, and then the guard stood to attention and relaxed as Carter headed away from the warehouse.

'Now what?' Adam asked.

'I'll hit him with my immobiliser, but I need to get closer. I don't want it to miss and cause a noise hitting another object,' Max replied.

'I thought that was for Deceptors?' Dazza challenged.

'It was, but thanks to some things Bobby's Dad had in his workshop, I've improved it so it works on humans. As you saw with Avery,' Max replied. 'Now you guys wait here. I'll signal when I've immobilised the guard.'

'But—' Adam started to say, but Max shot forward at full speed. Within seconds the guard was on the floor, and Max was summoning them.

Dazza and Adam ran down to Max.

'Uh, guys, what just happened there?' Avery said. 'It looked like someone sped up the film. How can anyone move so fast? Max talked about immobilising the guard one minute, and just a few seconds later, the guard was on the floor.'

Dazza tapped his earpiece, 'I think our signal got sped up too. What you just described is exactly the same as we saw.'

'That was lucky.' Max said, explaining that the guard didn't even glance his way as he crept towards him.

'Crept towards him?' Adam replied, 'I think you just covered several metres in a little more time than it took me to blink.'

'*This is the second time someone has said I moved very fast. I don't get it,*' Max thought.

'*Something must have happened when that whip hit you. Maybe it messed up your energy soul somehow.*' Bobby replied.

'*Maybe. Either way, this will be a rather useful skill.*'

'I'll have this,' Dazza said, picking up the guard's rifle. 'Pops used to have a tenant farm, so we often went out with his shotgun.'

'That looks a bit more complicated than a shotgun,' Adam stated.

'I'll figure it out,' Dazza replied.

'Avery, let the others know we are ready to enter. And don't forget to warn them it's us at the end of the corridor,' Max said.

Avery relayed Max's message, and Danny replied, 'OK, Avery, tell Max it's showtime.'

17

CONFRONTATION

Carter nodded to the armed guard who opened the door to the old office block. He strolled upstairs feeling smug with himself. Even though that old doctor they initially captured wasn't Max Janus, and the attempt to then use him as bait to capture Janus had failed, there was no doubt grabbing the boy's mother and sister would make it impossible for him to stay away. He was sure there was no way the infamous Max could avoid capture at his country house, and once they got him back to the power station, Janus would fully comply with J to save the lives of his host's family.

'The more sentimental they are, the weaker they are,' he thought.

The two doors opened at either end of the warehouse corridor, and Max and Catherine waved to each other in acknowledgement.

Approaching from opposite ends, the six friends, or should that be seven, with Max and Bobby being one body but two souls, crept along the corridor. Their senses heightened and alerted for any sign of danger.

Max entered first, followed by Adam and then Dazza looking around and waving the gun at anything he thought suspicious. At the other end of the corridor, Abi was at the front with her gun poised, followed by Catherine and Danny.

As they passed the offices to the front of the warehouse, they looked through the internal windows into the offices, but they were greeted by long-forgotten abandoned desks, filing cabinets and chairs. The dust across every surface made it apparent that nobody had set foot inside them for many years.

Max reached the doorway into the warehouse bay first and indicated to Dazza and Adam to stand still. Abi, Catherine and Danny joined them, and after a brief exchange with Abi, he asked her to stand ready to open fire.

'What about me?' Dazza asked.

'Keep an eye on that door we came through. If it starts to open, shout,' Max replied.

Max eased open the door into the warehouse bay, and finding nobody there, he beckoned the others inside.

At first glance, the room seemed full of scattered and stacked packing crates, with the wall behind them taken up by an old computer bank of dials and switches. Only the hum of electricity gave any clue to it not being deserted. As they passed the first set of stacked boxes, an extraordinary sight stood before them within the vast expanse of the dimly lit warehouse. Dominating the space stood a colossal Faraday Cage; its intricate metal framework was meticulously constructed to create an impermeable shield against the flow of electric energy within.

'Dazza, close your mouth. You're catching flies,' Adam said, equally in awe of what they were looking at.

A towering Tesla Coil pulsating with energy stood at the centre of this fortified enclosure, with its distinctive spiral form and crackling arcs of electricity. Also contained within the Faraday Cage was a Magnifying Transmitter harmoniously collaborating with the Tesla Coil to form a lifeline of power for the Daxson, who stood there unmoving and staring at them silently.

The interplay between the Tesla Coil and the Magnifying Transmitter produced an intricate dance of energy transfer. The Tesla Coil unleashed powerful bursts of electrical energy, resonating within the surroundings of the cage. These energetic waves coursed through the airspace, guided, and amplified by the Magnifying Transmitter's radiant fields. The symphonic hum of electricity provided a baseline for the crescendos of crackles from the electric arcs.

As the electromagnetic waves pulsated through the cage, the Daxson absorbed this vibrant energy to sustain its existence. The resonant frequencies of the system aligned with the creature's insatiable appetite, enabling it to draw sustenance from the electrified ambience surrounding it.

While the Tesla Coil and the Magnifying Transmitter offered the Daxson an energy source to survive, it was also trapped and unable to roam freely, leaving it tormented. As Max and the others came into view, it suddenly leapt forward, lashing out with ferocity and resentment, radiating a sense of anguish and a profound desire for liberation, shrouded in a twisted perception of its surroundings.

'The screaming, I can't stand it,' Max cried.

The others looked at each other and shrugged.

'What screaming, Max?' Catherine asked.

'Can't you hear its cries?' Max wailed. 'It's in agony.'

'All I can hear is that distinctive electrical hum and all the crackling of the electrical arcs, Chief,' Danny said.

Max doubled over in pain from the noise.

'We need to get him out of here,' Adam said. 'This can't be good for Max or Bobby,'

'How are our guests?' Carter asked.

'The mother is confused and worried, but the little girl seems excited by the adventure,' Claudia replied.

'Take the guard outside the door and the one downstairs and take our guests to the warehouse. I need to go and meet J and bring them to the warehouse.'

'I still haven't heard from Sabina, sir. Have you?'

Carter turned and looked at Claudia, 'Your sister is a loose cannon. Why would I have heard from her?'

'What if they've uncovered her?'

'If you want to investigate where she is, do it after today. If you think your Daxson is bad, try upsetting J.'

'Yes, sir.'

'Get them down to the warehouse. I want them both ready to be sacrificed to your Daxson when the Captain and his team bring the mighty Max in on his knees.'

Claudia entered the neighbouring room, furnished like a bedsit, 'DS Carter has just given me the good news. DI Fallon has met Bobby, and they're on the way. I'll take you down so you can meet them.'

'Are you sure?' Pat replied, 'I just want our life back.'

'It's fine, Mummy,' Lily said, holding Pat's hand. 'The kind lady is helping us.'

'What a fine young lady you are,' Claudia said to Lily. 'Now let's get going, and don't worry, the guards will protect us.'

Claudia escorted Pat and Lily downstairs and headed towards the warehouse, accompanied by the two guards.

Carter marched towards the main power station entrance. Grabbing a walkie-talkie off his belt, he said, 'Captain, update now.'

'Target apprehended. We'll be coming to you shortly,' a Scottish voice replied.

'Who is that?' Carter snapped.

'Sergeant Wallace, sir, the Captain is with the target.'

'Good work Wallace, over and out,' Carter replied, smiling broadly. Today was finally his day. Since J first approached him, he felt acknowledged for what he could do. Finally, someone realised his talents and rewarded him for it, and this was his moment to prove it. He walked towards the main entrance with a spring in his step.

'I bet you're so excited to see your boy,' Claudia said to Pat as they walked towards the warehouse.

Fallon released the walkie-talkie button and smiled as he turned to face the police sergeant by his side.

'The op has been a success, sir. Only five of our officers sustained minor injuries, and all surviving operatives have been placed under arrest,' the sergeant said.

'Well done, sergeant. Have we ascertained where Carter is?'

'Yes, sir. He is at the nearby Upper Wheatstone Power Station.'

'Excellent news. Get the local police to take those mercenaries in, then let's go and have a long conversation with our wayward colleague.'

'They are already being handed over, sir. We should be ready to leave imminently. May I ask you a question, though?'

'Ask away.'

'Who is Sergeant Wallace, and why the Scottish accent.'

'Sergeant Wallace was a fine man. When I joined the force, he took me under his wing and taught me everything I know, including how to mimic his accent to the point where some people couldn't understand what he was saying,' Fallon chuckled.

Adam and Dazza grabbed Bobby and tried to lift him.

'Please, make it stop,' Max wailed.

Danny moved over to the control desk and scanned the old-fashioned dials, levers, headphones, switches and buttons aplenty, 'This is so old school I don't know what does what.'

Max slipped through Adam and Dazza's hands and curled up on the floor.

As Claudia approached the warehouse, she heard the Daxson wailing. Pulling some earplugs out of her pocket and inserting them, she asked one of the guards, 'Where is the sentry?'

'Please, wait there, ma'am,' the guard replied, cautiously approaching the warehouse door. He looked around and spotted feet protruding behind some industrial bins. He ran across with his gun primed and ready to open fire. Slumped against a wall was the unconscious guard. After unsuccessfully trying to revive him, he pulled the pistol from the guard's holster and looked around before returning to Claudia.

'Someone has rendered the guard unconscious, ma'am. I suggest we make our way to the other entrance and pick up the other guard for support,' the guard said, adding as he handed her the other guard's handgun, 'Take this, ma'am.'

'What is going on?' Pat asked, pulling Lily close.

'We think those bad actors connected with that diplomat may have got on site,' Claudia said. 'Come this way.'

'Danny, throw me those headphones,' Catherine shouted urgently.

Danny pulled the headphones from the computer bank and tossed them to Catherine, who immediately put them on Bobby. They seemed to help as Max stopped screaming.

'Max, Bobby, can you hear me?' Catherine asked.

Bobby's eyes opened, and he looked at Catherine, nodding weakly.

Avery turned to Agathe in Glenthonre Crescent, 'I feel so helpless and guilty as well.'

'Why should you feel guilty, my dear?' Agathe asked.

'Because I brought all this on them. If I'd only fought harder, I might have been able to stop that Deceptor getting inside me or at least warned you all that she was here.'

'Regret does nothing but torture your future with unchangeable events of the past,' Agathe replied, 'Our successes give us confidence, but our mistakes give us power.'

'How are you feeling?' Catherine asked, holding Bobby's hand.

'I can still hear its cries, but they are bearable now. Thank you,' Max replied.

'What next, Chief,' Danny asked.

'I don't get it. The tracker and the find my phone both say Claudia is in this room,' Max replied, sitting up.

'Maybe this is why,' Abi replied, holding a handbag.

'Abi, can you hold it in front of your bodycam,' Avery asked.

Abi moved the bag, and Avery confirmed, 'Yes, that is Claudia's.'

'In which case, she is somewhere nearby and may be on her way back. Dazza, carefully open that door and tell me if you can see anything,' Max instructed.

As they reached the other door into the warehouse, the two guards heard muffled cries coming from the building behind them. They rushed over and found the other guard bound and gagged.

As they released him, the guard said, 'It's a young guy in a wheelchair. He zapped me with his chair. So be careful. It seems to be more of a weapon than a wheelchair.'

The three guards returned to Claudia and whispered something in her ear.

'It seems like we have quite a welcome party,' Claudia said.

The black limousine cruised up to the power station gates.

'Open the gates,' Carter ordered.

'But I need to know who it is,' the Cranside security guard protested.

'That's above your pay grade. Just do it,' Carter shouted.

The security guard opened the barrier, and the limousine glided onto the site and stopped with the rear nearside window level with Carter and the window lowered.

From the darkened interior, J asked, 'Do you have him?'

'Yes, we do. My team captured Janus at his country property, and they are bringing him over,' Carter replied proudly.

'Is everything prepared with the Daxson?'

'He's as angry as ever, and Claudia is taking the boy's mother and sister over to the Daxson now. Janus will have no choice but to comply, or else his host's family will be thrown to the Daxson.'

'That's going to happen anyway once I have injected Max, and he has to follow my orders,' J replied with a sinister laugh. 'We never leave witnesses who may come looking for them.'

'Of course, J. Everything is under control, and no loose ends this time.'

Dazza slowly opened the door and looked into the corridor. He looked to his left and then scanned across the office windows before ending on the door at the far end of the passage. He was just about to say all clear when he noticed a gun being pushed through the slowly opening door.

'Someone's coming, and they're armed,' Dazza hissed.

He looked out again, and a bullet ricocheted off the door frame behind him.

'Flipping heck, they're trying to shoot me,' Dazza shouted as Abi rushed over to him.

'Try shooting back, big man,' Danny yelled.

Dazza aimed his rifle and pulled the trigger. It clicked. 'The gun's faulty,' he shouted.

Abi turned to her left and flicked the safety catch on Dazza's gun, 'Try again.'

Dazza poked his gun out through the doorway and pulled the trigger. The recoil sent a stream of bullets up the door at the end of the corridor and into the ceiling. 'Flipping heck, this thing has some kick.'

'Just be careful with that,' Abi instructed. 'There are only about 30 bullets in each magazine. Assuming they are full. We can't afford to waste them.'

There was a crash of old glass as another bullet tore through the office windows and into the door where Dazza was standing.

He fired back, but the shots were wide of the mark.

Abi pushed Dazza aside but couldn't see the guard who had fired at Dazza. Then a head briefly appeared above one of the office windows. Abi aimed at the thin tin and plasterboard wall and shot a line of bullets across it. This startled the guard, and he jumped back, giving Abi a clear line of sight. She breathed in, then exhaled, and at the point where she stopped breathing for a millisecond, she took her shot. The bullet flew through the shattered office windows hitting the guard squarely in the pelvis, sending him crashing to the floor.

'Blimey, Abi, remind me to take you with me the next time the funfair is in town,' Dazza chuckled before another bullet from the end of the corridor sent them both ducking for cover again.

Max joined Abi and Dazza. He looked into the corridor and saw two more guards coming their way, with Pat Morris cuddling Lily and Claudia at the rear.

'*Cowboy, there is no way we can open fire now. It would risk hitting Mum or Lily,*' Bobby thought.

'*I know,*' Max replied, saying aloud, 'We can't risk hitting Pat or Lily. Catherine and Danny, you go behind those boxes by the control desk. Once they are inside, start flicking levers and buttons. Hopefully, it may cause some mayhem for the Daxson and distract them. As you're the better shot Abi, stand at the far end, aiming towards the door and take Dazza's gun as a spare. Only fire if you get a clear view. Dazza and Adam, you stand in that corner behind those boxes. Get ready to pounce.'

'Where are you going to be, Chief?' Danny asked.

'I'm the bait. I'll be standing near the Daxson's cage,' Max replied, grabbing a fire extinguisher and standing in front of it. 'All of you try to stay hidden until they are all in the room. Then, I'll let you know when to let rip.'

'How?' Catherine asked.

'When I say the word,' Max paused for a second, then said, 'Banana, go on the word banana.'

'That gunfire doesn't sound like everything is under control. Grace, we're leaving,' J replied.

'Please, J, give me a few minutes. I'm sure I can get it sorted. My team will be here shortly, so we can easily overpower whoever it is,' Carter pleaded.

'Carter, my family has spent a long time building what we have. We don't take risks; we manage or neutralise them. Grace turn this car around. I've heard enough. Oh, and Carter, if you don't have this sorted by the end of today, you'll be the one I neutralise. Understood?'

'Yes, J,' Carter replied dejectedly. He watched the limousine pass through the open security barrier and head off, then turned and started running back towards the warehouse, pulling out his handgun.

The door from the corridor slowly opened, and the first of the two remaining guards entered. Abi had him clearly in her sight, but she knew Max was right. They needed everyone in the room to minimise the risk to Mrs Morris and Lily.

Max could hear the door open, but the stacked boxes blocked his view. He glanced at Abi, and she nodded, confirming they were coming in.

'Mummy, what's going on? I'm scared,' Lily cried.

Bobby's heart sank hearing his little sister and knowing their danger.

'Shh, Lily, it'll be alright, I promise,' Pat replied soothingly.

As the guards cleared past the boxes, they were greeted by the sight of Bobby with his hands up.

'Well, I wasn't expecting to see you surrender so easily,' Claudia said, smiling. 'I like the headphones. It's a nice look, and it helps when my boy gets a bit noisy.'

'Your boy?' Max asked.

'Yes, that's what made my partner's death so hard to bear. We had just become a little family, and thanks to a wealthy benefactor, we've been able to bring him up here for the last seventeen years,' Claudia replied. 'If it weren't for you, my Daxson would have a mother and a father.'

'But, it's in agony. Can't you hear the screams?'

'That's only when it's scared. I make sure it has plenty of energy, and it really enjoys dispatching unwanted visitors. So how come you surrendered?'

'I ran out of bullets,' Max replied.

'Really? Do you take me for a fool?'

'I wouldn't even take you for a curry. But once a fool, always a fool,' Max replied glibly.

'You're going to regret saying that, but right now, I want to know where are your friends?'

'I came here alone. I didn't want to risk anybody else.'

'You may be a bit of an actor, but I know you're lying because Jimmy here had a shocking experience with your four-wheeled disabled friend earlier,' Claudia smiled, looking around the room. 'I know he's here somewhere.'

'Remember to press and flick everything you can,' Danny whispered to Catherine before appearing from behind the boxes. 'I'm here. Max asked me to help with the computers, but these are ancient.'

'Jimmy, help our friend out of that device,' Claudia ordered.

'I'm not going near it. Stan, you go,' Jimmy said to the other guard.

'Hold my rifle,' Stan said before approaching Danny cautiously. He leant forward and tentatively lifted Danny out of the chair before dropping him beside it.

'Oww, I'm reporting you to Social Services. That was abuse,' Danny smirked, rubbing his back.

Claudia turned to Danny and said, 'Oh, don't worry. You'll soon be in far more pain than that.'

With one guard holding two guns, the other guard walking back unarmed except for his holstered pistol, and Claudia facing Danny, Max said, 'This is getting silly. I'd even say a bit banana.'

Abi stood up, decided the guard nearest to Danny was the safest shot, and hit him in the back, sending him sprawling. Catherine started flicking switches, which caused the lights to flash, the equipment inside the Faraday Cage faltered, the Daxson began to rage, and the cage door clicked open.

Dazza and Adam lunged at the other guard knocking him to the floor as the two rifles flew across the floor.

Max picked up the fire extinguisher and threw it. 'Dazza, catch,' he said as he lunged at Claudia.

Pat froze in the melee as her brain tried to process what was happening around her. That confusion allowed Claudia enough time to grab Lily out of her arms and swerve Max's dive.

'Everybody freeze or the girl will go for a long sleep,' Claudia shouted, waving her handgun around.

The room fell silent, with only the hum and crackles of electricity as a backdrop, along with the Daxson raging almost inaudibly.

'You, the girl with the rifle, throw it this way and come from behind those boxes. You drop the fire extinguisher, and both of you let Jimmy get up,' Claudia instructed. 'And whoever is controlling that panel get out here.'

Catherine and Abi moved in front of the crates that were protecting them.

With a clang, the fire extinguisher fell from Dazza's hands as he backed toward the cage, and Adam stood, freeing Jimmy. As he got to his feet, the guard swung a punch which sent Dazza crashing against the cage, and he fell to the floor facedown. Jimmy swung another punch at Adam, knocking him out.

Then Jimmy picked up the rifle near him and walked over to Dazza, planting his foot in the middle of Dazza's back and pointing the gun at Dazza's head.

'Let me shoot this one, please,' Jimmy asked with a smirk.

'You know what Carter said,' Claudia replied, 'not until they are here.'

'Who's they?' Max asked.

'Just Carter and his friend. You'll soon meet them.'

'I'm pretty sure I already have,' Max muttered.

'You, get over there with those other women where I can see you,' Claudia said to Pat whilst waving her gun.

'Please, give me Lily. We'll do whatever you ask. Just give me my baby,' Pat begged.

'Move it,' Claudia shouted. 'There's one of you missing. Where is that lovely young friend of yours? Avery, isn't it,'

'That voice is giving me the shivers,' Avery said to Agathe.

'She's certainly not a nice woman,' Agathe agreed.

'Avery is very safe, thank you,' Max smiled.

'You need to tell me where, so I can rescue my sister,' Claudia said, lowering Lily with one hand and easing the door to the Faraday Cage open with her foot, allowing arcs of electricity to escape the compromised structure.

'Hasn't anyone told you?' Max asked in mock surprise.

'Told me what!' Claudia demanded, threatening to shove Lily into the cage.

Max looked around the room, 'It's like this. All of these people are good friends of Avery, as indeed is my host Bobby.'

'What's your point? Max,' Claudia snarled.

'Their friendship means, even now, Bobby is inside me asking if everyone is OK. Pat, Catherine and Abi look fine, but how are you doing, Danny?' Max asked

'I'm good, thanks, Chief,' Danny replied.

'Bet you'll be glad to get back to making that wheelchair fly,' Max joked.

Danny followed Max's gaze and replied, 'Oh yes, Chief, absolutely.'

'Dazza, how are you doing?' Max asked.

'I'm OK, but Adam is out cold,' Dazza replied.

'Reckon, you'll need to be a bit faster at lunging next time, big man,' Max laughed.

Dazza watched Max's eyes flicking from him to Lily and back, 'Maybe that bag of chips you promised earlier makes it a certainty.'

'They'll be over here waiting for you,' Max chuckled.

'Will you lot just shut the love fest up? Where's my sister? Or does my boy get a new ragdoll?' Claudia said, edging Lily closer to the cage door and opening it wider so arcs of electricity hit the floor inches from Lily's feet.

'*Lily, if you can hear me, don't be afraid and don't talk out loud. We are about to save you. Try to loosen your grip on that person's hand,*' Max thought.

'*OK, Max,*' Lily replied.

'Alright, we discovered your sister was transmuting inside Avery, and, oh my word, look at that on the wall,' Max said, pointing at the wall behind Claudia.

Jimmy turned, but Claudia sneered, 'You realise that trick only works in corny books and movies.'

Max smiled, 'I wasn't trying to trick you. I was just surprised to see a banana.'

Dazza leapt upward and forward, sending Jimmy flying backwards and lunging towards Lily with such speed she easily slipped out of Claudia's hand. He held her tight and went into a roll, almost knocking Bobby over.

As soon as Danny saw Lily was clear, he blinked twice and looked quickly from his chair to the inside of the Faraday Cage. The wheelchair shot forward, hitting Claudia en route until the chair and Claudia were inside the cage. Max shot forward and slammed the cage door closed as Abi grabbed her rifle and aimed it at Jimmy.

Claudia climbed out of the wheelchair, trying to get her bearings, 'Daxson, my boy, it's your Mumm—' but, unfortunately, she never finished her sentence as the Daxson grabbed her body and tore her energy soul from its shell. Unlike the gentle dissipation of Sabina, Claudia's energy soul exploded with an almighty scream.

Catherine ran over to Adam, who was starting to wake up, as Bobby and Pat ran across to Dazza, who handed Lily over to Pat.

'Weren't you a brave little champion,' Dazza told Lily.

'Dazza, you were amazing. How can we ever repay you,' Pat said, hugging Dazza, Lily and Bobby.

There was a crash behind them, with large flashes inside the cage. They turned to see the Daxson throwing Claudia's lifeless shell at the Magnifying Transmitter.

'We need to get out of here now. You too, Jimmy, and don't even think about going for your gun,' Max yelled, 'Dazza can you help with Danny?'

They rushed out of the warehouse. Dazza had Danny in his arms, and Pat was carrying Lily, then Jimmy walked out with Abi keeping her gun aimed at him whilst Catherine helped Adam.

Max stopped at the doorway and lifted his headphones. The noise from the Daxson throwing Claudia around and destroying the equipment in the cage was deafening, but Max realised the Daxson wasn't screaming. It was quiet.

He ran outside and yelled for everyone to get down just as there was an incredible explosion from inside the warehouse, sending debris in all directions, and the roof flew back like a can being peeled open. The area lit up from an explosion of incredibly bright light before it descended into the late afternoon gloom of a cloudy day.

Carter arrived just in time to see people pouring out of the warehouse. He recognised Bobby Morris and crouched down, carefully aiming his gun when the warehouse explosion sent him sprawling onto his back.

When he looked up, he saw a Cranside security guard leaning over him. 'You OK? I heard the explosion, so I hopped on my scooter to come and check out if we needed to evacuate.'

'Give me your scooter,' Carter barked at the guard.

'Oi, this isn't company property. It's my scooter. It's just quicker to get around this place than the crummy bike they give us,' the guard protested.

'Do I look like I care,' Carter snarled, waving his gun at the guard.

Jimmy looked around and realised the explosion had made Abi drop the rifle, so he grabbed it and stood up.

As Bobby stood up, Jimmy pointed the gun at him, 'Stay where you are.'

Bobby raised his hands, glancing around at his friends slowly sitting around him, and then he stepped forward.

Jimmy stepped back and shouted, 'I said stay where you are, and that goes for the rest of you.'

Bobby nodded and took one more step towards the guard.

Jimmy stepped back again, shouting, 'If you take one more step, I'm going to—ugh.'

Pat Morris swung her leg upwards between Jimmy's legs with all the force she could muster, and he crumpled forward onto his knees.

Abi reached over and snatched the gun from Jimmy's hand, 'I'll have that thank you.'

Pat pulled her leg out from under Jimmy and stood up, picking up Lily simultaneously. She walked in front of Jimmy and used her foot to push him onto his back, 'I am sick to death of people threatening my children today, thank you.'

Max looked past Pat and saw the commotion between Carter and the security guard. He ran across to Jimmy and pulled his handgun free of its holster.

'Catherine and Mum, take care of everyone. I need to get Carter,' Max yelled.

Carter saw Max heading his way, pushed the guard over, jumped on the scooter, and headed back towards the main entrance.

Max began to give chase, running as fast as he could. Carter was fast and had a good headstart, but Max was relentless.

Carter swerved to his left, disappearing into a dark alley between office buildings. Max hesitated momentarily, knowing Carter could be waiting to ambush him. But he couldn't let him get away. With a deep breath, Max entered the alley, his hand clutching the gun tightly. He crept forward, his senses on high alert passing industrial bins and other passageways and footpaths between buildings.

A shot whistled past him hitting a pipe and causing steam to pour out. Max spun around to see Carter heading away from him, ducking under some of the lower pipes, and Max started running again. Max's speed and agility meant he was soon closing the gap on Carter, and he risked taking a shot. Unfortunately, the bullet hit another pipe, releasing more steam and obscuring Carter in the mist.

Max slowed down, looking left and right. He could hear the scooter but couldn't see it. Suddenly he heard a loud crash behind him and turned just in time to see Carter heading towards him with his gun pointed straight ahead. A bullet hit his left arm as Max dived to his right, and Carter flew past.

Carter slowed down and grabbed his walkie-talkie, 'Captain, where are you?'

'Sergeant Wallace again, sir. We can see the power station in the distance. Our ETA is under five minutes.'

'What's taking you so long? It's only twenty minutes from Janus's safe house to here,' Carter growled as a bullet caught him in the shoulder.

'Sorry, sir, there was a wee skirmish, but it's sorted now.'

'I need backup now,' Carter bellowed as he accelerated away.

'You can't escape,' Max shouted, shooting towards Carter but missing.

Carter headed towards one of the chimneys, and Max chased after him but then stopped and looked around, realising the only place the road went was around the chimney. Max looked around and spotted a suitable place to crouch and wait.

Tapping his earpiece, Max said, 'Avery, how are the others?' But there was no response. So he tried again, 'Avery, Agathe can you hear me?'

'Max, Bobby, sorry Catherine was just telling us Adam seems fine now, and they've tied up the security guard,' Avery replied.

'How's Mum and Lily?'

'They're OK. Your Mum says her foot is a bit sore, but the pain was worth it for the satisfaction she got from doing it,' Avery replied. 'How are you doing?'

'Max has gone one better than my driving lesson. Instead of being shot at, I've now been shot,' Bobby said.

'It's only superficial,' Max replied.

'That's easy for you to say, cowboy, but I've never been shot before.'

A scooter started getting louder, and Max said, 'Got to go.'

Max crouched lower as the scooter approached, and as Carter drew level, Max dived forward, dragging him off the scooter.

They rolled across the ground with both guns going flying. Carter punched Max and tried to scramble to his feet, but Max swung his foot, taking out Carter's legs.

Carter fell facedown as Max scrambled to reach one of the guns, but Carter grabbed his ankle and pulled him down. Max lashed out, catching Carter in the face with his foot, sending the policeman rolling across the ground.

Max lurched forward and grabbed the gun. He turned, landing in a sitting position and pointed towards where he expected Carter to be, but Carter had snatched the scooter and was accelerating away. Max fired at Carter, but the bullet went sailing past him.

Max jumped to his feet, puffing heavily.

'Sorry, cowboy. Now I know why you wanted to get fit,' Bobby said.

'No need to apologise, buddy. You're doing way better than I ever thought you might,' Max replied, bent forward with his hands on his knees.

'Come on, he's getting away,' Bobby said, breaking into a run.

Carter sped towards the main entrance, pursued by Max, shooting at him. As they approached the power station's main gate, police vehicles started swarming in. Max fired again and hit the rear tyre of the scooter, sending Carter sprawling across the concrete.

The police vehicles screeched to a halt, and armed police officers swarmed out of the cars.

Max skidded and stopped, his gun still pointing at Carter on the floor.

A familiar voice shouted, 'Armed police, drop your weapon.'

Max looked up to see DI Fallon, and his heart sank. 'Carter is a crook,' he shouted. 'He tried to kill us.'

'Bobby Morris, drop your weapon, NOW!' Fallon shouted. 'Please do not force us to take action.'

Carter looked at Max, 'The game's up, mate. Hand over the gun.'

'Final warning Bobby, trust me,' Fallon shouted.

'*We don't have any choice, cowboy. Look at all those guns. There's no way we can escape,*' Bobby thought.

'*I'm sorry, Bobby. You don't deserve this. I hate losing, but even more, I hate hurting those I care about,*' Max sighed.

Max threw the gun on the ground towards Carter, who grabbed it and stood up.

'Drop the weapon,' Fallon shouted again.

'I have,' Max protested, 'Carter has it now.'

'DS Carter, drop the weapon now and turn around slowly,' Fallon shouted.

'John, it's OK. I've got him covered,' Carter shouted back.

'Carter, this is your final warning. Drop the weapon, or we will open fire,' Fallon replied.

Carter's face went pale. He held the gun out to his side and dropped it before slowly turning.

'What is on your belt? Remove it slowly and throw it down as well,' Fallon shouted.

'It's just a two-way radio,' Carter replied as he slowly unclipped it. Then, as he lifted it into the air, he pressed a button, and half whispered, 'Where are you? I need backup.'

He threw it to the ground, and a familiar Scottish voice crackled back, 'Och, I'm sorry, sir. Ye see, we got into a wee fisticuffs with some bothersome police officers, ya know.'

Carter moved his gaze from the walkie-talkie to Fallon, who was waving, and the radio crackled again, 'Surprise!'

Carter realised he was trapped. His mind raced through various scenarios, ultimately deciding that taking a hostage was his only chance. He dived towards the gun on the ground, intending to turn and aim it at Bobby, but several shots rang out before he'd even fully grabbed the weapon. His body jerked as the bullets hit him, and he collapsed onto the floor.

'Stay where you are, Bobby. I'm going to walk towards you,' Fallon shouted as armed police officers swarmed around Carter's lifeless body.

'OK, Bobby, you can lower your arms. It's all over,' Fallon said as he reached him.

'But how....' Max started to say.

'I've been working undercover for the last eighteen months. Well, more of a Trojan horse than strictly undercover. We knew Carter was involved in some illegal activities, so I was assigned to head up the department, befriend him and find out what he was up to. I am sorry I've been so hard on you, but I had to make him believe I was willing to be as corrupt as he was.'

'You certainly managed that. But I've got so many questions,' Bobby replied.

'There's plenty of time for questions later, but let's go and see what havoc you've been causing,' Fallon said, escorting Bobby to the back of an unmarked police car.

In Glenthorne Crescent, Michael walked into the Drawing Room to hear Agathe and Avery talking excitedly whilst some crazy images flickered across the screen, 'Where is everyone, and have I missed anything?'

Agathe looked at Avery then they both looked at Michael and laughed.

'Maybe if you'd not been snoring, you might have seen it all going on,' Agathe said.

'I've been working, not snoring,' Michael replied indignantly.

'Would you like to explain why there's a sticky note stuck to your face then?' Agathe asked.

Michael felt his face and pulled it off, 'Well, I might have nodded off for a second.'

Fallon pulled over to let two ambulances pass, 'That reminds me, we need to get you checked over, lad.'

'I'm fine. I've had worse,' Max absentmindedly replied.

'If you've had worse days than today, maybe we need to have a long conversation at the station,' Fallon laughed.

By the time they had parked and rejoined Bobby's friends, police were dragging away Jimmy and the now-conscious guard Max had immobilised. Catherine was with two paramedics treating the guard Abi had shot in the pelvis. The other paramedics were treating the cuts and grazes sustained by all and checking for more severe injuries.

Pat saw Bobby approaching and ran up to him, throwing her arms around him and knocking Fallon back in the process.

'I guess I deserved that,' Fallon said.

'You think so?' Pat replied sarcastically.

'It's OK, Mum. Fallon saved my life,' Bobby said. 'I'll explain it all later, but he is one of the good guys.'

'In which case, thank you,' Pat said, shaking Fallon's hand. 'But I reserve the right to wreak a mother's anger on you if I find out differently.'

'From what I've seen of your family and friends, I expect nothing less,' Fallon smiled.

Bobby noticed they had got Danny up on a stretcher chair and went over to talk to him, but before he got there, Lily intercepted him, 'Hey stinky, hiya Max,'

'Hello, squirt,' Bobby replied, 'And Max says hi too.'

'He said thank you,' Lily said.

'Who did Lily?' Max asked.

'The light man,' Lily replied. 'Just before he went flash in the sky, he said thank you.'

'And you heard it?' Bobby asked, crouching down to Lily.

'Course I did, silly, didn't you? He was scared and angry inside, but when you gave him his Mummy, he was happy because she had been a bad Mummy,' Lily giggled as she ran off to her Mum.

Bobby stood for a few seconds as he and Max considered what Lily had said.

'*I thought you said Daxson were just frenzied killers*?' Bobby thought.

'*They are. Maybe Lily just thinks she heard the Daxson say that. Young children do have remarkable coping mechanisms.*' Max replied.

'*I guess so. Come on, let's join the others.*'

Bobby walked over to Danny, who was talking to Adam, Dazza, and Abi.

'Blimey, bro, you look rough,' Danny told Bobby.

'Thanks, Danny. I thought I'd try to look more like you,' Bobby laughed.

'You wait until I get my wheelchair back. Then, I'll make you pay for that,' Danny said, smiling.

'Not sure your wheelchair is ever coming back by the looks of that place,' Abi said, nodding towards the warehouse.

'I'd say it's well and truly barbecued,' Adam laughed.

'Don't mention food. I'm starving,' Dazza said. 'Hey, I wonder if that chippie is still open?'

'I'm not sure we can wander off,' Danny said. 'Especially with me sat in this thing.'

'Fallon has just said we can go, but can we stay local as he wants to see us tomorrow,' Pat said, joining the group.

'We can all stay at mine. But we don't have enough cars to get us there,' Max said.

'Fallon offered to take Lily and me back, but he said you reprobates can sort yourselves out,' Pat laughed.

'Hey, Max, are we invited?' Michael asked over their earpieces.

'Hello, Michael, you missed all the fun,' Max laughed. 'Of course, the three of you can come too.'

'Your attendance comes with a condition, though,' Danny said.

'I dread to think, but hit us with it,' Avery replied.

'Nip to my place on the way and ask my folks for my number two chair, please?' Danny asked.

'No problemo, Danny,' Agathe said.

'Hey, that's my line,' Danny laughed.

Dazza pushed Danny back to his car, followed by Adam, Abi, Catherine, and Bobby. As they approached the vehicle, Bobby noticed the door to one of the huts was open, with hats and jackets inside.

'Adam, you go in Danny's car and Dazza and I will grab some hats and hi-viz jackets and walk out,' Max said.

As Danny drove off, Bobby and Dazza walked into the huts and picked up a hard hat each and a pair of hi-viz jackets.

'The jackets don't fit. Is everyone here a midget?' Dazza grumbled.

'It looks fine,' Bobby lied, 'Let's go.'

Eric Williams rushed to the barrier as Danny's car approached, 'Did you see that explosion, Thomas?'

'Who's Th..., Oh, yeah, erm, Eric. It was deafening. I reckon they had a little accident next door,' Danny lied.

'I hope it didn't stop you from making a good impression,' Eric said with a conspiratorial wink.

'Oh, yes, we made an impression,' Danny laughed. 'With my boss, of course.'

Eric went to open the barrier but then said, 'Stop right there. This doesn't seem right, not right at all.'

'What's wrong, Eric?' Danny asked.

'Who is the other man? There were just three of you when you came in,' Eric protested.

'I think that explosion got to you, Eric. Don't you remember this is my boss Melanie Ting and this is her husband, William?' Danny said with a puzzled look.

'Uh, well, I guess,' Eric replied, opening the barrier and scratching his head simultaneously.

As they drove past, Danny gave Eric a thumbs-up and a cheery wave which Eric returned.

Catherine and Abi started laughing.

'What is it?' Adam asked. 'Is this post-traumatic shock or something?'

Abi wiped her eyes and said, 'No, Adam, this is post-Danny shock.'

Catherine said, 'Abi, stop, please. Well, Mr Ting, I'm your wife, Mel, and you're my husband, Will. Now you work it out.'

Eric stood at the barrier as the two builders passed him. He glanced at them and shouted, 'Excuse me, guys.'

Bobby and Dazza turned.

'Your jacket is torn up the back,' Eric said, pointing to Dazza.

'I know, cheap junk,' Dazza replied, ripping it off.

'This place is all about cutting costs and corners,' Eric agreed, returning to his security hut.

18
THE DECISION

Did yesterday happen, or was it a dream? That was the first thought that went through Bobby's mind as he woke up. He stretched and looked around him. Adam was curled up next to him on the bed settee, Danny was snoring on a reclining chair, and Dazza was on his front with his feet hanging over the end of a sofa, fast asleep.

'*It happened, buddy,*' Max replied.

'*It's been insane. Is this really your life?*'

'*Well, I wouldn't say it's typical of my eat, work, relax and sleep lifestyle, but it does happen every so often.*'

'*I think someone is in the kitchen.*'

'*Any bets on your Mum or Agathe?*' Max laughed.

'*I can smell bacon and or sausages,*' Bobby chuckled. '*I reckon that's Agathe.*'

'*I've put you, your friends and your family through so much.*'

'*You've just tried to survive, cowboy. It's the Deceptors and Carter who made everything happen.*'

'*I'm still so confused about Fallon and Freddie. I was sure they were as crooked as Carter.*'

'*Me too,*' Bobby said. '*After all, Freddie planted that tracker on Danny. I know he said he was undercover, but how could Fallon not be involved?*'

'*Fallon is a mystery. Talking of Danny, he's a genius, but he dances to the beat of his own drum in a totally unconventional way. I can't believe he got away with those names to that security guard.*'

'*Whereas I can believe Dazza insisted we buy him chips from that chippie,*' Bobby laughed.

'*And as for your sister, Lily.*'

'*What about her, cowboy?*'

'*The fact that she can hear us telepathically, project her replies back and even understand Daxson is extraordinary.*'

'*But you said it was because of her age.*'

'*Seeing my aura, and maybe even hearing me, possibly. But understanding Daxson is very rare. I'd say almost unheard of even by most Shadowers,*' Max answered.

'*We never found out who the 'they' were that Claudia mentioned besides Carter either.*'

'*I just assumed it was Fallon. But obviously not. There are so many Deceptors out there. Maybe one day we'll find out.*'

Adam rolled over and looked at Bobby, 'Good morning, sweetheart. Did you sleep well?'

'Yes, thank you, hun,' Bobby replied, kissing Adam.

Agathe walked into the room and half-whispered, 'Anyone hungry?'

Dazza's hand shot up as Bobby and Adam replied, 'Yes, please.'

Before long, Adam, Bobby and Dazza were tucking into a fried breakfast when Abi and Avery walked into the kitchen.

'Morning,' Avery said, kissing Max.

Adam scowled but said nothing.

Abi noticed Adam's reaction and said, 'We've just been through a couple of crazy weeks, and I don't know about you, but I'm done in. So you guys need to accept you've just over five months of sharing Bobby and Max until they finally have separate bodies, right? I bet it's as tough for them as it is for you.'

'But,' Adam started to say.

'The only 'but' we have time for are the ones ending in 'ter' and spread on the toast Agathe is putting my scrambled eggs on. OK?' Abi said firmly.

'Can I point out I've already got my own body. It's this, what did Fallon say? Ah yes, it's this reprobate inside me who doesn't have one yet,' Bobby smiled.

'*Does this mean you still want me to go*?' Max thought.

'*Not now, cowboy, let's talk later. But, for now, let's enjoy the morning*,' Bobby replied.

Over the next hour, everyone got up and enjoyed Agathe's hospitality.

'I should be cooking, really,' Pat said, eating some marmite on toast.

'You need to relax, my dear,' Agathe replied, 'I've been through what you're going through, so accept all the help you can.'

'It's going to be a hot day according to the weather forecast on the radio,' Michael said, sipping his coffee.

'I didn't know people still did that,' Dazza queried.

'Did what, weather forecasts?' Abi asked.

'No, I mean listen to the radio,' Dazza laughed. 'It must be an oldie thing.'

Michael laughed and said, 'Oi, you cheeky devil. Firstly I'm not old, and secondly, I hear this is the correct response.' Michael gave Dazza a friendly punch in the arm.

'How are you getting on with the wheelchair?' Avery asked.

'Amazing, I'd forgotten how much fun it is relying on others to help you up and down steps and kerbs,' Danny replied sarcastically.

'Cheer up, Danny. Look at it as an opportunity to build an even more advanced one,' Catherine replied.

'We could work on it together,' Max suggested.

'I've seen your engineering, Chief. Knowing you, if I tried to make it go forward, you'd have it opening the fridge and turning the washing machine on,' Danny chuckled. 'But I'm happy to let you be my apprentice.'

'You know, if you weren't differently abled, I'd sort you out,' Max replied, winking.

'You'd probably stand more of a chance if I weren't differently abled,' Danny laughed, 'and once I've got New Dawn 2 up and running, I will be invincible.'

'You mean insufferable,' Avery replied.

'Oh, no, he's that already,' Abi added.

'Welcome to my fan club,' Danny giggled.

'Why did you call your first wheelchair New Dawn anyway?' Catherine asked.

'Because I intend to create a New Dawn for all differently-abled people,' Danny replied. 'With technological advances and AI, I don't see any reason why we can't resolve most challenges.'

'Very noble sentiments, dear boy,' Michael nodded. 'Although I struggle to see how artificial insemination can help. Well, unless—'

'Eww, Papa, don't even go there. Danny means artificial intelligence,' Catherine explained as the rest started laughing.

'Michael, I swear sometimes you're a dinosaur,' Agathe chuckled.

Later that morning, they all sat outside on the patio, chatting with music playing in the background and enjoying the warm weather.

'Mummy, can I go swimming?' Lily asked.

'In a while, munchkin. We want to enjoy the sun, not stay inside all day,' Pat replied.

'Why does it have to be one or the other?' Max replied as he picked up a computer tablet. Max pressed some buttons on the tablet, and the large bi-fold doors behind them parted, opening the pool room to the patio.

'See, some of my technology works,' Max laughed.

'I think I've got a plan,' Danny said.

'Oh, no, Danny's got a plan. Everyone hide,' Dazza interrupted.

'Hilarious big man,' Danny laughed, 'I reckon if Max manages the major engineering and I do everything else, we could start a business, D and M Incorporated.'

'Not bad, but M and D has a better ring,' Max laughed.

'Max, do you mind if I ask you a question?' Adam asked.

'You can ask me anything you like,' Max replied.

'If you've got a place as fabulous as this, why do you live in Michael and Agathe's basement?' Adam queried.

'Because having nice things is great, but having nice friends, no matter how many or how few, is better and being with them always beats being alone,' Max said.

The doorbell rang, and Max looked at the computer tablet, 'It's Fallon. I'll go and let him in.'

'You stay right there, Max. You've put Bobby's body through enough these last few weeks. I'll let Fallon in,' Agathe said.

A minute or so later, Fallon joined them on the patio. 'Morning, everyone. I hope you all feel better than most of you looked yesterday.'

'Are you going to need to take witness statements from us all? I've got a room we can use if you do,' Max offered.

'Thank you for the offer Bobby, but if this were an official investigation, we'd be doing it down at the station,' Fallon replied.

'So why are you here?' Danny asked.

'Ah, if it isn't Mr Windbag White,' Fallon laughed. 'I thought you might have a few questions, and I've got plenty.'

'Windbag White,' Dazza spluttered. 'That's going to stick.'

'Watch it, big man,' Danny laughed.

'Woah, there, Windy, you're frightening me,' Dazza chuckled.

'Should I call my solicitor?' Michael asked Fallon.

'That won't be necessary, sir,' Fallon replied, 'This is totally off the record.'

'Here's your coffee Mr Fallon,' Agathe said, putting a cup on the table.

'Thank you, but please call me John,' Fallon replied.

'Well, I've got a big one for you, John,' Bobby growled, 'Why did you turn against Carter when you were on his side until yesterday? How real is this undercover story?'

'Did you injure your throat in that explosion yesterday?' Fallon said, 'Your voice keeps changing.'

'That's a long story,' Avery said, 'How about answering our question?'

'OK, I'm detecting a little tension,' Fallon replied.

'Wow, no wonder Greater London Police made you a Detective Inspector. You'll be Commissioner by the end of the month,' Abi added.

Fallon sighed, 'Look, I'm sorry I seemed a bit unpleasant, but I've been investigating Carter for quite a while. So I had to make him believe I was on his side. I did explain a little to Bobby yesterday.'

'Why have you been investigating Carter?' Adam queried.

'We had a report that he'd been acting suspiciously,' Fallon replied.

'In what way?' Abi asked.

'He kept getting involved in investigations and turning up at shouts, sorry police call-outs, that didn't involve him. Plus, he started spending money a Detective Sergeant with his background wouldn't have.'

'So why were you at the Oliver Clinic and the Lamasery,' Danny asked.

'Carter told me there was an emergency at the Oliver, and we had fifteen minutes to get there. But he said he'd dispatched someone to confirm what was happening.'

'Sorry if I sound cynical, but that dispatched person was your son, Freddie,' Avery said, crossing her arms.

Fallon looked down, shaking his head, 'I'm afraid our Freddie has a bit of a vivid imagination. Carter found out Freddie claimed I was a secret agent and played him. Carter told Freddie that he would be an intermediary for secret information between Freddie and me.'

'But you're his Dad,' Abi said.

'Sometimes Freddie's lift doesn't go all the way to the top if you get my meaning. Carter had convinced him we couldn't speak about this directly, or it would blow my cover.'

'So he was doing whatever Carter asked but never told you anything, so he didn't blow your fictitious cover?' Danny laughed. 'This is classic.'

'That's why he put a tracker on your wheelchair,' Bobby said to Danny.

'So I understand. I caught him upset, and he said Carter had told him off for not telling them soon enough that the tracker showed you going to St Ethelbert's. After calming him down, I managed to get him to tell me the truth. That was how we found out about this hideaway you're in and that Carter had been watching the place. But I'd like to hear your side of events.'

They explained the tracker, Freddie's behaviour in the High Street, and his appearance at the Oliver Clinic.

'Someone is getting grounded tonight,' Fallon said. 'Talking of the Oliver Clinic. Mr Thomas, can I ask if you know of a consultant called Richard Mueller?'

Michael looked at Max, who shook his head, 'I used to, but he retired years ago. Why?'

'Oh, it's probably totally unrelated, but as I was driving up here, there was a report on the radio of an esteemed consultant from the Oliver Clinic who died in a car accident early this morning,' Fallon replied.

'Oh dear, that is a shame. Did he have any family?' Michael replied.

'None that we are aware of. That's why I asked. I wondered if you might have known of any, that's all. Especially as you'd all be involved in an incident there,' Fallon shrugged.

'What about why you guys went to the Lamasery?' Dazza asked.

'That was a weird one. Carter said he'd had a tip-off involving a major celebrity and some scandal, so we were heading to the Lamasery anyway. But on the way, he took a phone call, and suddenly it became an emergency. When we arrived, it was just some rogue person who had been impersonating a nurse and had been knocked out.'

'What happened to the nurse?' Adam asked.

'Carter had a conversation with her, and the next thing we are taking her home like some personal taxi. Carter reckoned he would be giving her a police caution, but I never saw it happen. But why the interest in the Lamasery anyway. You weren't there, were you?'

Danny looked at Dazza and Bobby, 'No, of course not. I've never been there. Have you, Bobby?'

Bobby shook his head, 'Me? Why would I want to go there? But, Dazza works there, and he mentioned that the police had been, isn't that right, Dazza?'

'Yeah. My Pops said there had been some incident involving the police. A wheelchair almost got stolen, too,' Dazza replied.

'Talking of wheelchairs, our scene of crime officers think a wheelchair may have been involved in the explosion,' Fallon said.

'Really?' Danny said, feigning surprise, 'What makes them think that?'

'Parts of it were found close to the explosion's epicentre.'

'Only parts of it?' Danny said with interest.

'Yes, it was so close to the explosion that other parts of it were blown into the foundations of the building site next door,' Fallon replied, showing them a picture of a wheel, handle and a few other parts jutting out of wet concrete.

'It's not mine, as you can see,' Danny replied, tapping his chair.

'But weren't you in a stretcher chair yesterday? Which, by the way, the ambulance service would like back,' Fallon smirked.

'Ah, well, that's because my chair got a bit damaged in the explosion. But as you can see, it's fixed now,' Danny replied. 'I'll make sure the stretcher chair is returned to the ambulance service.'

'Do you have any idea whose chair that was?' Abi asked.

'We don't know, but if I zoom in, you can see it had DIG stickers on it,' Fallon said.

'They look familiar,' Adam laughed.

Danny stared at Adam, then said, 'Oh, yeah, wasn't it to do with that archaeology thing we saw in town.'

'We also found the remains of a known associate of Carter's in the warehouse,' Fallon said, 'The strange thing is her DNA matched someone registered as dead by the Oliver Clinic a couple of weeks ago.'

'That's very strange,' Max replied.

'On the subject of strange, I don't suppose you could shed any light on what all that electrical equipment was doing in the warehouse, can you?' Fallon asked.

'I'm only guessing, but electrical equipment in a power station is probably quite common,' Max replied.

'OK, enough games. Who are you really, Bobby, and what has been going on?' Fallon asked.

'What do you mean?' Bobby asked.

'When Freddie mentioned your little fight, or as he put it, the three of them against ten of you, he said you moved impossibly fast. I thought he was lying until I saw you chasing Carter on his scooter,' Fallon said. 'I've also seen the CCTV footage of your driving lesson and had a full conversation with Ian Prosser. Even he couldn't perform some of the tricks you did. Also, Mr White has definitely been to the Lamasery, as Freddie's tracker shows him there.'

'Mum, would you get our guest a beer, a whisky, or maybe both,' Bobby said.

'I'm fine with the coffee, thanks,' Fallon replied.

'I'll get you something anyway,' Pat said, 'Just in case.'

'John. What I am about to tell you goes against all my privacy rules, but you saved Bobby's life and potentially mine,' Max sighed.

'Anything you say will remain confidential,' John assured him, 'Besides, after all my years in the force, nothing would surprise me.'

'I think this just might,' Bobby laughed.

Over the next hour, Max and all his friends explained Max's background and how they ended up where they were.

'And you were Julius Ceasar's chef?' Fallon queried.

'I think chef is overdoing it. I was one of his personal cooks,' Max laughed, 'But finally, someone who knows his history.'

'I've no choice,' Fallon said, 'My wife studied Ancient History with a specialism in the Roman Empire at Leicester University.'

'I was wondering about doing that, but I think I prefer politics,' Bobby replied.

'If you pick up even a fraction of Max's political acumen, you'll do well,' Michael said.

'This is all so surreal. I came here expecting a slightly strange conversation about how a teenage lad, his friends, and family helped us catch a dishonest copper,' Fallon replied, taking a large sip of whisky.

'I think we've achieved the strange conversation bit,' Michael laughed.

'What will happen to us?' Adam asked.

'I've been informed no further action. The record will show we caught a corrupt officer involved in an underworld group. Unfortunately, the officer was killed during the arrest process, and his accomplice was interfering with some equipment in the warehouse resulting in the power plant explosion and her death,' Fallon replied.

'That's good to know and a relief,' Avery said.

'What about you and Bobby, Max?' Adam asked. 'You said you'd leave him when this was over.'

'I'm still happy for you to transmute in me. Although, if we could have a little less drama, that would be nice,' Catherine replied.

'*It's your choice, Bobby. I've always said I'm honoured that someone would host me, but I've also put your family and friends at so much risk I'll leave if you want me to,*' Max thought.

'*You certainly can't transmute into Catherine, knowing she might be your daughter.*'

'*Funnily enough, the dinner at the Willow, which started this whole adventure, was about Michael and me explaining that I would need to find a new host. We would say it was because I needed new DNA after generations of having her forebears hosting me. I can still look for a new host if that is what you want, my friend.*'

'*You can read my mind. Well, you are in my mind, so you know the answer.*'

'*I should do, but it's like you're black walling me,*' Max said.

'*I don't even know how to do that. But here's my view.*'

'Adam, do you love me no matter what?' Bobby asked.

'I will love you forever, Bobby,' Adam replied.

'Avery, will you wait for Max?' Bobby asked.

'Well, I'm a bit busy, but I guess I can,' Avery laughed.

'Catherine, thank you so much for offering to take this squatter off my hands, but I think we've reached some acceptable terms,' Bobby chuckled.

'I'm so proud of you, champ,' Pat said.

'Thanks, Mum, I love you.'

'I'll always love you more,' Pat said, winking.

'John, will you join us for lunch?' Agathe asked.

'If I'm not an inconvenience, I'd be happy to stay,' Fallon replied.

'Can I ask one more question?' Adam asked.

'Of course,' Fallon replied.

'I may have overstayed the parking time outside the chip shop by the power station, and I wouldn't want Catherine to get a parking ticket,' Adam said.

'If you or Catherine can give me the registration number, I'll get that sorted for you,' John replied.

'I've got a request, too,' Dazza said.

'Hit us with it, big man,' Danny replied.

'Can we play some music that's not forty years old,' Dazza chuckled.

'It's not forty years old. It's quite modern,' Michael said. 'I remember grooving to this in the nightclubs.'

'Me too,' Max replied.

'I've always said you were old, cowboy,' Bobby laughed, checking the internet on his phone; he added, 'And yes, this tune is 42 years old.'

'If you think that's old, when we first hosted Max, it was Rock and Roll meets Beethoven,' Agathe said with a smile.

'Really? My Simon, Bobby and Lily's Dad was just like that. Mozart meets Metallica,' Pat laughed.

'But in Max's case, he'd hung out with Beethoven,' Agathe replied.

'I wouldn't go that far, but I did meet him a few times,' Max laughed.

'They say it's a funny world,' Fallon said, 'But today I realised it's even madder than that.'

'Any requests for lunch?' Agathe asked, 'I've got some beef pepperpot on for our Dazza.'

'And I've got plenty of fruit and sandwich fillings in,' Pat added.

'I'll have a banana and salad cream sandwich, please, Mum,' Bobby replied, putting on his sunglasses.

'Why are you putting on your sunglasses when the sun has gone in?' Abi asked.

Bobby smiled, 'As a wise person once said, everything looks better in sunglasses.'